The Palace of Shattered Vessels

THE PALACE OF SHATTERED VESSELS

Summer in the Street of the Prophets
AND
A Voyage to Ur of the Chaldees

NOVELS ONE AND TWO OF
The Palace of Shattered Vessels

DAVID SHAHAR

Translated from the Hebrew by Dalya Bilu

WEIDENFELD & NICOLSON
New York

Published by Weidenfeld & Nicolson, New York
A Division of Wheatland Corporation
841 Broadway
New York, New York 10003-4793

Summer in the Street of the Prophets was originally published as *Hekhal ha-kelim ha-shevurim* by Sifriat Poalim, Tel Aviv, in 1969. First published in English as *The Palace of Shattered Vessels* by Houghton Mifflin Company, Boston, in 1975.
Chapter 3, "Moses and the Ethiopian Woman," was translated by Dennis Silk.
Chapters 2, 3, and 4 originally appeared in *News from Jerusalem* by David Shahar,
published by Houghton Mifflin Company, Boston, in 1974. Copyright © 1974 by
David Shahar.
A Voyage to Ur of the Chaldees was originally published as *Ha-massa'le ur-kasdim* by
Sifriat Poalim, Tel Aviv, in 1971.

Library of Congress Cataloging-in-Publication Data

Shahar, David.
    The palace of shattered vessels.

    Translation of: Hekhal ha-kelim ha-shevurim; and,
ha-Masa' le-Ur-Kaśdim.
    I. Shahar, David. Masa'le-Ur-Kaśdim. English. 1988.
II. Title.   III. Title: Summer in the Street of the Prophets.
IV. Title: Voyage to Ur of the Chaldees.
PJ5054.S33H413   1988   892.4'36   88-5719
            ISBN 1-55584-068-X

Manufactured in the United States of America
Designed by Irving Perkins Associates
First Weidenfeld & Nicolson Edition

10   9   8   7   6   5   4   3   2   1

For my daughter, Dinah, with love

Summer in the Street
of the Prophets

For the Elevation of the Soul of Eviatar

Points of Reference

1.

The Fathers of Memory

LIGHT AND CISTERN WATER, the mouth of the cave and the rock at its side: these four have been connected in my memory with the figure of Gabriel Jonathan Luria ever since the time he came to stay in our house when I was a child. From Paris he came straight to our house, and since he entered the yard just before the King of Abyssinia entered the Ethiopian Consulate across the road—which is to say, just as I was drawing water from the cistern—his figure was fixed in my memory as rising from its mouth together with the pail of water splashing radiant, dancing light in all directions, which I was drawing up with a peculiar kind of pleasure from its bottom: rising and opening like the Japanese paper flower in its glass of water, which he himself was later to buy me from Hananiah's toy shop. The cistern water is deep and soft and dark and smells of ancient stone and iron and moss and the paraffin poured into it to protect it from malaria mosquitoes. The mouth of the cistern raised like a miniature altar in the corner of the yard is covered with an iron cap. I lift the lid and peer down at the skin of the dark water. The oily film of protective paraffin makes a rainbow-colored halo of light around the shadow of my head rising from the water

and hiding its depths and surface and giving me back my
voice "Ho ho" chilled with the stone and the iron. I let the
pail down with the rope wound tightly around my hand to
prevent its slipping from my grasp and sinking to the bottom of the cistern. A shudder of anticipated pleasure runs
through me as the pail lands on the skin of the soft, submis-
sive water and rests there bobbing lightly for a moment
before I thrust it down with an abrupt, vigorous movement
and make it penetrate the skin. The pail starts sinking with
the weight of the water filling it and I give it more and more
rope. The pail is full but I go on letting out the rope because
I want to feel it hitting the bottom of the well and hear the
metallic clang of the tin on the stone floor. Immediately I
begin to pull the rope until the pail returns full of female
waters, breaking through the upper skin and rising in the
narrow neck of the well, banging against the walls, spilling
and splashing drops of water and scattering splinters of
light everywhere. If I'm not careful half the water will be
gone by the time the pail emerges from the mouth of the
well. With an energetic heave I empty the pail into one of the
tanajeas, the two potbellied water jars nearly as tall as I
standing in the kitchen in square tins because their rounded
bottoms are too narrow to enable them to stand firmly by
themselves. Old Pnina, Gabriel's aunt, peers anxiously into
the cistern mouth and lets down a rope to measure the water
level, which is dropping at a surprisingly rapid rate despite
all her efforts to economize, for the month of Tevet is behind
us, the Feast of Lights has come and gone, Arbor Day is just
around the corner, and of rain or even clouds there is no
sign. If no rain falls during the next two or three weeks we
will have to call in Arele the King of the Dogs, the water
drawer. The water cistern was a source of constant worry to
Aunt Pnina, and the frown which creased her forehead
every time she peered into it infected me with her anxiety
too. The year before we had worried about floods: the whole

courtyard stood over the cistern, its floor serving as the cistern's roof, and on nights when the rain came down hard I would be filled with fear that the cistern, unable to contain the abundance of water flowing ceaselessly into it, would burst and we would all be drowned. The next morning Pnina would hurry to divert the water from the roof gutters directly into the drainpipes by the simple expedient of transferring the drainpipe plug to the pipe leading to the cistern. But this year was dry and rainless and Aunt Pnina looked deeply into the cistern mouth with frowning forehead and worried eyes, as if she meant to make it start filling up of its own accord by the sheer concentration of her gaze.

I let the pail down into the water once more, and when I pull it up again the voice of Gabriel Jonathan Luria and the light of his countenance rise with it. At once all anxiety about the cistern being emptied leaves me, just as the fear that it will burst with the pressure of the abundance, flooding and drowning and sweeping everything before it, leaves me later at the sight of his face and the sound of his voice, although it is not he but Aunt Pnina who diverts the rainwater from the cistern to the drainpipes. Aunt Pnina's activities, for all their practical importance, were insignificant compared to the reassuring radiation emanating from Gabriel Jonathan Luria, from the look of his face and the sound of his voice and, strangest of all, even from the words whose meaning, so far from calming, should have had exactly the opposite effect—that of confirming a dimly felt apprehension, clarifying it, and intensifying it into a cosmic dread.

He stood at the window smoking one of his flat Latif cigarettes and looking out at the rain pouring down in a steady beating rhythm as if it would never stop. "We must transfer the plug to the cistern pipe," said Aunt Pnina with her worried, frowning forehead and her frightened eyes. "After all, we're all standing on top of the cistern," and I saw in my imagination what she had refrained from putting into words: in a little while the floor we were standing on would collapse beneath us and we would all sink into the cistern waters and be drowned. "Yes, yes," he said, showing no signs of making ready for the necessary plugging operations, "the vessels will never be able to contain the abundance," and I was for some reason reassured, sinking into a strange kind of calm acceptance that this, in fact, was the way things were. Just as my anxiety lest the cistern be emptied left me now at the sight of his face appearing suddenly as if rising from the pail and the sound of his voice saying, "Yes, yes. The vessels are emptying." But what if Aunt Pnina failed to send for Arele the water drawer from his perch on the public water cistern, even after our own cistern was left without a drop to drink? And last year, would I have been able to stay so calm if she hadn't done what was needed, and we had all started sinking like lead in the abundance that the vessels couldn't contain? The same question came up again at a later stage, and more insistently, with regard to Gabriel Jonathan Luria himself, when his eyes were no longer able to bear the abundance of the light. With the passing of the years his sensitivity grew so great that, even inside the house, a single slanting ray of light filtering through the blinds and landing on the page of his book would be capable of felling him with a stroke of light, which he for some reason called a "reflex," and once his eyes had been dazzled in this way he had no option but to lie flat on the couch with dark glasses over his closed eyes and wait for the attack to pass. At this stage he stopped going out, and no longer took me with him on walks to the Old City and Mount Scopus or even the caves of the Sanhedrin tombs, which was the place he liked best and which has remained connected with him in my memory to this day. All this, however, happened many years later.

Here I must add only this with regard to this later stage, that when I saw him stretched out on the couch with dark glasses on, and he said to me, indicating his eyes with the

hand in which he held his cigarette, what he had said twenty
years earlier looking out of the window at the pouring rain,
"The vessels will never be able to contain the abundance," I
failed to see the connection between the cisterns, which
could not contain the water, and his eyes, which could not
bear the abundance of the light, just as I failed utterly to
remember then the favor he had done me in the distant days
of my childhood, before he became a prisoner, when he
opened my eyes to the miracle of the light.

My mother and father had gone to the Edison Cinema not
far from our house, and he remained at home with us children. I don't know why I had stayed up after my usual
bedtime. The house was quiet. A paraffin lamp burned on
the table, and its green china shade, in addition to the
yellowish-white pool of light it shed on the table around the
stem of the lamp and its base, diffused a dim green glow.
Gabriel Jonathan Luria sat reading a French book. When I
approached him he rose from his place, took me in his arms,
and went outside with me into the night.

The first meeting with the night sky shocked me and filled
me with muffled dread. I saw the sky and suddenly it was
black with tiny points of light in it. "Those are the stars,"
said Gabriel, and added, "the hosts of heaven." Somewhere
a door creaked open and a stream of light poured out of the
crack which opened in the blank dark wall, reaching the foot
of the cypress tree that stood in our yard and wrapping its
trunk in a mantle of day. Soft chill tongues of wind whispered between the branches, bringing with them from afar,
from beyond Mount Scopus, a smell of dampness of earth
and small, humming, clicking, buzzing voices, the voices of
night animals suddenly signaling and suddenly stopping.
The Old City walls and the mountains around them, the
Mount of Olives and Mount Scopus, were present in the
darkness and heavy with the weight of an ancient-breathed
quality, terrible in its dimensions which were beyond the

dimensions of man, and its eternities which were beyond the
eternity of man, and its indifference to the little men stirring
on its back. The same quality of mountains and sky, dimly
perceived on my daytime rambles along the mountain paths
between the thistles and the rocks, oppressed me now more
strongly in the night world revealed to me. The mountains
and the sky at night became more tangible in their distance,
more oppressive in their tangible presence in the darkness.

I clung tightly to Gabriel's neck, to the strong pleasant
smell of his tobacco. "Come back in," I said to him. "Let's go
back inside." He looked at me and said, "Good, let's go
inside." He understood that the fear of the elements in the
night had overcome its power of attraction, and with his first
surprise had come the awareness that I was not yet old
enough to live in both the world of the day and the world of
the night. As soon as we had returned to the shelter of the
four walls and the soft light of the green lamp shade, a heavy
weariness fell on me, as if I had just returned from a long
journey into an unknown land. After some time had
passed—whether it was a matter of days, weeks, or months
escapes me—I asked him to take me out again into the
mountains and sky of the night. I think I was resentful. I felt
a kind of anger, a kind of insult, because he had hidden
from me until now the other world of whose existence I
knew nothing and in which he continued to live after I had
gone to sleep, the night world in which he liked to take what
he called "midnight walks." He would often wander about in
the streets at night, especially in the narrow lanes of the
older quarters of the town. I wondered if he went as far as
the Sanhedrin caves on these midnight walks of his but I
never asked him, both because of a muffled apprehension of
that other world which had suddenly gaped like an abyss,
and also because of a childish reluctance to trespass in
another's soul or even peep into it through a window opened
unintentionally, a reluctance which is the basis of all true,

natural courtesy. On fine days during my school vacation he would take me for walks to the Sanhedrin caves, and the thought that these same caves went on existing in the night world too and that Gabriel himself perhaps wandered about in them in that same world, was a frightening revelation to me. Even in the daytime, when the sun in the naked sky encompassed and enveloped the whole world with its great light, going into the caves was a pleasure tinged with fear for me, fear of the dank, cold air, and the dark corners where all sorts of dangers in the shape of repulsive creeping creatures, or even predators, might lie waiting—let alone the danger from those other hidden beings which had no bodies at all. The spider spinning its web in the corner of the entrance to the cave, between the mezuzah and the lintel stone, had nothing dangerous about it, but of all creatures creeping on the face of the earth it was the most loathsome and disgusting to me—and this despite the magical beauty of the geometrical forms it spun out of its body. I loathed and detested it, it filled me with horror, long before I had ever heard the story of the "black widow," the female spider that devours her mate after coupling with him.

Regarding spiders, Gabriel told me in one of my last meetings with him a few years before the writing of these lines, after he had already stopped going out and begun to suffer from the blinding strokes of light, that it was old Rosa, Señor Moïse's sister, who came to clean his room twice a week, who had opened his eyes to one of the primary visual experiences of his life. She had finished her work and the two of them sat down to take a glass of arak together. This wise old woman who could neither read nor write had a great fondness for arak and Gabriel would tease her affectionately with cajoling, gallant little speeches as he placed the glass in her hand, for instance: "My dear Rosa, you must look after your health—if not for your own sake then at least for mine, for what would become of me if, God forbid, you were to fall ill and take to your bed? I beg you therefore to take a few sips of this arak. You know what the doctor says—there's no medicine in the world to compare with arak!" And Rosa would blush with girlish confusion and laugh with delight in the unspoken understanding of a seasoned partner in crime as she took the little glass in her rough, clumsy, callused hand and said, "Your life, Gabriel Bey. May God bless you and grant you health." And the two of them would sit there smoking flat cigarettes and drinking arak and chatting of this and that until one day the conversation turned to a certain niece of Rosa's.

"A pretty girl," said Rosa, "but she had a spider in the corner of the ceiling," and she tapped the corner of her forehead with her finger to make her meaning clear. Gabriel laughed with her, and it was only a moment later that he paused to consider what she had said. In order to indicate that something had gone wrong in the depths of this young girl's soul Rosa had said not "she had a spider in the corner of her mind," but "she had a spider in the corner of the ceiling." After Rosa had taken her leave Gabriel lay flat on his back and closed his eyes in order to prevent the attack of eye-dazzling which he felt was about to overtake him. Suddenly he saw himself peering into the opening of a ball like one of those glass bowls used as aquariums for keeping fish in, and in fact he thought at first that he was indeed looking into a huge goldfish bowl, only because of the vapors rising from it the fish, if that was what they were, looked blurred. As soon as he realized that they were not fish, but spiders, he was filled with disgust. "Such a world," he said to himself, "is really too loathsome to exist," and as he wondered at himself for allowing the Spider God to gain control of the world he was filled with rage, which escaped from his nostrils and turned into birds and cats which began to devour all the vermin infesting the world. And Gabriel saw that the birds were beautiful, and the cats found favor in his sight, and in his goodness and benevolence cows began to graze in the meadows. The birds listened to the disembodied spirits roaming the world and sang to them, and Rosa milked the cows and brought Gabriel a jug of warm frothing milk. She begged him not to destroy the spiders entirely in the fierceness of his anger, but to leave a few of them alive for healing, since spider webs were a good remedy for wounds and sores. Not only that, but they also trapped the flies of death beating against the windowpanes in their webs and ate them up. She reminded him too of the spiderweb that saved David when he was hiding from King Saul in the cave, and Gabriel drank the milk and granted her request. The milk she offered him to drink and the milk of human kindness shining in her face were more pleasing to him by far than her learned advocacy of the spider's cause, or than the beauty of the web that the spider had spun on the mouth of the cave.

I would leap into the mouth of the cave before Gabriel, and the muffled fears of disembodied spirits (the ones the birds listened to), together with the horror of creeping vermin, would merge with the shudder of anticipated pleasure which ran through me at the thought of the buried treasure I was going to discover in the mysterious world of the caves, giving it a powerful extra kick—like the sharp, bitter spices which, added to food, give it taste, although to eat them by themselves would be unbearable. The very fact of Gabriel's presence behind me dispelled not the dangers themselves, which seemed to me to exist, but my reluctance to face them—just as the sight of his face dissolved my anxieties about the cistern drying up or bursting under the pressure of the abundance. My leap into the cave entrance was a leap from the arid summer heat and the naked light into the cool darkness, preserving in its hidden depths the treasure buried there long ago—for the same people who thousands of years before had hewn and carved the caves from the rock

and deposited in their niches the sarcophagi of their dead
had deposited hidden treasures too, which were still there
waiting for me to come and dig them up and reveal them to
the light of day. The sarcophagi, and all the articles placed
beside them for the use of the dead, had been plundered
centuries before—the last of the fragments of the sarcophagi, on which the name "Yizhak" had been engraved, was
sent to the Louvre Museum by a French archaeologist in the
year 1869—but I knew that the treasure itself, buried deep
down, was still there, just as the burial niches were still there,
the same as they had always been, preserving the being of
the stone intact through the centuries, like a time-reserve in
space. This knowledge was the reverse side of the sensation,
muted and obscure yet deeply rooted, which overtook me
when I stood on the pointed rock at the right hand of the
entrance to the cave and looked across at the minaret of the
mosque in the village of Nebi Samwil, the Prophet Samuel.
It whispered that if only I could find the strength to look
with total concentration, I would see the prophet Samuel
coming home after making his circuit of Beth-el and Gilgal
and Mizpeh, just as it said in the Book of Samuel in the
Bible: "And his return was to Ramah, for there was his
house, and there he judged Israel . . ." I stand and look at
the path leading up to Ramah to his house, and all I have to
do for the wheel of time to complete its circuit and come to a
stop here, on the rock where I am standing now, and where
the prophet himself might once have stood, is concentrate
on it in the right way. The difference between the path and
the being of the stone present in the burial niches inside the
cave is only one of velocity, since the cave is like a brake
holding back the wheel of time in its revolutions and slowing
it down, and in the depths of the darkness beyond the burial
niches the action of this brake is so strong that fragments
of time are torn from their wheel and stick to it, fluttering around it with their living and their dead and their

birds listening to disembodied spirits and their buried treasure too.

Both the treasure and the bodies of the dead stored away in the sarcophagi in the burial niches of the caves seemed to me something natural and self-evident, a concrete example of everything I had learned at school about the cave of Machpelah, which was a burying place for Abraham, and Joseph who was embalmed and placed in a coffin, and the sepulchers of the House of David, and Asa who was buried in a "bed which was filled with sweet odors and divers kinds of spices prepared by the apothecaries' art" and the High Priest Hycarnos who opened a chamber in the tombs of the House of David and removed three thousand gold ingots which he gave to Antiochus to lift the siege from Jerusalem. Which is why I was so shocked and horrified when Gabriel and I emerged from the darkness of the caves into the glare of the naked sky over the cracked earth and the scorched thorns and I actually saw a person being buried with my own eyes for the first time in my life. The funeral procession was approaching the Sanhedria Cemetery from the slopes of the Bucharan Quarter, and among the mourners were the camellike Señor Moïse, absentmindedly disposing his long legs here and there, and Rosa, old and shuffling and stunned and crying, for it was her niece—the one of whom she was to say, "a pretty girl, but she had a spider in the corner of the ceiling"—who was being buried. Dumbfounded, I saw the corpse itself lying on the stretcher in its shroud without any coffin at all, unprotected and exposed to the world. The stretcher-bearers were climbing the dusty road and chanting the verse of the psalm: "They shall bear you up in their hands, lest thou dash thy foot against a stone," and every time their own feet stumbled on the stones of the path the thin little body was thrown up and down, from side to side, its head falling about distractedly as it was violently jolted backward and forward. And then to my

horror I suddenly saw its left foot poking out of the winding-sheets. This stiff greenish-yellow foot, which gave a concrete meaning to the phrase "a lifeless body," which I was to
hear some time later, hit the dry, crumbling ground when
the corpse was thrown into the hole, which the gravediggers
hurried to fill up with earth again. Gabriel watched the
burial in silence, and I too could not, dared not, open my
mouth. It was only when we were on our way home that I
asked him what had happened here, and why they had
buried her without even a coffin, because I had not yet
grasped that I had been a witness to the accustomed way of
doing things, and I thought that something out of the ordinary had taken place before my eyes. "The Jews here," he
said, "are in a hurry to break the vessel the moment it is
emptied of its contents, so that it will return as quickly as
possible to the dust from which it came." At first I thought
that he had paid no attention at all to my question, but was
returning for some reason to the water cistern which was
drying up for lack of rainwater and about which he had said
the day before, when he came into the yard just as I was busy
drawing water from it, "Yes, yes. The vessels are emptying."
But this time too, as soon as I understood what he was
referring to, the muffled dread aroused in me by this inevitable emptying melted away, just as my anxiety about the
emptying of the cistern had vanished at the sight of his face
appearing the day before as if rising out of the pail and the
sound of his voice saying, "Yes, yes. The vessels are emptying," and just as my fear that the cistern would burst under
the pressure of the abundance flooding and drowning and
sweeping everything away disappeared when he said, "Yes,
yes. The vessels will never be able to contain the abundance."

2.

The King's Eye

I SAW GABRIEL JONATHAN LURIA for the first time on a great
and strange day in my life, the day on which my eyes plainly
beheld, on the other side of the street, the King of Kings
Haile Selassie, Elect of God, Conquering Lion of the Tribe
of Judah, the Emperor of Ethiopia. It was the middle of
summer in the year 1936, and I was then a child ten years
old, carrying water from the cistern onto the broad front
verandah of our house, overlooking the Street of the
Prophets. In front of me I saw the Emperor, stepping briskly
up to the Ethiopian Consulate opposite the house, and then
when I turned to face the other way, I discovered a man
sitting on the wicker chair next to the verandah table,
regarding me and the scene before me with smiling eyes. On
that very day Mr. Luria had returned from Paris to his late
father's house—for our house was, in fact, his father's house,
and the well we drank from was his childhood well.

It was his mother who had rented their house to us,
leaving nothing to herself but the room we called the "stair
room" because it was built under the stairway leading up to
the house, with its ceiling serving as the front verandah's
floor. Although there was no connection between this underground room and the water cistern, which was located

19

under the paving stones of the backyard, with the house
itself separating them, his mother complained that a chilly
dampness from the cistern was seeping steadily into her
room and was bound to give her rheumatism in the end. It
was thanks to her misfortune and the straitened circumstances which obliged her to live off the rent from the house
that I was lucky enough to spend my childhood years in the
very same house, at the bottom of the Street of the Prophets,
in which Gabriel Jonathan had been born in the first year of
the twentieth century—twenty-six years before I myself was
born—and in which his own childhood had been spent. A
round window, like an eye opening to the east, peeped out
beneath the red-tiled roof, while the other windows of the
house were arched. The windowpanes at the front of
the house, opposite the main entrance in the Street of the
Prophets, were made of colored glass which I loved to look
at from outside in the nighttime, when the thick, opaque
stone walls were soaked in darkness, and the light stored up
in the house filtered out in a kind of calm desire through the
rose of lights in each of the windows. Around the paved
courtyard standing on the water cistern was a plot of land
intended for a garden, but in the days of my childhood no
flowers were grown there and there was nothing on it but an
ancient olive tree whose trunk was so scarred, fissured, and
cleft that its heart had been torn out, leaving an empty
hollow in its place, and a row of pines and cypresses standing
along the high stone wall which surrounded the house on all
four sides. On summer afternoons I would stretch out full
length on the round windowsill—the walls were so thick—
and look out toward Tur Malka at the top of the Mount of
Olives and the section of the Old City walls facing the
crowded square in front of the Damascus Gate. Horse-
drawn carriages stood side by side with the Arab company
buses to Ramallah and Jericho, and a few taxicabs as well, as
throngs of Arabs in long robes and keffiyehs and tarbooshes

milled and jostled between them. Fragments of Arab tunes
floated up to my window on Arab-smelling breezes. The
first wireless sets had just started appearing here and there
in Jerusalem and the first sounds from them to reach my
ears were these tunes, endlessly spiraling in the long-winded
cycle, quaking with longings, of Arab love songs. The circle
of Arab life which was revealed to me through the telescope
in whose tube I lay—the tumultuous life swarming against
the background of the Mount of Olives and the tower of Tur
Malka, with its haggling and shouting and singing and
smells, and its whole being which was dipped in a dream
despite all its uproar—was like a direct continuation of
everything I had learned in the Bible about the lives of our
forefathers in Eretz Israel; it was in some sense a materialization of those lives, awakening ancient chords like those of a
long-forgotten melody in my heart. But this materialization,
despite its being a direct continuation, was not a natural
continuation, for it was I who was the scion of the stock of
Abraham, Isaac, and Jacob, the natural and lawful heir of
King David's dynasty here in David's city. Sometime, somewhere, something had gone wrong, as if a prince and a
beggar had changed clothes in a masquerade; the beggar in
the prince's clothes had settled in the king's palace, while the
prince had taken up the beggar's staff and set out on a long
journey whose vicissitudes had transformed him beyond
recognition.

In the cellar of the house, where the rags of all the years
lay piled in rotting heaps and their junk lay rusting, I found
new treasures every time I went down with the landlady to
help her carry the folding wooden bed, which she would
bring up and take down at regular intervals for mysterious
reasons known only to herself. Once I found a music box,
which despite its hoary antiquity played, to the accompaniment of groaning and creaking from its rusted metal and
frozen cogs, the "Marseillaise" when I turned its twisted

handle, and another time I discovered a Turkish shoub'ria in its sheath underneath a pile of sacks.

A little farther down the Street of the Prophets, on the other side of the road, was the building that housed the Consulate of Ethiopia. Above its entrance, inlaid in a skillful mosaic design, was an angry-faced lion holding a scepter and wearing a crown on his head. Next to the lion was written—so I was informed, in impeccable Hebrew, by one of the monks belonging to the Ethiopian community of Jerusalem—in Ethiopian letters: "Menelik the Second, Emperor of Ethiopia, descendant of the Lion of Judah." This Menelik preceded Haile Selassie on the throne of Ethiopia. When the Italians invaded Ethiopia and conquered it the Emperor went into exile, and during his sojourn in Jerusalem he stayed in the Ethiopian Consulate opposite our house. From the verandah I saw the members of the Ethiopian community waiting for their king, and standing at their head were the tall monks, whose black faces fused with the black of their robes and the black of the cylindrical hats which added inches to their height, making them look like black poles come to life. A number of British policemen were keeping order, as usual, and a little throng of passersby had collected about them, Arabs and Jews, including several scholars with sidelocks and beards from nearby Meah Shearim on their way to the Old City.

When the Emperor emerged from his car my face burned and my whole being was buffeted by a wave of feeling in which shades of strange conflicting sensations whirled about like a kaleidoscope of shifting forms and colors spinning around very quickly on its axis. It was as a Negro dressed up as a British general in a comedy that the King of Ethiopia revealed himself to me for the first time—for the uniform he wore was the uniform of an English general in all its minutiae. From the insignia on the buttons to the leather strap slanting from the shoulder to the belt at the waist; from

the two rows of medals on the chest to the decorations on the
visor of the cap, not a detail was missing—except for the
English general himself. The neck emerging from this general's attire was like the black polished marble whose gleam
is grayish white, and so were the hands dangling from the
general's sleeves. The erect slender body, supple and muscular, which ascended the steps with an agile grace, was not
distinguished by its height, and it seemed that every one of
the monks—whose king was swallowed up by the building
before they had time to kneel and bow down before him—
was taller than he by the height of his hat. For one moment,
before he turned into the doorway, I saw his profile in the
shadow of the general's cap. It was adorned with a short
pointed beard and an abundance of hair growing down his
neck, and for all the delicacy of his features and the fine film
of spirituality overlaying them like a varnish, the expression
on his face was businesslike and brisk, as if he knew what
needed to be done because he was firmly anchored in this
world, and had no time to waste because he was in a hurry to
implement all the schemes hatching under the general's
visor, thanks to which he would eventually overcome all the
obstacles standing in his way.

The shade of his skin was actually far lighter than the skin
of his subjects who were crowding about the gates of the
Ethiopian Consulate, and had he been wearing a black robe
like one of the Coptic monks he might even have seemed
pale by their side. It was the light-colored British uniform
that made his skin so dark, and it was this uniform too that
was mainly to blame for the disappointment that played so
prominent a part in the wave of mixed feelings that over-
powered me. I had expected something altogether different: I was looking forward to a kind of radiance emanating
from Divine Grace, which was specific to the being of a king
to distinguish him from ordinary flesh and blood, and
which would flow far out of him and be sensed by everyone,

like the fragrance of orange blossom or the light of a lamp or the sound of a violin. The clothing of a king's body was suited to the splendid majesty of his soul, and if the king was Ethiopian, and the radiance of his kingliness flowed from the essence of the Negro soul, why then his clothing would be suited to this same essential Negro being, and in my imagination I could see no more fitting apparel for the Negus than a crimson cloak whose edges were trimmed with the fur of the silver fox, and on his head a crown of brightly colored feathers from the wings of the rare birds that inhabit the thickets of virgin forests.

This British-officer fancy dress in which the Emperor of Ethiopia appeared, innocent of any mysterious kingly radiance, not only made him just like any common mortal, but more than that, and unexpectedly, it brought him excessively close to me, and this precisely with regard to the secret longings of the soul; for in the depths of my heart I too saw myself as a kind of British officer, noble and proud and strong and brave, granting favors to his friends and wreaking vengeance on his enemies, for his was the power and his was the glory. This emperor had realized what for me was still a secret dream: he wore the uniform of war and stood at the head of an army that took orders from him and fought his Italian enemies, and all that remained was for him to change his skin.

The crowd stood watching in respectful silence and the Coptic monks knelt and bowed and the British policemen stayed at attention and the sergeant at their head kept saluting until the Emperor disappeared into the door of the building. At this moment a slight mishap occurred. One of the policemen winked at his mate standing by his side. Whether this wink was directed at His Imperial Majesty or whether it alluded to the private affairs between one British policeman and another, I don't know. In either case it was taken up by Itzik the American Watchmaker, who immediately raised his coarse and hairy hand in an insinuating gesture and called "Sambo" at the door closing behind the Emperor.

Itzik the American Watchmaker was neither an American nor a watchmaker. He was nothing but a bully about twenty-five years old who worked as an assistant in the big fish shop on the corner of the alley turning into the Meah Shearim marketplace. In his childhood it had been his ambition to be a watchmaker, because he was fascinated by the watchmaker who wore on his eye the black tube of a magnifying glass which revealed a secret world to him, and held in his hands the delicate instruments which probed the innermost parts, hidden from the naked eye, of the smallest of ladies' watches. And indeed, as soon as he had failed for the second time to pass the fifth grade of the Tachkemoni school (at the time pupils of his sort could still spend two years and more in the same class even in primary schools) he found a job as an apprentice to a watchmaker, and from that day forth he declared himself to be a watchmaker, even though he spent only a few weeks cleaning the watchmaker's shop and flat and carrying heavy clocks from customers' houses to the shop and back to their owners again. He also liked announcing, with a triumphant expression on his face, that he was registered on the American passport of his father, who had once spent a number of years in America. Just as he had never succeeded in mending a watch, so he never succeeded in getting to America, but as he was a great success, on the other hand, at lifting heavy loads on his back and moving herring barrels around in the fish shop, his bosses lavished every form of hard labor in the shop and outside it upon him, even lending him to the owners of neighboring shops for the same purpose, which filled his heart with professional pride as a rare expert, unique and unrivaled in his field.

However, the essence of his greatness and the main reason for his fame with all the children of Jerusalem derived from the holy war he declared on cats. Without being ordered to do so by his boss, and without demanding payment for the performance of this godly deed, he called of his own free will, his own private initiative, for a war of extermination not only on the cats lying in wait outside the fish shop, but on every cat he came across, great and small, old, pregnant, or day-old kitten. In the course of these cat-battles he invented and perfected a number of tactical ploys, and I myself with my own eyes once saw him walking down the road to the Damascus Gate with a crate of fish on his head, when his practiced eye suddenly fell on a gray cat curled up on the fence of the Italian Hospital. Without putting down his burden, holding himself almost erect, he gradually bent his knees until his free hand reached the pavement and gropingly found a piece of broken brick, having taken firmly hold of which the American Watchmaker straightened up again and stood. With one hand supporting the load on his head, without deviating from his erect posture to increase the momentum of his free throwing hand, he aimed the brick at the cat basking in the sun and hit him, and with the short, piercing, angry howl of pain which burst from the fleeing cat, the victorious warrior gave vent to a kind of gurgle of physical pleasure. He molested the Arab women coming to town to sell their wares too, upsetting a basket of eggs here or pulling a lock of hair there, but ever since the time he was locked up in the police station in St. Paul's Road (today its name has been changed to the Road of the Tribes of Israel and the building that once housed the police station now serves as a border emplacement next to the Mandelbaum Gate) and beaten up by the British sergeant for his pains, he was careful to conduct his operations in secret, which circumstances did not always permit.

Now, with the bawdy mocking sign he had made with his hand, and the cry of "Sambo" he had thrown at the exiled king's back, he fixed his eyes on the British policeman with a smile of mutual understanding in the expectation of gaining approval and further encouragement, but the latter shot

him a look of angry contempt and moved off with the
sergeant and the rest of the platoon in the direction of the
police station. For a moment the hulking youth stood rooted
to the spot with the smile congealing on his face, running his
eyes back and forth over the Consulate windows as if considering whether it were incumbent on him to cast a stone at
one of their panes. Then he extricated himself from his
dilemma with two perfunctory cries of "Sambo" which he
barked at a small child being towed after his mother, who
was walking toward the Ethiopian church in the wake of the
monks.

Together with the helpless rage and depression which
flooded me, I suddenly experienced, terrible in its certainty,
the sensation that I myself was being closely watched.
"There is an eye that sees and an ear that hears and all your
deeds are written in a book"—when I first came across these
words two or three years later this same sensation rose up in
me again together with the memory of the situation as a
whole, how I had turned around and seen Gabriel Luria
sitting on the wicker chair and watching me, the spectator of
the play. He was sitting with his legs crossed, leaning back in
the chair, his one hand holding a cigarette and his other
hand resting on his silver-knobbed cane. He was regarding
the whole situation like the spectator of a play in which I,
like all the other actors, played an unwitting part. A good,
reassuring calm radiated from him, and it was this, together
with the engaging smile twinkling in his eyes, that relieved
me of the terror of the seeing eye whose regard was quite
unique: it was very far away and very close at one and the
same time. So far away that it turned me (and with me all
the other participants in the play who were unaware of the
seeing eye) into a little midget, a tiny dwarflike creature, and
so close that every passing shade of thought and feeling
and every slightest movement took on an extraordinary importance against the background of an ancient, hidden
meaning.

3.

Moses and the Ethiopian Woman

MANY YEARS AGO I lost my joy on waking, the joy that summer when we moved to the house of Mr. Gabriel Luria and I first saw his father, the old Turkish Bey, and his mother with her dreaming eyes. Joy on waking endures only in memory, and in my silly hope of its return.

One summer day, a great and strange one in my life, Gabriel Luria returned from Paris, but I'd heard about him, since his mother had let us a flat in their house on the Street of the Prophets several weeks before he got back, and I knew the house where he had been born, and his mother also, before he himself was displayed to me with his mustache square as a die, and his cane and Panama hat. As for the old man, I can't say I knew him. I hadn't seen him more than two or three times at most. Yehuda Prosper Luria, Gabriel's father, that old Sephardi Jew, was in several ways unusual: quite apart from the occasional mistress, he had two wives, and in this resembled our fathers in that golden time when the Children of Israel still lived in tune with their nature. One wife, Hannah, belonged to the Pardos, an aristocratic old Sephardi family, and everyone said she was unusually kind and gentle. They lived together in his Jaffa house, where the three sons and the two daughters of his marriage grew up. Gabriel's mother, the second wife, belonged to a very poor Ashkenazi family from the Old City. The old man installed her in his Jerusalem house in the Street of the Prophets, and every now and then he'd stay there a week or so. In the last years of his life, he'd stay there only once every three or four months. In addition to his two wives, the old man had another distinction: the title Bey, conferred on him by the sultan. Moslems and the Jews of the old Yishuv continued to address him by his Turkish title, Bey, even after the sultan was deposed and his entire empire dissolved. I don't know whether he was given that title because of his office or that office because he was a Spanish national in Jaffa with a Turkish title; in either case he was the Spanish consul in Jaffa till the arrival of the British, and Europeans used to call him Monsieur le Consul. He died several weeks before the return of Gabriel, his youngest son.

In regard to the age of "the old Spaniard"—that's what his Jerusalem Ashkenazi wife would call him, but when she flared up she called him "the lecherous old Turk"—in this as in everything there were differences of opinion between her and her rival, the first wife. His Jaffa wife said—and Gabriel believed *her*—that the old man was eighty-nine when he died, but his Jerusalem wife, Gabriel's mother, maintained he'd achieved his century two or three years before he deserted this world. Gabriel himself didn't know the precise age of his father and he told me years later his mother had always had a tendency to exaggerate the number of years marking her off from her husband, and one could safely assume the years she had subtracted from her own age she had added to her husband's. With time she widened the chasm of the years between them till, on his death, it was clear to herself and her audience that fifty years separated her from "that old Turkish devil," who seduced her into marriage when she was "an innocent girl of fifteen" and he "an old lecher of sixty-five." Her son calculated that twenty years at most separated her from her husband, and Yehuda Prosper Bey was fifty-five years old at the time of the birth of his youngest son, Gabriel.

The old Bey still held himself straight, on those few occasions I saw him in the last year of his life, but an old man's stiffness had been poured into his joints. His head, under its hat, was shaved, as were his cheeks, except for a thick mustache overhanging each side of his mouth and black as his thick eyebrows. His quivering belly preceded him, and at his side, tall, thin, and a little bent, disposing his camellike legs here and there, walked Señor Moïse, his friend, who, it emerged, shaved him every day and dyed his mustache and eyebrows when that need arose. I didn't know, then, that the brave black color of the mustache and eyebrows of the old Bey was one of Señor Moïse's achievements. He was an artist in barbering and hair dyeing, secret and anonymous as the nameless great, retaining their anonymity because they thought of their art and not their name. I assumed that Señor Moïse's real function was to fend off the attacks on the consul by his Jerusalem wife.

Once he had taken off his hat and overcoat, the old Bey would seat himself on the verandah in the red plush armchair Señor Moïse had fetched up from the cellar, tell his beads, and hum away drearily, while his wife, with her gentle look and dreaming eyes, in increasing anger, from the doorway hurled her sharp complaints at him, in a Ladino laced with Yiddish curses, or a Yiddish decorated with Ladino insults. Señor Moïse would interpose himself, calming her down with soft words and gestures, begging her pardon but it's not right, it doesn't reflect well on her husband or herself. During all this time he was waiting for that moment when the verbal attack would end, to be followed by the bombardment of the clothes, which he caught with the agility of long service, and in order of flight: first the hat of the old man, next his scarf, and last his coat. His hat, for some reason, was a favorite target, and she would crush it in her hands and work it over with her feet. In the first bombardment I witnessed, she managed to snatch the hat from the old man's head just as he was going out the door, and to hurl it over the balcony and the stone wall into the street. But the hat had a stony strength and endured all the woman's inquisitions. After Señor Moïse had retrieved it, brushed it with a small brush, he took out of his inside jacket pocket—where, it seems, it was kept for any eventuality—and with his long hands smoothed away every wrinkle, as innocent and undamaged as before, that hat returned to the shaven head like a washed pumpkin of Yehuda Bey. Her real anger, it is said, had its source in the tarboosh her husband wore in Turkish times, and with the transition from the Ottoman to the British Empire, there was a "transference," as the psychologists would put it, in her feelings from the red column with the black tassel to the black pot with the brim. Long-legged Moïse—so she told me—had only a few years back been raised to the dignity of a "Señor," since that time when he'd managed—according to her—with his cunning and his stratagems to snare her husband's soul and to subdue it to his own will; for "the old Turk" doesn't lift a finger till compelled to by that "slave who reigns" over the soul, body, and money of his former master. Even those few miserable coins the old man throws her from time to time—"as one throws a bone to a cur"—and this only after the waters have overwhelmed her soul, after rows and threats that if he doesn't pay her the alimony due her she'll sue him, she'll reveal to the judge and the entire world "his concealed virtues"—even those worn coins paid for with her heart's blood aren't given her personally by her husband, they're passed on to her through Long-Legs, who all his life was a base domestic. He had been an orphan in Turkish times and died of hunger three times daily till the consul felt sorry for him, took him in, and when he grew up made him his kawass. The servant of a dignitary was called a kawass in Turkish times. When the consul went out, his uniformed kawass preceded him, and cleared a way for him with his staff.

Our landlady's stories were the only source of information about the old Bey and his friend Señor Moïse, so it is interesting that all her name-calling did not diminish him for me, just as her stories about "Señor Moïse's intrigues and cunning," through which "he acquired control of the body, soul, and money of the old Turk," did not prevent my observing the elements of respect, gentleness, and love in Señor Moïse's service. The attack repelled, and with no further need to defend the Bey from his wife, Señor Moïse would sit at his master's side on a stool, and together they would watch the setting sun. I once overheard snatches of conversation they had about the greatness of Moses. "Our master Moses"—so the old man said—"had the power to breathe the breath of life into dumb things. He cast his rod on the ground and it became a serpent. He told Aaron, 'Take thy rod, and cast it before Pharaoh, and it shall become a serpent,' and it became a serpent. You see, Señor Moïse, only God can breathe the breath of life into dumb things, and God conferred a little of his power on our master Moses, the man of God."

"But Prosper Bey," Moïse answered, the effort at deep thought corrugating his brow, "the Egyptian magicians also had the power to breathe the breath of life into a rod, for it's written, 'Now the magicians of Egypt, they also did in like manner with their enchantments. For they cast down every man his rod, and they became serpents.' "

"Of course, you're right"—the Bey sat up, and with an enormous red handkerchief wiped away sweat beads giving off sparks from his well-shaved head in the setting sun— "the Egyptian magicians got their power from their gods, and our master Moses his from our God, so there was war between their gods and our God, but the Lord our God overcame the Egyptian gods in that war, for it's written: 'But Aaron's rod swallowed up their rods.' "

"Just listen to His Holiness," his wife shouted from the

doorway. "You'd think he spends his whole life doing good and Bible-reading. All he can think about is Moses, Moses." She held an old checked scarf in her hand, and she crossed the porch to wrap it around her husband's neck. "Tuck it in carefully," she said. "All I need now is for you to get pneumonia. You should know there's a freezing wind in Jerusalem in the evening. You look like some street-boy in your open-necked shirt." That was the last time I saw him. Several weeks later we heard of his death in his Jaffa house, and in my memory he still sat there on the verandah of our house in the checked scarf his Jerusalem wife wrapped around his neck, his hoarse old voice, in impotent rage, repeating, "Our master Moses, our master Moses," and sweat beads on his shaved head shooting fireworks at the sunset.

But I saw Gabriel's mother almost every day, over the years we lived in the house she inherited from her husband. Into that tangled inheritance I cannot enter, if only because she herself and the old judge alone knew its details. Years later Gabriel told me his mother had defrauded her enemy who, according to the old man's will, was the legal heir to all his property. The old man left all his property to his Jaffa wife and his children by her, and nothing to Gabriel's mother save the tenancy of his house on the Street of the Prophets for the remainder of her life, and the income from its rent. He didn't mention Gabriel in his will, which was not inadvertent, though Gabriel had the impression, when he last saw his father just before going abroad, that he didn't remember him, and that in the old man's muzzy brain Gabriel had been confused with his father's brother David. Yehuda Prosper's older brother had been called David, and when they were still children Yehuda followed him around like a shadow till David died suddenly on the day of his bar mitzvah. His father would unexpectedly hug Gabriel when he was a boy, saying, "You're exactly like my brother David, God bless him; you've his face and movements. He didn't live long enough to be your uncle, he died suddenly on the day of his bar mitzvah." The old man was in a blur when Gabriel said good-bye before going off to Europe. He plucked at his black mustache, his black eyebrows reared like two crests of one somber wave, and in a hoarse old voice he growled, "David, I've told you already you're not to go to Bethlehem." He cleared his throat, hawked, his face got very red. "On the way you can go to Rachel's tomb, but don't stay long, or you'll have to sleep there overnight." Gabriel was not struck out of the will, I've already said, from inadvertence. It was because of Gabriel's behavior, or rather because of the way he squandered his father's money in Europe, for years neglecting his medical studies, despite his father's letters threatening to stop his allowance and disinherit him if he kept up his prodigality. So if Gabriel had a roof over his head when he got back penniless, it wasn't because of the father he so much loved—and Gabriel never loved anyone more than he loved him—it was because of the chicanery of his mother.

I would see her, as I said, nearly every day when we lived there, especially during the long school holiday, since I spent most of it on our verandah. There weren't very many children's summer camps at that time, and we would play in the yard and change our books at the B'nai B'rith Library, which I believe still survives, in the same building in an alley off the Street of the Prophets. I would read on the verandah, and she would interrupt me at some crisis in the story. She would ask me to take the folding bed down to the cellar, or fetch it up from the cellar, or to shift the commode so she could get at some remote corner with her broom, and then shift it back once she'd swept that corner. She would confer on me errands not requiring overmuch skill, for instance, buying matches or a can of olive oil or clothespins or some other article not likely to decay or rot, and independent of that perishable scale of values with its innumerable rungs of good and evil. It was for this reason I was never sent to buy a loaf of bread, or a rotel or oquia of tomatoes, which demand

an innate talent for fine distinctions in addition to the requi-
site experience, though it was in this connection I received
from her a protracted and well-thought-out lesson: a bread
must be well baked, for there's nothing worse for the digestion than underbaked dough, which shouldn't be over-
baked, either, because then it infringes on the zone of the
burnt. And she'd known loaves whose dough hadn't been
properly kneaded or leavened, whose crust was burnt and
whose insides were soggy. Then how is a man to do right,
that is to say, to choose from all the loaves the properly
kneaded, leavened, and baked loaf? He must first have
sharp senses, then exercise them, and hone them with life
experience. He needs an eye for the glow of the right loaf, a
nose for its warm smell, a hand to probe the tension of the
crust covering the soft flesh of the bread, and an ear alert to
the tiny crackling voices of the bread's guts pressed against
its skin. Even she, with all her experience and her fastidious
senses, sometimes had to go back to the shop and change
her bread. And at the end of all these lessons, enlivened by
demonstrations of the color, smell, touch, and crackling
voices of the right loaf, chosen by her, she would send me out
to buy a cake of laundry soap, or of carbolic, thereby deepening the insult that in her view I was not equipped to buy a
loaf of bread. Years later, when I laughingly told Gabriel his
mother had slighted my matured senses, he told me I'd no
idea how grateful I should have been to her for not sending
me on those errands, which were the nightmare of his childhood—that nightmare of returning rotten tomatoes, burnt
bread, rancid butter, wormy rice, kerosene-smelly cheese.

"Gabby," she would say, "take this rancid butter back right
away to Red Ear." This was her name for the grocer; she had
a good eye for the distinguishing peculiarities in a man, for
his general look and his specific defects. And his right ear
was red, even when he paled. Nobody saw it till the old Bey's
wife took a hard look and delivered that verdict, which stuck

to him the rest of his life. Something trivial, hidden, entirely unremarked became a focus, a point of reference. Everyone interrogated by her eye—shopkeepers, domestics, friends of her husband—was awarded a nickname, and not only that but an impersonation also, for she was a natural mime. When she told, for example, the story of her quarrel with the Black Cockscomb, that is to say, Dinah the Persian washerwoman, awarded that name for her general look and particular hairdo, she would give you not only what Dinah said but her way of saying it, gestures, voice, intonation.

Sometimes, inspired, she would imitate her interlocutor in the actual course of their conversation: she would adopt a Yemenite accent when talking to the Yemenite plasterer, and with Red Ear, a Galician Jew, she would have pronounced Galician intonation, which gave her the twofold pleasure of satisfying her innate craving for drama and for imitation of a man of two unusual qualities: he was both a shopkeeper and a Galician. She considered all shopkeepers thieves, all of them anxious to unload the shoddiest goods at the highest prices. All Galicians were born crooks. "You're a foolish boy," she would tell Gabby when he winced away from returning some purchase. "What stops you giving Red Ear back his rancid butter? A Galician shopkeeper isn't ashamed to cheat a child—he palmed off last week's butter on you—yet you're ashamed to return it. What kind of world are we living in? You're ashamed to tell him he cheated you. Well, of course, it's nice for a shopkeeper when a fool falls into his shop."

In defense of the Bey's wife, I must say she did not send only her son back with shoddy goods, or her husband to change the present he had given her. Like all perfectionists she was stricter with herself than others, and spent a lot of time returning purchases that displeased her, or about which she had changed her mind. She was a perfectionist also in her cooking. But because she was so fastidious her meals came into the world rather late, which is why her husband, when they still lived together, complained that he never got his food at the right time, and there was no sequence to the dishes. Really to enjoy one of his wife's masterpieces, the old man said, one had to devote the day to it: the salad was prepared in the morning, the main dish at noon, the soup arrived at Minha, and at Ma'ariv the dessert. Of course he was exaggerating but he did convey some notion of his Jerusalem wife's life rhythm. She suffered, like all perfectionists, from the flawed reality around her, and in her good times even, when she had the whole house to herself and a Moslem maid, she would complain. Then how much more so at the end of her life, when she rented the house to us and descended to live in the basement. She was then a woman of over sixty, with astonishing changes of expression that kept pace with her moods. She had been dark and delicate when young; it was her delicacy and gazelle-brown eyes (for oddly enough Gabriel inherited his blue eyes from his Sephardi father, not from his Ashkenazi mother), her graceful movements and laughter that captured the heart of the Spanish consul when he paid a ceremonial call at the Evelina de Rothschild School for Girls, where she was about to complete her studies. It was she who presented him with flowers on behalf of the graduating class. After many years of marriage, he still thought himself physically and spiritually gross in comparison with her. Gabriel was thirteen before he heard his father, in one of their quarrels, call his mother a delicate viper; the Mishnaic caution against the law students, he commented to Señor Moïse, referred really to the Jerusalem wife, who bites like a fox, stings like a scorpion, hisses like a snake, and whose words are like live coals. She kept that delicate look in old age, though now she was bent and slow and stiff. Usually she seemed immersed in a distinct and distant world, even when making her rounds of the market; her movements were slow, and she had a tendency to sink into long, remote thoughts and reveries, so she never had time enough even for her routine needs. She was always occupied with cooking, mending, cleaning, though she lived entirely on her own and did not keep up connections after her husband's death, till a late friendship sprang up between her and her sister, Pnina.

She would sit for hours outside her door on the verandah, with an abstracted look, polishing rice in a siniyeh, a flat copper dish. Sometimes she would sing softly and pleasantly, and it always surprised me that those songs and the hysterical abuse of her husband issued from the same mouth. The ancient, animal sound of her abuse gave me gooseflesh. No one who heard her singing could have guessed at the wild beast inside this delicate, gentle woman, just as no observer of the deep friendship that developed between her and her sister, Pnina, after the death of the old Bey, could ever have imagined the atrocious war she waged on her sister thirty years back, on discovering she was the mistress of her husband, Yehuda Prosper Bey. It belonged to Gabriel's saddest and most shaming childhood memories. His adoring and attentive mother became a tigress. "Mother, please, I can't bear any more." She didn't listen. In the rush to finish off her sister who claws back but retreats, her blind anger can bring down her son. She held on like a wildcat, all nails, to her sister's hair, her neck veins bulged, she shrieked, "Madonna! Who ran after the fat prick of the Turkish adulterer? You shrinking spinster, I'll scratch your eyes out." Her scream didn't have a human sound; it was more of a hiss. Pnina was her elder sister, a pious spinster who had never left home but lingered there for years after the disgraceful marriage of the younger sister to that "Turkish adulterer." In the sisterly quarrels preceding the discovery of her affair, Pnina held her sister responsible for her spinsterhood, that infidel sister who was the slave of "the fat prick of the Turkish adulterer" and became his "concubine." And what God-fearing Jew would marry a woman whose sister was the concubine of a Turkish adulterer? This is what Pnina said in her prolonged spinsterhood for as long as the affair continued in secret with that same Turkish adulterer. But when the affair came to an end following its discovery, of course it was a God-fearing Jew she found itching to marry her. After the death of the old Bey, his widow grandly allowed herself to be reconciled to Pnina, who became a kind of lady's companion, especially when her sister's bouts of headache and her mysterious backache began. She would lie back in bed, swathed in a turban to prevent dizziness, and permit her elder sister to fuss over her, even send her sister on errands. Pnina may have gotten a scolding from time to time; occasionally she became an object of teasing, but in general the sisters enjoyed a good gossip.

She would sit for hours at the door, peeling ba'miah, and sing children's songs to herself in a soft, clear voice at sunset, or tell me stories about Gabriel if I asked. I would ask, and she would respond, but of herself she would not volunteer anything, for I knew her at the end of her life, and her reverie was given to herself, her aches and pains; her feelings to her own childhood and adolescence. That is why I heard the first time of his childhood studies, of the period when he still attended the tiny yeshiva of Rabbi Avremale in the Old City, not from his mother but queerly enough from Yitzhak, the son of Red Ear, when I went to the grocer for half a rotel of granulated sugar and a dozen clothespins. Gabriel was sent first to the cheder and then the yeshiva of Rabbi Avremale, and from there he went on to Kol Yisrael Chaverim, the Alliance school. After graduating he joined the Teachers' Seminary established by the German-Jewish society, Ezra. Of all people it was his father, the Sephardi Jew with the Turkish title, who decided he should begin his studies at an Ashkenazi cheder. He wanted his son, he said, "to strike roots in the inheritance of his fathers," and he preferred the Ashkenazi cheder to the Sephardi Talmud

Torah because "the Ashkenazis are more exacting than the Sephardis."

When he had sent his long roots down into his fathers' inheritance (as interpreted by Rabbi Avremale, whose yeshiva later on fostered generations of Netorei Karta*), his son Gabriel—the Spanish consul thought—could offer his branches to any wind without risking his soul.

Reb Yitzhak, Red Ear's son, who after the establishment of the State of Israel became one of the supporters of Netorei Karta, appeared to me a prematurely old Jew, though he couldn't have been forty, since he went to the same cheder as Gabriel. Red Ear's own name for his son was not Yitzhak but Reb Yitzhok. Reb Yitzhok was a big man, and he had an enormous beard blown every which way like a horse's tail at a gallop, but his sidelocks exerted the principal charm. I have never seen sidelocks as grandly long as his among any Jews I've encountered in the Meah Shearim market or the Hungarian Quarter. There are dandies who braid their sidelocks but he let them grow as they liked, so they streamed into his beard like two frothing rivers into the sea. On an errand to his shop for my landlady, I would address him in Hebrew but he would answer in Yiddish. Of course he knew Hebrew but he thought it was spoken only by atheists, who had drunk from the waters of "that troubler of Israel, Eliezer Ben-Yehuda, may his name and memory be wiped out." I told him to charge the half-rotel of sugar and the dozen clothespins to the account of Mrs. Luria. He looked severe. When he had noted down the purchase, he asked me, with lowered eyes, whether her son Gabriel had got back from abroad. "He's clever," he said, "but wicked. He has a pagan soul. You don't often find such a soul even among the goyim. They've suppressed their cults. He was still at cheder when he set up his cult."

When a man was called a renegade, or a goy, by a religious Jew, or a woman a whore, I had never thought of that man as

---

* Netorei Karta—The most bigoted and fanatical of Jewish religious sects.

a real goy, or attributed the actions of a whore to that woman. Passing through Meah Shearim without a hat, I had several times been called such a goy, and my sister had been called a whore because of her light summer frock. Such terms don't carry any private weight, and I took them for what they were, as a general designation for anyone not religious.

So if after all I was impressed by Reb Yitzhok, it was because both words and tone implied unusual wickedness in Gabriel, a kind of savagery marking him off from the usual run of atheists and even from goyim; but such phrases as "the soul of a pagan" and "the work of star-worshipers" didn't give me a clear notion of what he had actually done. Even Gabriel's mother would not explain that when I got back with the half-rotel of sugar and the dozen clothespins, and recounted part of what Red Ear's son had said about her son. Of course I would repeat only what was least likely to offend her, phrases like "working the sun and stars." "What did Reb Yitzhok mean," I asked her inquisitively, "saying Gabriel worked the Zodiac when he was a boy?"

"He can go to hell," she said calmly, quite unruffled by what he'd said, and I was amazed that an old man with such a beard and sidelocks could be consigned to hell. "Like father like son. A Galician thief. Look what dirty sugar he gave you."

She poured the sugar into a bowl, put the clothespins into a drawer of the commode, then went out onto the terrace to cut choorfesh—that's the Arabic name for this vegetable, and that's my name for it as I don't know its Hebrew name even today. In France it has a domesticated cousin, the artichoke. As she seemed occupied with the choorfesh, I thought she hadn't heard my question about the strange cults of her son in his childhood, so I cast around for a way of getting back to the subject. Talking as if to herself, she anticipated me.

"So Gabby did 'foreign' work as a child. Any kind of work is foreign to those schnorrers. He was full of fantasy when he

was a boy, like the old man; you know the old man is Oriental, all Orientals are dreamers. He was soaked in their fantasies, especially about Moses, anything about Moses. Now
what did Moses really do? He took over a rabble, sons of
slaves, and made a great nation out of them. Why did he
drag them around with him forty years, where a decent man
wouldn't show his face? I say he did it because he was
ashamed to appear in public with them; he couldn't be seen
among decent people together with that mob of slaves with
their first-day-out look. That old Turk never stopped thinking about Moses; I think if he'd had an Ethiopian woman
he'd have become a Moses. And Gabby is flesh of his flesh.
He got his strong body from his father, his strong body and
his imagination also. Every day he'd get back from cheder
with a new story about something wonderful happening to
him on the way. He daydreamed so much I began to worry
about his health. He had such pictures in his mind. You
know, there should be a limit to everything, you can hurt
yourself carrying things too far. Dreamers stumble, they get
lost. And look what happened to Gabby. He was talented.
He was never short of money. His yeshiva head, his teachers
at the Lemmel School and the Alliance, they all said he had a
good grasp of everything. He had a sharp mind. And we
gave him everything. The Jerusalem poor in their wildest
dreams never saw what we gave him. And none of his friends
went off to Paris like him, sent off like a prince to finish his
studies. If he'd returned when he should have, he'd be the
biggest doctor in the country. He'd be bigger than Dr. Ticho,
Dr. Mazia, and Dr. Wallach all squeezed into one. And what
did he do there? I ask you, what did he do there, all that time
in Paris? What's he doing now? Wandering around like a
tramp. He squandered his father's money. It's all because of
his fantasies. I can't sleep at night, thinking about him. He
gave his life to his fantasies; he got them from his father. I
told you he's flesh of his flesh."

Her thoughts reverted to Yehuda Bey, and in discoursing on her late husband she forgot about her son. The more she expatiated, the more impatient I became, and I felt saddened by the knowledge that I would get nothing out of her to give me a clear picture of the pagan cult of Gabriel's childhood—what she called his Oriental fantasies. Her reveries revolved around herself; she was full of the story of her life with the old Bey. Her dead husband had the real claim on her thought; she left her living son only a place in the margin. I tried several times to direct her back to the "Oriental" fantasies of the young Gabriel, but she had nothing to add, she would only emphasize they were a kind of Oriental sickness contracted from his father. Her old-woman's talk annoyed me; it flowed along such a different riverbed from the one I had had in mind, but echoed peculiarly in my soul, not by day but at night, in a recurrent childhood dream which coiled itself around the conversation, just before his death, of the old Bey and long-legged Señor Moïse. Old Red Ear sits dozing as always at the door of his shop, his son Reb Yitzhok stands with wild sidelocks in front of the balance, and directs an angry look at the scales. It isn't the grocery shop, it's our verandah, and old Red Ear is Pharaoh. I'm surprised that Pharaoh, exalted over all the kings of the earth, builder of the pyramids, of Pithom and Rameses, in fact is merely the Galician grocer, that helpless old man. I'm disappointed, saddened by this gray, small, old, helpless reality. The chief magician, that is to say, Reb Yitzhok, whispers in the red ear of Pharaoh, "Wake up, open your eyes, sit up straight. Here he comes. Stop snoring." I learn from his whisper that this uninterrupted snoring sending out ripples over the world originates in the nostrils of the red-eared Pharaoh now compelled to wake up because Moses the man of God advances along the terrace in his black London bowler hat and carrying his cane, breathless and puffing from the steep climb. Señor Moïse supports him under the arms, stands at his side, disposes his legs here and there, scouts around with his eyes, alert to any ambush. And at that moment the old woman emerges from the basement, makes for the old man, snatches the hat from his head, and works over it with her feet. The head magician is surrounded by a crowd of Hassidim energetically praying. Their eyes are closed in intense concentration, their mouths are wide open, but no one can hear them because of the snoring of Pharaoh, who has relapsed into deep sleep. "Don't believe him," the old woman cries to the magicians, pointing at the old Bey. "They're only Oriental fantasies, he's not Moses, he's not Moses. He doesn't have an Ethiopian woman." Señor Moïse interposes himself, calming her down with soft words and gestures, begging her pardon but it's not right, it doesn't reflect well on her husband or herself. The old man, who's now sitting in a red armchair, wipes the sweat beads shining in the sunset from his skull, calls Señor Moïse over, and whispers something in his ear. The excitement among the magicians increases. They stand on tiptoe, rock to and fro on their heels, violently tremble. They beat their chests with their fists. The weight on my chest disappears, I feel refreshed. On waking I have the joy of knowing clearly beforehand that Aaron's rod, cast down at the command of Moses, will soon swallow the old woman and overcome Pharaoh's magicians and every windmill.

I must stress here that this clear knowledge was no longer part of the dream itself, which ended with the old Bey's whispering in Señor Moïse's ear, the one that so excited the magicians and lifted the weight from my heart, but a logical conclusion I came to when I woke, stemming from the contents of the dream and adding the downfall of Don Quixote's windmills to the defeat of the old woman and the magicians of Egypt in the dream, and the happiness that was born out of that knowledge mingled with the joy of all my awakenings that summer, and the laughter.

The joy I had on waking that summer left me over twenty-five years ago. The moment of waking, this transition from the reality of consciousness in sleep to the reality of consciousness when awake, is the hardest and most painful of all—even when the opening eyes of the flesh liberate the soul from the terrors of the closing eyes of the spirit—because like the creation of the world, illumination, birth, and death, it is one of those leaps over the void in which the agony of birth encompasses both the creator and the creature, the woman in labor and the newborn babe, the world and its redeemer.

When I myself began to suffer the agonies of waking, morning after morning, I remembered what Gabriel told me once that same summer of the joyful awakenings, when we were walking down Abyssinian Road together after one of the attacks of light which dazzled his eyes. When he was a boy attending the Little Yeshiva he had read something in a midrash*—or maybe in one of the commentaries on the Book of Genesis, I don't remember exactly—about the verse "and God said, Let there be light: and there was light": "and there was," *vayihi*, comes from *vayi*—the cry of pain of the creation of light and the world. Gabriel said that he had only begun to understand the meaning of these words twenty-five years after he read them, when he began to suffer from the strokes of light; and it seems to me that I myself began to grasp something of their meaning, since, as with all true meanings, only a person who has experienced them first-hand can grasp and contain them, twenty-five years after Gabriel told them to me, when I began to suffer from the pain of waking, which came to teach me by the long hard road of suffering the meaning of the lost blessing of the joy I once had on waking—a joy which no longer exists except in the longings of memory and the fatuous hope that it will come back one day.

* Midrash—An early Rabbinic legend or homiletic commentary on the Bible.

It may be that it is all only a question of age, and that then, when I was a child, the transition from the consciousness of sleep to the consciousness of waking was very quick and unconscious, so that the pain too was unconscious. Or possibly—and I incline to believe in this possibility, perhaps because I want to believe in it—there was no abyss gaping then between these two states of the soul—the abyss of birth and death—and I would run back and forth between sleeping and waking, and waking and sleeping, as if I were passing from one room to another in an enchanted palace, bubbling with the joy of the wonderful surprises awaiting me in every corner and at the top of every flight of stairs. It must be stressed, and stressed and stressed again, that the consciousness of the soul in sleeping and the consciousness of the soul in waking are not identical with the consciousness of night and day, even though sleeping usually comes at night and waking in the daytime, which can, and often does, lead to confusion between the two. When, for example, I first became conscious of the night in my first encounter with the night sky, it happened at night but the consciousness itself was a waking consciousness, and it seems to me no exaggeration to say that the world of the night and the world of the day are both only different aspects of the waking consciousness, whereas the consciousness of a man asleep, like the consciousness of the soul before birth and after death, exists beyond both day and night, and even dreams don't always penetrate into it and reach it, unless they belong to a certain kind, the kind we don't even remember having forgotten. And the remembrance of this essential reality which is above and beyond day and night depends precisely on the awakening of the waking consciousness, an awakening from the reality of man in his waking state which must also be counted among those leaps over the void which are the creation of the world, illumination, birth, and death.

4.

The Dove and the Moon

OUR LANDLADY, Mrs. Luria, didn't like going into the pharmacy because of the pharmacist, Dr. Blum, who always—so she said—gave her either an oppressive feeling of guilt for having disturbed him at his important work, or else an unnatural sensation of strain, as if she were a little girl who didn't know the right questions or the right answers either. Her sensations on those rare occasions when he deliberately set out to be nice to her were twice as oppressive, strained, and annoying, and so she used to send me to him instead.

At the beginning I was of the opinion that he went about quite naked under his white coat, and that he had nothing on his skin but the spectacles pinching his nose, like a kind of scientific Gandhi, because nothing peeped out of the opening of this coat on top but the faded fair hair on his chest, and there was nothing to be seen below but his bluish-white knees. Later on, however, I discovered that this initial impression was due to the fact that he wore no tie around his neck during working hours, and his trousers were khaki shorts—not the kind that everyone wore then, but the kind worn by the British officers and soldiers, which were stiffer and more ironed. (Only now, while writing all this, does it occur to me that since the establishment of the State, short trousers have almost entirely disappeared from the country.) To complete the picture of this scientific Gandhi, he wore nothing on his feet while he worked but a pair of worn-out sandals, which had turned into slippers ever since the straps of their heels had fallen off and slapped the floor with his every step.

He was always busy transferring the contents of the Separanda and Toxica compartments from one cupboard to another, and rearranging the jars in each compartment. Since he had recently returned from the University of Beirut, where he had qualified as a pharmacist, and his pharmacy was as new as his diploma on the wall, I supposed at first that he would bring this activity to an end as soon as the place of each bottle of medicine had been finally fixed. But days, weeks, and even months later—in fact for the whole of the period during which he served as a pharmacist—he continued to transfer the drugs from one place to another with the same expression—concentrated in its vacillations, brisk in its tortuousness, frowning and pursed—he wore when he paced back and forth in the cage of his laboratory, his face turned to the ceiling and his hands folded on his backside, holding the little book open at the place where he was supposed to be reading. When he was not trying to determine the right place for drugs, he was searching the heights of the ceiling for the meaning of the verses of the little book peeping through the fingers of his hands folded on his backside, and between the two he had to find time for the unavoidable nuisance of concocting eye drops for Mrs. Luria, his regular customer, who in spite of everything remained—through my good offices—the only one loyal to him to the end of the pharmacy's days.

"Ha, what does the younger generation say?" he would ask me twice a week without looking at me, since his eyes were busy examining the new Toxica compartment. "Who will save us?" Sometimes he would change the formula and ask,

"Who will bring salvation to the world?" and once he said, "Who will save me?" Once he suddenly roused himself to look at me and ask, "And Gabriel, how is he? When did you see him last?"

"I've never seen him," I said. About an hour before, I had tried in vain to evoke some sort of picture of Gabriel in the days of his childhood from the words of Mrs. Luria, and I didn't know yet that I was to see him for myself in less than a month's time with his sudden return home.

"He must have gone abroad before you were born," he said. "That's the way of the world nowadays. A man doesn't see his brother."

"He's not my brother," I said, "and Mrs. Luria isn't my mother. She's our landlady." Apparently he didn't hear what I said, or else my words made no impression on him at all, for he fell to examining my face and said, "Yes, yes. You can see it at once. You're alike as two peas in a pod, except for the clothes. When we were children we studied Torah together in the cheder, and that Torah, that strong drug, is at the root of all his troubles. I told your mother so. 'Mrs. Luria,' I said to her, 'please give me your son Gabriel's address. I want to write him a letter. Do you know what is at the root of all your son's troubles? The Torah! Yes, yes—it was the Torah that poisoned his mind!' I tried to explain it to her, but she got up and ran away. She said she had no time for nonsense, and since then she's been afraid of coming in here. She's filled her mind with straw and chaff, there's no room in it for the things that are really important. Forgive me for talking like this about your mother, but there's no need for you to feel insulted—most mothers in our day, and in fact most human beings, are exactly the same. That's why they give the impression of people so busy with important affairs. She refused, naturally, to give me your brother Gabriel's address. If you knew Gabriel's address, I would ask you to give it to me, but it's as clear as daylight to me that she's never disclosed it to you, just as she's probably succeeded in keeping secret from you certain events that happened years before you were born, when Gabriel was still a child and used to go down to the Kidron Valley on moonlit nights with his doves."

On moonlit nights with my doves, which I never had, to the Kidron Valley I never went down, but once I went up to Mount Scopus on a night when the full moon floated up beyond the mountains of Moab, orange-veiled in a broad ancient silence charging the Judean desert night with the high tension of an existence beyond, lapping the pillars of the world with the waves of the mountain shoulders in a line of latitude from the peak of Nevo to Tur Malka, and afterward I dreamed a dream. In the recurring dream the moon would rise above the mountains of Moab and advance toward the Mount of Olives and grow bigger and purpler and suck up and absorb into itself the juice of the world, until I woke up terrified and throbbing with the awful knowledge that the soul of the squeezed-out world was about to expire. It was the terror of the other world that surrounds the manifest world as the sea envelops the ship that dares to cleave with its prow the foam licking its bows, that great immeasurable sea whose primeval splendor can be enjoyed by the voyager only when he feels the deck firm beneath his feet and knows that his craft is in no danger of capsizing. It was the same terror that gripped me when I sensed the ghosts who filled the room in the dark of night, as I fell into the sleep which awakened me to their blood-curdling call, and when I mentioned it to Dr. Blum at our landlady's funeral, he told me something he had once read in a certain little book, whose name and author had both slipped his mind: namely, that it was always the way of the spirits of the dead to terrify us with their presence, unless we had loved the dead person when he was alive on earth. When it happened, not only did I not know whose spirit was terrifying me, I didn't even know if it was the spirit of anyone in particular. The very sensation that a being that filled the house existed, although it could not be grasped with the senses of time and place, was very terrible to me, like the terrible moon in the recurring dream that came back to me with the first allusion to the moonlit nights on which Gabriel had gone down to the Kidron Valley with his doves. "Yes, yes," he added, looking steadily at the shrouded body of the landlady, who looked much smaller and more shriveled up in her death than in her life, "it's only after a person dies that we find out whether we really loved him."

I was suddenly unnerved by the thought peeping out of his eyes and his voice that it was her ghost that had come to haunt me on that night—a hasty and basically untenable conclusion on his part, since the night of terror had preceded the night of her death by seven weeks at least—but I was too experienced to try to argue with him, and went on listening in silence. Now, when it was undeniable that her soul had departed from her body, Dr. Blum felt himself at liberty to acquaint me with those details concerning the events in her son Gabriel's childhood which in his opinion she had deliberately kept secret from me, and which for the sake of the truth he himself should have proclaimed in season and out, but which he had repressed for her sake, not because she was worthy of it, but because he felt himself bound by some sort of elementary decency in human relations. Precisely at this point, and in spite of my experience, I tried to show him his mistake and prove to him that the landlady had made no attempt at all to keep the said events a secret, if only for the simple reason that she knew nothing about them, and to the little she did know she paid no attention at all, and to my questions about the moonlit nights on which Gabriel had gone down to the Kidron Valley with his doves she had responded with astonishment and said, "Ha? To the Kidron Valley? With his doves? The rascal must have been trying to sell them to the Arabs of Silwan! Well, really! So now at last, after all these years, the great mystery of where our doves disappeared to is solved! And to think that it never once occurred to me to suspect him! Ha, ha, he was the one for mischief when he was a boy . . ."—which shows that in her eyes it was nothing but a childish prank of no importance at all, deserving of no more than the forgiving smile she bestowed on it from a distance of thirty years.

"A childish prank of no importance at all!" The pharmacist repeated the words of the landlady, transmitted to him by me after a certain delay, and a bitter smile spread over his lips. "Almighty God! I've always known that she stopped up her mind with straw and chaff, but during all this time that I concocted eye drops for her I never realized that she was so blind. I tell you straight, I'm sorry for every drop of effort I wasted on her during all these years. You know what the trouble with me is? The trouble with me is that I know there's no one to talk to, that I'm wasting my words on deaf ears, and in spite of everything I go on trying to explain."

His anger seethed and grew with every word he uttered, and when the funeral procession reached the cemetery, his eyes behind their pince-nez spectacles were already misted with helpless rage against the landlady, who so long as she stayed in her bodily abode had allowed him to hope that if only he could burst his way into one of the blocked-up openings with his tireless knocking, he would reach her at last. But from the moment she made up her mind to disappear completely, she had robbed him of all hope of finding her, even were he to succeed in tearing her deaf ears open with his words and breaking into all the orifices of her untenanted body; the landlady no longer peered through the weary eyes or eavesdropped behind the curtains of the deaf ears, and as he walked by the side of her abandoned house which was returning to the dust and the stones from which it had been taken, her address was more unknown to

him than the address of her son Gabriel, which she had
hidden from him, although certain events of his childhood
were hidden from her, and the details known to her she had
regarded merely as a mischievous prank, deserving of no
more, from a distance of thirty years, than a forgiving smile.

As for me, I don't know whether the events deserve a forgiving smile or not. Because they reached me from the pharmacist's mouth and not from hers, and at a time when his eyes
were blurred with a mist of helpless rage at her demise, I
don't know not only what they deserved, but even how he
himself regarded them, he who was at least once an eyewitness to them. But ever since they had fallen from his mouth
like fragments of ancient pottery, awakening with their muffled sound the memory of that other existence, existing
beyond the oblivion which is born with our birth, I could
never see the new moon rise without there being born in me
the image of the boy Gabriel, who on his thirteenth birthday
became bar mitzvah and therefore went down with his dove
to the Kidron Valley, not at the new but at the full moon.

When he lay down on his bed the room filled with longing
and the window wide open to the east grew lighter from the
sill upward, and the wings of his dove fluttering outside
played on the string strung onto the moon, until she
dropped like a spark from on high and landed on the windowsill, a silhouette against the moon floating up from
below to be an orange halo for her. He rose to the murmur
of her call and dressed himself and went out after her to the
moon shedding her reddish gold onto the mist surrounding
the mountains of Moab and growing rounder and more
silvery as she climbed higher. His foot did not stumble and
his head did not smash into the abyss at the foot of the wall
along whose battlements he sped from the tower of David
above the Valley of Hinnom and the Ophel and the Gihon
spring and the Kidron stream toward the Valley of
Jehosophat; and no harm befell him, nor could it, so long as

his soul, bound up with the life of the dove and beating
between her wings, remained intact. When a stone from a
catapult had once damaged her wing, he had fallen ill and
recovered only when the wing had healed, and he knew too
that with her death his soul would die, so that his only care
as he raced above the ancient chasms was for the dove fluttering before him, until he jumped down at the corner of the
Ophel and crossed it and turned aside into the bed of the
creek following the course of the Kidron stream and passing
between Zacharia's tomb and Absalom's tomb until he
reached the rock altar which no iron instrument had hewn.
The dove landed on the head of the rock in the direction of
the invisible line beating inside her and extending from the
Kidron stream through the Valley of Jehosophat to bisect
the point where the eastern slope of Mount Scopus hits the
western slope of the Mount of Olives at the angle of the
moon, and he lay on his belly with his arms at his sides and
his legs pressed together, in line with the dove and the moon.
On the fullness of the broad ancient silence, fragrant and
merciful in its indifferent coolness, the moon strings
vibrated in a trembling crescendo of desire and the longing
of one world for another, until the pipeline of the spheres
opened and the stream of abundance surged out of him and
into the breath of the moon, inhaling the red of the high
hills and exhaling the violet and silver effulgence in which
he rose, and holding her pulsing and cooing above the altar,
stretched forth his hand to slay his dove. No ram was caught
by its horns in a thicket, and her blood gushed out and
spilled onto the altar, bare of wood for the fire. From the
corners of the altar the blood dripped blue in the light of the
moon, drop after drop, and no fire took hold of the
twitching corpse to offer it up as a sweet savor in the nostrils
of the Lord, to please Him and revive His spirits with the
gift of the soul which had perished with her sacrifice and
did not forgive him.

"I'll never forgive myself for not getting Gabriel's address out of her," said the pharmacist on our way back from the landlady's funeral, removing the spectacles from his nose so as to polish away the vapors of his rage. Naked and bereft of their lenses, his eyes were sunk deep into their sockets and stared out helplessly at a world not theirs. "Now there's nothing left for it," he said with the same expression, concentrated in its vacillations, brisk in its tortuousness, frowning and pursed, that he wore when he was busy transferring drugs from one compartment to another, at the same time returning his spectacles to their usual place, clearly marked by the red groove running around the bridge of the nose, "but for me to try to study Torah at the university. Who knows? Maybe there they understand the law of the priests better than the rabbi who taught us Torah with Rashi at cheder when we were children. After all, I'm no greenhorn any longer, and at my age I should see things with a calm mind and a tranquil spirit."

With this last point I fully agreed, but his biblical studies on Mount Scopus didn't bring him much tranquillity, this qualified pharmacist who, once he had removed his white coat and revealed to the world the trousers above his prominent bluish-white knees, looked more or less like any other civilized member of society, since in those days many respectable citizens were in the habit of wearing short trousers. The helpless rage to which he had first succumbed at the landlady's funeral, and which had appeared to be connected—to use the language of calm minds and tranquil spirits—with a certain change that had taken place in her abode, and seemed likely to pass when he had adapted himself to this same change, not only did not disappear, but actually increased the more he attended lectures on the Torah on Mount Scopus and the more he discussed them with his teachers and his fellow students. In fact, he was no longer capable of stating his views—and not only in the matter of the Tabernacle and its appurtenances and the Tent of the Presence and the Ark of the Covenant, but about anything at all—without shouting and throwing his hands about in the void of the world like a man drowning in mighty waters and searching in vain for something to hold on to. His voice, which had once been clear and loud and pleasing to the ear (at least to my ear, sensitive to this day to the soft cadence peculiar to the speech of those who were born in this country and started speaking Hebrew in the days of the Turks), became hoarse from all his shouting, and like water streaming from a half-blocked pipe would sometimes spurt out thin and high, and sometimes splutter and bubble and cough, and it in itself was enough not only to alienate the teachers he put to shame in public, but to grate on the ears of anyone who was not hard of hearing. Even I avoided him several times in the street, pretending to be so busy with urgent affairs of my own that I was blind to what was going on around me. What exasperated him most about the Higher Academy of Sciences on Mount Scopus, infuriating him to such a degree that it ruined his voice, was the unfortunate resemblance he discovered between his professor, alive and kicking and propagating knowledge, and our landlady, may she rest in peace. "This terrible resemblance between them," he would say, "will drive me out of my mind one of these days." And like her too, this same professor was of the opinion that the whole business of the law of the priests and the Tent of the Presence and the Ark of the Covenant and the various sacrifices was a mere piece of childishness, deserving of no more, from a distance of three thousand years, than a forgiving smile. What could be forgiven her, however, a simple woman with no pretensions, could not be forgiven him, a man who wore a crown of academic honors and went forth to propagate knowledge in the name of unfettered science. From what he said, I understood that it was in the name of unfettered science, too, that

the most serious of his disagreements with this same professor arose. In the opinion of the pharmacist the methodology employed by the professor was not sufficiently scientific,
and it was this opinion of his—which he did not take the
least trouble to conceal—that cut the Torah professor to the
quick and decided him to get rid of his pharmacist student,
come what may.

Of the precise form taken by the termination of the pharmacist's studies on Mount Scopus I was ignorant at the time,
since it coincided with the period during which I was avoiding him; but from what he told me later, at our last meeting
in the Café Atara, I gathered that the two of them had
conducted their farewell celebrations on a joint trip to the
biology laboratory, which they had reached locked in a close
embrace, to the sound of cheers from the male students and
shrieks of laughter from the females. The biology laboratory
itself was irrelevant to the expulsion of the pharmacist from
the university, which had been decided upon long before
they reached its precincts, and its involvement in the affair
was due entirely to the insistence of the pharmacist, who
needed it, by way of illustration only, in order to demon-
strate what he meant by a scientific approach to the Torah.
Anyone wishing to investigate the law of the priests on the
basis of a truly scientific methodology must conduct as many
exact experiments as possible—so he repeatedly insisted to
the professor and the students and, in fact, to anyone who
was willing to listen to him. In one of his classes he
expressed the opinion that the Hebrew University should
erect the Tent of the Presence and the Ark of the Covenant
and the Tabernacle with all its appurtenances in all their
minutiae, and that the professor and all his assistants and
students should officiate as priests therein, offering up the
sacrifices in strict accordance with all the rules laid down for
them, and only then, after many years of exact experiments,
would we have the right to express an opinion worth any-

thing from a scientific point of view on the power of the rituals described in the Torah to make the God of Israel dwell amongst us, so that we would once again become His people and He would once again reveal Himself to us, and to the whole world, in all His miracles and prodigies, His mighty signs and portents.

While he was delivering himself of these remarks, his hoarseness dissolved and melted away, and the more he seemed to discern on the face of his professor an echo of agreement to what he was saying, so there returned and sounded again in his voice the pleasing cadence it had possessed in days gone by. Not only was the professor nodding his head in agreement, he was actually beaming with joy. For a long time now he had been waiting only for a favorable opportunity to expel the pharmacist from his classes, and now that the right moment had arrived he was determined not to miss it. Congratulating himself heartily on the manner, at once elegant and entertaining, in which he was about to rid himself of his burden, the professor rose to his feet and solemnly announced that he had no objections at all to the methods employed by his colleagues in the Department of Biology; on the contrary, he had nothing but the greatest respect for them, mingled with admiration for their heroic bravery. Only once had he himself ever dared set foot in the biology laboratory, and when he had seen with his own eyes a toad being dissected and skinned, he had fainted and recovered only after being treated with valerian drops. Fortunately for him, they had not been busy sacrificing at the time, slaughtering the bull, for example, and sprinkling its blood, for then even valerian drops would not have helped him. And now, since the esteemed student Dr. Blum had expressed the wish to offer up sacrifices experimentally, and since the sacrifices, as all those who had listened attentively to the words of the lecturer were well aware, came from the animal kingdom, and to be more precise from five species only—from cattle and sheep and goats and turtledoves and pigeons—and since the animal kingdom in all its species and subspecies, including the five species mentioned above, belonged exclusively to the Department of Biology, where his friends the biologists officiated with such praiseworthy courage, it was clearly incumbent on Dr. Blum to transfer himself to the Department of Biology forthwith, at once, and without a moment's delay.

The pharmacist, who was usually rather quick-witted, did not understand at first what this speech was leading up to, so moved and excited was he by the mistaken impression he had received while he himself was still speaking, that here, at long last, he had succeeded in opening the ears of the Torah professor, up to now as deaf as those of the landlady, Mrs. Luria. He even greeted with enthusiasm the idea of inviting other departments to participate in the great experiment. Only when all the students burst out laughing did the full significance of his new status in the Department of Biblical Studies dawn on him, and then he was shaken by a fit of rage the like of which he had never known before, not even at the funeral of the landlady, may she rest in peace. It was this rage of his that brought the elegant opening to a violent conclusion, although as far as the entertainment of the audience was concerned it detracted nothing at all, and even added an unexpected turn to the proceedings. "In everything you've said," cried the pharmacist in a loud shrill voice, ending in an ominous gurgle which intimated that he himself would very soon be in need of the valerian drops alluded to in his teacher's remarks, "you've justified my contention that you have no idea at all of scientific methodology. You yourself openly confess that only once in the whole of your life have you ever set foot inside a laboratory, and therefore you should draw the only possible logical conclusion: not I but you are the one who needs to go to the biology laboratory. I—I'm a Doctor of Chemistry. I, thank God,

already know what a laboratory is. Not I but you are the one
to go!"

"It's not I who'll go but you!" shouted the professor in
reply; and thus they stood facing one another, each sending
the other to the same place with outstretched hands and
glaring eyes, and who knows how long they would have
remained frozen in these exhortatory postures had not the
pharmacist roused himself and, passing from words to
action, rushed up to his opponent, grabbed hold of him, and
dragged him outside. It was thus that the two of them, as
has already been mentioned above, arrived at the biology
laboratory locked in a close embrace for their final farewell
celebrations.

As is also mentioned above, these details concerning the
circumstances of his graduation from the Department of
Biblical Studies on Mount Scopus I heard from the pharmacist himself some years later at our last meeting in the Café
Atara. To be precise, I should point out that this was not
only our last meeting in the Café Atara, but also our first,
since up to then I had never seen him in any café at all;
evidently he had been too busy in those frenzied days transferring the contents of the Separanda and Toxica compartments from one cupboard to another or else arguing
desperately with his professor and his fellow students about
the rightful place of whole offerings and shared offerings.
At first I didn't recognize him, although I sat down at a table
near his and looking in his direction saw a gentleman in a
gray suit. Only when the waitress approached him and he
ordered a cup of tea and a plain cake, an echo awakened in
me to the sound of the soft pleasing cadence of his voice. I
turned to look at him once more, after having identified him
by the memory of this cadence, and found him as pleasant
and attractive to the eye as he was to the ear, and this not only
because of the tremendous change wrought in his whole
appearance by the light gray suit, but mainly because of the

confidence-inspiring expression on his face. His pince-nez spectacles had at last found their rightful place in the world in the company of the blue tie peeping out between the starched collar shining whitely above the well-cut light gray suit, which made him look tall and broad-shouldered and lent him an air of respectability and reliability. From the careful elegance of his attire and the benevolence of his countenance, brimming over with the self-satisfied air of a man firmly anchored in this world, it was patently clear that he had at long last found not only the calm of mind and tranquillity of spirit which he had sought in vain in the law emanating from Mount Scopus, but also a respectable portion of the goods of this world. He was chatting easily in French, with a smattering of expressions in Arabic, with a bald, fleshy man who had entered the café and sat down beside him, and who looked far more self-satisfied, prosperous, and worldly than he. From the heavy mustache of this fat bald man, as well as the gestures of his hands and his appearance in general, I concluded that he was one of the Arab Christian merchants from the Nashashibi Quarter of Jerusalem, and I proved mistaken only in the address. When he had taken his leave the pharmacist told me that his corpulent companion was one of the wealthiest notables of Beirut, and that he was visiting the country in connection with his business interests, which extended over the whole of the Middle East. The two of them had studied together at the University of Beirut, where a friendship had been inaugurated which had only recently begun to bear fruit, for it was only recently that the pharmacist had finally responded to the persistent propositions of his friend. When they were still students this friend of his had offered him a partnership in his business, which dealt with the production and marketing of pharmaceuticals, and now they were working together. I asked him if he was still a student in the Department of Biblical Studies, and then he told me, in detail and with a good-humored air, the story of the dénouement recounted above, in which he had dragged the Torah professor with him to the biology laboratory. "When all's said and done," he said, "all that miserable creature deserves is a forgiving smile. You'll forgive me, I'm sure, but I must go and speak to that chap sitting and waiting for me over there in the corner. He's still a greenhorn in the hashish trade, and that's why he's so nervous and tense. We're already producing synthetic drugs that are far superior to hashish, but our Palestinian clients aren't used to them yet and still prefer hashish."

He stood up to go over to the nervous greenhorn, and when he gave me his hand in farewell, he suddenly roused himself to look at me and ask, "And Gabriel, how's he? I never got around to seeing him that time he came back from Paris. When did you see him last?"

5.

Pulsations in Abyssinian Road

WHEN I STARTED taking books out of the B'nai B'rith
Library I learned that the librarian, who was short, bespectacled, and cross-eyed, had also gone to school with Gabriel
Luria in the Old City when he was a child. I liked the
librarian mainly because of the gateway he opened for me
four or five times a week: in the long school holidays I was
capable of finishing almost any book in one day's reading,
and whenever I had nothing new to read I would return to
Bialik's translation of *Don Quixote* which I had received for a
birthday present, and the clear and certain knowledge-in-
advance of everything that was going to happen on the next
page not only did nothing to lessen my interest in it but, on
the contrary, added the extra enjoyment of the tremor of
expectation with which I looked forward to renewing the
taste of the pleasure I knew to be lying in store for me,
waiting to materialize as soon as I turned the page. This was
a stream of expectation flowing in a well-known and well-
defined riverbed, in contrast to the surging sea of breakers
which engulfed me whenever I opened a new library book, a
sea whose first ripples had already started running through
me the moment I passed the garden gate on my way to the
library to change my book.

My way to the B'nai B'rith Library lay through Abyssinian Road, which curved twice like two waves chasing one another and suddenly turning to stone as they flowed past the garden walls of the houses standing on their shores. These thick, opaque, stone walls, entirely surrounding the life stored up inside them, were like the stiff covers of the books come back from the binder's, standing dumbly side by side on the library shelves in a uniformity which was only outward and apparent, since each and every one of them sheltered a separate flow of life, unique and distinct in its color and sound and flavor and individual twists and turns. I longed to enter the gates in the garden walls, just as I was eager to open the covers of the library books, because I yearned for the wonderful, unique world of the life hidden behind their blank, protective outer coverings; but just as some books had something about their names or appearance or print that made me feel bored even before I began to read them, and I therefore hurried to return them to their places on the shelf, so there were certain walls I would run past, averting my eyes, because the very thought of penetrating the house shut up inside them sent a disagreeable shudder through me. The first house was one of these, the corner house with one side facing the Street of the Prophets and the other side facing Abyssinian Road. Its garden wall was of stone, like all the others in the street, but the house itself was for some reason made mainly out of sheets of tin, like a kind of garage that was amazingly neat and clean and free of oil stains or rust because it had never performed the function for which it was clearly intended, or like an army barracks that had lost all its soldiers and was therefore visited from time to time by solemn men in black suits coming to console it in its bereavement. Because of the tin itself—its feel and look and especially its voice, including the entire range of notes of which it was capable—no utensil made of tin, whether it was a water pail or a washbasin, was ever agree-

able to me, never mind a whole house made out of sheets of
tin which seemed to me not a real house at all but a scare-
crow of a house and sent a shiver of revulsion right through
me, like the touch of a lemon I once wanted to smell. Instead
of the glowing peel, hard and soft at once, surrounding the
flesh of the living fruit and giving off the cool, sharp,
refreshing smell I had expected, my fingers suddenly found
themselves clutching the dead celluloid of which that hollow
toy of a lemon was made. Next to this house, arching and
turning to stone along the double wave of the lane, stood the
wall of the Abyssinian Compound with its green-domed
church and monastery and houses, and into these too I had
no desire to penetrate in those days, although for a completely different reason. The stream of Coptic life welling up
beyond these walls was, I imagined, so strange and foreign
that peeping in from outside or even dressing up in the
robes of a Coptic monk would not be enough to penetrate it.
In order to really know what lay behind these walls I would
have to change my skin and actually become an Ethiopian,
and this idea had no attractions for me at all at the time, just
as the idea of plunging into an adventure story about climbing Mount Kilimanjaro did not attract me then, because I
had already been seduced by the South Sea Island Nights. I
put off reading about Kilimanjaro to some later date, just as
I put off looking into the world of the Abyssinian Compound until such time as my soul would be in the proper
state to undertake so long a journey, but when the South Sea
Island Nights were over and the African adventure story was
already in my hands I heard something about two Coptic
novice monks that rid me forever of any desire whatsoever
to penetrate the world of Coptic monks in general, although
this piece of information referred, as mentioned above, to
these two only. I was climbing the library steps behind the
librarian when, like a pair of black giraffe necks gliding
high above a wall, two stripling Coptic monks with cylin-

drical columns of hats crowning their heads passed before our eyes. They were arguing with each other in whispers but their thin voices floated up to us on the air, high and clear as the thin twanging of mandolin strings quarreling with the wind. Under their hats their heads were apparently shaved as clean as their necks and temples, which were as smooth and shining as the polished black marble of their cheeks. The faces of these giant cubs, perhaps because their bodies were so tall, looked astonishingly young, like those of little boys, but I suppose they must have been about seventeen or eighteen years old. "You realize, I suppose, that those two poor wretches are eunuchs. They must have been castrated when they were small children."

There was something about the librarian's voice I always found pleasing to listen to, something about its accent and timbre he had in common with the pharmacist and my father and mother and all their generation who were born in Jerusalem and started speaking Hebrew in the days when the country was still under Turkish rule. This pleasantness padded his words even when their content was abrasive and might have scratched without it, but this time no padding in the world could have softened the shock of their blow—the shock of pain: it seemed that they still bore, these two monks, shut up in their blood, the pain of the cutting off of their testicles which had cut them off with one blow from the tree of their lives whose seed was in them to bear fruit after their kind, and that once they had been sentenced to life imprisonment, each in the cell of his own solitary confinement, they had been cut off from the tree of life in general, whose roots were embedded in all the generations that had gone before them and whose branches waved in the breezes blowing over all the generations to come, and having thus been cut off from the past and the future—deaf to the music of the pulsing tide flowing abundantly from cell to cell—they were cut off from the body of life in the present as well, like two cells in a cold empty space meaninglessly suspended on nothing.

Long after the librarian had suddenly disappeared in a cloud of rumors about something terrible that had happened to him and forced him to flee the country in secret, Gabriel told me a story about castrating pigs in the village of Carnac in the province of Brittany in France. Before he came home Gabriel had hired himself out as a farmhand to a woman farmer and performed every kind of hard physical labor on the farm and in the house for her until the question of castrating the pigs had come up. Although Gabriel had a natural aversion to this animal, which increased as he became increasingly familiar with its nature and habits, still he could not bring himself to castrate the males of the species. An old farmhand, one of the local peasants, took hold of a little piglet and showed him how to cut off its testicles with an instrument that looked like a pair of pruning scissors. Gabriel watched with his hair standing on end and immediately gave notice that he would have nothing to do with the job of castrating the pigs. If it had been a question of slaughtering the pigs, putting an end to their lives in any way whatsoever, he would not have hesitated an instant, just as he had not flinched from killing all kinds of fowls and beasts up to then at his mistress's request. But castration, even the castration of the loathsome swine, filled him for some reason with dread as an act of cruelty to which he could on no account be party—as either perpetrator or witness.

Scarcely had I recovered from the librarian's words, which had opened my eyes to the outrage perpetrated by human hands on the two young Ethiopians walking along the pavement below us, than I was startled to hear high, ringing laughter, like the pealing of silver bells, proclaiming the astounding fact that it was possible for these incurable eunuchs to laugh and be happy. The happiness started bubbling up in their voices as they were about to enter the gate leading to the green-domed Abyssinian church and encountered a priest with frizzled gray hair on his way out, and after he said something to them they both broke into

peals of laughter which continued even after he had parted
from them and started off in the direction of the Street of
the Prophets. That the latter was no eunuch was abundantly
clear from everything about him, from his beard whose
curls were like coiling silver threads of filigree and the
robust build of his body to the lustful gleam which
appeared in his eye at the sight of the little girl in the pleated
tartan skirt who was zigzagging down the street on skates.
He said to her in Hebrew, "Give my regards to your father,"
and when she mischievously skated around him in a rapid,
dangerous circle he put out his hand to catch her and called
out in a Hebrew which he had picked up from the street
urchins and which sounded very strange and vulgar and out
of place coming from the lips of this silver-haired black
priest: "You'll be sorry when I get hold of you, Missy! Just
you wait and see!" They both laughed, and his frankly cov-
etous glance followed the dance of the skirt on the legs
gliding on the roller skates in figure eights on the asphalt
until skates and legs and dancing skirt all disappeared into
the green-painted iron gates in the garden wall of the little
girl's house, the gate I always longed to enter on my way to
the library and on my way back from it and on my bed in the
clear summer nights, when the sounds of the piano hidden
in the innermost recesses of the house secluded behind the
high garden wall floated all the way down the Street of the
Prophets and in at our windows, opened wide to the sky and
the stars. Sometimes notes dropping from the piano would
trickle into the Arab tunes borne upward from the Damascus Gate and Mussrara and flowing into the round window which looked out to the east, and then the night air
would vibrate with a growing tension because the Western
notes dropping into the Oriental tunes did not blend with
them to create a smoothly flowing harmony, as sometimes
happens when music absorbs a melody from a foreign culture and succeeds in swallowing and digesting it, but splash-

ing into the territory of the foreign rhythm they produced instead an explosive compound which needed only a spark to ignite it.

The first casualty in the nocturnal battle for control of the airspace over the Street of the Prophets (which raged between the Chopin waltzes emerging from the home of Dr. Landau, the eye specialist, and the love songs of Farid el-Atrash blaring from the newly installed radio sets in the Arab cafés) was our landlady, Mrs. Gentilla Luria. As soon as the first notes fell from the piano like cool, smooth marbles into the tremulous vibrato of the guitar strings accompanying the Arab crooner (some said that he wasn't an Arab at all, but an Egyptian Jew), Mrs. Luria would succumb to a violent headache, requiring the immediate attention of her sister, Pnina. "Hurry up and soak the handkerchief in cold water"—this was the handkerchief that would be bound around her head like a turban to relieve its sufferings—"and close the windows! Hurry, hurry! Can't you hear—the doctoress's Polish owl is at it again! I'll see him in hell, and his lady-friend with him! Such a thing could never have happened if my husband were still alive. He would have told the mayor, Ragueb Bey Nashashibi himself, to stop that creature from banging on the piano and preventing the whole street from getting a decent night's sleep. Have you ever heard such a thing? An entire street should suffer just because the only lover Dr. Landau's wife can find is a Polish owl who's good for nothing but thumping on a piano! At least if he would play a proper tune to warm a person's heart. But no, he's not capable of that either. And what's the wonder? If he was a proper pianist he wouldn't need that hysterical cat who's never managed to find herself a real man—nothing but broken vessels who imagine their moanings and groanings are works of art."

I never met any of the "broken vessels" who had sheltered under Mrs. Landau's wing before the "Polish owl," but with regard to the latter's musical ability Mrs. Luria's description did justice to only one part of the external truth, and had less to do with his actual talents than with his relations with the public—in other words, his stage fright. So great was this stage fright that it paralyzed his arms and made his fingers play notes that were forced and frozen, and sometimes even wrong, giving him a bad reputation. Alone in his room, however, especially at night, he was wonderful. Half awake, half asleep, I would suddenly hear a clear note falling into the open window frame like a star coming out, immediately filling the empty blackness with waves of secret longing, vibrating to the bottom of my being and stopping my breath with the materialization of the second note in the light of the second star, and then another and another, until the whole of space filled up again with rhythmic waves of longing for the missing points of light needed to complete the constellation of a sign of the Zodiac: the sign of Gemini. But scarcely had this been done than the piano began to play again, scattering here and there, in no discernible order, droplets of sound which crystallized into points of light on the trembling threads of longing to draw another sign—the sign of Aries, and next to it the signs of Leo and Taurus and Virgo. Only when the music died away did the dread come slowly back to take its place, the dread of the infinite spaces of the cold, dark void separating the stars which were meaninglessly suspended on nothing.

Her sister, Pnina, having shut the window against the great dread of the Polish owl's piano-playing, Mrs. Luria began to suffer from suffocation in the narrow, closed room, and all the wavings and fannings of the water-soaked white handkerchief could not restore her, so long as the window remained closed, just as bound about her temples like a turban the same wet handkerchief had been unable to relieve her headache so long as the window remained open. "No, no. Things simply cannot go on like this. You see, Pnina, what things have come to when I can't live with the window open and I can't live with the window shut? Why, it's hell on earth when a person feels sick with the window open and sick with the window shut, and all this has come about simply because Yehuda Prosper passed away and I've got no one to protect me from the hellish inquisitions of the Polish owl of the doctor's wife, who should have been thrown out by her husband long ago, together with all her broken vessels. But of course he would never do such a thing because he's a saint. If he wasn't a saint, would he have taken pity on that miserable creature and made her his wife? You see, Pnina, how these saintly characters with their mercy and compassion make it easy for all kinds of bitches to take over the world? Yes. And now my headache has affected the optic nerve. I can't see a thing already. Well, it's plain to me that I won't have any alternative but to get up early tomorrow morning and go to Dr. Landau's clinic. In any case it's time for me to go to him again and have the hairs taken out of my eyes. And don't you forget to wake me early so that I can go and get a number in time, or else I'll have to spend the whole day sitting there in the line with the armies of Persia and Media and the stinking Arabs. That's right, open it wide. I feel better now." And indeed, so great was Mrs. Luria's relief at the thought of visiting Dr. Landau's eye clinic (which was then situated in St. Paul's Road next to the police station) that she was able to meet with composure the renewed invasion of her open window by the hammering of the Polish owl on the doctor's wife's piano. All the armies of Persia and Media (as she called the Persian, Bucharan, and other Oriental Jews whose countries of origin had formed part of the glorious kingdom of King Ahasuerus in biblical times) besieging the hospital entrance and camping in its corridors could not have prevented her from observing the sacred ritual of going to see Dr. Landau once a week at least, a ritual she performed wearing the best dress she kept for this and one other occasion only, that of her weekly visit to the home of Judge Dan Gutkin.

6.

The Old Judge's Visit

THE UNEXPECTED VISIT the old judge paid to our landlady, Mrs. Gentilla Luria, shortly after she lost her husband, suddenly implicated me in a murder which had been committed in the Old City twenty years before I was born. The judge himself had no way of knowing that at the very moment he brought up this murder case of bygone days the ancient dagger was lying underneath a pile of copybooks in my desk drawer, and he may not even have been aware of my presence in the corner of the verandah. I found the dagger, as I've mentioned before, in the cellar, where the rags of all the years lay rotting and their junk rusted away. This ancient Turkish shoub'ria was all that survived of the different kinds of weapons, decorated saddles, bracelets and earrings, and other trinkets and ornaments which the Arabs left in pawn with the master of the house when they came to borrow money from him in the days when the Turks ruled the land and Yehuda Prosper Bey was at the height of his power and greatness.

After the old man's death Mrs. Luria stopped visiting all her friends and acquaintances and went out only once a week to call on Judge Dan Gutkin, who helped her wind up the affairs of her late husband's estate to her complete satisfaction, just as he had always helped the old man himself to settle his business and legal affairs in the most satisfactory way. This Supreme Court judge, the friend of her erstwhile husband, was a famous man in the Palestine of those days, much sought after by dignitaries and notables of both the Jewish and the Arab communities because of the influence he was supposed to have with the British Mandatory authorities. He remembered not only the days of Mrs. Luria's greatness, when she was the wife of a consul and took her place among the wives of all the other pashas and beys of the Ottoman Empire, but also the days of her beauty, when she felt on her back the eyes of the men turning their heads to look at her as she passed. However, she soon began to return from her visits to the judge's house disappointed, because of the dark alleyways into which his conversation tended to stray. Instead of dwelling on the memory of the days when she had been singled out from all the other girls and chosen to present important visitors to the Evelina de Rothschild School for Girls with bouquets of flowers, he began returning in his thoughts and conversation to the days that had preceded that golden age, to the depths of poverty and misery in the obscure early childhood of a down-and-out carpenter's daughter in Midan Street in the Jewish Quarter of the Old City, to the ragged, barefoot little girl peeping out of the attic window above her father's workshop, where the whole family lived in a kind of box room reeking of carpenter's glue, sawdust, and turpentine. All his life Yentele's father (for this was her name, Yente, until the Consul Yehuda Prosper Luria Bey had come to pay a courtesy call on the Evelina de Rothschild School for Girls, and she had been chosen to present him with a bunch of flowers on behalf of the graduating class) lived in abject poverty, although he was the best carpenter in Jerusalem, who had studied cabinetmaking in the metropolis of Vienna and made the Ark of the Law for the Kahal Zion synagogue

(which had an underground passage leading directly to
Mount Zion and the sepulchers of the House of David), as
well as for the Stambuli and Nissan Bey synagogues. From
the top of the wooden stairway leading to the attic she would
look down on her father standing meekly and humbly in his
own workshop, bowing his head before the synagogue wardens and diffidently, timidly hinting that they might give
him a a few pence to buy food for the Sabbath on account of
the money they owed him for the Ark of the Law (which had
cost him months of backbreaking work to make and for
which his payment was in any case inadequate), while they
put him off with vain excuses and mollified him with subtle
new interpretations of the law and wonderful midrashim
instead of paying him his due. In contrast to these worthies,
the rich Bucharan Jews who commissioned him to make
them huge cabinets as broad as bridal beds suffered from a
certain poverty of language and scholarship, and since they
were unable to sweeten the pill of their reluctance to pay
him his due with the sayings of the sages, they glared angrily
at him instead and abused him roundly for the impatience
and impertinence of his demands. From the bottom of the
pit of hunger and disgrace and humiliation the carpenter
was saved thanks to the intervention of certain religious
fanatics, who set his house on fire because of the cross he
made for the Russian monastery on the Mount of Olives.
From time to time the Father of the monastery would give
him various carpentry jobs to do, but the carpenter resolutely refused to carve crosses for him until the situation
became so desperate that he did not even have a farthing to
buy candles for the Sabbath. After he had finally given his
consent he began to carve the big olive-wood cross at night,
both because he felt uneasy in his own mind about what he
was doing, and because he did not want passersby to see that
the hand that had carved the Arks of the Law was also the
hand that was carving the cross. One night, when the work

was done, little Yentele woke up and, peeping out of the round attic window, she saw the big cross spread out on the paving stones shining in the moonlight, creeping slowly toward its destination on the Mount of Olives. But her father's worst fears were realized, and sooner than he thought. A few yards from the shop a group of Jews on their way home from midnight prayers at the Western Wall encountered the carpenter carrying the cross on his back, and the next night his house was set on fire. They escaped from the Old City to the Nahalath Shiva Quarter in the dead of night, and the carpenter's wife made up her mind to revenge herself on the people who had burned her house down by sending her children to the Christian Mission school. He implored her not to do it, and after much pleading on his part she relented a little and compromised by sending them to the schools of the Jewish heretics and atheists outside the Old City walls.

Memories of happy days began for Gentilla only after the tongues of flame began licking at the wood in the shop downstairs: her father pulled her out of her bed next to the round attic window and carried her through the flames in his arms and fled with her from the fire and the Old City, and her mother sent her to the Anglo-Jewish school. Her father's life too, it seemed to her, became a little easier, for although he was at first convinced that he and his excommunicated family would starve to death, orders for plain school desks and benches soon came to take the place of the elaborate cabinets and Arks of the Law. The carpenter no longer dared show his face inside the Old City walls and he never set foot on the paving stones of its streets again until the day he died. Sometimes he would suddenly run into the dark little kitchen adjoining his new workshop and hide, because he thought he saw the synagogue warden passing in the street—the same one who still owed him half the money for the Ark of the Law and who might even have had a hand in the burning of his house. He would run away and hide like a shamefaced, guilty child, ashamed of himself for what he had done, and ashamed of himself before his wife and children for being ashamed. And another relic of that moonlit night on which he had carried the big olive-wood cross on his shoulders was a double rupture of the groin which remained with him for the rest of his life. Every few days, while he was at work, his intestines would slip down into his testicles and he would fall to the ground in terrible pain, writhing and clutching and screaming, and his wife would rush to heat up the flat stones which were always kept next to the stove for this purpose, and put them on her husband's groin to ease the pain and make the intestines return to their place. And now it seemed that Judge Gutkin had nothing better to do than try to carry her back to those terrible times.

The last time she had called on him all he could think about were the gloomy alleyways of the Old City, and however hard she tried to turn him back onto the glorious highways of his life (from the day he returned from Oxford University with the imposing degree of an English barrister at law and was appointed a judge and succeeded in everything he did and climbed higher and higher and became a Member of the British Empire and sat on the bench of the Supreme Court and was awarded a distinction still more exalted than its predecessor, becoming an Officer of the British Empire at whose approach the British officers themselves jumped to attention and saluted), he insisted, stubborn as an old mule, on returning to the dark, twisting alleyways of his childhood in the Old City. "Do you remember," he said to her, "when you lived in Midan Street, we lived in the almshouse called the German Compound, 'Der Deutsche Platz'?" "What are you talking about?" she cried indignantly. "Are you trying to tell me that I'm as old as you are? When you lived in the German Compound I hadn't even been born, and the little girl you remember from Midan Street was my sister, Pnina, who's seven years older than I am. Don't forget that you're at least fifteen years older than I am, and I was born when you were already a pupil at the Little Yeshiva—and in any case please stop reminding me of the dirty, stinking streets of the Old City. What am I talking about fifteen years? You're at least twenty years older than I am! You were Yehuda Prosper's friend, so you must be older than I am by twenty years at least."

"It was only when I was a pupil at the Little Yeshiva," he said, without paying any attention at all to her remarks about the difference in age between them, which grew greater every time she thought about it, "that I dared to enter the Karaïte Compound at the end of the alley on the border of the Moslem Quarter. And not by daylight either, God forbid, but after evening fell, stealing in as if I wanted to commit a crime. These Karaïtes* were so ostracized and outlawed that the rabbis refused to convert a Karaïte Haham who wanted to become a Jew and promised to donate all his money to the Jewish religious charities. Any goy in the world, Moslem, Christian, or heathen, had the legal right to convert to Judaism, but not a Karaïte. In those days they used to be called 'Zaddokites' too. The synagogue in their compound was buried deep in the ground and when I started to descend the cold, dark, stone stairway leading down to this synagogue, which was a thousand years old and contained the oldest Torah scroll in the world, the 'Mik-dashia,' in its Ark, I felt that I was committing an even greater sin than the time when I peeped into the Church of the Holy Sepulcher. I took off my shoes and placed them, as they did, at the head of the stairs next to the water cistern. I had a big hole in the heel of the black sock on my right foot.

* Karaïtes—Jewish sect dating from the eighth century A.D. that rejects rabbinical tradition and the Talmud, and bases its teaching solely on the Scriptures. It survives only in Jerusalem, Egypt, the Crimea, and Turkey.

You remember how we used to call holes in the heels of our
socks 'potatoes'? With every stair I descended I felt waves of
fear rising and engulfing me and the cold kiss of the naked
stone on the heel of my right foot. I knew that every step was
leading me one degree further down into defilement, but I
also knew, without for some reason feeling any surprise at
the apparent logical contradiction, that precisely here, at the
very bottom of the pit of sin into which I was gradually
sinking, our holy ancient law lay hidden in its original purity
unencumbered by exegesis and interpretation, and when I
reached the bottom of the abyss of terror and stood on the
floor of the synagogue, I knew that only God could save me,
and my heart cried out to him in prayer—not one of the
prayers from the prayer book, but the song of degrees:

> *Out of the depths have I cried unto thee, O Lord.*
> *Lord, hear my voice:*
> *Let thine ears be attentive*
> *To the voice of my supplications.*
> *If thou, Lord, shouldst mark iniquities,*
> *O Lord, who shall stand?*
> *But there is forgiveness with thee,*
> *That thou mayest be feared.*

And while I was repeating this mute prayer to myself, without so much as moving my tightly shut lips, I was answered.
All at once I was lifted up to a great height, through all the
layers of sin and the spheres of defilement, and I found
myself breathing pure, clear mountain air, free of any fear
or anxiety or dread, free of the need to pray to any god at
all. The moment I was answered I didn't even feel the need
to thank Him—He had done his job and He could go. How
did the light get into the Karaïte synagogue? It was a cellar,
after all, buried deep in the ground. It's funny—when I was
standing there inside it I never gave the matter a thought,

and now fifty years later this trivial question suddenly pops into my head in the middle of a complicated property case when I have to give all my attention to the arguments of the contending parties, and it hasn't stopped worrying me since. I can't seem to remember there being any windows, but windows there must certainly have been, somewhere up in the ceiling beyond the pillars supporting the roof. What do you say, Yentele, where did the light come from? Do you remember how Ali Ibn Masrur tried to escape to that same Karaïte synagogue after the famous murder in the suk Elatarin? I don't think he knew where he was running to. He just ran through those winding streets until he came to the Jewish Quarter, and like a hunted animal he dived for shelter into the first hole he came across. But maybe he knew very well that that cellar was a synagogue, and he believed that its sanctity would protect him—you remember how the Moslems believed that Jews had all sorts of magic powers: he probably thought that there was an altar in the middle of the synagogue and that sacrifices were offered to God on it, and all he had to do was reach that altar, hang on to it, and be saved! What do you say, Yentele? Why are you getting up to go already? Stay a little longer, you aren't in a hurry to go anywhere, are you?"

"And what have I got to go on sitting here for?" she retorted angrily. "There was never a truer word said than that the old are like children. Here you are returning to the nonsense of your childhood and youth like a stubborn old horse returning to its stable, and if I go on sitting here any longer I suppose there's nothing to stop you from returning to the days when your mother wiped your backside for you. And now good-bye, good-bye until next week." And just when her displeasure with the judge's conversation had grown so great that she was considering whether it wouldn't be best for her to stay away for a month or two until he recovered his senses, he started coming to visit her, turning up at unheard-of hours in the middle of the day or in the evening on his way to or from the courthouse, when she was quite unprepared to receive visitors of any description at all, let alone people with important positions in society. On one of these unexpected visits he gave rise in me—unwittingly and unintentionally, as I've mentioned before, since it is extremely unlikely that he even saw, or if he saw, gave a second thought to, the strange child sitting in a corner of the verandah apparently engrossed in Bialik's translation of Cervantes's *Don Quixote* into Hebrew—to a violent storm of emotion, shameful, terrifying, and embarrassing at once, as I found myself, while listening to him reminiscing in his calm, deliberate voice (to Pnina, since her younger sister, Gentilla, had shut herself up in her room and refused to receive him) about how he had been implicated in a murder which had been committed in the Old City twenty years before I was born, and all because of the dagger I had discovered in the cellar and stolen. This terrible storm, whose reverberations were to pursue me, both waking and sleeping, for days to come, descended like a bolt from the blue on a wonderfully clear, calm summer's day. Gentilla was sitting, as was her habit in the early evening, at the entrance to her room and sorting rice in a wide copper basin with a detached, distant look in her eyes, humming to herself the tune of an English nursery rhyme she had learned in her schooldays at the Evelina de Rothschild School for Girls, "Three blind mice, three blind mice, See how they run, see how they run, They all ran after the farmer's wife, who cut off their tails with a carving knife . . ." and I was reading my book in the corner of the verandah, when the sound of the judge's car was heard approaching from the direction of the Russian Compound, where the courthouse was situated, and drawing to a stop at the gate. "Oh my God": the cry of despair broke from Gentilla's lips as she stopped sorting the rice and sat frozen in her seat, paralyzed by the catastrophe which was about to overtake her—the catastrophe of being discovered by her important visitor in her disheveled daily wear with untidy wisps of gray hair escaping from the handkerchief bound around her head as on one of those inferior nobodies, the pious Orthodox women she hated with all her soul. "Pnina, Pnina, hurry up and receive the judge here, on the verandah. Don't let him into the house whatever you do. Tell him I'm not at home. No, tell him that I don't feel well, that I've got a headache. Hurry up, for God's sake! Until that woman moves her fat behind the whole world can return to chaos."

Despite the chaos that the sound of the judge's approaching car had produced in Gentilla's soul, she nevertheless kept a clear enough head to change the command of "Tell him I'm not at home" to that of "Tell him I don't feel well" in case the unexpected visitor stayed long enough to enable her to change her clothes and if not dye her hair, then at least paint her naked face and put a decent covering on her shames and humiliations and make all those changes in her external appearance which were so closely associated with changes in the state of her soul and which, therefore, took so inordinately long to effect. After Pnina had moved her fat behind and placed the three-legged iron table in the middle of the verandah and next to it the red plush armchair which had been reserved in its time for the old Bey, her younger sister, who had shut herself up behind locked doors in her room, was still lying flat on her back on her bed with closed eyes in order to recover from the palpitations of her heart, compose herself, and gather strength for the effort of changing her clothes while she listened in, half awake, half asleep, to the circlings of her soul in its revolutions until the proper face for receiving important visitors should reach the borders of the body and overlap it. If the fundamental purity (which was connected with the desire for perfection) in the make-up of her soul—that same purity that prevented her from mixing threads of different kinds in the fabric of her daily life, from diluting the attention needed for select-

ing the properly baked loaf of bread with negotiations about
the rent, or combining her weekly visit to Dr. Landau with
taking a pair of slippers to be mended to the Arab cobbler
who sat on the pavement outside the eye clinic, or from
lending herself to any of the thousand and one other hybrid,
mongrel deeds to which the secular necessities of daily life
subject us—if this fundamental purity stood in direct relation to the slowness of the rhythm of her life, then she could
have attained the perfection she aspired to in receiving her
guest only by stopping the course of time and freezing it
until her preparations were completed. But the sun, which
stood still upon Gibeon and hastened not to go down about
a whole day at the command of Joshua, was not about to
stand still at the command of Gentilla, and scarcely had she
shut the door behind her and dropped onto her bed than
the judge's Arab driver leapt from his seat, hurried around
the car, and opened the door for his long, lean master, who
emerged in a dark blue suit and a stiff white collar and a
black tie and a black London hat on his head, like all the
other British masters busy keeping law and order in all the
other colonies and dominions and mandates and protec-
torates of the British Empire all over the world. His square-
jowled bulldog face fitted his clothing to a nicety, exuding so
distinctly British a chill that no one who was not familiar
with his past could ever have imagined that the possessor of
this face not only could quote chapter and verse in Hebrew
from his mouth which drooped downward at both its corners, but had been born and bred in the Old City of Jerusalem and had gone to school at the Yeshiva of Hebron. It
should not be hastily concluded, however, from the attributes of his person or the correctness of the attire in which
his lean flesh was clothed that it was due to these alone that
he attained to the exalted degree of Officer of the British
Empire, since there is no doubt whatsoever that he owed not
a little in his climb to the top to the manner in which he

comported himself on the bench itself. In everything he said and did in the courtroom he observed the strictest letter of the law, always maintaining the same severe expression on his face, which remained cold and impassive throughout, with never the shadow of a smile or a twitch of impatience or a frown of displeasure either side could grasp at to guess which way the wind was blowing. Because of the cold, impassive formality with which he, with infinite patience, conducted all the cases that came before him, his sentence always came as a surprise—and not always because of its severity. He would sometimes search until he found a technical flaw in the manner of the presentation of the evidence, or an irregularity in police proceedings, or mitigating circumstances that had escaped even the counsel for the defense, in order to pass lenient sentence on an Arab murderer who had cruelly stabbed his friend to death for failing to pay a ten-grush debt or for making love to his wife. On other occasions, no less surprising to the defendants and their lawyers, he would suddenly come down with the full force of the law on devious business transactions where nothing was at stake, in the last analysis, but money.

The climax of these surprises, which threw the whole of the Jewish community into an uproar and incited politicians of all shades of opinion against him, was the famous sentence he passed in favor of certain Arab tenants who refused to move from the land the Jewish National Fund had purchased from their effendi landlords residing in Beirut. During the course of this famous case His Worship the Jewish judge, to the horrified disbelief of the lawyers representing the Jewish national institutions, discovered and drew up from the depths of the sub-subparagraphs of Ottoman law a tiny clause so insignificant that it had escaped the notice of generations of Turkish legal experts, and on the basis of this obscure legal quibble he passed sentence in favor of the Arab defendants. Among the other accusations hurled against him in the aftermath of this shocking sentence, a rumor swept the community that this reactionary who served the interests of the British and the Arabs, this traitor to his people for the sake of an Imperial decoration, was no more averse to receiving bribes than any British or Arab official, and that in the very case in question he had certainly not refused the presents and gifts generously heaped upon him by the Jewish National Fund. In other words—he took his fill of bribes but gave nothing in return, and therefore not only was he corrupt from the point of view of national, social, and legal morality, but even from the point of view of the honor of thieves he was more shameless, contemptible, and unprincipled than the Arab and British officials, who had the decency at least to keep their side of the bargain and play by the unwritten rules of the game of give and take. When the legal advisers of the National Institutions tried to put pressure on him by veiled threats to prosecute him for taking bribes, they discovered to their consternation that he had done his work so well, so expertly and elegantly, that there was not a trace of incriminating evidence against him, and for this feat alone—as the wits among them were quick to remark—he fully deserved the title of Officer of the British Empire.

The Officer of the British Empire climbed the steps to the home of his old friend the Officer of the Ottoman Empire, who had departed this world only a few weeks before, reaching the verandah just as the Jerusalem widow of the de parted was shutting herself in her room and her sister, Pnina, was drawing up to the three-legged iron table standing in the middle of the flagged floor the red plush armchair which had been kept up till then for the exclusive use of Yehuda Prosper Bey. As soon as he had seated himself in the armchair with his face toward the setting sun, Pnina hurried off to bring him some biscuits and a cool drink. Not forgetting the driver who was sitting and waiting in the car below, she took him too a tray of refreshments on which she placed, between the cool drink and the plate of biscuits, a five-grush coin. This coin, which was then considered a very handsome tip for a driver of any description, was accepted calmly and casually by the Honorable Dan Gutkin's Arab driver, with none of the grateful thanks and obsequious bowings and scrapings befitting the insignificant drivers of lesser masters: he thanked her with a slight nod of his head and a polite smile, as behooved an important driver who was honored by the honor of his famous master, and repaid him by behaving in strict accord with the rules of etiquette and good manners in all circumstances and at all times.

Meanwhile I was flooded with a sense of uncomprehending wonder, delightful and frightening at the same time, as if I had suddenly stepped into a magic palace, at the sight of the judge with his mane of white hair combed severely back from his forehead on both sides of the middle parting above the square-jawed assertiveness of his lean face, lowering his long limbs into the armchair of the old Bey, sitting up excitedly and calling out "Of course, of course" as he drew a large red handkerchief over his smoothly shaven, shining head to wipe away the beads of sweat sparkling like fireworks in the setting sun. The picture of the old Bey, as I had last seen him before his death, sitting on this red armchair with the checked scarf his Jerusalem wife had wrapped around his neck, his hoarse old voice shouting in impotent rage, "Our master Moses, our master Moses," superimposed itself on the picture of the judge sitting on the same verandah in the same armchair without either picture blotting the other out, blurring or erasing its lines to the slightest degree, and my heart expanded in joyful wonder and awe in the palace in which I suddenly found myself standing. But the palace vanished as suddenly as it had appeared, and with it the picture of the old Bey, and I said to myself, "No, it's quite impossible that this red chair should have

room enough for both of them, the old man and the judge as
well—and besides, the old man's dead and gone." Still,
something strange and wonderful had happened to me
here, seeing Judge Dan Gutkin sitting in the chair instead of
the old landlord. "You know," said the judge to Aunt Pnina,
who came and sat down beside him after bringing back the
tray she had taken to the driver, "he was only ten years older
than I and yet he belonged to a different empire, the Ottoman Empire." Pnina sighed and wiped her nose with a lot of
noise and fuss and her eyes grew moist. "No, no," she contra-
dicted him. "Yehuda Prosper, may he rest in peace, was
fifteen years older than you, or maybe twenty. You were a
young man, no more than a boy, when you left the yeshiva
and asked him to find you a job. By then he had been
married to my sister for a couple of years already. You're my
age, or two or three years older at most. Don't you remember
how we stole into the Karaïte Compound together to see the
Turkish police arresting Ali Ibn Masrur after the murder in
the suk Elatarin? People talked about it for years, but what
exactly happened I can't remember at all, except for the
Turkish police arresting the Arab in the Karaïte Compound.
I don't know if you remember."

"But of course I remember. I remember it all very well,
Perele. After all, it was the first time in my life that I actually
saw the law in action with my own eyes," said the judge, who
went on looking straight in front of him at the setting sun,
which shed a reddish-blue light, like burnished copper
veined with steel, on the white hair combed severely back
and the inscrutable face which seemed utterly detached not
only from what was happening around him, but also from
what was happening inside him, and even from the melodious voice issuing from his mouth, the lion's mouth turned
down at both its corners.

When I went down the steps to the Ancient Egyptian Wing
of the Louvre Museum, I saw a polished flintstone lion filling

the hall in which it crouched with an orange glow, an expression of inscrutable power, self-generated and flowing in its own closed circuit, on its face. The blue-uniformed guards and the few tourists strolling around in the field of the sphinx's radiation were completely indifferent to the radiant energy encompassing them, not because their powers of resistance were particularly strong, but simply because they were made of an insulating clay, like light little sticks of wood which remain immobile in a powerful electromagnetic field while huge iron poles rush headlong to cleave to the magnet. I passed my hand over the smoothness of the sphinx's cool stone and looked at its face gazing straight ahead, ancient and calm and inscrutable, and a soft, melodious voice flowed from the cold kiss of the polished stone and ran right through my arm until it penetrated my ear, for the sphinx was singing a song that told an ancient tale without moving a muscle of the petrified stone of its face. It was only after I emerged from the museum, still trembling with excitement and awe and full of the same sense of uncomprehending wonder, that I suddenly became aware of the fact that the voice that had penetrated my ear was the voice of Judge Gutkin, as I had heard it some thirty years before on the verandah of the house. The next day I hurried around to the museum again and went down the steps to the Egyptian sphinx's hall, but the voice did not come back to sing in my ear. I placed my hand on its flinty face and encountered only the cool, smooth stone. It made not a single sound, neither then nor on all the subsequent occasions when I returned to wake and rouse it. If the sphinx had had the mouth of a lion, it would have resembled the judge.

As in the case of the sphinx so too in the case of the judge there was no connection at all between his voice and the inscrutable expression on his face. This soft, melodious, even-tenored, and reassuring voice always came as a pleasant surprise when it emerged from the cold, withdrawn face of its possessor, but now as I floated gently on its waves I was suddenly flooded with waves of terror—as if I were sliding down a rope stretched between two mountain peaks and the least deviation from the rhythm and equilibrium of the slide might send me hurtling down into the depths of the abyss gaping below. The voice dived thirty years backward in time to the tale of the deed of Ali Ibn Masrur which had opened Dan Gutkin's eyes, for the first time in his life, to the workings of the law.

At dawn Mahmoud Effendi, a leading citizen of the city of Bethlehem, rose to travel in his carriage to Jerusalem, where he intended purchasing fine linens and perfumes and jewels as presents for his new young fiancée. This girl seemed to him the living embodiment of the description of the Efreet's mistress in the Second Kalandar's Tale in *The Thousand and One Nights,* which he had read as a young man and never forgotten: "There stood a damsel like a pearl of great price, whose favor banished from my heart all grief and cark and care, and whose soft speech captivated the wise and ware. Her figure measured five feet in height, her breasts were firm and upright, her cheeks a very garden of delight, her color lively bright. Her face gleamed like dawn through curly tresses which gloomed like night, and above the snows of her bosom glittered teeth of a pearly white. As the poet said of one like her:

> Four things that meet not, save they here unite
> To shed my heart-blood and to rape my sprite:
> Brilliantest forehead; tresses jetty bright;
> Cheeks rosy red and stature beauty-dight."*

The youngest of his first wife's sons, little Daoud, who was his favorite child, begged his father to take him with him to

---

* Richard F. Burton, *The Book of the Thousand Nights and a Night: A Plain and Literal Translation of the Arabian Nights Entertainments* (New York: The Heritage Press, 1934).

the Holy City in his carriage, and he granted him his wish because he loved him dearly.

After Mahmoud Effendi had finished his business in the markets of Jerusalem he was strolling leisurely through the suk Elatarin, which is the perfume market, on his way back to the carriage waiting for him at the Jaffa Gate, with his son trailing behind him and lingering to watch the goldsmith at his work, when Ali Ibn Masrur (who up till then had been considered an upright man who feared God and eschewed evil) suddenly broke away from the crowd and stabbed him to death with a dagger. Before the child had lifted his admiring eyes from the cunning fingers of the goldsmith hammering the pure gold, his father fell to the ground, his blood spilling red on the paving stones. Afterward, during the entire course of the trial, the child Daoud, sitting next to his mother with the rest of the murdered man's relatives, the only eyewitness to the murder among them, kept his eyes fixed expectantly on the judge, waiting with the utmost concentration to hear what he would say. The judge, who felt the eyes of the child fixed on him, called him gently to the witness stand to deliver his testimony, and the child sprang up and stepped forward eagerly. As soon as he began to speak the judge and all the other people crowding the courtroom realized that he imagined that it lay in the judge's power to bring his father back to life and that the whole of the trial being conducted before his eyes was nothing more than a kind of ceremony which he needed to enable him to exercise his magic powers, a kind of ritual for remedying the injustice and restoring the murdered man to life, a necessary formality at the end of which the judge would stand up in his place and call out, "Let Mahmoud Effendi of Bethlehem enter!" and the door behind the judge's back would open wide and he would come into the courtroom, to the great joy of all assembled there—his father in all his glory. About the murderer he did not think at all, and showed no desire to see him punished or be revenged on him. When the judge persisted in performing his rites and rituals around the irrelevant figure of Ali Ibn Masrur, delaying the utterance of the magic words which would resuscitate his father until he could bear it no longer, the child decided to take matters into his own hands. He suddenly ran to the door behind the judge's rostrum, opened it wide, and cried in a voice choked with tears: "Oh my father, come to me, come to me already." Morning broke the next day and Ali Ibn Masrur was taken into the courtyard of the Kishle prison to be hanged by the neck until he was dead. The moment the prisoner gave up the ghost there was a burst of laughter from the prison guards and the people who had come to watch, because of a slight mishap that occurred. His belt came undone and his trousers fell down, and the whole of his body from the navel to the knees was exposed to view. The moment the rope throttled him and his neck broke under the weight of his body, his penis stood erect and ejaculated.

Pnina sat erect in her chair, dried her eyes and wiped her purplish nose with a big handkerchief. Next to the bony, long-limbed judge, all Pnina's roundnesses were emphasized—the beads of her eyes, the button of her mouth, the rotundity of all her forms in the skins of their clothing—like those of the old Russian woman who cleaned the windows in the Orthodox church, who had been privileged in the twilight of her days to shelter the noble master of her youth, now fleeing for his life, in her home in the Russian Compound and offer him the hospitality of her table. And like this Russian mother sitting on the terrace outside her front door of an evening and sighing into the silences of the indigent aristocrat opposite her, Pnina too sat stealthily shedding tear after tear, trying to disguise her weeping by twisting her face into a smile as she listened to the old judge telling the story of how he had seen the way the law worked with his own eyes for the first time in his life, and how he had made up his mind to get to the heart of the matter. "You don't know what a good man the late Yehuda Prosper was and how much good he did in secret," she said to the judge after putting her handkerchief away in her apron pocket, and he gave her an inquiring look as if to ask what possible connection there could be between the secret goodhearted-ness of his late friend and the body of the hanged man which ejaculated living sperm the moment it gave up the ghost. His look was not one of surprise—for he had long since ceased to be surprised at any manifestation of human behavior—nor yet the injured or angry look of one who suddenly realizes that he has been wasting his confidences on deaf ears, but the look of a man emerging from the web of his thoughts in which he has long been caught, and examining the outside world in order to discover exactly where he is at this particular point in time, and this exam-ination—or perhaps the desire itself which arose in him to investigate his context in the external world—forged for a moment a living link between the expression on the judge's face and the voice coming out of his mouth with the ghost of a charitable smile as he perceived the nature of the rever-berations his words had awoken in the heart of his listener: "After Señor Moïse's father was murdered in the night in Lifta and the murderers robbed him of all his money, Yehuda Prosper, that saintly man, took pity on the poor abandoned orphan and took him into his home and was like a father to him, a real father who left him money when he died. And that's only one of all the good, merciful deeds he did in secret without anyone in the world knowing the first thing about them, like one of the *lammed vav** righteous men on whom the world rests. In fact, I wouldn't be in the least surprised if he himself was actually one of the *lammed vav* of his generation."

The loud peals of Gentilla's laughter bursting hilariously out of the closed room behind the judge's back were so

* *Lammed vav*—Thirty-six.

infectious that they succeeded in etching lines of gaiety even on his face and in bringing to his lips the ghost of a smile that was almost happy. The landlady (who, all the time she had been lying flat on her bed in the seclusion of her room, waiting for the right mood for the reception of the uninvited guest to arrive, and with it the strength and the will to change into the appropriate clothes for the occasion, had been listening to every word of the conversation being conducted on the verandah without removing her attention from the fine shades and nuances of her own innermost sensations, as if she were listening to two separate wavelengths on a set of earphones without preferring either one to the other) was so prodigiously amused by the very idea of Yehuda Prosper being numbered among the *lammed vav* righteous men that she was swept away on the peals of her own laughter and, rising from her bed, opened the door and joined the conversation just as she was without changing a single item of her clothing—for once she had actually been overtaken by the right mood she no longer paid any attention to the external formalities of dress, and in fact her fits of merriment (which were becoming increasingly rarer) changed her whole being completely, sweeping her audience off their feet and impregnating her features and movements with a kind of youthful ferment which did more to blur the signs of age than any illusory effects of outer apparel.

"Well, Dan, I ask you, have you ever heard the like? It's lucky for Sholem Aleichem that Pnina has never thought of collecting all the gems that come out of her mouth and putting them into a book. Imagine, all these years I've been living with a saint by mistake—one of the *lammed vav*, no less! I set out to catch a titled Turkish gentleman and found a saint hiding underneath a red tarboosh instead! What a dreadful mistake, what a disillusionment, what a disappointment!"

"That reminds me of a wonderful midrash," said the

judge, and as he spoke the landlady's gaiety evaporated and her face fell. "Do me a favor and don't start telling me midrashim!" she interrupted. "It was those cursed mid-rashim that were the ruin of my father, those Talmudic paradoxes, those thumb twisters and turners, all those casu-istries of the crooked Jewish mind that I detest! My poor father, in spite of the scandalous way he was cheated and underpaid, in spite of everything he suffered at the hands of those sanctimonious crooks, went around to his last living day with the feeling that that gang of pious humbugs, the rabbis and the wardens and all the rest of the religion-mongers, owed him nothing for the backbreaking work he put into their Holy Arks, on the contrary—he owed them his grateful thanks for condescending to talk about the Torah with him, for every one of the honey-sweet midrashim that they poured over all the rotten things they did to him, for the great honor they did him by allowing him to make them Arks of the Law free, gratis, and for nothing! Just as that saint in disguise, Yehuda Prosper Bey, lusted after women, so my poor father lusted after midrashim. Those were his only pleasures in life—listening to midrashim and making Arks of the Law."

The judge, who had spoiled her good mood with the single word "midrash," which he had dropped like a spot of black ink into a cup of clear water, immediately shut the memory of the wonderful midrash away in his heart and returned to the subject of Yehuda Prosper, but because of the sudden change in her mood the effect of his words was only to stir up ancient suspicions lying dormant at the bot-tom of her heart and start them fermenting until their hissing and seething filled the whole cup.

"One of the *lammed vav*—" said the judge, "I don't think that Yehuda Prosper himself would have been too pleased with that compliment. On the contrary—it was Moses who fired his imagination, Moses, who at the beginning of his life struck down the Egyptian, the little villain, and at the end of it Pharaoh himself, the head of the evildoers—not secretly and stealthily and anonymously, but with a strong hand and an outstretched arm and signs and portents manifest to the whole world. The man who with thunder and lightning and a great noise transformed a rabble of slaves into the chosen people."

"Well, I for one think that Pnina's right. After all, who knows if she doesn't what good deeds he did to her in secret in his lifetime, and even more so after he died, for why should she get less than Señor Moïse?" The bitter drop that had clouded the water in the cup and fermented its sediment soured Mrs. Luria's smile and transformed her into a shrewish old woman. The suspicion that Pnina had gotten her hands on the old man's property in secret and come up with a good slice for herself, having been awakened from its long slumber, was taking hold of her again and growing into the terrible certainty that this pious old hypocrite was in fact the principal benefactor of the old Turk's estate.

In contrast to the bitterness that had invaded the landlady's smile, voice, and words, the judge's face, for the first time since he had arrived on the verandah and taken his seat on his late friend's red armchair, broke into a real smile. But even this smile still remained within the closed circle of a man enjoying an exclusive private joke, which he had no intention of sharing with anyone else. "Yes, yes. You're right. Pnina's right. One of the righteous men on whom the world rests—maybe Yehuda Prosper would have been pleased with the compliment after all. When we were standing and watching Ibn Masrur being hanged, Yehuda said of it—the righteous member—that it was the foundation of the world—only then I didn't understand what he was getting at.* After the sentence had been carried out, a clerk of the

---

* The reference is to Proverbs 10.25: ". . . the righteous is an everlasting foundation." This verse received a later occult explanation in the Jewish mystic tradition of

Turkish court brought the hanged man's belongings out for public auction. Among all the rubbish spread out in the sun on the paving stones there was only one object of any value that drew the eyes of all the bystanders to it—the dagger with which the hanged man had killed his victim. But no one responded to the opening bid which the auctioneer offered again and again in a tremendously loud voice, in a kind of singsong rising and suddenly breaking off, like a ram's horn blowing shevarim, and what was even more surprising, no one put out his hand to feel the shoub'ria being offered for sale and examine it, as was the custom in those days. A rumor had swept the crowd that there was a curse on this shoub'ria, which had once belonged to the murdered man himself, Mahmoud Effendi, who had sold it to his future murderer, and like its two last owners so too all the previous owners of this accursed dagger had come to a sudden, violent end. I remember how all that rabble split in half to make way for Yehuda Bey, who started walking very slowly and solemnly between the two walls of eyes fixed silently upon him toward the auctioneer standing on the other side, who was holding the shoub'ria in the hand of his outstretched arm. The baksheesh he gave the auctioneer was more than the whole of the opening bid for which he bought the shoub'ria, and as he started on his way back to his place, a king in all his glory with the shoub'ria stuck in his belt, the crowd seemed to expand as it caught its breath in a gasp of excitement, like the audience at a circus when the animal trainer puts his head into the lion's jaw."

"He was a shrewd businessman all right," said Mrs. Luria, "cunning as a snake." And Pnina's eyes began to fill again, stealthily shedding tear after tear while her face twisted into

the Kabbalah, according to which there are ten spheres of divine manifestation in which God emerges from His hidden abode. These are symbolically described in a diagram of the human body. One of these spheres, called "Foundation," corresponds in the symbolical diagram to the sexual organ.

a strange, apologetic smile. "Yes, yes"—she sighed—"he was stronger than iron, a hero, and weaker than a fly."

I drew my head back just in time, jumped off the verandah, and ran to the tap in the corner of the yard. The bitter-tasting dryness in my throat, the weight pressing down on my chest, and the difficulty I was having with my breathing had all descended on me as soon as I realized that the shoub'ria would have to be returned at once to its place on the cellar floor, between the music box and the folding bed. As I was drinking, however, I realized that the thing was impossible: the judge, the landlady, and the landlady's sister, Pnina, were all sitting in the middle of the verandah, next to the stairs descending to the cellar, and I was allowed to go down to it only when the landlady herself required my assistance in conveying the folding bed up these stairs or down them again. I therefore had no alternative but to postpone the return of the dagger to the middle of the night when everyone was asleep, and although I still had a long time to wait I immediately made a wide detour around the verandah and stole into the house through the back door in order to make sure that it was still lying where I had left it, at the bottom of the desk drawer. Improbable and even incredible though this may sound, it is nevertheless true that the oppression that had descended upon me with the knowledge that I would have to return the shoub'ria to its place was not accompanied by any consciousness of fear at the curse that lay on this dagger, but rather by a growing recognition of the necessity for its return to its rightful owners, by a feeling that when I had stolen it from the damp cellar floor and placed it in my warm trouser pocket I had broken into the framework of a life that was not mine—a feeling which grew, as the judge's words conjured up the picture of the old man defiantly declaring war on the devil's curse in full view of the whole town, into an actual sense of sin, as if I had forced my way into a holy shrine and violated its sanctity by my presence: I would return the dagger to its place in the dead of night, and tomorrow morning I would go down to the landlady and ask her to sell me the ancient dagger lying abandoned and unclaimed in the depths of the cellar so that it would be mine by right, openly, lawfully, and publicly— like the old man who had dealt with a high hand and an outstretched arm. "He was stronger than iron, and weaker than a fly"—Pnina's words came back to me when I removed the little dagger from the bottom of the drawer, and its chill touch on my palm, coming together with the smell of the moldy green metal, suddenly flooded me with the same sense of uncomprehending wonder I had felt at the sight of the judge sitting in the old man's chair, but differing from it, nevertheless, if I can put it this way, with regard to the shade of the light and the sound of the voices filling the palace, which was now bathed in a clear translucent green, its voices echoing as in a long corridor situated not inside any building but in a forest strewn with the sunlight penetrating the branches of its trees and caught in their net, illuminating the palace from within in all the different shades and nuances of green. The sense of an enigma posed by this incomprehending wonder was not accompanied by any of the anxiety or strain usually involved in the search for the solution to a riddle. On the contrary, the very act of wondering about the meaning of the enigma was in itself imbued with a marvelously pleasant sensation, which was very remote and at the same time very familiar, like a melody coming from afar to pluck at thin, forgotten strings of ancient longings woven like tendrils into the landscape of the words: "He was stronger than iron, and weaker than a fly." Together with the knowledge that he was already gone while the dagger still existed, and parallel to it, came the clear certainty, fragrant as a breath of wind in the Judean mountains on a spring day, delicate and sharply refreshing as a draft of sparkling wine, that this little dagger, this blade which was no bigger than a man's finger, this dull, cold, helpless, inanimate bit of steel, was powerless to put an end to the old man's life, or to his thoughts on the subject of his master Moses, or to the life of Mahmoud Effendi and his great love, just as its stabbings were powerless to harm the waters of a mighty flood, and just as it would never be in its power to put an end to this dream forest in which I was wandering, with its abundance of memories and desires and hopes and lusts and longings and pictures and songs—a great ocean which all the stabs of all the daggers and all the blows of all the swords and bayonets in the world would never be able to extinguish.

Outside, the old man's red plush armchair creaked as the judge stood up at the end of his visit to return to the motorcar waiting for him at the gate, and the quiet groaning of the ancient wood immediately extinguished the green palace, which vanished into thin air with all its marvelous sensations. I returned the dagger to the drawer, underneath the copybooks and the textbooks, and wondered at the peculiar ideas that sometimes took hold of me. The old man had died in his bed at a ripe old age, and this dagger—if it was indeed the same dagger the old man had purchased thirty years before at the public auction of the personal possessions of the hanged man Ibn Masrur (and this too was a nonsensical idea, for hadn't his own wife, Mrs. Luria, just borne witness to the fact that he was a shrewd businessman, "cunning as a snake," who had spread the rumor of the curse on purpose, in order to buy the dagger for next to nothing and sell it afterward for its full price? What was more, during the thirty years that had gone by since then hundreds of shoub'rias and swords and all kinds of other weapons, which he had received as security for the money he lent to his Arab customers, had ended up in the cellar, and this particular dagger, which had found its way into my hands by accident, was almost certainly among the last of them)—this dagger had murdered not Yehuda Prosper Bey but Mahmoud Effendi of Bethlehem, before whose eyes floated only the image of his beloved, in milky ribbons of steam rising from the lakes of pale blue vapors filling the valleys of the dawn road to Jerusalem, a road he traveled never to return.

7.

Between the Testaments

As I WRITE THESE LINES I am reminded of something that the pharmacist, Dr. Blum, once told me about the son of the Bethlehem effendi who was killed for love, Daoud Ibn Mahmoud. Or perhaps it was not about him but about the old judge's Arab driver, who was also called Daoud Ibn Mahmoud, and who was also destined to be killed.

If I knew where to find the pharmacist of my childhood years I would go and ask him to set the matter straight, but ever since the time I met him by chance in the Café Atara many years ago I have never seen him again. I don't know what has happened to him since then, or even if he is still alive. As far as age goes, at any rate, there is no reason to suppose that he is not still alive and kicking and thinking as furiously as ever along his own peculiar lines, since when I first saw him, which was when he returned from Beirut and opened his pharmacy, he was not yet forty, and from that day to this no more than thirty years have passed. This means that if he is still alive he is not yet seventy years old. It may well be that during all the years that have gone by since that chance meeting in the Café Atara he has been obliged, because of the peculiar nature of his business enterprises, to cover his tracks or even to leave the country in secret, but it is equally possible that he may have taken up another line of business and that during all these years he has been living among us, going around and around in his own circles which are not tangential to my circles, in which case he may suddenly appear before me one of these days on a street corner, like a memory looming up from the dark: in all of my encounters, not only with people but even with houses and trees and alleys and streets and sights and smells, I have always sensed something of the essence of the advent of memory. For all of them go on existing and living their lives year after year, even though they are situated outside the circles of our daily routines—dead to us because they are external to us, outside our ken. Suddenly, their routines brush up against ours, and here they are rising up before us like Lazarus from the dead, to show us that their being dead to us was merely the result of the narrowness of the torch's beam, capable of illuminating only a small part of our path through the big, broad fields that lie outside our ken because of the curtain of darkness cutting them off from our field of vision, even when their abysses gape inside us.

Dr. Blum I did not see again but I did suddenly see, springing up like an apparition in front of my door, another of the flowers that had bloomed in the fields of Gabriel's youth—Dr. Shoshan.* When the bell rang and I went to open the door he was standing on the threshold like the materialization of a dim childhood memory: the librarian from the B'nai B'rith Library, where I used to change my books as a child, standing before me with a book in his hands. I had not seen the little librarian shooting sparks from his Chinese-slanting eyes behind the thick lenses of his glasses for over thirty years, and out of sight for all these years, he had been out of mind for most of them too. My distant childhood years, which no longer existed except in occasional dreams or thoughts, took on a tangible form at

* *Shoshan*—Hebrew for "rose."

the sight of the bespectacled little man standing at the door, as if they had been there all the time, existing in the substance of the material world, but in a different place, which had given them a different flavor. The man was the same man, but he had a different flavor, and not only because of the thirty years that had been added to his age. He didn't recognize me, of course. How could he have? To him I had been only one of hundreds or perhaps even thousands of children coming to him to change their library books. In time which runs forward memory runs backward, and children remember the grownups who preceded them while grownups forget the children who come after them.

Despite the thirty years that had been added to his age in the meantime he now looked not only neater and more elegant than before, but also more vigorous and energetic, in spite of the malignant disease that had taken root in his body in recent years. This impression of vigor vanished abruptly as soon as he started to speak and was left open-mouthed, gasping for air to breathe like a fish floundering on dry land. Each fresh spurt of speech started out in a burst of optimism only to peter out in hawking coughs and end up in the handkerchief waiting in his hand to receive the phlegm. He had come to offer me some translation work. Not just any translation work, but the translation of the book he was holding in his hand, which was a biography of John Calvin, originally written in French and subsequently translated into English with the assistance of the World Centre of Calvinist Congregations. He had arrived at my door through a mistake he had made regarding his own new address. A month ago he and his wife and his son and their dog had come to live in a house next to our own, and since the two houses stood side by side and their entrances were similar, he had entered our house by mistake. Once inside the lobby he sensed something different, and in order to set his mind at rest he decided to look at the names of the tenants on the letter boxes and find his own. If he found his name—Dr. Shoshan—it would mean that he was not mistaken and had come to the right address. He did not find his name, but he did find mine. When my name jumped at him from the letter box he remembered having once come across a book about Zen Buddhism which had been translated into Hebrew by someone with that name, and if I was indeed the man who had translated the book *The Wisdom of Zen* into the Hebrew language, why then there was no reason why I should not also translate into Hebrew the biography of Calvin, who was incomparably more important to the world in general and to the people of Israel in particular than Bodhidharma, who had spread the teachings of Zen in the East, especially since, besides the spiritual benefits I would certainly derive from translating the book, the World Centre of Calvinist Congregations of which he himself, Dr. Shoshan, was the general secretary, would see to it that I was handsomely rewarded for my labors in hard cash as well.

"Yes, I am the man who translated *The Wisdom of Zen* into Hebrew," I said, and was about to go on and tell him happily that I still remembered him from the distant days when he was working as a librarian in the B'nai B'rith Library, when a renewed fit of coughing made him press his handkerchief to his mouth again and I hurried to offer him a cup of tea instead. While I was busy in the kitchen making the tea, I was suddenly reminded of the back of a man I had seen stepping briskly out of the gate to the Lepers' Hospital one summer's evening when the whole of the western sky from horizon to horizon was the color of a ripe orange, and the black silhouette of the doctor—for I assumed that the man was one of the doctors working in the hospital—dwindled into the distance on the dusty path running along the stone wall and leading to the road to Salameh Square.

For some years the assembly point for my reserve duty battalion was in the old British barracks called after Major

Stone opposite the Lepers' Hospital: recently the lepers have
been removed and taken somewhere else—where I don't
know—leaving the place empty and deserted; the high stone
wall surrounding the wooded grounds has started to crumble into disrepair, and the battalion has begun to assemble
among the ancient pine trees beneath whose shade the
lepers once strolled. But on the evening I am speaking of,
the high stone wall had not yet begun to crumble, and it still
enclosed the Lepers' Hospital on all sides, and we assembled
in the Stone Barracks opposite. As on all previous call-ups
and practice call-ups and routine reports-for-duty and emergency mobilization exercises, on this occasion too I withdrew into my shell and waited for the time of my subjection
to the authority of the army to be over as quickly as possible,
so that I could sink back into the best of my dreams in the
routine of waking sleep to which we are all subject in our
threefold chains—the dream of freedom.

As was only to be expected, and as usual on all previous
call-ups, time dragged on interminably in the uniform gray-
ness of the world of external activities. However, as was not
to be expected, one moment—the moment when the man
came out of the gate in the wall—suddenly detached itself
from the course of time: this moment appeared before me
like the vision of an orange sunset in which everything—the
stone wall and the treetops beyond it and the dusty path and
the black figure of the man—was immersed in a strange,
wonderful, ample calm, as fixed and unchanging and outside the course of time as a picture hanging in a museum
that you can go back to look at whenever you like and find
exactly as it was when the artist finished painting it, without
having to worry about the changes that may have taken
place in the landscape during the passage of time—whether
the sun has set and the sky darkened, or the wall collapsed
and its stones scattered, or the man reached the end of the
dusty path and turned off onto the main road and disap-

peared. The strange and wonderfully calming and uplifting flavor of this certainty that it was possible to return to this orange-colored moment of spacious sunset detached from the race of time, just as it was possible to return to a picture hanging in a museum, or to a place where you had already been before, remained with me even after I had returned to the course of time and the little black figure had turned the corner and disappeared. "I suppose you know who that is," said one of my fellow reservists who was standing next to me and must have noticed me staring in the man's direction. When I said that I supposed he was one of the doctors working in the Lepers' Hospital my companion laughed and said that he was no doctor but a Christian priest, and no ordinary Christian priest either, but a Jewish Christian priest. When I asked him how he knew he told me that a little while before he had read an appeal in the newspaper asking for contributions of old books for the patients of the Hansen Hospital. He had collected some books from his shelves which dealt with neither statistics nor economics, books in other words he did not need in his work, and taken them to the hospital. The nurse who met him at the door was a Swedish nun who knew no Hebrew, but at the sight of the books in his hands she understood what he had come for and led him to the priest who was responsible for the spiritual well-being of the patients, and spoke a few words to him in her language. The priest answered her and then, as he was glancing through the books, he turned to my companion and thanked him, to his astonishment, in fluent Hebrew. Most of the books were translations of English, French, and Russian novels, but among them was also the translation of *The Wisdom of Zen,* which at once caught the eye of this Christian priest who looked after Jewish lepers and knew how to speak Hebrew better than any of them did. As he was leafing through the book and commenting on the differences between the religious faiths of the Far East and Christianity, the priest became aware of the donor's bewilderment and straightaway, without waiting to be asked, he told him that he himself was a Jew, born and bred in the Old City of Jerusalem. He had studied Torah first at Rabbi Avremale's Little Yeshiva, and then at Rabbi Kook's Yeshiva, and he was still as much of a Jew as ever, and the only change that had taken place in him since then was that his eyes had been opened to the divine mercy of the redeemer of mankind, the Messiah Jesus of Nazareth.

Jesus of Nazareth seemed to me to have been a kind-hearted man, full of compassion for suffering and pain, who wished well to all mankind and wanted to save the wretched and miserable, the oppressed and humiliated of the earth, just as the New Testament, which is the sole source I have ever consulted on the matter, tells us. With respect to his attitude toward women and married life, I received no definite impression from what I read there and the few hints I did pick up were not always to my liking, but at the same time my heart went out to this great soul tortured with its great love and pity. In his love and his pity and his hatred for all institutions and authorities, especially religious institutions which by their very nature kill the holy spirit even as they preserve the external form of the word of God, he seemed to me to maintain and continue the ancient tradition of the biblical prophets. Unfamiliar as I am with the various Christian churches and ignorant as I am of the writings of their founders and saints, I am unable to understand where they see the connection between themselves and the prophet Jesus, especially in view of the fact that any ruling power, especially temporal religious power, seems to me to contradict by its very nature the personality and essence of the life and death of Jesus, and it was about this that I wanted to talk to Dr. Shoshan as I stood pouring the tea in the kitchen, full of amazement at the situation itself and the curious chances and accidents of time: on the day of the emergency

mobilization exercise I had not known that the black silhouette vanishing into the ripe orange sunset was that of the
librarian of my childhood, who would one of these days
arrive at my front door as a result of a mistake in the address
of his new apartment, without his remembering me from his
librarian days or knowing that the silhouette of his back had
helped to create the picture of an extraordinary time-tran-
scending moment in my life.

As I carried the tea into the room from the kitchen it was
about these things that I wanted to talk to him, not only
because they interested me from the human point of view—
for Jesus the man interested me as a human being, just as
Moses and Buddha and Bodhidharma and Mohammed interested me as men, quite independently of the truth or
falsehood of the doctrines they brought to the world—but
also because I thought that Dr. Shoshan, because of the very
nature of his occupation and interests, would be eager to
give me the benefit of his thoughts on the matter. When I
entered the room and sat down opposite him, however, our
conversation took a different turn. After I opened by recalling childhood memories he took over and started telling me
with growing excitement and enthusiasm, between trouble-
some fits of coughing and throat-clearing, about his own
childhood days. He had suffered great distress as a child
because his sidelocks stubbornly refused to curl. In those
days the little cheder scholars of the Old City had prided
themselves upon the possession of nice curly sidelocks—the
curlier the better. He himself, then as now, was the unfortunate possessor of straight, flaxen hair, and the sidelocks
falling straight as a die on either side of his face had ada-
mantly refused to curl, although he rolled them diligently
around his fingers all day long as he sat poring over the
Pentateuch with the commentaries of Rashi. This disgrace
of straight sidelocks dogged him throughout his childhood.
When he left the cheder and entered Rav Kook's Yeshiva

someone told him—he could not quite remember, but he thought it was probably Gabriel Luria, who was his best friend then—that there was a secret remedy for his affliction. The remedy was beer. You had to dip the tips of your fingers in a glass of beer and twist the resistant locks around them while they were still dripping with it, and this he did three times a day, morning, noon, and night, until he was forced to the sad conclusion that this remedy too had failed him and that the straightness of his blond sidelocks was incurable.

As Dr. Shoshan spoke he laughed repeatedly at the silliness of the troubles that had made him miserable as a child, and the laughter twinkling mischievously in the eyes and lending a childlike expression to the face of the aging man (like a double negative of two photographs, one of a child and one of an old man, taken on top of each other and developed into one picture which looked one moment like an old man turning into a child and the next like a child turning into an old man), this laughter was interrupted by attacks of choking, throat-clearing, and coughing which ended up in his handkerchief and wiped every trace of childishness or mischief from the lined old face turning red and white by turns.

He himself told me—and I heard it too from the statistician who had donated books to the lepers—that two years before in Amsterdam he had undergone a difficult and dangerous operation to have a cancerous lung removed, and now his one remaining lung was infected with the same incurable disease. Just as he had known what he was facing then, so he knew now what it meant when he choked and coughed and spat blood, and yet the moment he recovered from one of these attacks his face would light up again, and he would explain that he was getting better all the time and that within two or three weeks he would be rid of "this stupid cold," and he would say these things in an upsurge of faith that was no less certain, perfect, and sincere than the certain knowledge that his days were numbered.

Even when he stopped coughing his voice remained hoarse and breathless and he whispered huskily as if he were confiding some intimate secret in me. He clutched the little book he wanted translated into Hebrew like an opera singer imploringly clutching the candle illuminating her path in the dark dungeon into which she has innocently been cast, as a pretext for straining the muscles of her arms and chest to help the muscles of her throat reach the high notes of her aria. Only unlike the opera singer's, Dr. Shoshan's hands clutched the little book unconsciously and without any deliberate theatrical design, and if they helped him bring any sounds forth from his tortured throat, they were not such as to delight the ear of the listener. His face too was already showing signs of weariness, and he returned to the subject of the translation. I had neither the time nor the inclination to translate the life of Calvin into Hebrew at that time, and he did not try to persuade me to begin the work at once. He simply left the book with me with the request that I read it in my spare time and tell him what I thought of it when I had finished. "We've got plenty of time," he said as he got up to go. "There's no reason to hurry."

When I went out to see him to the gate I heard a little boy on his way to the Music Academy with a violin case under his arm whisper to his companion: "Look—there goes the missionary!" How could I, a child running down Abyssinian Road to change the book under his arm at the B'nai B'rith Library, possibly have imagined that the man who seemed as much a part of the library as the smell of the ancient wood of its shelves and the shape of its rooms, that the bespectacled little librarian who seemed to have been created by nature for the sole purpose of being a librarian, and not just any librarian but the librarian of this library in particular—

that in days to come this same man would look like a missionary born and bred, to other children in another time and another place? There was no reason to suppose that this little boy had received any sort of religious education at home, since he was the son of the same statistician who had first told me about the Jewish Christian priest, a man of a rationalistic, scientific cast of mind, who behaved as if the Sabbath and the Holy Days of Israel had come into the world for the sole purpose of enabling him to put his wife and children into his motorcar and drive them to the beach. In this respect he was no different from any of the other children in the street who all went to the neighborhood school of which his mother was the headmistress, and, this being the case, I wondered: from whom could this child have learned to be suspicious and afraid of missionaries? I don't know if he knew exactly what the word he whispered in his friend's ear meant, or the kind of people it described, but from the look in his eyes and the tone of his voice it was quite clear that he felt they were dangerous and had best be avoided.

The boy with the violin hurried past us with his friend, and Dr. Shoshan to my relief noticed neither him nor his remark which, I felt then, might well have hurt or offended him. How misplaced this feeling was I discovered the very next day, when I met Dr. Shoshan as I was emerging from my front gate and he joined me and started telling me, with obvious satisfaction, about all the bitter humiliations he had suffered, and all the terrible trials and tribulations he had endured in his lifetime for the sake of his savior. This time no fits of coughing and cawing and blood-spitting interrupted his speech, and it seemed that he may have been right when he explained to me the day before that he was getting better all the time and was about to recover from the "stupid cold" that was plaguing him—although there was still no change in his voice, which remained dull, shallow, and whispering. In his well-pressed tailor-made suit and erect, vigorous bearing he looked more like a successful British businessman who had served in his youth as an officer in His Majesty's armed forces than a Jewish Christian priest who had served in his youth in the B'nai B'rith Library. The improvement in his health, the clear fine weather, and his own good mood had apparently combined to open the doors of memory to a succession of pleasing images from the past, in all of which he appeared as a unique, exceptional individual courageously defending the True Faith against a cruel, ignorant, benighted mob which mocked him and howled for his blood. For example, a few years before he had happened to see an announcement advertising a mass protest meeting against missionaries to be held in the Great Synagogue in the Zikaron Moshe Quarter. He knew, of course, that in going to that protest meeting he would be like Daniel entering the lions' den, but even this certain knowledge of the terrible dangers in store for him could not prevent him from doing his duty and going to the defense of his faith, and in fact it never occurred to him for a moment to stay at home. As soon as the people gathered in the synagogue saw him, before he even had a chance to open his mouth, they all began spitting in his face and cursing and reviling him and some of them even went so far as to lay hands on him, slapping his face hard on both cheeks, pulling the spectacles from his nose, and tearing his coat. Once his glasses were gone, their lenses trampled into dust by the heavy feet of the maniacs surrounding him, he could no longer see anything or find his way out, and if it had not been for a certain merciful person with a true Christian heart in the audience, who had helped him to escape the clutches of the ravening mob, who knows what would have become of him? And who had outdone them all in heaping insults and abuse on his head? None other than Reb Yitzhok, who had gone to school with him at Rabbi

Avremale's cheder. That blockheaded Yitzhok, whose brains the years had done nothing to improve, that ignoramus who couldn't even read a simple page of the Gemarah to this very day! And how could you expect someone who had never succeeded in getting to know a single verse of the Pentateuch with Rashi by heart and who couldn't even understand the meaning of the words in the prayer book to open a page of the Gemarah and understand even the simplest matter discussed there? Actually, Dr. Shoshan's weak, whispering voice continued in a more speculative vein, there was nothing to be wondered at in the fact that this Itzik had shown such extreme fanaticism and militancy, since in order to be a true fanatic, never mind in what cause—communism, capitalism, Buddhism, psychoanalysis, Orthodox Judaism, or left-right-right-left Labour Zionism, a man had to be stupid. That stupid Yitzhok had continued to pursue him after he had escaped from the hall, spitting at him and shouting abuse after him. It so happened that Dr. Morning-Rose, an American pastor of the Presbyterian flock, and his good friend since the days of his studies at the Theological Seminary, was passing by and witnessed this disgraceful spectacle. He immediately proposed sending for the American ambassador and making a big fuss in Israel and America and taking Reb Yitzhok and the rest of that criminal mob to court, but he, Dr. Shoshan, had implored him to leave them alone and forget the whole incident.

Dr. Shoshan stole a quick sideways glance at me from behind his spectacles to see how I was taking this tale of a latter-day Daniel in the lions' den, and I looked back admiringly at the little man whose single surviving lung was bringing him nearer every day to his fast-approaching end, although to tell the truth what really struck me in his story was not the terrible lions who had trampled his spectacles in the dust and slapped his face, nor the Daniel who had discovered among the ravening beasts one lion who had gone to cheder with him and another who was possessed of a true Christian heart, but the contempt of the Christian missionary for the ignorance of the Jewish religious fanatic Reb Yitzhok, who was incapable of reading a page of the Gemarah.

Nor was this contempt reserved solely for the ignorance of Reb Yitzhok and his fellows. Having mentioned the desire of his friend Dr. Morning-Rose to bring the United States government to his rescue, Dr. Shoshan went on to add tolerantly, "A good man with his heart in the right place, but the biggest ignoramus I've ever come across. I simply can't understand how the American Presbyterian Council came to send such an ignorant man to Israel. A man who's never read the *Institutio Christianae Religionis* in the original and doesn't even know the difference between the Augustine and Thomist conceptions of predestination, never mind appreciating the importance of Calvin's contribution to the question."

As he uttered these words about the importance of Calvin's contribution to the doctrine of predestination, his wife emerged from their front gate. She turned out to be a big woman with a lot of flesh which was not, however, distributed evenly over her frame but all concentrated in one place, thickening her waistline and bulging above it and totally depriving her scanty buttocks and thin legs, left to bear the burden of all that upper flesh with a shocking kind of intrinsic injustice which reminded me of the outrage I had once felt as a child on seeing an emaciated little Arab porter carrying a fat, bloated effendi on his back into Dr. Landau's eye clinic with the same unprotesting stoicism now displayed by Mrs. Shoshan's skinny legs. She said a few words to her husband in Dutch, and throughout the subsequent exchange which took place between them, bringing an angry flush to his cheeks and choking his hoarse voice with a

renewed outbreak of gasping coughs, her own red face
remained calm and expressionless. Their two faces shone
ruddily at each other, like two sheets of water reflecting the
same sunset, but whereas the surface of her face appeared
to rest on depths of motionless tranquillity, the surface of his
seemed no more than the skin on top of a furious whirlpool.
As I listened to them talking in a language at once strange
and curiously familiar to my ears, like a dialect of Yiddish I
would have been able to understand if only the words had
not somehow gotten mixed up with each other, I kept on
catching the word "Hartal," which was the name of a very
rich Jew. Since I have never seen this Hartal or even a picture
of him, I have no idea what he looks like, but at the sound of
his name coming out of Mrs. Shoshan's mouth there rose
before my eyes the image of the back of the man stepping
briskly out of the gate of the Lepers' Hospital and I recalled
the conversation I had had on that same evening with the
statistician-economist who told me that the silhouette vanishing into the sunset was that of the Jewish missionary.
When the silhouette disappeared around the corner and
there was nothing left but the long, high hospital wall, I
remarked that I had always liked stone walls and that it was a
pity that people had stopped building them around their
houses. My companion replied that it was all a question of
economics. Building garden walls of stone cost a lot of
money nowadays, and only the very rich who were prepared
to waste capital on unprofitable investments, like the millionaire Hartal, for example, could afford them. The stone
wall that surrounded the whole of Hartal's garden, concealing its swimming pool and dance floor and summer house
and other amenities from inquisitive eyes, was even longer
and higher than the wall surrounding the hospital grounds
opposite, and it alone—according to the simple calculation
of building costs per running meter—must have cost Hartal
a couple of hundred thousand liroth. I myself, who have

never in my life thought of costs per running meter at the sight of a stone wall, am no judge of the matter, but when it comes to money you can rest assured that this economist knows what he's talking about.

It was the name of the millionaire Hartal coming out of his wife's mouth that was responsible for the angry twitching of Dr. Shoshan's face. As soon as she started walking down the street he muttered furiously to himself, his lips trembling with anger, illness, and age, "Hartal, Hartal, Hartal!" After this he became a little calmer and said that now that his wife, as I had seen for myself, had gone out to visit her friend Mrs. Hartal, he had no reason to hurry home: he was at liberty and at my service to take me anywhere I wanted to go in his motorcar and he was even ready, if I had the time and inclination for it, to take me for a short drive into the countryside. The mention of a short drive in the countryside removed the last traces of wrathful twitching from his face, and when we got into the car and he started the engine he said with a smile, and without the least sign of bitterness or anger, that his wife had one peculiarity: she loved rich people. This love, he informed me, was a pure love; she had never requested any favors from her rich friend in the past, nor did she cherish any secret dreams of benefits to be bestowed in the future. Her love, if he might be permitted to use the phrase in this context, was a Platonic love. Take today, for instance. She was supposed to be sitting and waiting for him to come and give her her daily Bible lesson, and today's lesson was to be on a subject of exceptional interest, which was St. John of Damascus, one of the fathers of the early Greek church, and his approach to the problem of predestination. This St. John of Damascus had asked a great question: how was it that God, who was infinitely good, had predestined some people from the moment of their conception to end up in Hell? And now just because this Mrs. Hartal had called up to invite her to tea, his wife immediately lost her head completely and forgot all about her husband, her Bible lesson, St. John of Damascus, and the damnation awaiting the wicked. This rich friend—or any other friend for that matter, as long as her husband had plenty of money—had only to whistle and his wife would drop everything and run. For how could St. John of Damascus or Louis Molina or John Calvin himself compete with the force of the Platonic love aroused in her bosom by Mammon? The truth of the matter was that his wife's indifference to the problems of religion had long since ceased to surprise him. Her father, his late father-in-law, who was a great man—a leader of the Church in our times, a brilliant scholar and polemicist, a professor of casuistry and the author of a number of monographs which were among the cornerstones of the Dutch Reformed Church in our day, had once warned him in a lighthearted way against the bad influence his daughter was likely to have on his spiritual development: "Beware of my daughter Paula," he had said. "She may yet change your predestination!" And everybody had laughed at the joke. It wasn't that his wife was guilty of any actual sins; she did everything that the Church expected of her—but with an indifference so total that it never even gave her occasion for heretical doubts. Unlike his wife, her childhood friend Henrietta van Eckern was truly devout. In fact, if it hadn't been for his love for Henrietta, he would never have married Paula—and here Dr. Shoshan broke into silent laughter which was interrupted by a fit of coughing and retching that ended up, as usual, in his handkerchief and obliged him to stop the engine just as the car began to pull away from the curb.

The truth of the matter is that if I had stopped for even a moment to consider, I would not have accepted his invitation to take me for a short drive into the countryside. One little fit of coughing like the one I had just witnessed—and this was nothing compared to what he was capable of, as I had already had ample opportunity to observe—while he was driving would be quite enough to shake his whole body, jerk the steering wheel off its course, and send us straight into the giant gasoline carrier coming toward us. Why precisely a gasoline carrier I don't know, but in my mind's eye I already saw the huge red truck with "Paz" written on its side advancing on us with all the force of its 200 horsepower, and Dr. Shoshan with one little cough sending us straight into it with a terrible crash and explosion of smoke and flames. But instead of doing what plain logic told me to—which is to say, apologize politely and get out of the car with some plausible excuse—I remained seated in a kind of paralysis of the will and relaxation of the instinct of self-preservation. I sank into apathy and delivered myself into the hands of chance, feeling only the slight suspense of a spectator wondering what will happen next in a play in which he himself plays no part.

The attack of coughing proved short-lived, and when he had recovered Dr. Shoshan started up the motor again, whispering the name of Henrietta to himself as he did so. "Henrietta, ah yes, Henrietta, as I was saying—" and the silent laughter came back to plough furrows around his sunken mouth and bloodshot eyes behind the spectacles which had misted over from his coughing, obliging him to shut the engine off again. From another pocket he took out a new, clean handkerchief, with which he proceeded to clean his spectacles while he told me the story of his love for Henrietta. He told the story like someone standing outside it, as if he himself had not been involved, and not he but someone else had been in love with Henrietta. This Henrietta was the only daughter of Theodore van Eckern, the famous banker, the Old Lion of Amersfoort. After graduating from the Theological Seminary with distinction Dr. Shoshan had been appointed, on the recommendation of his professor, to the pastorship of the Amersfoort congregation, where he soon made a name for himself as an outstand-

ing preacher, thanks to the excellent sermons he preached
every Sunday morning in the Amersfoort church. This was
nothing to wonder at, since these sermons in their content,
scope, profundity, and scholarship were far superior to anything the Amersfoortians had ever heard before, it being no
secret to anyone that the town of Amersfoort had not been
graced before his coming with pastors of any stature worth
mentioning. "But what will probably come as a surprise to
you," said Dr. Shoshan, blushing, "is the fact that at that time
I had a very pleasant voice. You probably find it difficult to
imagine that this hoarse, coughing, breathless old man . . ."
Perhaps I should have told him not only that did I not find
any difficulty in imagining, but that I actually remembered
his voice from the days that had preceded his sermons in
Amersfoort, but I said nothing and simply nodded my
head, perhaps because I felt that the memory of the pleasant
voice of the librarian at the B'nai B'rith Library belonged to
the world of my own childhood memories more than it did
to the old man sitting next to me. There was another reason
for my silence too: from the moment he started talking
about Henrietta I had the distinct impression that it made
very little difference to him who the man sitting next to
him was or what the thoughts passing through his mind
might be.

Thanks to these excellent sermons which he preached in
his pleasant voice Dr. Shoshan had been accorded the greatest honor that lay in the power of the town of Amersfoort to
bestow, which was to be invited to dine on Sundays and other
public holidays, as well as on the occasions of the private
celebrations of his host, at the table of Theodore van
Eckern, the old lion whose money and personality dominated the whole town and its environs from the suburb of
Soest to the village of Spakenburg. In short, from the very
first dinner at which he first set eyes on the Old Lion's
daughter Henrietta, he fell head over heels in love with her,

and so did she with him the very first time she ever heard him preach—that is, before he even knew of her existence. This great secret, which filled his heart with the greatest happiness he had ever known, Henrietta disclosed to him only after they had known each other for several months, on the eve of the fateful day on which they made their love known to her parents and asked them for their blessings on the match. The Old Lion and his lioness seemed to have been expecting the happy event no less than the lovers themselves, and all would have been well if not for a slight mishap, a kind of basic misapprehension which immediately came to light. Because of the foreignness of his accent Henrietta's parents did not know exactly what the origins of the young pastor were. The old man was of the opinion that he hailed from Germany, from Prussia to be more precise, and that he was a Berliner, while his wife had come to the conclusion that he was a Frenchman from Paris. When he revealed to them that he had been born in neither Berlin nor Paris but in Jerusalem itself, not far from the site of the Last Supper, and that he was neither a Prussian nor a Frenchman but belonged to the nation that had given birth to Jesus Christ, they were overcome with panic and dismay, and the old woman fainted and almost had a heart attack. It is possible that the old man, who had nothing but contempt for public opinion, since the members of this public were all under his thumb in any case, and who was a brave and fearless man, would have come around in the end, but his wife was on no account prepared to resign herself to the terrible disgrace of such an alliance. "Henrietta will never marry a Jew!" she declared, and in the quarrels that broke out after this declaration, every time the young priest met the hatred in the old woman's eyes he felt as if he himself had nailed Jesus to the cross with his own hands. The old man would sink into a heavy silence, his wife would threaten to commit suicide because it was only over her dead body that this disgraceful marriage would take place, and the tears would well up in Henrietta's eyes and flow without stopping. This Henrietta was like a delicate hothouse flower who had bloomed all her life in the warmth and security of her family's love and whose only wish in everything she did was to please her parents and make them happy. The thought that in gratifying her heart's desire she not only would not make her parents happy but would destroy their happiness and might even be the cause of her mother's suicide was unendurable to her. Dr. Shoshan, who really loved her and wanted only what was best for her, solved her problem for her with Christian charity, Christian mercy, and Christian love by leaving Amersfoort and disappearing from her life. His last letter to her, in which he explained everything, he sent by the hand of her best friend, Paula, who was within the year to become his wife: the same Paula who had just canceled her daily Bible lesson because her rich friend Mrs. Hartal had invited her to tea, and because of the Platonic love she bore for all rich people.

This Platonic love, as he had already told me, had long since ceased to surprise him. The truth was that if we really thought about love we would discover that it was always, by its very nature, Platonic, and that the words of the sages regarding the duties of religious observance applied to it too: the reward of love is love, and the punishment of love is love, and in this world the punishment of love is always greater than its reward, and the greater the punishment of the lover in this world the greater his reward in the world to come. On the other hand, there was something about this woman—his wife—that did surprise him. His wife, to his great astonishment, was growing more like Henrietta's mother every day. Sometimes when he woke from his restless sleep at night and looked around him, he saw her face in the light of the oil lamp which burned dimly all night long, and it reminded him of his Amersfoort days and the home of the

Old Lion. On the night of the day on which he had seen my name on his letter box as a result of his mistake in the address (the mistake from which our acquaintanceship had grown), when he got into bed and prepared himself for what he hoped would be a good night's sleep—more or less— because he felt pleasantly tired, his eyes fell on his sleeping wife and his heart started beating wildly in the awful fear we feel at the sight of something uncanny: the woman lying next to him was not Paula but Henrietta's mother. Nor was this an illusion created by the dim light of the oil lamp, for he could assure me that even in the middle of the day Paula's face tried its best to look like the face of the Old Lion's wife—only in the daytime it didn't scare him so much.

Interesting that he couldn't remember the old lady's name. He remembered her husband's name well enough, Theodore, like the Zionistic prophet, and of course the name of her daughter, Henrietta. But the old lady's name he had forgotten entirely, it was quite gone. Her name was gone, but not her memory, which was sometimes much sharper, clearer, and more alive than Henrietta's. He remembered every single detail not only of her face, but also of the way she walked and the sound of her voice. He had to say this for the old witch, that her voice was easy on the ear— soft, but clear and full of nuances—and it was here that the similarity between her and Paula came to an end. Of his wife it could be said that the voice was the voice of Paula, but the face was the face of Henrietta's mother. In this sweet, soft voice of hers Henrietta's mother would threaten her daughter with suicide. Yes. As for the old witch's threats to commit suicide, on him they had made no impression at all—but since he knew from his own experience the terrible distress produced by such threats in the person against whom they were directed, a distress that rational arguments and logical proofs could do nothing to remove, he did not even try to reassure Henrietta and prove to her that her mother had no

intention at all of committing suicide and that her threats
were nothing but emotional blackmail and terrorism of the
most despicable kind. The particular flavor of that misery
and distress he remembered from the days when his own
mother had employed the same terrorist techniques against
him on finding out that he intended changing his religion
because his eyes had been opened to the truth of the Mes-
siah-King-of-the-Jews: it was his fate, it seemed, to turn
mothers into terrorists and blackmailers-by-threats-of-
suicide with the truth of his faith and his love. His sister was
a more serious opponent than his mother. She had not tor-
mented him with words, or persecuted him with ultimatums
and threats—she had simply thrown a red-hot iron at his
head. His sister was a nationalist, a Revisionist, a disciple of
Vladimir Jabotinsky's. She was standing and ironing her
blue and brown uniform when he came to visit her to talk
about the questions of religion and faith which she found so
boring because she was an atheist who believed in nothing
but nationalism. When he opened his heart to her and
revealed the truths of his faith, that new faith filling the new
heart which was bursting in his breast, her face paled and
she froze in her place and her hand holding the iron pressed
it down on the brown shirt until it scorched the material and
wisps of smoke began to rise from the ironing board. "Traitor!" the cry escaped from the depths of her being. "You are
a traitor to your people!" With that she picked up the iron
adorned with scraps of her scorched shirt and hurled it at
his head. She was saved by a miracle from hitting him with
the red-hot iron, which could easily have killed him and
made her into a murderer. When he saw what things were
coming to, that by the truth of his faith he might yet be
responsible for turning his sister into a murderer, he picked
up his heels and left the country and went to Egypt, where
he was baptized.

By the time he reached his baptism Dr. Shoshan was

bathed in perspiration because of the combined efforts of speaking, which fatigued him even in the absence of any further choking attacks, and of driving, in which he did not display any great expertise. Speaking and driving went together in him, in Dr. Shoshan, during our short drive to the outskirts of the town, like a baby and an old man walking hand in hand with faltering steps: one tottering with sickness and old age and the other stumbling and falling because he had only recently learned to walk, and the art of walking had not yet become second nature to him. In speech he was at the end of the road, and in driving at the beginning. Because all the activities involved in driving a car were new to him and he was not yet accustomed to performing them automatically, smoothly, and in time, his car progressed along the road to Ein Kerem in a rhythm of its own, out of step with the rest of the traffic and the pedestrians, stopping with hellish screechings and starting up again in a series of violent hiccuping jerks, frightening the drivers of all the other cars on the road and especially all the pedestrians. Twice, in two of these wild leaps forward, he almost killed first a child and then a woman pushing a pram, and on both occasions he stopped the car with a desperate grinding of brakes and teeth and an outburst of rage against the two pedestrians who had almost made him into a murderer. It never occurred to him to admit that there was anything wrong with his own inexperienced, unskilled driving—perhaps because knowledge and erudition, in any field, were of such great importance to him, and just as there was nothing he condemned in a man more than ignorance, so there was nothing more praiseworthy and superior in his eyes than knowledge and cleverness, and no one he admired more than a clever, erudite man. For a long time this was a great wonder to me, and I never ceased marveling that this man, whose whole life had been dominated by faith, by the loss of the faith of his childhood and his fathers, and the adoption of the faith of the enemies of his childhood and the enemies of his fathers and forefathers, not only never brought up the subject of faith in his conversation, but even in his behavior in church, where I accompanied him on the Sunday of the week following the trip that placed my life and the life of everyone who crossed our path in danger, he made not the least attempt to put on a show of reverence and piety: he did not look piously heavenward, or soften his footsteps reverentially in the house of his God, but knelt and bowed and made the sign of the cross in a dry, brisk, businesslike manner, like a man performing routine operations which are necessary to his purpose and which are no longer a burden to him because he no longer pays them any attention—like someone, for instance, who has to take a bus to get to his destination and hurries to the ticket seller, hands over his money, gets his ticket and his change, stands in the right line, and gives his ticket to the conductor to be punched without stopping for an instant to think about any of these activities, which are in themselves of no importance at all and whose only purpose is to enable him to get on the bus traveling to where he wants to go. So Dr. Shoshan in church crossed himself at the right time, and knelt at the right time, and sang to the best of his ability with the rest of the congregation lifting up their voices in the hymn, "The Lord's my shepherd, I'll not want, He maketh me to lie down in green pastures, He leadeth me beside the still waters, He restoreth my soul . . ."; but in contrast to the traveler in my allegory, once Dr. Shoshan had finished the business of buying his ticket with an energetic, almost angry, briskness, I did not see him seat himself for his inward journey and soar to the heights of holiness like his coreligionists communing with their Savior and restoring their souls to the right and the left of him—some with the closed eyes and bowed heads of Christian meekness, and some standing silently to attention in their devotions like soldiers of the Church Militant—but rather turning his head impatiently from side to side as if he were trying to assess the varying degrees of stupidity and ignorance hiding behind each and every one of the Sunday suits surrounding him. In his conversation too, whenever he touched on the cardinal articles of his faith, such as the Divinity of Christ or the Grace of God (which was very rarely), he never so much as hinted at faith or personal experience of religious ecstasy, but confined himself to a sort of technical scientific jargon instead.

On one occasion and one occasion only Dr. Shoshan did say something that gave me the kind of shock you might get if the door into a blank stone wall suddenly opened for a second to reveal an undreamed-of abyss, something that could, I think, be described as a manifestation of faith. This was when I called on him to return the book about the life of Calvin. While I was apologizing for the fact that I did not intend to translate this book into Hebrew, he remarked with a faint smile: "Yes, yes. I have already ordered my wife in my will to have the following words engraved on my tombstone and nothing else: 'Here lies Israel Shoshan son of Rivka until the resurrection of the dead.' In Hebrew, of course. It was in Hebrew that Jesus Christ said before his death: '*Eli, eli, lama sabachtani?* My God, my God, why hast thou forsaken me?' And I too, and I too . . ." Here he was interrupted by the need to cough and clear his throat, and it was only after he had recovered and spat blood into the basin offered him that he completed his sentence and said: "And I too, Hebrew was my mother tongue and it will be my tongue too when I arise in the resurrection of the dead." The owner of the hand that had offered him the basin understood not a word he said because she spoke no Hebrew at all, but still she gave him a smile full of kindness and goodwill as he announced his intention of continuing to speak the Hebrew language after his death and resurrection. She was a nursing sister from one of the northern countries who had come to look after him when his condition worsened. Paula, his wife, I did not see, perhaps because she had been called away to have tea with her friend Mrs. Hartal, but it was obvious that she was not missed by the invalid, since the nun never stopped caring for his needs for an instant, doing her best to efface herself as she worked so as not to disturb her patient and his visitor: she emptied the basin and brought it back with a shining aluminum lid, stirred mixtures in glasses and offered him various ear, nose, and throat drops, adjusted the pillows beneath his head, dusted the furniture, and in general bestowed on both the room and the invalid as decent and inviting an air as possible under the circumstances—an air of health and civilization which covered up and concealed from view the gross matter in which the soul is clothed in the material world, the flesh and the blood: the flesh and the blood of Dr. Shoshan, neatly attired in a clean pair of pajamas and a spotless dressing gown.

The room in which Dr. Shoshan was spitting out the remains of his last lung, of the flesh and the blood which had become his enemies from the moment they ceased to serve him as a vessel for his life and which were to drive his soul from his body before the week was out with their total assimilation into the world of matter, this room in all its details was a contemporary room: in other words, it was a modern room with modern furniture which left no impression on me at all and was forgotten as quickly and completely as a telephone number, because it was as meaningless, as impersonal, and as outside the frame of human reference as a telephone number. All I remember about Dr. Shoshan's room is the picture hanging above his head and the two books lying on his bedside table, and I remember these rather for the expression they gave to his personal tastes and preoccupations at the end of his life than for their incompatibility with the contemporary note struck by the rest of the room. The picture showed a Jew sitting and studying

Gemarah, and on the table, next to the Bible which alone
gave off the odor of Christian sanctity from the little gold
cross stamped on its back (for the room as a whole was an
impeccably Orthodox Protestant room, free of cross or icon
or sacred Christian image of any kind), lay a large volume
which on closer inspection proved to be one of the tractates
of the Vilna Talmud, the Sanhedrin Tractate if I am not
mistaken. The Bible—which included, of course, the New
Testament—was, as it were, the instrument of his profession,
while the Gemarah was his hobby, which he pursued whenever he had any time to spare from his work in the church
and the Lepers' Hospital and wherever else he labored to
convert souls to his new faith. He gave me to understand
that if he had enjoyed playing card games such as bridge or
poker, or if he had taken an interest in chess, he would not
have needed the Talmud, but since all these games bored
him to death, and so did solving crossword puzzles and
reading novels, studying a page of the Gemarah a day filled
the space in his life which was filled for other people by card
games and novels and theaters and cinemas. His greatest
enjoyment came from reading the Gemarah aloud to the
singsong of the ancient melody he still remembered from
his days at the yeshiva, but since in recent years he had to be
careful of his throat, he was obliged to read his daily page to
himself, shaping the words silently with his lips while in his
inner ear he heard the melody of his inner voice, which still
sounded the same to him as it had in the days of his youth.

Now while the instrument of Dr. Shoshan's work was clean
and shining with newness, the instrument of his amusement, the Talmud, was so worn with age, so tattered and
stained and musty-smelling, that it looked as if it had served
not only its present owner in the days of his youth, but also
his grandfather before him in the days when he too was a
young yeshiva scholar.

"A fine picture, eh?" whispered Dr. Shoshan when he saw

my glance slide from the Gemarah on his table to the Jew
studying Gemarah in the picture hanging above his head,
and his pursed face melted for a moment in a smile of
satisfaction in anticipation of the admiration his beloved
picture was sure to arouse in my breast.

Like the kings in certain pictures who always hold the
scepter of monarchy in their hands and bear its crown upon
their heads lest the beholder might otherwise suspect that
they are not really proper kings at all, the Jew in this picture
too was studying Gemarah wrapped in a prayer shawl and
crowned with a fur-brimmed Sabbath hat, and his whole,
person was enveloped in a kind of halo of romantic sweetness, bubbling queasily out of him like belches and hiccups
from a belly surfeited with too many good things to eat. I
don't know the name of the painter, but reproductions of his
works portraying synagogues and Jewish weddings in a similar style are familiar to me from the homes of certain prosperous Jews from Germany, and sometimes from Eastern
Europe too, where they merge with the smell of heavy food
and faithfully reflect the bourgeois tastes of their owners.

If, for example, Dr. Shoshan had suddenly pulled a lol-
lipop out of the pocket of his dressing gown and started
sucking it with great enjoyment, announcing that there was
nothing he liked better in the world than that pink lump of
sticky sweetness whose appearance alone is enough to make
me sick to the stomach, it would not have surprised me more
than the discovery that in the art of painting the taste of this
Jewish priest was indistinguishable from that of the busi-
nessmen mentioned above, and not because I am of the
opinion that there is any necessary connection between a
man's intellectual powers and his aesthetic sensibilities, or
because I imagined that a picture of a Christian martyr
crowned with a halo painted by the same hand, or by one
like it, would have been more appropriate to his room. What
surprised me was that all the trials and tribulations of Dr.

Shoshan's life, with its great crises and its courageous and extraordinary revolution, had left no mark at all on his taste in art, which remained what it had been in the days when he was a little boy attending Rabbi Avremale's Little Yeshiva in the Old City and the greatest treat he could imagine was the sugary confection which looks like pink cotton wool and is called in Arabic *sha'ar il banaat,* meaning "girls' hair." Even his face behind its dry network of wrinkles took on a childish expression as he turned to look at the picture on the wall and began telling me about the vicissitudes that had brought it from Amersfoort in Holland to his apartment in Jerusalem. He had first set eyes on it when the train in which he was sitting and thinking about the first sermon he was to preach before his first congregation drew into the Amersfoort station. When he rose from his seat and reached for his suitcase on the shelf above his head he saw, through the steamy glass of the carriage window, this very picture on display in the window of a secondhand-furniture shop on the corner of the little lane leading off the entrance to the railway station. Then he had forgotten all about it, and it was only when he made up his mind to part from Henrietta and leave Amersfoort forever that he remembered the picture. All the way to the railway station he thought about it and asked himself if it was possible that it had not yet been sold. When he reached the station he turned his head to the left to face the little lane, and there it was just as before, waiting for him in the shop window.

He was starting to tell me about the owner of this furniture shop too, when his face suddenly fell and its childish expression disappeared, leaving only the dry wrinkles of old age which deepened and twisted viciously at the sound of the footsteps of his wife, Paula, coming into the room, and whatever else he had to say was choked to silence in his throat.

I thought that I would never hear the rest of the story, for in the helpless rage that overcame him at the sight of his wife he hardly noticed my hasty departure and did not even answer me when I said good-bye. Besides, I was afraid that the violent fit of coughing that overtook him as I left might well be the last and that he would soon, perhaps that very night, give up the ghost. The next morning, however, I saw him sitting on the balcony of his apartment in his dressing gown and he smiled and beckoned me to come in. He remembered exactly where he had been interrupted the previous evening, namely at the furniture shop, and took up the story of the picture clearly and lucidly from there. The owner of the shop, who to his astonishment was not a Jew but, on the contrary, a faithful member of his flock, who had never missed a single Sunday sermon, was eager to be of every possible assistance to him in the transportation of the picture to its destination, and insisted on sending it, by registered post and insured against damage, to wherever he was going.

And where was he going, this talented young pastor who had been obliged to cut his ministry short and abandon his innocent lamb, Henrietta, together with the rest of his flock before his appointed term of office was up? He was going to France to the city of Noyon, the birthplace of John Calvin, to wait there until the ministers and missionaries of his church were sent out to take up whatever posts fell to their lot in the new division of office. It was his master and teacher and father-in-law-to-be, in other words Paula's father, who had authorized him to go there and wait, and also to make his modest contribution to the Calvinist congress which was about to take place in the city of Calvin's birth. His modest contribution to that great congress included, besides participation in the debates and voting rights, a sermon on Calvin's interpretation of the Last Supper, and the preparation of this sermon sucked him, so to speak, dry. At first he thought that the sermon was ready and all that was missing were the ears to hear it, but the closer he came to the day on which he was to deliver it, the more clearly he realized how far from ready he actually was. In the end he was obliged to absent himself from the lectures and debates of the congress in order to make up everything that he felt was still lacking. On the eve of the day of his sermon, as he was pacing back and forth in his room, from the table to the window and back again, trying to put things in their right sequence and order, he saw through the opening in the curtains a van belonging to a well-known furniture removal firm draw up outside his inn, which was the Huguenot Hostel.

The name of the firm, Calberson, which was painted in big yellow letters on the side of the van, was also printed on the back of the blue overalls and on the peak of the cap of the porter carrying his load from the van to the hostel door. For some reason the name of this firm printed in large letters all across the porter's back (and not the load in his hands, which did not appear to be very heavy) reminded Dr. Shoshan of the Crucified One carrying His cross on His back, giving rise to the curious reflection that even in our day and age few people actually advertised the names of the crosses they bore printed in large letters on their backs.

If only this porter carrying his modern cross on his back would come into his room, he would be able to confide the main points of his sermon in him and see by his reactions whether it went home to his heart or not. But this too was a nonsensical reflection, since his was no popular sermon but a professional lecture at the highest level, intended only for the experts among the heads of the Calvinist congregations and dealing with the subtle distinctions between the concepts of transubstantiation, consubstantiation, and virtualism, stemming from the different approaches to the sacrament of the Eucharist instituted by Christ at the Last Supper. The nonsensical thoughts that were passing through his head revealed an absentmindedness which was

certainly not appropriate to the evening before this important lecture, but luckily there was no danger of their being
put into practice, since it was not to his door that porters
were bringing parcels, and they were not bringing parcels to
him because there was nobody in the whole world who
would want to send him a parcel. This being the case, he
closed the shutters and went back to pacing from the table to
the window, shuttered against the events and contingencies
of the outside world which led his thoughts astray and cast
them on the mercies of every passing wind, and from it back
to the table, collecting his scattered thoughts and disintegrating ideas and bringing them back to the point. But
just as his straying thoughts were beginning to gather
around the point again, there was a knock at the door, and
there stood the porter carrying the modern cross printed on
his back and in his hands a parcel which proved to be none
other than the picture he himself had purchased in the shop
opposite the railway station on his departure from the town
of Amersfoort, the very same picture that was now hanging
on the wall at the head of his bed.

The moment he saw the shape of the parcel in the porter's
hands he knew that it was his picture, and he hastened to
rummage in his pocket for a tip, or a *pourboire,* as they called
it in France. And then, when he approached the man and
looked into his face, he felt that he was taking leave of his
senses. Under the peak of his cap the porter bore the face of
Gabriel Luria, the friend of his youth, and when he opened
his mouth and Dr. Shoshan realized that the man standing
in front of him was not a French porter wearing the face of
Gabriel Luria, but Gabriel Luria wearing the uniform of a
French porter, he felt his whole being jolted by a sudden
shock of fear at the insubstantiality of this world, founded
on the nothingness of the senses. Although his fear had
started to dissolve with Gabriel's first smile and had vanished entirely once the chain of circumstances leading to

their meeting in the Huguenot Hostel had been explained and they had begun to discuss the Last Supper together, ever since then, at different times in his life, he had felt an echo of that same fear gripping his heart—like the times, for instance, when he woke up early in the morning and saw his wife, Paula, sleeping beside him, with Henrietta's mother's face.

Gabriel had spoken very queerly about the Last Supper, very strangely and queerly indeed. What had he said? He would tell me next time we met. I promised to come and see him on the Tuesday of the following week, but as things turned out I couldn't make it. On the day that I was supposed to go and visit him I was called up for an emergency mobilization exercise.

At twilight I sat leaning against the wall of the Lepers' Hospital, watching the sun setting behind the cypresses and bathing the dusty path next to the wall in an orange halo of light which swallowed up the silhouette of the doctor emerging from the gate and making his way to the main road. I remembered the same moment of sunset in the same place on my previous call-up, but this time nothing happened to transcend the dull monotony of the march of time. The statistician sitting next to me asked me if I remembered the Jewish Christian priest who had come out of the hospital gate the last time we were there. "Of course I do," I said, and added that it was only the call-up that had prevented me from paying him a visit that very day. The statistician smiled and said that in any case I could not have visited him today because he had died on Friday evening. He had heard about it from Mrs. Hartal, who was the best friend of Paula, Dr. Shoshan's widow.

To Paula I spoke only once, and that was after her husband was already dead. I asked her where he had been buried. He was buried in the Protestant Cemetery in Emek Refaim Street, and I went down there to visit his grave. It

was only after I had started walking up the rows of tombstones with their inscriptions in Latin characters that I
remembered Dr. Shoshan's promise that he would go on
speaking Hebrew after his resurrection from the dead and
his behest to his wife to have his tombstone engraved in
Hebrew with the words: "Here lies Israel Shoshan son of
Rivka until the resurrection of the dead." I hurried on,
eager to see with my own eyes this singular Hebrew tombstone, which would have been strange enough in itself but
would be a hundred times stranger still all alone in the sea of
Latin-lettered tombstones surrounding it. When I reached it
I felt my heart contract in anxiety at the sight of the terrible
mistake someone had made. It was not in Hebrew that I saw
Dr. Shoshan's name engraved on his tombstone, but in
English, and of the resurrection of the dead there was no
mention at all even in English. I left the tombstone with the
same haste I had shown in reaching it. I was in a hurry to
inform the widow, Paula, of the mistake made by the tombstone-engraver, and it was only when I reached the gateway
of the cemetery and was brought to a halt by the crowds in
the street that I realized there was no need for haste here—
there would be time and enough for the tombstone of Israel
Shoshan son of Rivka to be put to rights before the resurrection of the dead. Nevertheless, from that moment on I was
oppressed from time to time by the sense of an urgent duty I
had to perform, a duty to go and tell Paula about the mistake that had been made in the inscription on her husband's
tombstone. Instead of performing this duty, however, I put
it off from day to day and week to week until, two or three
months later, I suddenly saw her coming toward me on the
street. Coming not alone, but in the company of a certain
man upon whose arm she was leaning with all the weight of
her upper body, and to whom she was talking with a liveli-
ness and an enthusiasm the likes of which I had never seen
in her before. Acting on my first impulse I quickened my

step and hurried toward her, but at the same time I also felt a certain hesitation about bringing up the matter of the mistake in her husband's tombstone, which was clearly of a private and intimate nature, in the presence of a third person, and this doubt gave rise to another, more serious suspicion regarding the origins of the mistake itself. Maybe it wasn't the tombstone-engraver who had made the mistake, but she herself, and at the look she proceeded to give her escort all my doubts disappeared at once. This look convinced me that whatever she had done in the matter of erecting a tombstone on her husband's grave she had done with a clear head, in cold blood, and with her eye on the engraver to see that he carried out her instructions to the letter.

The insubstantiality of this world which is founded on the nothingness of the senses and bursts like a bubble and rises again with all its illusions and mirages like a dancing bubble in the air was brought home to me when I heard the voice of Dr. Shoshan about three months after his death, a few days after the look in the eye of his widow as she gazed at her gentleman companion released me from the pressing duty of informing her of the mistake-that-had-never-happened in the matter of the inscription of the tombstone she erected on her husband's grave. His voice rising up as if from the depths of my childhood I heard not in the dark of night in a closed and shuttered room but in the middle of the street at midday. I was on my way home when I saw the statistician's son—the same boy with the violin case under his arm who had whispered to his friend, "Look—there goes the missionary!"—getting into his father's car to show this friend the new radio they had installed in it, and as he was playing with its knobs the voice of the librarian of my childhood was heard announcing in clear mellifluous tones: "This is the Voice of Good Hope from Monte Carlo bringing you the Gospel of Salvation," and opening the daily lesson with a

sermon on the meaning of the concept "Servant of the Lord"
in the Bible. The broadcasting station bringing the word of
salvation to the world from a house near the gambling
casinos of Monte Carlo had chosen one of the first sermons
the recently deceased missionary had ever preached in the
Hebrew language for a repeat broadcast, and the child carrying the violin who had known the missionary only in the
last years of his life did not recognize—even after I had
approached him and hinted that he had heard it before and
that its owner had lived on our street—the voice which
sounded after his death as it had in the time of his life before
his throat and lungs had been devoured by cancer. He
stared at me with a pair of wide, childish eyes, full of innocent wonder, as I told him that this voice was the voice of the
dead missionary, and that I had known him a long time ago
when I was still a child and he was still a librarian. And there
was something else in the eyes of the child carrying the
violin which while deepening the sense of the insubstantiality of our dancing bubble of a world deepened in me
too—not by contradicting, but by complementing it—the
sense of an existence continuing its being through all the old
bubbles that had already burst and through all the bubbles
that had not yet been born, as well as the sense of all the
changing shades of color in the mirage of dancing lights: he
looked at me as if he were seeing me for the first time in his
life, and out of his look there arose in me the memory of the
first time I saw Gabriel Jonathan Luria on a great and
strange day in my life, the day on which my eyes beheld, on
the other side of the street, the King of Kings Haile Selassie,
Elect of God, Conquering Lion of the Tribe of Judah, the
Emperor of Ethiopia, in the middle of summer in the year
5696 from the Creation of the World, 1936 according to the
Christian calendar.

8.

The Return of the Prodigal Son

SINCE UNTIL THAT DAY (until, that is, I actually saw Gabriel Luria with my own eyes) I had only heard about his great physical strength from the little librarian, about his "Oriental fantasies" from his mother and the pharmacist, and about his pagan soul from the grocer Reb Yitzhok, I saw him in my imagination as someone like the Turkish carpet-seller, a big, strong man with a drooping mustache whose eyes looked out from under his black fur hat with a strange wild glint in them, striking terror into my heart whenever he removed his black hat and revealed to the world a head as bald and smoothly shaven as the head of the old Bey himself. It was rumored that he had once been a dancing dervish and that he possessed magical powers, and when he came knocking on the door with his bundle of Persian carpets hoisted casually on one shoulder despite its great weight, some of the neighborhood women would panic and slam the door shut in his face while others would gladly purchase not carpets (I don't remember a single housewife ever buying a carpet, even a small one) but good advice and recipes for magic charms and spells.

This was why, when I turned away from the Ethiopian Consulate and saw Gabriel Luria sitting on the wicker chair

and watching me, the spectator of the play, I was so surprised by his appearance, which was very different from
what I had imagined and had nothing at all in common with
the appearance of the Turkish carpet-seller. In his hard,
round, white straw hat with its black ribbon, called by him a
"Panama hat," his blue cloth jacket with its gold buttons, his
faultlessly pressed white trousers, and his silver-knobbed
cane, he looked exactly like a French dandy who had
stepped out of a film starring Maurice Chevalier to come
and sit on the verandah of our house. And this French actor,
because he had stepped out of the film screened in black-
and-white and arrived on our verandah in all the colors and
dimensions of his body, brought his own smell with him
too—a smell compounded of his own body odor, the aroma
of his English cigarettes, and the perfume of the French
after-shave lotion called Moustache. Yes, even the little black
mustache sitting square as a die in the center of his thin face,
between the prominent high cheekbones and the square
chin, was apparently there for no other reason than that it
was needed to complete the mosaic of fashionable male
elegance in Paris that season, and shortly afterward, when
fashions in Paris changed, the mustache disappeared
together with the silver-knobbed cane and the white Panama hat.

It was no Hercules then, with wild Oriental fantasies rising in clouds of smoke from a pagan soul uprooted from its
home in the quarries of stone gods, who sat before me in the
wicker chair, but a man firmly, complacently, and cheerfully
anchored in the very heart of the world of fashion, bearing
its claims with an easy grace and a nonchalance which surprised not only me but also his mother, whose astonishment,
however, which was even greater than mine, soon turned
from an outburst of joy into one of bitter and violent rage.
She was climbing the stairs from the street to the verandah
with a slow, heavy tread, due to spiritual negligence and

sloth rather than any inertia of the flesh (since her body was still quite light and slender for its age), with a loaf of bread and a packet of butter in her hands. When she saw the fashionable gentleman reclining on the wicker chair an expression of panic crossed her face, an apprehensive look lest some important, uninvited guest should see her in the slovenly state which had become almost permanent with her since the death of her husband, the old Bey. And then suddenly her face beamed and her eyes shone with a joy which, breaking open the shell of her withdrawal, utterly transformed her blank, remote expression, bestowing upon her a kind of reflection of the youthful gaiety that had captured the heart of the Spanish consul in years gone by. She hugged and kissed and embraced him as if he had been not a man of forty but a child of four, and in fact she actually called him "Gabby, Gabinke, Gabilu," cooing and clucking at him as if he were a baby in diapers in her arms. "I'd forgotten already how handsome you are—" she said, "as handsome as an Italian."

Ever since the day two naval officers from an Italian warship docked in Haifa Bay had appeared among the guests at a reception given by her husband, Yehuda Prosper Bey, Mrs. Luria had made up her mind that Italians were the best-looking men in the world—although the Italian consul in all his ugliness had appeared at the same reception, and she later made the acquaintance of a number of other Italians, such as the doctor at the Italian Hospital and the Italian antique dealer at the bottom of the road, the sight of whose faces alone might have been enough to shatter any such conviction in a weaker mind than hers. With the passage of the years the verdict "as handsome as an Italian" was reserved for men whose appearance awoke ancient longings in her heart, or for those rare moments of sentiment and nostalgia powerful enough to dissolve even the bitterest of her grievances against her husband, grievances even his death had not been able to mollify. In one such moment of grace she bestowed this special mark of her favor on the memory of the old man himself, saying to her son, Gabriel, "You know, when your father was a young man he was as handsome as an Italian."

Gabriel responded to his mother's welcome warmly and wholeheartedly, but the more emotional she became in her endearments and embraces the further he withdrew into himself with an impatience which turned into actual resentment when she in the violence of her joy went so far as to announce: "And now I'm the happiest woman in the world." This resentment immediately found an outlet in his answer to the question "And now what shall I get you—tea or coffee?" which was: "There's no need for you to get me anything. I'll do it myself."

"No, you won't do it yourself. I'll do it for you," she insisted with sudden vehemence, and her gentle, melodious voice hardened. "In the first place, you must be worn out by your journey. Why, you've only just arrived from Paris." She bent down and began inspecting his face with an anxious, apprehensive look, as if she were trying to discover the signs of some serious illness he was hiding from her. "You're terribly pale!" she pronounced. "And what are those black circles around your eyes? Now tell me the truth—is there anything the matter with you? And why are your eyes so red? It must be because you smoke so much! You should read what it says every week in the medical column of the *Daily Post* about smoking: why, smoking's the cause of all the diseases in the world, heart, lungs, stomach, liver, even—God preserve us— cancer! Please take that cigarette out of your mouth this minute and throw it away—it makes me feel quite ill to look at it. You don't have to follow in your father's footsteps in everything, you know. He never stopped smoking cigarettes and drinking Turkish coffee all day long, drinking Turkish coffee and smoking cigarettes while I begged and implored him to stop poisoning himself, but of course the old man was never prepared to give up any of his pleasures, he was ready to poison himself with smoke and coffee so long as he wasn't deprived of his pleasures—until in the end his pleasures came and deprived him of his life! If he hadn't smoked and drunk coffee all day long, he would never have had the stroke that killed him. And you—how can I possibly allow you to make yourself a cup of coffee when I know perfectly well you'll make it so strong that with the first sip you'll start having palpitations! Now just you throw that disgusting cigarette away immediately and I'll go and make you a nice weak cup of coffee with a lot of milk that can't do you any harm."

Gabriel closed his eyes and pressed his fingertips to his eyelids as if he were making an effort to shake off the heavy weariness that had descended upon him with the endless flow of words emerging from his mother's mouth. Having resigned himself to drinking the tasteless cup of coffee she was about to press on him for reasons of health, all that remained for him to do was implore her not to force him to drink a health-giving beverage that would actually make him sick. "Just a little milk, please," he said with his fingers still pressed on his closed eyelids, "a very little—and no skin."

"Oh what a fool you are," she said with a tender smile, and a resurgence of sentimentality beginning to gleam in her eye. "Why, the skin's the most important part of the milk! Every morning I spread it on my bread for breakfast. It's not only healthier than any condiment—it's tastier too."

Mrs. Luria had begun to concern herself with the right road to bodily health even before Gabriel left for France, and this concern had left its mark on the taste of the food and drink served in her house even then, but to the refinements and restrictions that had succeeded in driving the last vestiges of taste from her food she had attained only during his absence from home, in the last year of the old man's life. Until then Gabriel's father had still been prepared to sit on the verandah in the red plush chair and wait for hours on end—despite his grumbling that he had never yet succeeded in getting his meals from her on time—until the rice and roast chicken and salad prepared with just the right combination of flavors and spices to please the most discriminating palate were ready, but gradually a healthy tastelessness began to dominate all her cooking and in the last year of his life he refused to eat or drink anything which she had prepared, even a cup of coffee or a sandwich—he would send Señor Moïse from the café on the corner to fetch it, since Mrs. Luria would not allow him to set foot in her kitchen.

At the beginning of the straight and narrow road to health she declared war on all food that was roasted or fried, it having been clearly demonstrated in the medical columns of all the newspapers she read that anything roasted or fried was the enemy of the stomach. Later the ranks of the stomach haters and destroyers were swelled by all things peppered and spiced, and after that the war was carried into the camp of salt. The strategists of health agreed, of course, that a "certain amount" of salt was necessary for the fortification of the body, but anything in excess of this "certain amount" turned, in the course of time, into an enemy too. This question of the "certain amount" of salt which had never been satisfactorily defined was a severe stumbling block to Mrs. Luria's progress on the road to health, and she devoted many hours of theoretical study and many practical experiments to its investigation. In the last year of the old man's life, when her discoveries were revolutionizing nutritional concepts, the determination of the "certain amount" of salt passed from the domain of the palate into that of the chemist's scales, and from then on it was impossible for anyone still dependent on the taste buds of a palate corrupted by the rottenness of contemporary civilization to enjoy anything cooked in her kitchen. The old man himself would sometimes have to avert his eyes from the sight of his Jerusalem wife eating a chicken boiled in soup with no salt or pepper or spice of any kind to give it taste so as not to be overcome by nausea. After the old man's death and before the return of her son, Gabriel, from Paris, she was listening to a lecture on the radio one day when she discovered a new and wholly unexpected enemy of health, a kind of fifth column dwelling in the very heart of the fortress itself—sugar. This lecture dealt not with health, but with questions of a philosophical nature, and the fact that she nevertheless continued to listen to it was not because of its contents but because of the voice and way of speaking of the lecturer, which were pleasing to her ear. She was generally more impressed by the timbre of a man's voice than by what he had to say, and it was enough for a person's voice to jar on her ear for her instantly to adopt the opposite position to his, even if he was expressing the very same opinions as she herself had always held up to then, and to which she returned the moment she was rid of him. This lecturer was giving a series of lectures over the radio in his pleasant voice and pleasing manner of speaking on the philosophies of the Far East, and on that evening he addressed himself to the subject of Zen Buddhism. Mrs. Luria, sailing peacefully along on the flow of his voice, suddenly sat up and began to listen excitedly to what he was saying. She discovered that this philosophical system was not a mere web of idle thoughts which made no difference to anyone one way or another and could be adapted to the needs or wishes or passing moods of whoever adopted it, but that it provided among other things vigilant safeguards for the health of the body and warnings against bad habits and corrupt practices. Together with the joyful emotion which flooded her at this important chance discovery, however, Mrs. Luria was thun-

derstruck to find all her previous conceptions overturned by
the first commandment of the Zen kitchen, which stated
that sugar was the principal enemy of man. Sugar, which up
till that moment had stood at the very center of her defenses
against the pollutions of spices, peppers, and salt.

For a week or two she was distressed, up in the air with no
solid ground beneath her feet, vacillating between an absolute faith in sugar and a total rejection of Zen Buddhism as a
collection of Oriental fantasies remote from common sense
on the one hand, and the acceptance of this teaching as an
absolute truth which had suddenly shone forth on the world
from the East, together with heartbreak and despair at the
treachery of her faithful ally sugar on the other. From this
chaos and these dark depths she was restored to tranquillity
when the right way suddenly revealed itself to her in all its
simplicity, unrelated to the truth or falsehood of the teachings of Zen, which were henceforth consigned to oblivion as
irrelevant and beside the point. Sugar would go the way of
salt: since a "certain amount" of this commodity was necessary to the body it too would be transferred from the
domain of the palate to that of the chemist's scales. She
wondered why this perfectly obvious solution had not
occurred to her in the first place.

Even before the old man died, during the period when he
would still sit waiting in the red plush chair on the verandah
for her to serve him food fit for the most discriminating
palate, she would take her meals alone (since she herself had
no time to eat when she was busy serving him, and in any
case his visits were not regular or timed to fit in with her
schedule) and after his death she never had any opportunity
at all of eating with anyone else. All through that summer,
until Gabriel returned from Paris, I would see her sitting
and eating alone and my heart would contract with a queer,
foreign pressure, like a breeze blowing from another world.
I would lift my eyes from the book I had received from the

little librarian in Abyssinian Road and see, from where I sat
at the end of the yard, the upper half of her body behind the
window bars rising straight from the floor, since her room on
the other side of the steps was lower than the level of the
verandah and her table stood next to the windowsill. She
would sit bent over as if completely absorbed in the plate
before her, and while she chewed her face looked through
the window bars growing out of the verandah floor, as if
through the prison bars of an underground dungeon, at the
wide, high, open world beyond, only the eyes directed
toward this world were not looking at it: their gaze seemed
to pass right through and far beyond it to another world in
which she had her being, or perhaps it would be better to say
which had its being in her, since the look in her eyes was as
withdrawn and isolated as the look in the eyes of a day-
dreamer. When she was eating she looked as if she were
partaking simultaneously of two activities which were not
only different, but would usually be considered contradic-
tory and mutually exclusive, since one was absolutely physical and the other absolutely spiritual. All the civilities of
eating in company, to the extent that she had developed
them in the distant days of her social eminence, dissolved
and vanished during the last years of the old man's life, and
after he was dead she paid no more attention to table manners than a cat with false teeth eating a chicken wing boiled
in soup, and since I have never seen a cat with false teeth
neither have I ever heard a cat at its meal making the kind of
noises Mrs. Luria made at hers. A belief in the virtue of
chewing was one of the basic tenets of her whole health
system and she was punctilious in its observation, chewing
and grinding and pulverizing every bite of food that entered
her mouth into atoms and ending every chew with a kind of
metallic clang. From time to time, when crumbs got stuck
between her false teeth and her naked gums, she would
remove the teeth and hold them in her hand while she

cleaned the crumbs away with her tongue, at the same time opening her mouth wide in a liberating belch, since belches and hiccups were good for the digestion. At least once during every meal she would stop chewing and begin sniffing the plate or bread or spoon in her hand with a sleuthlike expression of suspicion and mistrust on her face. She had an extraordinarily fine sense of smell, and more than once I saw her throw out a whole pot of soup she had labored for hours on end to prepare, because one little sniff had revealed a slight trace of laundry soap or paraffin to her sensitive nose. These traces were so slight that no one else in the world would have noticed them, except perhaps her son, Gabriel. Astonishingly enough, eating habits such as these, naked, explicit, and emphasized as they were by grimaces of lips and cheeks, blinkings of eyes, and sounds of biting, sucking, swallowing, and gurgling, with the grinding of false teeth to boot, did not make Mrs. Luria look vulgar. They had rather the look of a basic life activity to which the adjective *vulgar* could no more be applied than to a cat satisfying its hunger, and as with the cat so too with her, what was surprising was precisely the delicate grace with which this naked animality was overlaid.

Together with this naked animality, which was purely physical, and parallel to it, Mrs. Luria was subject as she ate to stirrings of the soul which were purely spiritual but were reflected in, or, as they grew more powerful, brimmed over into the world of the senses. Once she had overcome the initial obstacles of sniffing and belching and dislodging obstinate crumbs from her gums, and her teeth had started to chew as steadily and rhythmically as the engines of a smoothly sailing ship, Mrs. Luria would embark on a voyage to her innermost thoughts and reflections, like the captain of a ship who can allow his thoughts to wander after he has maneuvered his craft past the dangers of the coastline with its reefs, both hidden and exposed to view, and set sail for the open sea.

Sometimes she would be seized with joy in the course of the sharp and frequent changes taking place in the delicate shifts and nuances of her distant ruminations, and perhaps this joy was no rarer than the melancholy it replaced, but like the melancholy, so too the joy reflected in the expression on her face and the look in her eyes staring blindly at their surroundings pinched my heart like a breath of wind blowing from another clime. What upset me most, though, was the sight of her grief as she ate. Years after her body had returned to the dust from which it was taken, the title of a book in French caught my eye as I was walking past the windows of a bookshop. It was *Le sentiment tragique de la vie*, a French translation of Miguel de Unamuno's book, and as I read these words the face of our landlady looking out of the window of her room as she ate rose before my eyes. The book itself I have never read nor do I know what it is about, but to this day I always find myself muttering the phrase "the tragic sense of life" to myself whenever I remember the grief on Mrs. Luria's face as she ate, that basic, ancient, primary grief which seemed, as it were, to confirm the tragic nature of life on this earth, where the survival of one living species is forever dependent on the killing and eating of another living species; that same ancient grief which for all its primariness appeared to stem not from existence itself on earth, which is neutral, but from some other, distant world beyond it. And like this grief, the joy too which seized hold of her in the constant cycle of changes taking place in her moods as she ate, rooted as it was in the elements of nature, seemed nevertheless to emanate from a different, distant world in which her soul roamed while her mouth chewing the tasteless, saltless, boiled chicken wing ensured the survival of her body in this one. In the middle of eating she would suddenly burst into loud laughter. Sometimes she seemed to be laughing at the memory of some amusing incident which had happened long before, and which she was reliving now with great relish as she ate, and sometimes she seemed to be enjoying a joke someone invisible to everyone except herself was whispering into her ear, but above all there was something uncanny and not of this world about the peals of laughter breaking from her lips, as if she had suddenly come across an extraordinarily funny passage in a book she was reading, a secret, mysterious book she alone could see lying open in the sky above her.

In the long and short breaks she took during her meals— for she was usually obliged to stop eating before she had finished her meal, cover her plate, and lie down on the couch in order to recover from the "hot flush" that had overtaken her (ever since the beginning of her "change of life" she had suffered from these "hot flushes," as she called them, several times a day) or simply to rest from the labors of eating— during these breaks, once she had recovered her breath, she would sometimes hum softly to herself one of the songs she had learned at the Evelina de Rothschild School for Girls, and sometimes, when her exuberance grew, she would even sing out loud in a voice which was surprisingly clear and sweet for her years.

On days when she was particularly exuberant I sometimes saw her break her rules and eat roast beef and pickles and other salty, peppery foods dangerous to her health, and on these occasions she seemed not in the least bothered or upset by the contradiction between her theory and her practice. She seemed ready to risk her life at the very moment when she found most pleasure and relish in it, and on the other hand to observe the delicate and sensitive balance of her diet most scrupulously and be most strictly on her guard against the slightest suspicion of danger to her life on earth precisely at those times when this life was a burden to her, when she was most miserable, gloomy, and depressed: in short, precisely at those moments when she felt that her life was not worth living.

After she had reminded her son, Gabriel, that the skin

was the most important part of the milk and gone inside to make him a cup of coffee in strict accordance with the rules of health, her voice could be heard humming a little tune in the kitchen. When she returned to the verandah with the coffee she was still smiling, but nevertheless the prodigal son's welcome home was not to end in joy and gladness: as she sat talking to him she became more and more sentimental, and this sentimentality quickly gave way to an outburst of rage the likes of which had not seethed and boiled in her since the old man's death. It was the elegance with which he was dressed that sparked off this great wrath: the black ribbon round his white Panama hat, the gold buttons on his blue coat, the knifelike crease in his white flannel trousers— the same graceful, lighthearted, open elegance which had only a little while before melted the insulating shell of the remote, withdrawn expression guarding her face. At the climactic stages of this great rage she looked exactly as she had in the old Bey's lifetime, when her arms and the wisps of her hair flew wildly about and a thin film of hysteria veiled her eyes, only now it was not on that bald head with its dewdrops of sweat sparkling like fire in the setting sun that her yells of rage descended, but on the white Panama hat. It was as if time had stopped for her: just as she had stood shouting a year ago and two years ago she stood shouting still, and the only change to bear witness to the passing of time was the change in the occupant of the red plush chair, who had been transformed from a venerable relic of the Ottoman Empire into a kind of actor who had stepped out of a French film. Even the complaints and reproaches and accusations she hurled against him were the same despite their different variations on the central theme, which was money: her complaint against the old man was that he gave her no money, while her complaint against her son was that he had wasted the money she sent him on gold buttons and silver-knobbed canes like an empty-headed loafer. She reminded her son, as she had reminded his father, of the great and endless sacrifices she had made for him all her life, for which she had been rewarded by indifference, by criminal neglect, and even by being looked down on, despised, and "having her face spat on." For him, her only son, she had moved out of the big ground-floor flat and buried herself alive in a basement under the stairs with no sun or air, simply in order to be able to send him the few pence she could scrape together from the rent so that he wouldn't starve to death in Paris after the old man stopped his allowance. And all the terrible fights she had had with the old man during the last years of his life, was it for herself that she had been fighting, for herself she had spat blood and worn herself out body and soul over every single penny she managed to squeeze out of him? She herself needed nothing. Bread and water were quite enough for her, but even so she had not come into her own and reached safe harbors with the old man's death. On the contrary—suddenly she found herself alone in the world to face a hornet's nest, a swarm of repulsive leeches—the whole tribe of the old man's relatives who came down on her like a gang of murderers with daggers drawn to take everything away from her, even the house her husband himself had left her, while not only had he, her only darling son, not even troubled himself to come to the help of his sick old mother who was fighting singlehandedly for her life, and for his life too, he couldn't even be bothered to send her a few lines of encouragement since he was too busy, apparently, playing cards and flirting. And what had he done with the money she sent him? He had spent it on Panama hats and gold buttons and silver canes. And what was the wonder? When all was said and done the apple didn't fall far from the tree. He, Gabriel, was as like his father as two peas in a pod, bone of the bone and flesh of the flesh of that lecherous old Turk, that dirty-minded gambler who had suddenly begun put-

ting on holy airs in his old age and rolling his lewd eyes up to
heaven with pretended piety and talking about Moses! What
she had taken out of her own mouth to send him, her only
son—she a sick lonely widow in a damp cellar—he had spent
in Paris on getting himself up like a pimp, and all that was
left for her was to commit suicide and put an end to her
sufferings once and for all. In any case it didn't matter to
him whether she was alive or dead, and all he cared about
was her money. Only when she had taken her life by her own
hand, only then would he realize that he had waited for her
death in vain, that whatever she had deprived herself of for
his sake she had already given him while she was still alive.
Of course she knew very well that if it weren't for vain hopes
of getting his hands on all kinds of imaginary bequests and
inheritances he would never have taken the trouble to come
back to her at all, for wasn't he flesh of the flesh and bone of
the bone of his father, and wasn't any prostitute in the street
dearer to him than his own mother?

Ever since her husband's death, but especially since the
old judge had wound up the affair of her inheritance to her
own complete satisfaction, Mrs. Luria had become so worried about her finances that she had stopped sending her
son any money at all, and contented herself with sending
him parcels tied up with whole balls of string, which I would
carry to the post office for her. The parcels contained warm
underclothes—long woolen underpants and undershirts
with sleeves—and sometimes also socks and sweaters. "I
know him," she would say to me. "I know he's walking
around in that freezing Paris cold in thin, short underpants,
and it would never enter his head to go into a shop and buy
himself a pair of long woolen drawers." As long as she had
no property of her own she sent him money, and even
though these were only small sums saved from her house-
keeping money, still it never occurred to her to keep whatever she had left over after her own needs had been satisfied,

because the money itself was not important to her at that stage. In all the bitter wars she waged against her husband the real issue was not money but her suspicions that he was giving other women what was due her, and since what she was fighting for was not the money, but the principle of the thing, her wars with her husband could be said to have been, in a certain sense, pure ideological wars, innocent of the desire for gain. It was only after she inherited the old man's property, and with it the great fear of poverty and what the morrow would bring, that she started hoarding her pennies and suspecting everyone, especially her son, of having designs on her money and trying to get their hands on it by deceitful, cunning tricks. Nevertheless, after Gabriel came home she was ready, when she was in one of the happy moods during which she would hum the tunes of her school-days to herself and reminisce nostalgically about the good old days when she had seen life with her husband who had been "handsome as an Italian and a dear man," to give him, Gabriel, the lot, and she would even urge him to "go and buy everything you need, because money, thank God, is no problem." But Gabriel never took advantage of her moments of generosity—which usually ended in an expedition to the market to buy him another two pairs of woolen socks and half a dozen pairs of long underpants which he would never wear—even though he knew very well that this would not be remembered to his credit in her moments of anger, and that with the first spark of rage to arise in her breast all her suspicions about his designs on her money would come back to life.

He said not a single word in his own defense during her outburst of maternal anger against the golden buttons on his sport jacket and the silver knob on his cane, but went on sitting in the red plush armchair, smoking and sipping his mother's tasteless coffee by turns, looking straight ahead with a patient expression on his face. I did see him lose his temper and answer her back on other occasions, but to these outbursts of his we will return later, in their proper time and place. I don't know if *patient* is the right word to describe the expression on his face; it was an impatient patience, a resigned acceptance born of experience and relating solely to the phenomenon of the eruption of anger itself, which was an inevitable feature of the volcanic terrain of the meetings between them, and not at all to the content of the words which burst out of her and hurled themselves against him like the by-products of this eruption. Not only did he refuse to accept these words, he pulled down all his shutters against them, and all that could be heard was an endless flow like that of rain falling outside but not penetrating the house. Her words stayed outside him and he stayed outside them, tired and remote, the look in his eyes as isolated as the look in her own when she was eating her meals.

When her rage had spent itself and she sat down beside him and began speaking to him softly with words that were like an echo of her reflections on him and his fate, they were very alike in the remote, withdrawn look in their eyes. They looked like two people sitting opposite each other in a railway car carrying them far, far away on the tracks of their own thoughts, but the very remoteness that brought them together also set them apart. The quality of his remoteness differed from the quality of hers: they sat facing each other and traveling great distances at the same time but in different directions, leading them into different landscapes strange and foreign to each other. She spoke to him about himself, and began with the old judge. When Dan Gutkin had gone to study law in England he had not been a young man. He was a middle-aged man already and had started his studies in England at an age when most men are already well established in their careers. "Father, may he rest in peace—" (when she was speaking to Gabriel she would say simply "Father," and of her own father she would say

"Grandfather." She used the words "your father" only when she was in a rage and all her grievances against her late husband were as sharp and fresh in her mind as if he were still alive and sitting in the chair opposite her. "You're as like your father as two peas in a pod, bone of his bone and flesh of his flesh—" this formula was reserved for the resemblance between their bad qualities, while the opening "You're like Father in this respect" or "In this respect Father was like you" was a sign of her satisfaction with whatever good Gabriel had inherited from his father). "Father, may he rest in peace, who was such a kindhearted man, too kindhearted for his own good the way he threw his money around on all kinds of charities and good deeds, Father was the one who encouraged Dan Gutkin to go abroad in the first place and helped him with money and connections and letters of recommendation. Of course, what he sent him was nothing to what he sent you all those years you were in France. I still remember what a sight he was when we went to see him off, Father and I, at the port. He could only afford to travel steerage, the worst class, and in those days the poor people in steerage didn't get any food on the journey. They all had to bring enough food with them for the whole voyage, and he took a tin of olives and two packets of matzoh with him to keep him alive until he reached England. And you should have seen how he came back! Even before he came back he had already been appointed a justice of the peace here in Jerusalem, and before you could turn around he was already a Supreme Court judge and an Officer of the British Empire. But what am I telling you about Dan Gutkin for? Look at your own generation—your own friends who went to school with you. Itzik Blum, for example, who's not fit to tie your shoelaces; and which of all those boys who went to cheder with you was fit to tie your shoelaces? You were head and shoulders above them all. Itzik Blum, the son of that stupid, revolting schnorrer, went to Beirut and studied at the university there, and came back a Doctor of Chemistry and opened a pharmacy and became an important man in the world. And look how you came back. You, who grew up like a prince in comparison to all those Jerusalem beggars and schnorrers and who set out for Paris like a prince and lacked for nothing until you stopped your studies. Tell me the truth, how did you manage to live there when Father stopped sending you money? How did you live for three years in a big, cruel, foreign city without a penny to call your own? It sends shivers down my spine just to think of it. I only hope that terrible life in Paris didn't ruin your health. The main thing is to take care of your health, and all the rest—diplomas, titles, important jobs, money in the bank—are really of no importance at all."

As the days went by and Gabriel continued to spend his mornings sitting in the same red chair smoking cigarettes and drinking cups of coffee I would often hear his mother sing the same tune—opening with a note of sorrow for all the secret greatness latent in her son which had not yet emerged into the manifest world, denouncing in passing all the inferior and contemptible creatures who had clawed their way to the top of the dungheap of external honor, going on to sing the praises of the superior qualities that had been bestowed on him, Gabriel, at birth, and ending with a statement of the principles necessary for the maintenance of human life in the manifest world, the principles, in other words, of how to keep healthy.

Because of these same principles necessary to the maintenance of human life on this earth, she would sometimes even express her satisfaction with the fact that Gabriel had not as things turned out, completed his medical studies in Paris, that is, with the very same failure in his career she usually deplored. She could thank her lucky stars—she would say—that Gabriel was not a doctor, for if he were a doctor his life would be in constant danger from the relatives of all his patients who took it into their heads to die. The bereaved families of these patients would put the blame on him and bear grudges against him and try to be revenged on him. Take for example the case of the dentist Dr. Melman, who had pulled a tooth by mistake when all the surrounding tissue was infected, and the patient had succumbed to blood poisoning and died. And when this patient's family, who were some kind of Persians or Kurds from some godforsaken hole in the back of the beyond behind Mount Ararat, got to hear of it, the whole clan descended on the dentist to revenge their relative's blood. The long and the short of it was that the dentist had been forced to flee for his life, in the dead of night and by the skin of his teeth, all the way to America. He dared to come back only after many years had passed, with a different name—Dr. Yarkoni. There were lots of patients who never got better and died. Some died in spite of the treatment they got from their doctors, and most died because of it, and in both cases they placed their doctor's life in danger, even when they didn't come from Persia and Media but from Europe and America. Except for the eye specialist, Dr. Landau, she didn't know a single doctor who could be trusted and whose judgment she could have confidence in. And even Dr. Landau himself, who had cured the eye diseases of all the rabble from India to Abyssinia, hadn't he been ambushed in the 1929 riots and stabbed in the back by an Arab? An Arab who had been saved from blindness solely because of the devoted care of Dr. Landau! And if you asked how such a thing could be possible, it only went to show that you didn't have any conception of the power of incitement among the Arabs: it was enough for an Arab sheik to get up in the mosque on a Friday and explain to the congregation that all their troubles were due to the Jews and call on them to *"etbach el Yahud"*—in other words, "kill the Jews"—for the whole lot of them to rush straight out of the mosque and go and murder the Jews in the street, even if they themselves had been cured of their diseases by Jewish doctors.

And it was a good thing too that he hadn't studied law and become a lawyer, because that was another sure way of making enemies. A lawyer never saw things the way his client wanted him to see them, and that in itself was enough to make bad blood between them. Right from the start the client would begin to suspect his lawyer of conspiring with his enemies against him, and if he happened to lose his case in the end then of course his hatred knew no bounds. Just as Mrs. Luria discovered hidden enemies to health in every food and spice, so she exposed to view the dangers lurking behind every profession that came up for her consideration. In the end, she decided that the best job for a man to have was that of consul of some foreign country across the sea, like the late Yehuda Prosper who had been the Spanish consul in the days of the Turks. Even this job, however, was not quite free of dangers, the main one being jealousy: the honor and prestige attached to the title of consul inevitably made other people jealous. She who had been the wife of the Spanish consul in Jerusalem in the days of Turkish rule knew very well what it meant for a man to be a consul; no one could pull the wool over her eyes. All that was demanded of a consul was to go to parties and balls and receptions and enjoy himself, and the more parties and receptions he went to the better. The only trouble was that in order to become a consul in the first place you had to have lots of money and be a practical man who knew something about politics and understood the ways of the world with all its secret machinations and intrigues: in other words you had to know how and when and to whom to give the right baksheesh. In short, you had to be a respectable man with connections in high places and friends in the government like the old Turkish adulterer himself. Anyone who thought the old man was a dreamer full of Oriental fantasies about himself and Moses simply didn't understand him or know what he was really like. The old fox was a businessman second to none, a unique expert in the art of hunting with the hounds and running with the foxes. All his Oriental fantasies were kept locked away in a special compartment, strictly separate from the rest of his life. They didn't control him—he controlled them, and he never let them out of hiding except in the privacy of his home. It was only to her that he gave himself up to his fancies, pretending to be some idealistic visionary whose only wish in life was to liberate his people and lead them from slavery to freedom like Moses. If only Gabriel had been a man of action like his father everything would have been all right. Then she would have been able to rest easy in her mind and know that he would find his way in life and succeed in everything he turned his hand to. In the first weeks after his return home, when her remote, withdrawn gaze fell on Gabriel sitting in the red plush chair, she would stop eating and say, "If you had been a man of action like your father, and not a loafer like your grandfather, I could die in peace." Together with the sorrow and anxiety in her words, there was also a note of anger against this son of hers who had not known how to select, from the genealogical abundance bequeathed him by his fathers and forefathers, the right characteristics for leading a happy, successful life. Why couldn't he, for example, have inherited a practical turn of mind and the power to impose his will on others from his father, and a talent for some specific profession from her father? In which case nothing could have stopped him from making a brilliant success of his life and telling the rest of the world to go to hell. But no: Gabriel Luria was not the man to bring a little comfort and joy into his sick old mother's life. Instead he had to act without thinking in his usual reckless, impulsive way, grabbing a fistful of his father's Oriental fantasies with one hand and of his grandfather's inconsequence with the other—of that same helpless passivity which was responsible for his dying without a penny to his name, despite the fact that he was the best carpenter in the whole of the Ottoman Empire, with people coming from Jaffa and Beirut and Damascus to ask him to carve furniture for them for nothing. Even the miserable pittance he agreed to work for they didn't pay him in the end, because they saw at once the kind of man they had to deal with. Her father was simply unfit for life in this world. He went around in a kind of open-mouthed admiration for all sorts of old wives' tales, all kinds of midrashim and fairy stories that the synagogue wardens and the rest of those crooks with their beards and sidelocks fed him instead of paying him what they owed him for their Holy Arks. And now her only son had seen fit to inherit that same disastrous inconsequence of her father's which had brought him, his wife, and especially his children so much suffering and misery. But her son who was not, thank God, bewitched by all that nonsense of fairy stories and midrashim; in what worlds was he roaming as he sat there on the red plush chair?

Gabriel spent the best part of his days in that red plush armchair, and he would even shave himself sitting in it every morning. I had also once seen his father the old Bey sitting in that same chair and shaving himself with an old-fashioned barber's razor shortly before he died. Actually it was Señor Moïse who was standing in front of him and shaving him, with his camel's legs slightly apart and an expression of total concentration on his face as he addressed himself to his exacting and exalted, his almost sacred task. Suddenly the old man muttered something angrily under his breath and ordered Señor Moïse to go and fetch the big mirror from the kitchen at once, because he had decided to shave himself. Moïse's face crumpled as if he were about to burst into tears, and he stood rooted to the spot with the razor hanging from his hand, stunned by the old man's request. It was years now since Yehuda Prosper had held a razor in his trembling hands, and even in the distant days of his prime when his hands were strong and dexterous and did whatever he told them to, he had always preferred to delegate the job of shaving his beard to a barber. It never occurred to Señor Moïse to defy his master's order, but at the same time it was clear to him that the moment he placed the razor, which he himself had sharpened on the leather razor strap, in those trembling hands he would be placing the old man's life in danger. The old man stretched out his shaking hand for the razor and Moïse recoiled. For a moment it seemed as if the servant's love and devotion to his master would lead him to refuse to do his bidding, and as long as his hand waved helplessly in the air in front of him the bald old man seated in the chair with the towel tied around his neck and the basin of soapy water in front of him looked exactly like a hairless baby, full of impotent fury because the nurse who was feeding him refused to give him the shining blade of the knife to play with. This moment of Señor Moïse's transition from a loyal servant who believed in his master and obeyed his orders implicitly to a nurse who dismissed his master's wishes and imposed on him the logic of his own love was as sharp and narrow as a razor's edge, but it lasted only a moment. The old man who was unable to control the trembling of his hands and the twitching of his throat succeeded in imposing his will on the strong hand of Señor Moïse, which gradually let go of the razor and placed it carefully in the outstretched palm waiting for it. The old man used a barber's razor for shaving to his dying day because he could never get used to a safety razor—which he saw as a complicated, awkward, and dangerous instrument, although it was explained to him that, on the contrary, it was designed to make shaving easier and do away with the dangers of the old "cut-throat" razor, as its name implied—and not because of any inherent conservatism or resistance to

change. On the contrary, he tried all his life, as the advertise-
ments put it, to "march with the times," and was one of the
first notables in the Ottoman Empire to exchange his red
tarboosh for a black bowler hat from London and his
hookah for English cigarettes. Gabriel didn't even know how
to hold a barber's razor but, like his father, he too used to
shave sitting down, and in the summer he would shave sitting on the red plush chair on the verandah in front of the
three-legged table. Unlike the old man, Gabriel recoiled
from the idea of being shaved by a barber, although he liked
having his hair cut and as far as I remember he used to go to
the barber, Haim Cohen-Zedek, at least once a month for
this purpose. He had a full head of hair despite the widow's
peak cutting deeply into his wide forehead—more deeply on
the right side than the left—and showed no signs of going
bald in spite of his forty years, whose only traces were in the
few scattered locks that had started going gray, according to
him, when he was still a boy in his twenties. His hair grew too
closely for a parting and he would comb and brush it
straight back, wetting both comb and brush beforehand so
as to prevent its springing wildly up again. It was this ambition to keep his hair in order that was at the bottom of his
monthly visits to the barbershop, where he would have it cut
very short and tell the barber to clip the back and sides as
British soldiers had theirs cut. "I don't want to look like a
philosophizing artist," he once said when the barber tried to
persuade him to grow sideburns. On another occasion he
said to this same barber, "Please don't try to make a Sunday
poet out of me. You know I want an English haircut" (which
in those days meant a severe, restrained military crop). Once
when he had not had his hair cut for longer than usual
because of illness he looked in the mirror at his hair waving
wildly in all directions, frowned, and said half anxiously,
half humorously, "And now I already look like a mad German composer." He repeated this expression, "I look like a

mad composer," whenever there was something amiss in his dress, when out of negligence or haste his shirt was not quite clean or his pants not properly pressed. He took such care not to look like a mad German composer that he looked instead, especially in the first weeks of his return home, like a French dandy who had nothing in his head except for pursuing women and the other pleasures of this world in their most banal forms, a French dandy of a stiff, military type—like an officer in civilian dress on leave in the city. The barber, who knew from experience that Gabriel was not prepared to entrust his face to a stranger's hands, nevertheless refused to give up, and every time that Gabriel came into the barbershop he would inquire with a brisk, businesslike expression, "Haircut and shave?" His professional pride was hurt by this stubborn resistance because he could not understand why Gabriel, who liked to feel the razor on the back of his neck and around his ears, recoiled from the touch of the same razor held in the same hand, on his cheeks. In general his skin was dark and healthy, easily tanned by the sun. At the same time, however, it appeared to be very sensitive to touch in the area of the face. If the razor failed to land at exactly the angle to which he was accustomed it would immediately give rise to a rash—and there were days, especially when he was upset or annoyed about something, that his own carelessness would be responsible for making this rash break out on his face. This extraordinary sensitivity of Gabriel's facial skin left its mark too on a series of relationships very different and far removed indeed from his relationship with his barber. These were his relationships with the women he would go to bed with and possess without kissing them and without allowing his face to approach their skin in any way at all. The only thing his relations with the barber had in common with his relations with these women was the insult—both the barber and the women came out of their encounters with Gabriel insulted.

There were some women, on the other hand, whom Gabriel had to meet only once in order to long to put his face against theirs and kiss them—but of this later. All I wanted to do here was describe the differences and similarities between Gabriel and his father with regard to their respective shaving habits.

During his preparations for shaving, while he busied himself about putting all the things he needed on the verandah table, and especially while he waited for the water to warm up on the little spirit stove, Gabriel would sing loudly to himself—usually without even being aware of what he was doing. It was due to this lack of awareness that he was so startled—startled and also annoyed—when his mother's head emerged from the window of her room turbaned in the wet white towel she used against her headaches, crying angrily, "Will you please stop singing so loudly? Why is it that you always have to start bringing the roof down with your racket just when I've got such a splitting headache I feel as if my head's about to burst? Your voice is just like your father's. More like a lion roaring in the jungle than a normal human voice. Just tell me one thing—what makes you any better than Mrs. Landau's Polish owl? And why have the two of you joined forces to make my life a misery? The minute one stops banging as loudly as he can on the cursed piano the other begins roaring like a lion!" The anger and bitterness in her voice and words would give rise immediately to a reciprocal anger and bitterness in him and do away with any desire he had to sing at the very moment he became conscious of the fact that he was singing.

On the mornings of his first days at home after he returned from France he would sing a French folk song for children while he waited for his shaving water to warm up on the spirit stove: *"Sur mon chemin j'ai rencontré la fille du coupeur de paille, Sur mon chemin j'ai rencontré la fille du coupeur de blé."* He sang in a soft, tender baritone, his voice rising as the beat quickened and tending from time to time to melt in pathos. He himself was never aware of the pathos in his voice, and whenever anyone drew his attention to it he was actually insulted, because he detested any manifestation of pathos in singing or anything else. While he sang and waited for the wick to take and the steam to start rising from the pot of water, he would drum his fingers on the table in time to the tune. "How beautiful it is," he said once after explaining the words of the song to me. "How much longing there is in the simple words 'On my way I met the corn-reaper's daughter,' yes, yes, 'On my way I met the hay-reaper's daughter.'" I couldn't see at first what there was to admire so much in either the tune or the words of this song. The tune left me cold and the words meant nothing to me, and the only thing that interested me in the whole affair was the story he told me about what had happened to him in the little village in Brittany where he had first heard it. It was only many years later, when I suddenly heard the same song bursting out of an open window as I happened to be walk-ing past in the street, that my heart contracted in a painful spasm of memory and my eyes were opened to the abun-dance of longings of which Gabriel had spoken. About every song he sang he would say that it was a stream of waves of longing. When he walked past the ancient peasant cot-tages behind their garden hedges toward the wooden bridge leading over the stream to the path through the fields beyond, he would be tense with expectation, awaiting the appearance of the girl who was about to materialize from the fields of wheat, from the wind blowing from the Bay of Carnac bringing the smell of the Atlantic Ocean to the country roads, from the water of the brook lapping around the roots of the garden hedges, from the stones of the ancient houses standing and dreaming the centuries-old dreams of all the generations who had been born and died in their four-poster beds with their lace curtains, from the giant oaks which were all that survived of an ancient forest, from the ruins of the fort on the crest of the hill, from the rhythm of this countryside's breathing and the stirring of its ghosts and the colors of its sunsets which had been poured into the melody of the folk song and the words: *"Sur mon chemin j'ai rencontré la fille du coupeur de paille, Sur mon chemin j'ai rencontré la fille du coupeur de blé."* The girl who would rise from the fields of wheat and walk toward him and meet him on the wooden planks of the bridge and smile at him with her eyes and give herself to him and reveal the source of her being to him and let him penetrate her secrets.

Like someone penetrating a secret he would get into his ancient bed at night in the ancient room in the ancient farmhouse at the foot of the ruined fortress on the hill. This ancient Breton bed was called by the local people a "closed bed," and it was made of wood carved all over like lace. When the sliding doors were closed it looked like a very big, deep, high cupboard with little peepholes and windows carved in it among the relief work and the tracery, and you had to climb onto a high wooden step to open it. This step which stretched all along the base of the bed was also carved all over in a pattern of interlocking circles and turned out to be a capacious box which you could pull away and open and use to keep linen in. When Gabriel climbed onto the box step and opened the sliding doors he discovered the bed, deep and secret, piled high with eiderdowns and pillows, surrounded by high walls and covered with a canopy, and when he got into it and closed the doors behind him, he found himself suddenly transported into a separate world, shut in on itself in a darkness in which soft lights from the little peepholes and squares and circles carved in the wood danced. Like the farmhouse itself, the bed was about four hundred years old, and the old woman who owned the farm told Gabriel that some of the other furniture was just as old. The bed linen, the pillow cases and sheets, on the other hand, were far younger, not even seventy years old. These things the old lady told Gabriel in French, for she was an educated woman, but to her servant who was even older than she was she spoke in the ancient language of Brittany. Until the Great War (the one we today call the First World War, the Second World War having broken out four years after this conversation took place, which was one year before Gabriel returned to Jerusalem), she told him, there was not a single one of her farmhands, nor of the laborers on the neighboring three farms (the whole of the village consisted of these four farms) who could speak French. It was only when the war broke out and they were conscripted into the army and spent four years fighting with French soldiers that they learned to speak this foreign language. From then on the girls of the district too had started speaking French and replacing their black dresses and embroidered aprons and lace caps with "vulgar Paris clothes." The first morning he opened his eyes under the canopy of the ancient bed, the old lady, who brought him his breakfast on a tray, told him the story of the beautiful Madeleine and what had happened to her three hundred years ago. So long as Gabriel was staying in her house as a rich student from Paris visiting the Carnac district to investigate the prehistoric megaliths, she herself brought him his breakfast in bed, since the old maidservant who prepared the strong coffee steaming fragrantly in its cup and spread the hot rolls with butter and jam was not considered worthy of the honor of serving this learned guest in person. One of her great-great-grandmothers who had been born in the very bed Gabriel was lying in now some three hundred years ago had been called "La Belle Madeleine" because of her extraordinary beauty, a beauty matched only by her great joy in living and lust for the pleasures of this world. Madeleine had had her pleasure of all the good-looking men in the countryside, but instead of confessing these sins of the flesh to the village priest she had kept them locked away in her heart. One day the devil had appeared to her in the form of an aristocratic stranger from Paris come to see the menhirs and dolmens for which the district was famed, huge stones surviving from the ancient temples of the sun- and moon- and star-worshipers who had lived there thousands of years ago. The beautiful Madeleine had taken this stranger to show him the rows of giant mono- lithic pillars, each carved of a single granite rock and some of them ten feet high, and the dolmen chambers which housed the famous "merchants' table"—a great flat stone with fruit and sheaves of wheat carved on it. There on the "merchants' table" she had lain with him and given him her heart. From then on La Belle Madeleine desired one thing only: to pleasure the dark stranger from Paris (who was none other, as we know now, than the devil himself in dis- guise) and let him drink his fill of her embraces, but he instead of enjoying her seemed to sink deeper into a heavy sadness every day. At the sight of her melancholy lover poor Madeleine was heartbroken. She knelt at his feet and begged and implored him to tell her what she had omitted to do for his pleasure and what she should do, let him only ask and she would give him anything, anything at all he asked of her. "If only I could have a piece of communion bread," he said, "it would revive my soul." "Is that all?" cried La Belle Mad- eleine, surprised and delighted. "Why, there's nothing eas- ier!" "If only you would give me a piece of the consecrated host to eat and a glass of the consecrated wine to drink you would revive my soul," said the devil, and Madeleine ran off at once to the church and stole into the vestry behind the curtain and broke off a piece of the host and poured out a glass of the wine and brought them to her lover to eat and to drink. And in her sinful infatuation La Belle Madeleine did not even stop to think that the consecrated host was the body of our Lord and the consecrated wine was His blood which He gave us to make us one body with Him and save our souls through the sacrament of the Holy Mass, as every Christian knows and reads in the Bible: "Jesus took the bread and blessed it and brake it, and gave it to the disciples, and said, 'Take, eat; this is my body.' And he took the cup, and gave thanks, and gave it to them, saying, 'Drink ye all of it; for this is my blood of the new testament, which is shed for many for the remission of sins.' "

"And what happened to her in the end?" asked Gabriel.

"She died in the very bed you are lying in now," answered the old lady. "I've already told you that it all happened three hundred years ago. She died and went to hell and from that day to this her soul has suffered torments of hunger and thirst, hunger for bread and thirst for water. The priest in our village church often returns to the subject of La Belle Madeleine in his sermons and tells us about the terrible hunger and thirst she suffers in hell. Everyone around these parts knows the story and it's not only here in our church that she is spoken of but also in Quiberon and Locmaria-quer and even in the city of Vannes. Sometimes her ghost haunts this house, searching for her lover to appease her hunger with bread and her thirst with water or opening cupboards and drawers and rummaging in baskets for something to eat. If you hear a door creaking in the middle of the night or someone poking about in the drawers you must cross yourself and call on the Father and the Son and the Holy Ghost or on the Virgin Mary to chase the ghost of La Belle Madeleine away."

"Is she seen too, or only heard?" asked Gabriel.

"Seen too," answered the old lady. "Seen too, of course! I saw her myself only twelve years ago. She was tall and firm-fleshed and very beautiful with big gray eyes and a straight nose with delicate twitching nostrils and a full, red little mouth with the lower lip thicker than the upper, and high cheekbones and black hair and white skin and a lace cap like butterfly's wings, standing so proud and straight with sparks coming off her from the devil in hell and the hunger and thirst burning up her insides."

When Gabriel climbed into his bed at night he concentrated all his thoughts on La Belle Madeleine, so that she would come and show herself to him when the clock struck midnight, and when he shut the sliding doors and lay down inside the dark box he waited for the sensations of a strange, distant world to envelop and engulf him. But instead of the strange remote soul he was expecting he felt a gentle warmth spreading through his limbs and a longing which flooded his open eyes with tears as he saw his grandfather sitting in his workshop and carving pomegranates and sheaves of wheat on a piece of olive wood for the cornice of a wardrobe. He was engulfed by an overpowering smell of wood—the smell of the walls and canopy of the ancient Breton bed in which he was lying—and as he inhaled the air of the strange bed he saw quite clearly the chisel in his grandfather's hand cutting into the flesh of the olive wood between its veins and heard the split wood squeak and the sawdust rustle beneath his feet, the feet of a child of six come to show his grandfather his new shoes, shining patent-leather shoes which made little popping noises when he walked. Grandfather stops his work, wipes his hands on his apron, picks him up, and seats him on his knee. Grandfather sings to him and jiggles his knee to the rhythm of the song. Grandfather sings, "Grandfather's going far away, Grandfather's going far away," and Grandfather did go far away before the year was out, and Gabriel never saw him again, because Grandfather died. Grandfather wipes the sawdust off Gabriel's new shoes and promises him that he too will give him a present, but it will be a few weeks before the present is ready. "What will you buy me, Grandfather?" Gabriel asks. "I won't buy you anything," says Grandfather. "I'll make you something." Grandfather made him a wooden box in the shape of a miniature Ark of the Law with a carved cornice supported on two pillars standing on either side of real doors he could open and close with a real key, a tiny shining key. Gabriel holds it in both his hands and fondles it with his fingers, feeling the fluting of the pillars and the moldings of their capitals, and the lines of the pomegranates and wheat sheaves cut into the cornice. He lifts it to his nose and smells the smell of the olive wood mingled with the smell of the lacquer which is not quite dry yet. He lifts it to his mouth and kisses it delicately. He presses it to his heart and suddenly begins skipping and singing for joy to have such a pretty, precious little box. A special box with no other box like it in the whole world. A box his grandfather had made especially for him. At the sound of the three light knocks with the polite, deliberate pauses between them, he sat up with a start on a frantic impulse to jump out of bed and run to look for the little box which had vanished from his life over thirty years before. On no account could he remember the circumstances of its loss, or when he had stopped seeing it among his other possessions. This box which had been dearer to him than any other present he had ever received had been completely obliterated, and however hard he tried to concentrate on the fragmentary pictures of his childhood he was unable to retrieve anything which had any bearing at all on its fate: he could not make up his mind whether he had lost it or given it away, whether it had been broken or stolen, or when exactly it had disappeared from his life and thoughts.

"Did La Belle Madeleine appear in the night to disturb Your Honor's sleep?" asked the old lady coming in with the tray, and it seemed to Gabriel that he could discern a secret smile hiding among the wrinkles surrounding her mouth. "No. I'm sorry to say that she didn't," he replied, without knowing why he had said that he was "sorry," whether he had used the phrase simply out of politeness or whether he really was sorry. "Well there's no chance of seeing her today," said the old lady. "It's St. Anne's Day today and she wouldn't dare come even if she could. You know of course that St. Anne was born and died here too, not in this bed exactly because she died hundreds of years before this house was ever built, but here in the neighborhood. I hope the blessed saint showed you something good in your dreams?"

"Something very good," said Gabriel. "A pretty wooden box."

"Yes of course," said the old lady. "That must be the very box which is used as a model for all the holy vestment chests in all the churches in Brittany. Joseph made it and sent it to St. Anne for a present after she left Nazareth and came back to Brittany, the land of her birth." Gabriel drank his bitter morning coffee (which was so strong that until he got used to it, it made his heart palpitate violently in a way that was both upsetting and pleasant) and listened to his hostess, who seated herself on the step of his bed and told him the story of St. Anne of Brittany and the chest that Joseph the carpenter of Nazareth had made for her. St. Anne d'Auray (called after the village where she was born) was the patron saint of Brittany and of all Bretons wherever they happened to be. She was a noble princess and her husband, who was a member of the royal household, treated her harshly and used her ill. She ran away from him to the Holy Land and settled down in Nazareth, where she gave birth to the Virgin Mary. When Mary reached puberty, her mother told her all about the terrible sufferings she had endured at the hands of her husband, Mary's father, and warned her not to marry anyone but a Jew, because Jews were good husbands to their wives and treated them kindly. And thus it came about that Mary, the daughter of a noble Breton prince, married the poor old Jewish carpenter of Nazareth, St. Joseph (who concealed from her, as he concealed from all the other inhabitants of the town, his noble descent, which could be traced all the way down to King David himself), who in his mercy and compassion adopted the infant Jesus, immaculately conceived and borne by his young bride, the blessed

Virgin Mary. When St. Anne had satisfied herself that her daughter, Mary, and her son, the infant Jesus, could be safely entrusted to the care of the old Jewish carpenter, she went home to die in her native land, in Brittany, and be buried with her ancestors. The infant Jesus, who was deeply attached to his grandmother, promised her that he would not forget her and that when he grew up he would come to visit her in distant Brittany, and he kept his promise. Before she died St. Anne was granted the joy of seeing her grandson, Jesus, who came to Brittany bearing a gift for her from her son-in-law, Joseph, a wooden box with a lock of her daughter Mary's hair in it. The box was placed in the Church of St. Anne for safekeeping, and since then it had been used as a model for all the holy vestment chests in all the sacristies of all the churches in Brittany. And Christ bestowed yet another favor on Brittany, his grandmother's native land. He struck the rock next to her house and a holy spring gushed out of it and was still gushing out of it to that very day, the sacred spring of St. Anne la Palou, which pilgrims came to visit every year on the day of the Grand Pardon. The important and learned guest from Paris had been granted a great privilege indeed! On the eve of her name day St. Anne herself had shown him in his dream the very box St. Joseph of Nazareth made to hold a lock of her daughter the blessed Virgin Mary's hair. The very same box that people meant when they said "touch wood," because anyone who touched it was healed of his sickness and protected from the evil eye and kept safe from harm and bad luck. And for this favor he should certainly give thanks to St. Anne and make the pilgrimage to her sacred spring, the spring of St. Anne la Palou, which was only a few minutes' walk from the very bed he was lying on, at the foot of the ruined fortress on the hill. And he should realize too how lucky he was (and she too, and all the other people in the village) since others had to make the long and weary pilgrimage to the sacred site from the four corners of the land, while they were right there on the spot. If he prayed with all his heart and soul, then perhaps St. Anne would find him worthy of an even greater favor still, and appear to him once more in his dreams and show him where the holy box was now.

"What do you mean where the holy box is now?" exclaimed Gabriel in surprise. "Haven't you just told me yourself that it was placed for safekeeping in the Church of St. Anne?"

"Yes, yes, my dear sir," said the old lady, "I did say that it was placed for safekeeping in the Church of St. Anne, but I didn't say that it was there now. Many years ago the box disappeared and now nobody knows where it is."

If the god of dreams had opened a window in his sleep to show him a dream, then maybe St. Anne would have taken the opportunity to come in and show him where to find her holy box, but no dream came to light his way through that night's sleep, or if he did dream then the outside light came to make him forget whatever he had seen through his closed eyes in the inner light which illuminates the way of dreamers. With the spirals of light, the loops and circles and arabesques bursting in through the openings carved in the walls of his bed, Gabriel woke to the smell of the ancient wood and the twittering of the birds in the old oak tree next to his window. An ancient pain woke with him, crouching on his chest and suddenly unsheathing a sharp pointed claw from its heavy paw to dig deeply into his flesh. He threw off his blankets, twisted and turned, stifled the groan about to burst out of his throat, and opened the doors of his bed to see if the old lady was eavesdropping before the three polite taps which heralded the arrival of his breakfast. If only his grandfather were still alive, perhaps Gabriel could somehow have made amends, but his grandfather had been in the world of ghosts for over thirty years now. He had died only a few months after making the wooden box as a present for his grandson. After showing him how to open and shut the little doors with the tiny, glittering key, Grandfather's eyes began to sparkle with the excitement of the great secret he was about to reveal to his grandson. "Come with me and I'll show you something," he said, gesturing toward the little alcove at the back of the workshop. "But first promise me that you won't tell anyone." Grandfather opened the curtain stiff with dust and carpenter's glue and showed Gabriel two great planks of wood lying side by side on the floor. They were carved to look like pillars and their capitals were decorated with pomegranates just like the two pillars supporting the cornice of the box Gabriel held in his hand. Grandfather was secretly making a new Ark of the Law for the same two crooked wardens who had still not paid him the money they owed him for the last Ark of the Law he had made for them twenty-five years before, when they were still the wardens of the Yeshuoth Ya'akov synagogue in the Old City, the very same two wardens whom he himself suspected of being implicated in setting his house and shop on fire on the night after he had carried the big olive-wood cross on his back to the Russian monastery on the Mount of Olives. He sat down on one of the two pillars and started stroking the grooves he had cut into the flesh of the wood with the swollen, callused fingers of his heavy old hands. "I know very well," he said— as if he were talking not to his little grandson but to his angry, accusing daughter—"I know very well that in their wickedness and stupidity and mean little tricks there's nothing to choose between them and the Russian monks on the Mount of Olives, but I don't give a damn—I'm not making the Holy Ark for them, and I'm not making it for the Jews who've grown rich and want to build themselves a new synagogue to show off with, either." He wanted to go on and say something else, but he fell silent instead, and Gabriel ran home to show his mother his present, and while he was demonstrating all the delights of the little box to her he betrayed his grandfather to his mother and told her all the old man's secrets—even the exact place he kept the two pillars he was working on inside the little alcove at the back of the shop. When Grandfather made him promise not to tell anyone Gabriel understood at once that the person he was not supposed to tell was his mother, because there was nobody else who was in the least bit interested in what Grandfather did. And after all the trouble he caused him by his betrayal Grandfather didn't scold him or reproach him or shout at him or even withdraw from him in silence. He went on smiling at him and loving him as he always had, and Gabriel went on accepting this great love and taking it for granted, and it didn't even occur to him to ask the old man's pardon. And when did his beloved grandson Gabriel wake up at last to the need for asking his forgiveness? Thirty years after his death, in a godforsaken village on the western borders of France. When he woke up and found himself in the ancient boxlike Breton bed he wanted to laugh, but the pain pressing down on his chest stifled the laughter while it was still struggling to get out of his lungs, the pain which grew worse and more oppressive as the pictures he was looking at grew sharper and their details clearer. Grandfather's face, paling at the sight of his mother bursting into the workshop, and his hand, trembling so hard that the chisel fell out of it and dropped onto the trestle table. And his thin, broken voice begging her not to make a scandal in front of all the world, and the expressions on the faces of all the neighboring shopkeepers and all the people passing in the street who gathered outside to see what was going on. "Senile idiot, wicked old man, Canaanite slave," yelled his mother at the top of her voice, to the delight of all the people crowding around the open workshop door. "So now you're making Holy Arks for the crooks who cheated you of your money and burned your house down! Oh, you miser-

able slave—why don't you go and lick your master's ass?"
After that Grandfather was unable to hold a chisel in his
hand, and once his trembling hands were no longer good for
anything the sight of his tools began to weigh so heavily on
him and make him feel so depressed that at the end of his
life he took to spending his days sitting in the sun on the
pavement outside the locked doors of his workshop. He
would sit on the pavement talking quietly to himself with
one eye closed and the little finger of his right hand stuck in
his right ear, and every now and then he would burst out
laughing. Sometimes the sight of the old carpenter sitting
outside his shuttered workshop with his finger in his ear,
muttering and laughing to himself, would attract a crowd of
street urchins who gathered around to tease him, scenting
the departure of sense from soul like the flies of death who
smell out from afar the departure of soul from body. Gabriel
on his way to visit his grandfather once saw from the corner
of the street a group of children teasing him, and immediately turned around and went off in a different direction
so that no one would suspect him of having anything to do
with the senile old man. This clear picture of himself as a
well-scrubbed and -brushed child wearing a blue jacket with
gold buttons and the arms of Paris embroidered on its
upper pocket, which he had received as a present from his
father's friend the French consul and which he had been on
his way to show to his grandfather, turning sharply away in
the direction of the Zion Cinema and hurrying past its
façade, pursued by the awful possibility that those rough
boys might find out that the old carpenter who talked to
himself in the street was none other than his grandfather,
came back to him so vividly that he could actually see the
sunlight playing on the texture of the gold buttons and smell
the new cloth of the splendid jacket as he rose from his bed
in the little village on the Atlantic coast (which the villagers
called the "Wild Coast") thirty years later, and caused him

such gnawing, suffocating pangs of pain that he suddenly found himself writhing at the foot of the bed and banging his head on the wooden floor which proved too shaky to bear the sharp new pain of his old cowardice and started to shudder and groan beneath the weight of its blows. One, two, three, came the politely spaced knocks of the mistress of the farm bringing him his breakfast, and he sat down quickly on the step in front of the bed, hurrying to wipe the dust off his forehead as he did so, while calling out as he did every morning when he woke up, *"Entrez, je vous en prie, entrez, Madame."*

"Monsieur's face looks different this morning," she said, and Gabriel's heart sank at the thought that the old lady had peeped through the keyhole and seen him writhing about and banging his head on the floor. "Your cheeks are so pink and your eyes are so bright—could it be that you have been granted a vision in the night? Perhaps it was St. Anne in all her glory who came to you in your sleep?"

"No, no," said Gabriel, amazed at the deceitfulness of his looks and glad that it had saved him from the old lady's poking and prying into the pain in his heart. "It was only a broken old Jew, a senile carpenter."

"Just as I said!" cried the old lady triumphantly. "It was St. Joseph himself, Monsieur, who was revealed to you in a vision. I expect you know that very few people are ever granted the privilege of seeing St. Joseph. He only shows himself to the good in heart, and the sight of him purifies the heart. They say that he appeared once in a dream to the charming Merlin and revealed the whereabouts of the box and all that had happened to it since it disappeared from the Church of St. Anne to him, and no wonder, since this Merlin was an exceptionally good and honest man. The only wonder is that the charming Merlin was none other than the brother of the beautiful Madeleine who fell in love with the devil and stole the consecrated host from the church for him, and St. Joseph appeared to her brother in a dream after she had fallen into the clutches of the devil. Merlin kept everything that St. Joseph told him in his dream to himself, and not only didn't he tell a single soul what he had seen in his vision, he himself never even tried to remove the box from its hiding place. He sent all the princes and counts who came from the king back empty-handed, and retired from the world to live the life of a hermit in the Brossliand forest which filled this whole area in those days from the fortress on the hill as far as the eye could see, all the way down to the bend in the river Odette. Today there's nothing left of it except for those few ancient oaks you can see from the window.

"In the depths of the forest the wood sprite Vivienne revealed herself to him and he revealed himself to her, and once they had revealed themselves to each other, love revealed itself to both of them. In her fear of losing the charming Merlin Vivienne drew a circle around him at the foot of an oak tree. If he had wanted to, Merlin could easily have broken out of this circle, but he didn't want to. He was glad to stay inside it, and all he wanted was to stay inside it. So from then on the charming Merlin stayed inside the oak forest and never set foot in the outside world again, although in those days a gracious and merciful king, a king close to God, was sitting on the throne of France—St. Louis. Now the works of St. Louis are well known, and the learned Monsieur is certainly familiar with them and doesn't need me to teach him, but still the good deeds which men do, especially kings, deserve to be recounted at all times—especially at a time like this when the young Monsieur's face is still shining with the light of the countenance of St. Joseph, who visited him in a vision in the night. You may wonder why I say 'especially the good deeds of a king'? Because it is harder for a king to do good than for any other man in the world, since a king has more power than anybody else to put his

evil inclinations into practice. This king devoted all his
wealth, his own and his country's, to acquiring the holy relics
of our Lord and Savior Jesus Christ. The beams of the cross
that Jesus carried on his back, the crown of thorns that was
placed on his head, and the sponge of vinegar that was
offered him to quench his thirst—all these relics of our
Lord, which contain sparks of the Holy Ghost because of
their contact with the body of Jesus, who was himself a vessel
for the Holy Ghost, were then in the hands of the Venetian
bankers, and the pious King St. Louis redeemed them. How
did these holy relics of Christ, sanctified and sanctifying by
touch, fall into the hands of the bankers of Venice, you may
ask? The way it happened was this: the Crusaders of those
days who sought to reach the Holy Land landed up in
Byzantium instead, and instead of capturing the Holy Sepulcher from the Moslems, they took the city of Constantinople from their fellow Christians of the East and ruled there
in their stead. They were soon encircled by hostile forces
and in order to wage war on these enemies they needed a
great deal of money. They therefore applied to the bankers
of Venice for a loan, but the latter were prepared to grant
them the loan they needed only in exchange for a very
precious pledge, the most precious pledge in the whole of
Christendom. In other words—the holy relics of our Lord
which were stored in the great church at Constantinople.
The Crusaders gave these holy relics to the Venetian bankers
in pawn for the money they needed to make war, but they
were unable to redeem them. In their distress they applied
to the King of France and asked him to help them. St. Louis
immediately realized what a great opportunity had come his
way and determined not to miss it. He collected all the
money in France and sent it to the Venetian bankers to
redeem the beams of the cross, the crown of thorns, and the
sponge of vinegar, and when the holy relics reached France
he went to receive them in the garb of a penitent, barefoot,

bareheaded, and dressed in sackcloth. He built the Sacred Chapel on the Ile Saint-Louis in the middle of Paris especially to house these relics. And all this time the charming Merlin stayed in hiding in the Brossliand wood, a willing prisoner in the enchanted circle of the wood sprite, with the secret of the hiding place of the box which was truly the work of the hands of St. Joseph and held a true lock of the true hair of the blessed Virgin herself, locked up in his heart."

"What do you mean by 'true'?" asked Gabriel, when he saw the same secret smile folded in the corners of the old lady's mouth and eyes again. "And the cross for which King Louis gave the whole riches of the kingdom of France, wasn't it the true cross of Jesus?"

"Only a muddled king, a pious fool like Louis," said the mistress of the farm, "could have imagined for a moment that he could buy the holy of holies from the tyrants of Byzantium and the merchants of Venice."

"And the box," said Gabriel, "how do you know that the box . . . ?"

"Really, Monsieur," said the old lady, "you surprise me. An intelligent, educated man like you, how can you think of comparing the words of the tyrants of Byzantium and the rascals of Venice with the words of St. Joseph himself, who appeared in a vision to a pure-hearted man and spoke to him face to face?"

This question of his apparently continued to bother her, for when he went out that evening for his nightly walk to the pillars of the ancient star-worshipers and the sea coast, she approached him again and said, "I suppose that your question this morning was intended to test me, to see if I knew the difference between true and false?" These words reminded Gabriel of the Tree of Knowledge, and between the pillars and the sea it occurred to him for the first time since he had first heard the biblical verse from Genesis in the domed room in the little alley in the Old City of Jerusalem, and on all the different occasions when it had subsequently popped up in his thoughts, that the knowledge that had banished Adam and Eve from the Garden of Eden was the knowledge of good and evil, and not the knowledge of true and false. If he had sought the knowledge of true and false instead of running after the conventions of good and evil he would not have thrown the Garden of Eden away with his own hands, now prickling into gooseflesh from the cold night wind blowing through him with all its might after crossing the vast darkness of the ocean. He pushed his cold hands into his trouser pockets after raising his coat collar against the chill damp air redolent with the fish and salt of the great sea: the great wide sea and the distant stars blowing the cold of the void and the dark into his face were as terrible to him in their indifference as the knowledge of truth and falsehood of the science-worshipers who had taken over the world to teach it the neutral laws of blind natural forces which existed without a cause and without a purpose, without reason, meaning, feeling, or value. The great pillars standing in their orderly rows along the lines of the rising and setting of the sun, which had required great knowledge on the part of the ancient star-worshipers who made them and set them up in these exactly calculated lines, these too, like the massive rocks of the bay and the waves of the sea and the stars in their courses, gave off a remote, indifferent chill, since they too belonged to the same neutral system of earth and sea and blind open-eyed stars turning unwittingly in the prison of their closed orbits, in blind obedience to the blind laws of the blind forces which in their blindness had created themselves.

As he turned to go back to his closed bed in the village the cold wind blowing in his face brought with it what sounded like fragments of warm human voices coming from the bay, and these voices, masked by the murmur of the sea, continued to pursue him with every gust of wind, until he stopped and turned in his tracks and saw that they really were human voices coming from the bay. There were a number of boys and girls from the village sitting in one of the fishermen's boats anchored along the quay, and they were singing a song which had a familiar sound, a folk song apparently, frequently heard in the single street of the village, whose subject was a young girl's disappointment in love. On his way back home to bed he kept on hearing the melody of the song's refrain in his ears and without realizing what he was doing he began to sing the words to himself, "It's written in the sky, it's written in the sky, it's written in the sky ..." Suddenly he felt a wave of wonderful happiness flooding through him and carrying him toward the secret which was written in the sky for anyone to see in holy letters of moon and Great Bear and Little Bear and Orion and Cassiopeia and all the points of stars all the length and breadth and depth of the scroll of the sky, like the Chinese poem written on the ancient piece of parchment.

This story of the ancient piece of parchment I heard Gabriel tell so often as an example of his way of looking at things—especially his way of looking at the truths of science, which he always referred to as "the knowledge of true and false of the science-worshipers who have taken over the world"—that I don't know anymore if it was something that happened to him in the days when he was still a medical student at the Sorbonne University, or if it was just a parable, a story he made up himself in order to illustrate his point of view. The expert on chemical analysis in the laboratory, who was not a Frenchman but a Jew from Alsace, had been asked to analyze some black stains on a piece of yellow parchment, and when the head of the department came into the laboratory accompanied by an elegant Chinese gentleman to hear the results, he presented him with a set of formulae containing the exact analysis of the chemical components of the

parchment and the stains, including what was then still a
great scientific novelty, their age. He modestly announced
that he now knew everything there was to know about that
piece of parchment with its black spots—and at that point
the Chinese approached him, bowed gracefully to the
ground, praised the profundity of his wisdom and the
extent of his knowledge, and then begged a thousand par-
dons for bringing to his attention the curious coincidence
that the same black spots that had the honor of being composed of exactly those elements which the honorable
learned doctor had mentioned could also be interpreted,
above and beyond the perishable black material of their
bodies, as a combination of ancient Chinese letters compos-
ing a love song of ancient times. The words of the folk song
"It's written in the sky, it's written in the sky," which Gabriel
had heard so many times during his stay in the little Breton
village of Carnac and to which he had paid no attention at
all (except to wonder in passing how this worn-out cliché,
the product of superstitious beliefs in weak minds, could still
be sung so enthusiastically by young people in modern
times), these simple words now dazzled him with an awesome, brilliant light as they suddenly drew back the curtain
that had been blinding his eyes. Not a metaphor and not a
parable and not an empty phrase but the plain and simple
truth—it was written in the sky in letters of light, in star-
letters, and not even the thought (which came close to a
certainty) that however hard he tried he would never be able
to decipher a single shining letter in a single light-word of all
that was written there for all to see could dim the awesome
light revealed with the falling away of a single veil of the veils
of that dividing curtain. Every schoolboy today knows far
more about the components and mechanics of the illumi-
nated writing of the heavenly bodies than the most learned
of the ancient Druids who made the calculations necessary
to place these giant pillars along the line of the rising and

setting of the sun, but even the least of the Celts whose bare feet trod this earth at the edges of the West thousands of years ago understood (what the learned doctor who knew everything there was to know about the black spots on the parchment did not understand) that these points of light in the sky, above and beyond any formula capable of containing them, were also the writing of a poem, and a poem moreover which he had his own way of interpreting.

I asked Gabriel if he remembered what the ancient poem that the distinguished Chinese gentleman had recited in the laboratory was about. He thought for a moment and said he had written the words down in a notebook which he had thrust into the bottom of one of the suitcases, which he had not even opened since his return home. When the time for the suitcase to be opened came around, he would take the notebook out and show me the words of the Chinese poem. In the meantime, if I wanted to read something that would give me an idea of the Druidical atmosphere that still hung about the ancient oak forest at the foot of the ruined fortress on the hill, he would show me a poem he himself had translated into Hebrew.

This poem Gabriel had translated sitting in the servant's room on the farm, which belonged to Leontine, the old maidservant who was even older than her mistress. Leontine, who had previously been considered good enough to prepare his breakfast for him, but not to serve it to him in his closed bed in the farmhouse bedchamber, had now herself become Gabriel's mistress. Gabriel's metamorphosis from the respected guest of the mistress of the farm to the servant of her servant had been rapid and abrupt, without any intermediary stages, and it had taken place the day after the night on which he had sensed that one of the veils covering his eyes had fallen away. It was caused by the letter (awaited no less eagerly by the mistress of the farm than by Gabriel himself) that came that same day from Jerusalem, from the old Bey. Instead of the usual money order it contained a final notification to the effect that, since Gabriel persisted in his refusal to continue the medical studies for which he had been sent to Paris, his allowance had been stopped. Gabriel then suggested that he would hire himself to work for the mistress of the farm in the house and on the fields and pay her what he owed her with his wages, while continuing to reside under her roof in the room with the ancient Breton bed which he had occupied up to now, but she thought differently. When she suddenly realized that he didn't have a penny in the world, and no hopes of getting any money through the postal services either, she turned pale, her hands began to shake, her wrinkled face broke up into shuddering waves, her mouth opened and shut like a fish out of water, and for a moment Gabriel stopped breathing in the awful fear that she was about to die of a heart attack all because of him, right there in front of him. "Impostor!" the word broke from her lips in a mighty yell. "You shameless fraud, you charlatan! A scandal, a scandal!" She was outraged by the scandalous, shameful deception which had been perpetrated upon her by this beggarly ragamuffin who under the pretense of being a rich student had been received in her house like a prince, and Gabriel's proposal that he should continue to sleep in the master's bed even after he had been relegated to the status of a hired laborer increased her sense of outrage even further by exposing the fact that he was not only an impostor, but a dangerous revolutionary who would not hesitate in his brazen impudence to overturn the very foundations of the natural order of things. "Leontine!" she yelled, and if he had not heard it with his own ears he would never have believed that so thunderous a roar could have emerged from the frail old lady standing trembling in front of him, "Leontine—take this charlatan to his proper place at once! Everyone to his place! Everyone to his place!" Her shouting was superfluous of course, because the old servant had been standing in the doorway all the time watching the amazing exchange taking place between her mistress and her mistress's high and mighty guest. The old lady's repeated command, firm and frightened at once, "Everyone to his place! Everyone to his place!" reminded him of the saying from the Ethics of the Fathers, "There is nothing which does not have its place," and gave him an insight into the panic that had taken hold of her above and beyond an old lady's fear of falling victim to the tricks of an impostor, an insight into the terror of confusion, the horror of the dark chaos into which the world would relapse the moment its established order collapsed, the moment nothing was any longer in its place, and what was even worse and more terrifying—nothing was any longer inside the form that fitted it and was the right shape and dimension for its essence, and no soul had the body that suited it. The possibility that one of her farm hands might really be a learned gentleman from Paris living in her house and sleeping in her ancestors' bed and receiving breakfast from her own hands was no less frightening to her than the possibility that Rexie, the curly little dog who fell asleep every evening in her lap, was really the soul of a poisonous snake inhabiting a puppy's body, or that Leontine was really the ghost of La Belle Madeleine inhabiting her old maidservant's body. After he had spent a month living in Leontine's room, Gabriel himself felt, in fact, that he didn't know who or what his servant-mistress really was, and if the mistress of the farm—who ever since his fall had avoided Gabriel, returning his greetings in the farmyard with a cold, distant *"Bonjour"* and a look of grim astonishment at the impudence of this unknown, inferior creature giving her a friendly, familiar greeting as if she knew who he was, or had ever had anything to do with him, or as if he were her equal—if she had told him that his mistress the servant Leontine was in fact La Belle Madeleine who had once upon a time fallen in love with the devil in the guise of a handsome young man, he would not have been surprised—just as he would not have been surprised to discover that she was really a reincarnation of St. Anne.

Leontine's room, which was not in the house but in a corner of the yard next to the back gate, was no different from the room in the farmhouse itself either in its size or its furniture: it was a very big room with antique beds lined up against the walls and an old black clock standing in the corner leisurely ticking the minutes away with its burnished copper tongue in the still, musty air, and a night-cupboard standing at the head of his bed. In this night-cupboard the only difference between the two rooms lay hidden, to be revealed to him in all its glory when he opened its doors before going to bed and found to his astonishment that it contained a chamber pot. Not simply a chamber pot, but a chamber pot such as he had never in his wildest dreams imagined to exist in the world. Unlike the chamber pots he remembered from his childhood, which were made of enamel-coated iron peeping with black eyes out of every hole in their white coats, this one was made of shining white china and encircled by a garland of red, pink, and yellow roses, with little posies of violets intertwined upon its lip. At the sight of this splendor modestly hiding in the night-cupboard he felt the whole room becoming warm and close and friendly, and when he took it out and placed it on the table he was overcome with bliss. What man may be considered rich? Rabbi Yossie said: He whose lavatory is close to his table.* A new pain born of his new insight cut through the ancient joy of the warmth rising from the depths of Abayeh's childhood,† which he had not understood in his own childhood when he went to relieve himself in his grandfather's lavatory. It was because of his excitement, apparently, at the

---

* Rabbi Yossie—One of the Talmudic sages.
† Abayeh—One of the Talmudic sages.

wonderful box his grandfather had made him for a present that he suddenly had to go, and his grandfather took him by the hand and led him to the lavatory, which was on the other side of the building, through a dark covered alley smelling of mold and urine. "You can go back to the shop," he said. "I know where the lavatory is." But Grandfather stayed outside the door, and all the time he was sitting on the toilet on one side of the door, the old man, to his distress, stood there humming on the other, as if he were a baby afraid of staying by himself in the dark lavatory. "I told you to go back to the shop. I told you I'm not a baby and I'm not afraid of staying in the lavatory by myself!" he shouted at the old man in angry resentment which momentarily banished all the joy of his wonderful present from his heart. Then Grandfather told him the story of Abayeh who had never seen either his mother or his father because he was born an orphan. When he was in his mother's womb his father died, and she herself died when he was born. The nurse who looked after him was an intelligent, kindly woman, and she took a little lamb and brought it up with him and let him take it into the lavatory with him to calm his fears. When he grew up Abayeh said that when a man enters the lavatory he should turn to his guardian angels and pray to them, begging and imploring them in these words: "Guard me, guard me! Help me, help me! Support me, support me! Wait for me, wait for me until I go in and come out, for this is the way of men." "But he was still a baby when he used to go to the lavatory with his lamb," said Gabriel to his grandfather, "and anyway, he was an orphan and that's why he felt so lonely. Because his mother and father left him and died, he was afraid that the angels would abandon him too. And besides, we know now that there aren't any angels, and that it's all a lot of superstition. His nurse told him there were good angels who kept guard over him and went with him everywhere that he went so that he wouldn't be afraid to go by himself. And besides—what's there to be afraid of in the lavatory?" "There's a devil in the lavatory," answered Grandfather. "That's what it says in the Gemarah. His name is Bar-Shirikai Pandai. This devil is born of the bravery of lions, and if you have a sharp eye you can see him on the head of the lion and the muzzle of the lioness. If a man is sitting in the lavatory and he suddenly sees this devil in front of him, he must say, 'On the mane of the lion and the muzzle of the lioness I found him, in a bed of vetch I beat him, and with the jawbone of an ass I slew him.' Saying this he becomes as strong as Samson, who rent a lion with his bare hands and slew a thousand men with the jawbone of an ass. The devil takes fright and runs away." "What does the devil look like?" asked Gabriel. "He looks like a satyr, a he-goat, and Abayeh wasn't the only one to be afraid of him. All the ancient sages were afraid of him. This devil is jealous of scholars and comes to torment them in the lavatory. Raba wasn't an orphan like Abayeh, but still he had a good wife who protected him from all sorts of evil spirits. When he went to the lavatory she would put a nut inside a copper jar and rattle it outside the door, and after he became head of a yeshiva she took even greater care of him and made a window in the lavatory door to put her hand through so that she could keep it on his head as long as he was inside."

Gabriel was so amused by this picture of Raba sitting on the toilet and doing his business with his wife's hand sticking through the door and resting on his head that every time he thought of it he burst out laughing. The first time he heard the story from his grandfather he laughed so much that he infected the old man too. Grandfather laughed and lifted him up into the air, laughed and kissed his head, laughed and danced with him in his arms, as he used to dance in the synagogue with the scroll of the law cradled in his arms. His grandfather was amused, but his mother wasn't.

"What's the lavatory devil's name?" Gabriel was so happy and excited that he couldn't wait for his mother to find the answer to his riddle herself and shouted triumphantly, "Bar-

Shirikai Pandai!" This riddle and its answer made his mother's face go white. "So your grandfather's been poisoning your mind with his old wives' tales again!" If there had been any doubt left in her mind at all, here was this lavatory devil come to give her conclusive proof that her senile father had set his heart on dragging his grandson down into the dungheap of idle superstition and insane hallucinations after he had already succeeded in ruining the lives of his own children with his idiotic midrashim. "That man will never set foot in this house again!" she yelled in prophetic wrath, and as for Gabriel, she gave him strict orders never to visit his senile grandfather again.

"Well, never mind, you can keep on going to visit him, and of course he can come here to see us whenever he wants to. After all, he is your grandfather, and he loves you, and he's a good man even though his mind's become a little confused with old age—" thus she recanted and backed down from her overhasty prohibition after a moment's reflection in which she apparently remembered the proverbial sweetness of forbidden fruits. "But you're not to take any notice of his stories about angels and devils and the rest of his old rubbish and midrashim. After all, you're an intelligent boy, and you know perfectly well that there aren't any devils and demons and evil spirits in lavatories or chamber pots or anywhere else."

So the learned gentleman from Paris is intrigued by the chamber pot, said the smile which lit Leontine's face as she entered the room and saw Gabriel holding it in his hand and staring at it, suddenly catching sight of her in the big wardrobe mirror opposite him, and blushing at her smile. As he explained to me many years later, this blush of embarrassment was not for himself, it was for Leontine, because he suddenly realized that in removing the chamber pot from the night-cupboard and putting in on the table and examining it he had unwittingly invaded the privacy of the old woman who in the kindness of her heart had taken him into her room instead of sending him to the barn where the seasonal workers slept. There was only one lavatory on the farm, in the farmhouse, and the old servant probably needed the chamber pot on winter nights when she didn't feel up to facing the walk to the farmhouse, or when it was too cold to go out to the fields beyond the garden gate. Most of the local peasants who had not been infected with the frivolous spirit of innovation spreading from the metropolis relieved themselves in the fields.

"A pretty pot," said Leontine.

"Very pretty," said Gabriel. "The prettiest pot I've ever seen."

"Yes, it's the prettiest one I've got," said Leontine. "I put it there especially for you. I said to myself, this delicate gentleman from Paris will certainly be afraid to go out into the fields at night."

"I'm not afraid of the night," said Gabriel.

Leontine looked at him and said, "That may be a good sign."

A light night breeze blew between his naked legs as he crouched low over the earth with his trousers down, lifting his eyes to the distant stars and holding his breath to move his bowels, when suddenly he sensed that there was someone standing behind him. The shivers of this disagreeable suspicion running up and down his spine turned into pincers of terror crushing his ribs as soon as he smelled the carpenter's glue and heard the voice singing, "Purify our hearts to worship you truly, purify our hearts to worship you truly . . ." and knew that the person standing behind him was his grandfather who had died thirty years before. The presence of the dead man behind his back transformed the whole of the solid tangible world stretching from the earth beneath his anus to the stars above his head into a thin, fragile web of fancy spun on the winds of nothingness, and he did not have the strength or the courage to turn his head around. All he dared do was get up and run for the gate in the fence with one hand holding the trousers flapping around his naked legs. Only when he was safely inside the yard did he stop to recover his breath and button his trousers in the light of Leontine's window. He pumped some water from the ancient pump to cool his face and neck and make himself present-able and peeped through the window before going into the room. He was relieved to see that the old woman was lying flat on her back sleeping soundly and there was no danger of her reading on his face that something so ridiculous had happened to him—as relieved as he had been to realize that the mistress of the farm had not seen him hitting his head on her floor. The picture of himself running for his life with his trousers around his knees now seemed very funny to him—even funnier than the picture of Raba sitting on the toilet with his wife's hand on his head had seemed to him when he was a child. Not wanting to wake Leontine by laughing out loud, he sat down and laughed silently to himself as his grandfather had laughed secretly to himself at the end of his life.

Leontine laughed too when he asked her on his return from the day's work (the same day that he had been sent to the pigsty to help castrate the pigs) if she believed in the immortality of the soul. Leontine laughed a lot because she was always in a good mood, and this would sometimes infu-riate her mistress beyond bearing. The mistress of the farm took everything very seriously indeed and therefore (since everything, from the leaking roof to the broken plates which slipped out of her servant's hands at the sink and the cows sick with hoof-and-mouth disease, was perishable by nature, bound to wear out, and doomed to extinction in the end) she always went around with a depressed and agonized expres-sion on her face, bent down beneath the burden of the suffering and disintegrating world. She would say about Leontine, "She's not serious, that Leontine, she's a frivolous woman," and when she was angry she would yell at her, "Get out of my sight, you heartless animal!" The first Sunday Gabriel arrived from Paris, and in fact the whole of that first week, he heard her muttering at Leontine, "Heartless animal. You heartless animal. Oh what a scandal—God almighty, what a scandal!" This was all because of the following incident. That Sunday a memorial service for the village men who had fallen in the Great War ("on the fields of honor," in the words of the priest) had been held in the Church of St. Anne. Because of Leontine—according to her mistress—the two old ladies had reached the church a little late and hurried silently to take their places beside the village doctor who was standing bareheaded among the rest of the congregation with his black Sunday top hat lying on the seat next to him. When the priest finished his memorial address in honor of the fallen and gave the congregation the sign to be seated, the mistress of the farm, who was excited and moved by the solemnity of the painful occasion as well as agitated by the late arrival for which, as mentioned above, her servant was to blame, sat down on the black top hat, which crumpled beneath her with a silken squeak. The doctor paled and gave her an angry glare as she hurried to straighten the hat and smooth its crumples as best she could, returning it to him with an expression of profound apology on her face. If it had not been for Leontine everything might have passed off quietly, but that heartless animal burst out laughing in her face so loudly that the whole congregation turned to look at them, outraged, and the priest interrupted his sermon to say, "It appears that certain ladies in the congregation need to be reminded of the fact that they are in a place of worship and in the middle of a service in memory of the fallen who died on the fields of honor." What hurt the mistress of the farm more than anything else was that the priest had said "ladies," that he had used the plural and included her in the scandal, when it was only Leontine who had laughed. In order to correct this mistaken impression she was forced to drag herself about the village, leaning on Leontine's arm, for a whole week, until she had visited every single house in it and explained to everyone that it was not she, but only Leontine, who had laughed in church.

It was probably this full free laughter without reservations or inhibitions that more than anything else made Leontine look so much younger than her mistress. When the latter told Gabriel that her servant was several years older than she was he found it impossible to believe her, and put it down to the same kind of exaggeration of other people's ages which was characteristic of his mother, but then Leontine herself confirmed it. She was nimble and agile in her movements, and even in her gait, despite the fact that she had a slight limp. Not a real limp exactly, but a kind of halt in her left leg as if the knee were stiff. Leontine would sing at her work, and it was from her that Gabriel learned the folk songs of the district like "On My Way I Met the Corn-Reaper's Daughter," and "It's Written in the Sky." She laughed too when he remonstrated (very mildly, it's true) with her for bringing him breakfast in bed and protested that it was not right that she, who had been placed over him by the mistress of the farm and told to keep him hard at work, should get up before him every morning to prepare the bitter, fragrant coffee and spread the hot rolls with butter and jam for him. Leontine gave him a number of reasons—some touching on health, that it was necessary for her health to get up early in the morning and exercise her body, and some on pleasure, that it was a pleasure for her to wake him up in the morning with the good, strong smell of coffee—all of which succeeded in convincing him that it was his duty to go on allowing her to bring him his breakfast in bed, especially since this duty was a very enjoyable one despite the feelings of guilt that accompanied it.

"I know it's a funny question," said Gabriel, "but still,

please tell me whether you believe in the immortality of the soul."

"What's it got to do with belief?" she said. "I see and I know what I see."

Gabriel was uncertain of the old woman's meaning.

"So then you don't believe?" he asked.

"Of course I don't," she said. "I thought you'd already realized that I was a heretic, and that's why the boss is always so cross with me. All I have is what my eyes see and what I know for myself." She burst into loud peals of laughter again and Gabriel found himself sympathizing for a moment with the mistress of the farm, who would sometimes be driven to despair by Leontine's laughter. She pointed to the night-cupboard holding the splendid chamber pot and when her laughter died away enough for her to talk she said, "You know, I put the chamber pot there for you because I thought you might be afraid of the ghosts in the night."

Gabriel tried irritably to bring her back to the point. "So your eyes see that a man is dead and buried, and you know that that's the end of it. He was and is no more." He left the room and went out into the night without waiting for a renewed outbreak of boundless laughter.

With the smell of good, strong coffee in the air, he woke to see Leontine bringing him breakfast in bed, her eyes smiling on a world that had not reverted to chaos at the sight of a servant reigning and bore without disquiet the maidservant who had inherited from her mistress the honor of bringing breakfast in bed to the guest of high degree, who had forgotten that he was no longer a guest waking in the mas-ter's bed but had fallen to the rank of servant of a servant. "No, no, Leontine. You shouldn't be bringing me breakfast in bed, I should be bringing you breakfast in bed. Oh my God, what's going on here?" The hands of the big black clock cut the hour nine in a right angle from its face, and he was supposed to be up at six. "You forgot to wake me for work!" he cried, and jumped out of bed. "I forgot nothing," said Leontine. "You forgot that it's Sunday today, the day of rest." Now he noticed the ruffled white lace apron on her dress and the traditional lace cap standing on her head like a pretty little tower, as well as the smell of the red and white and pink carnations she had picked in the garden and placed in a vase on the table and in little jars standing on the shelves.

Gabriel preferred the smell of carnations to that of any other flower except jasmine. "Carnations were my son Marcel's favorite flower," she said, "and he died twenty years ago today, at nine o'clock in the morning. He fell in the first battle for the Marne." Without any change in the smiling expression of her face and the light in her eyes she told him the story of that day twenty years ago. She was standing in the corner of the room in the morning, about to wind the clock which had just that minute stopped. When she touched the pendulum everything went dark and she stopped breathing and heard her son Marcel crying, "Mother, Mother, I can't breathe," and saw him vanish beneath a landslide of smoking earth. She saw him die eight hundred kilometers away and knew there was nothing for her to do but wait for his name to appear on the next list of the fallen. But it appeared instead among the names of the missing, and it was only several weeks later, when the shells of the German counterattack tore up the trenches of the first French attack that the body of her wounded son, who had been buried alive under the fallen earth, was discovered. She said nothing to her husband, who was ill in bed with his last and fatal illness and who was, besides, "afraid of ghosts," and had been ever since the death of their little girl, Lizette, who had died of pneumonia fifteen years before her brother was killed. One night, when her husband went outside to relieve himself under the oak tree beyond the fence, he saw the dead Lizette standing in front of him. He was so frightened that he ran for his life, leaving his trousers in the field behind him. The sweet little Lizette had been very dear to Leontine's heart and she too wanted to see her. Bathed in perspiration and trembling with fear, she went into the fields in the middle of the night and called, "Lizette, Lizette, come to me, Lizette, I want to see you, Lizette," but Lizette did not come. Every night Leontine went out into the fields in fear and hope crying, "Lizette, Lizette," until everybody said that she had gone out of her wits with grief for the dead child, but Lizette did not come. She stopped going out into the fields in the middle of the night to wait for her and she stopped hoping. One summer night, when she was sitting and embroidering a blouse, she lifted her eyes to the open window and saw Lizette standing next to the gate. She dropped the blouse and ran to her by the shortest, quickest, and most direct way—through the open window by her side. "I feel better now, Mummy," said Lizette. "The pneumonia's gone and I can play outside next to the river again."

"When will I see you again?" Leontine asked, but Lizette was gone. Leontine knew that she would come back to her as soon as she could, and she did come back on two more occasions until she put on a new body and came back to the world as a newborn baby, just as they said in the village—"one child dies and another is born." The soul of a child doesn't have to wait as long as the soul of a grown-up person, which may have to wander naked in the world for centuries. It was only when she came back home that Leontine began to feel the pain in her left knee, which had been hurt when she jumped out of the window, damaging the kneecap so that to this very day she could not bend it as she used to. Lizette's soul had put on the body of a baby born four months after she died, but Marcel, who had been a man of twenty-one when he was killed, had been waiting these twenty years, free to gladden his mother's heart and entertain her with his jokes and tricks. He was a great one for a

joke, was Marcel, and sometimes he also sang to her and
taught her the new songs he had learned in the regiment.
Her mistress who saw and heard nothing but herself and the
mooing of the cows and the crowing of the cocks and the
rubbish preached by that drunken old fool Père Legoffic in
church on Sundays, who always asked her, "Aren't you afraid
of all those spooks of yours? Now if my late husband were
suddenly to appear before me in the kitchen I would die of
fright on the spot." "So she says to me, and I say to her that if
she really loved her husband she would overcome her fear
and want to see him. The trouble with her is that she believes
in all old Legoffic's nonsense. When that old fool begins
pouring hellfire and brimstone on witchcraft and witches
who call up the spirits of the dead she goes pale and begins
to shake and she's afraid to look at me. And now she's all
ready to go to mass and I'm keeping her waiting." And the
moment the words came out of her mouth the voice of the
mistress of the farm was indeed heard calling in the yard,
"Leontine, Leontine, if you don't come at once we'll be late
for church again."

Gabriel looked out of the window and watched the two old
women walking arm in arm to church for Sunday mass. The
farther they got from the house and the closer they got to the
church the older the figure of the mistress of the farm
looked and the younger the figure of Leontine looked. Old
and weak and burdened down with the troubles of the farm
the mistress leaned on the arm of her servant (who strode
forward with a straight back and a sprightly air despite the
stiffness of her left knee), stopping every now and then
despite her fear of coming late to say, "Please stop galloping
like a horse on its way back to the stable. Have a little
consideration for my condition." On their way back, the
mistress of the farm looked even more bowed down and
Leontine even sprightlier than when they set out.

She came into the room humming the song "It's Written in

the Sky" to herself and with a dexterous flick of her wrist loosened the strings of her cap from under her chin and threw it up in the air as if she were liberating a giant white butterfly, which flew up to the ceiling and came to rest on the red carnations standing in the vase on the middle of the table. "She's got a green soul," said Gabriel to himself in Arabic. He had heard this expression used once in his life, in Arabic: it was when he was a child about ten years old listening to a conversation between his father and Judge Gutkin. His father bent down to whisper something in his friend's ear, and they both burst out laughing, and Dan Gutkin slapped his thighs and laughed loudly and cried in Arabic, "Yehuda Prosper Bey, you've got a green soul. Upon my word, you've got a green soul." Afterward his father explained to him that the judge had used an Arabic expression that meant that a person was young at heart, like a fresh young plant which was bright green and full of the sap of life. Now, watching the hand throwing the white cap up into the air, Gabriel realized that the age of Leontine's soul did not correspond to or depend on the age of her body: it belonged to a completely different cycle. When her body's time was up Leontine's soul would fly out of it as young as the day it had entered it, with an electric whir of green butterfly wings.

"I knew it, I knew it, I knew it!" she cried triumphantly. "I knew that I would have a happy meeting today!" And whom had she met in church if not little Charlot—Charles Letroquer, Marcel's childhood friend. Charlot and Marcel had gone to school together and joined the army together to fight in the Great War and they had even been together in the trenches in the first attack on the Marne. Now this little Charlot was an important man, head of the Breton office of the famous removal firm of Calberson, which was situated in the county town of Le Mans, and he had a special car to take him to and from work every day. It always made her happy to meet Marcel's friends, but especially little Charlot, who had such interesting stories to tell about what had happened once upon a time and what was happening now. Little Charlot came back the next morning with the smell of the coffee and the rolls. "Today," said Leontine to Gabriel, "you won't work in the yard or the fields. You'll go straight to little Charlot and he'll tell you what to do next." Strange sparks glinted in her eyes as she spoke, and it was these rather than her actual instructions (which were strange enough in themselves) that led Gabriel to conclude that the old woman had gone out of her mind. When he tried to bring her back to her senses, saying, "What on earth?" and "What in the world are you talking about?" she interrupted him firmly with "Don't start arguing," and left the room. It was from little Charlot, and not from Leontine herself, that he discovered what the old woman was about: since she knew what the farmhands earned she calculated that Gabriel would have to work three months on the farm to pay her mistress what he owed her, and since she knew her mistress, she knew that the moment those three months were up he would be turned off the farm without a penny in his pockets. She had therefore asked little Charlot to take Gabriel on as a porter with the removal firm, calculating that with what he earned there he would be able to pay off his debt within a month and still have something left over. When Gabriel tried to thank her the next day (for her kindness even more than for the material advantage which he would obtain from this arrangement) she brushed him off with a wave of her hand and a peculiar glint in her eye which made his heart contract inexplicably. "Hurry off to work now," she said. "Little Charlot is already standing and waiting outside his house for the car. If you don't run you won't arrive at your destination today."

Gabriel's destination that day was the north of Paris, where he had to load and unload crates which had arrived by rail from across the borders. "If you look sharp," said little Charlot with a wink to Gabriel and the other porters climbing into the giant truck that was to take them to the metropolis, "you'll have some time left over to enjoy yourselves in Paris when the job's done. But don't go to the Place Pigalle or the Champs-Élysées. They'll skin you alive there and you're not American tourists. Take my advice and go down to the bottom of the Rue St. Denis next to the Church of St. Eustache. You'll have lots of pretty girls to choose from over there and the prices are reasonable."

Before he arrived at the bottom of the Rue St. Denis by the Church of St. Eustache he went into the wrong entrance when delivering the last parcel of the day. He was sent to a town called Noyon on the northeastern outskirts of Paris to deliver parcels there, and the mistake in the entrance came about as a result of the high spirits which overtook both of them, him and the driver of the truck: because the day's work had gone smoothly and quickly and would soon be over and they would be driving full speed ahead for the Rue St. Denis and the *embarras de richesses* that awaited them there, they both began to sing at the tops of their voices, breaking into the Breton folk song "It's Written in the Sky" as they drew up at the entrance to the Huguenot Hostel, to one of whose residents their last parcel was addressed. The gates opened and two heads—belonging, as they discovered later, to the concierge and the messenger boy, respectively— peeped out amazed at the sudden burst of joy shattering the atmosphere of fixed, frozen calm in the hostel. As the gates opened, Gabriel's eye was caught by the high stone wall, which reminded him of his childhood love for the high stone walls of Jerusalem concealing their secrets from the world, only here he did not feel drawn toward the secrets of the foreign life going on behind the hostel wall because of the flavor of the atmosphere, which was disagreeable to him because of the peculiar smell it exuded, a smell of ancient sheets soaked in carbolic soap and stiff with the starch of a strict, cold, alien life: a life firmly anchored in the calculations of this world, padded by self-righteousness, and fortified by a pious conviction of salvation in the world to come. When Gabriel walked into the inner courtyard with the parcel in his hands, the manageress called out angrily to the concierge and the messenger boy, "What's going on here? Everyone to his place! Everyone to his place!" in the same panic-stricken tone and in the very same words the mistress of the farm had used when she threw him out of her house to go and live with Leontine. At the same time her eye fell on the strange porter who after confusing her subordinates with his wild singing was now standing in the main entrance to the hotel, parcel in hand, like the proverbial straw that broke the camel's back. She said sharply, "Hey, you, you Breton, the service entrance, please, the service entrance!" and when Gabriel turned on his heel and went outside and came back in again at the service entrance, she was there waiting for him. "Is that what they taught you in your country, in Brittany? To make deliveries through the front door?" This conclusion about his origins she had apparently come to from hearing him sing the Breton folk song with the driver in the pure Breton accent he had picked up during his stay in Carnac. As for the expression "your country," he had already had ample occasion to observe that the French called the province of their birth—and sometimes even the town—their "country." Thus, for example, the laundress who came from the city of Bordeaux would say, "In my country, in Bordeaux."

The hotel manageress already had her hand out for the usual tip when her eye fell on the address on the parcel and she realized that it was not supplies for the hostel, but a private parcel for one of the residents. "Room number nineteen, second floor on the right," she said curtly without a further glance in his direction, but as he began climbing the stairs she decided to add some further instructions for the edification of a person who in the light of his previous behavior was evidently sorely in need of it: "And don't knock too loudly on the door, and don't forget to take your hat off to the gentleman. He is one of the leading pastors of our church—a great man, a great man!"

Gabriel knocked three times on the great man's door. Politely, as the mistress of the farm had been in the habit of knocking on his door in the days of his own greatness, with knocks that were neither peremptory and impertinent on the one hand, nor unduly modest and self-effacing on the other, but respectful without surrendering self-respect. The knocks were the same and so were the measured pauses between them, but the door was different and its voice differed accordingly. His door in the farmhouse was a heavy antique door and made a dry, muffled sound whereas here there was a crisp, ringing echo to the lively tempo of his knocking which, he felt, augured well for the *pourboire:* he would get a decent tip, he thought, although nothing extravagant, since as far as he knew respectable clergymen were not in the habit of throwing their money around. This expectation of a tip put him in mind again of the great esteem in which he had previously been held by the mistress of the farm. Since she herself was the owner of the establishment she did not, of course, accept tips, and when on his first morning on the farm he had unthinkingly offered her something, out of the habits formed in years of living in Paris hotels, she had refused to accept it but had continued nevertheless to knock on his door every morning with the utmost politeness, respectful but dignified, the mistress of the house bringing her guest breakfast in bed with her own hands. As long as she thought he was a rich man, she held him in deep respect even when she herself was not actually getting any of his money, and when he handed over the money due her for his board and lodging every week the expression on her face reminded him of the prayer "Blessed be God who dispenses of his wisdom to flesh and blood," because she looked as if he were giving her not simply banknotes which passed from hand to hand but slices cut out of his own spiritual substance. When the notes were in her hands and before she put them away in a hiding place known to her alone, she would sit on the edge of the sofa with her mouth pursed and a fixed, devout look in her eyes, passing the banknotes slowly through her fingers with a kind of yearning rustle. She was very anxious about his spendthrift ways in those days, always on the alert lest he spoil her farmhands with extravagant tips for their occasional little services, but especially careful to warn him against the greedy Leontine who tidied his room every day and was therefore the recipient of regular tips. "Don't take any notice of her smiles—" she said, "all she's interested in is the *pourboire*."

Pourboire—the French word and its literal translation, "for drinking"—emerging from his father's mouth rose up in his memory from the depths of his childhood, floating on waves of heat radiating from the stones baking in the naked sun glaring down on the walls and houses of the street the Jews called "For the Sake of Zion" and the Christians called "St. Paul's Road," which led from the New Gate down to the bottom of the Arab quarter of Mussrara. They were sitting in a coach that was red inside and black outside, and two brown horses were driving them around the walls of the Old City and through the streets of the new city to show them to an important visitor who had arrived in Jerusalem. The visitor must have been important because his father was wearing all his decorations, both the Spanish and the Ottoman ones, and Señor Moïse was wearing the official livery of a kawass, and holding his special staff in the hand of his outstretched arm, to bang on the cobblestones and make way for them through the alleyways of the Old City as he paced ceremoniously in front of them. Back in the coach again his father explained the meaning of the word *baksheesh* to the visitor. *Baksheesh,* he said, was a Persian word meaning "give," and its translation was *pourboire.*

"What's *pourboire?*" asked Gabriel. *"Pourboire,"* said his father, "means 'for drinking' and is the French for *baksheesh.*" At this moment the coach drove up to the eye clinic which the famous young Dr. Landau had recently opened in For-the-Sake-of-Zion Street. Outside the coach the white walls baking in the sun hurt his eyes with their glare, and all along the pavements Arab beggars sat exposing their maimed and mutilated limbs for the benefit of the rich effendis in their carriages, shouting, *"Baksheesh, baksheesh!"* They alighted between a man whose legs were two stumps, dragging himself toward them on his hands and backside, and a young boy as thin as a dry twig, waving the raw stump of his arm at them. Gabriel felt sick at the sight of all this mutilated flesh and the stink of its filth and turned his face toward Mount Scopus. While his father was still busy lecturing the visitor from abroad on the subject of *baksheesh,* the latter, confused by the heat and glare and inattentive to the words of his host, made a fatal mistake and began distributing a handful of coins to the beggars and cripples nearest him. The attack was immediate and shocking. Suddenly they found themselves surrounded on all sides by stumps of arms and legs, amputated noses, crushed faces, and gaping wounds crying, *"Baksheesh, baksheesh"* in an increasingly menacing chant. Gabriel was forced to push the bone sticking out of the thin boy's arm away from him with all his strength, and then they had a moment's respite when the visitor flung another handful of coins onto the pavement a few feet away. The beggars fell on the scattered coins, scrambling and grabbing, and Gabriel was afraid for a moment that the one-armed boy, who in his agility had reached the money first, would be killed by the blows and kicks of his fellows. But these diversionary tactics did not prevent the main force from blocking their way, and they succeeded in

reaching the entrance to the clinic only after Señor Moïse
had used his staff to hack a path clear for them and unexpected aerial support had scattered their attackers and
given the suffocating Gabriel space to breathe. When he
lifted his eyes in amazement to see where his salvation had
come from, he saw the Arab coachman standing up in his
seat with his stomach sticking out in front of him and his red
tarboosh tilted over his left eye at a combative angle, crack-
ing his whip right and left onto the mutilated flesh gaping at
his feet.

When they were already standing in the entrance to the
clinic, a coach like their own drove past with an Arab effendi
and a child inside it. The effendi lifted his hand in a ceremo-
nious salaam to Yehuda Prosper Bey and Gabriel's father
responded with a string of congratulations on his approaching wedding and blessings on his head and house and cor-
dial wishes for his health and happiness and prosperity in
the days to come. "That's Mahmoud Effendi of Bethlehem,"
he explained to his visitor with a smile, "on his way to the suk
with Daoud, his first wife's son, to buy presents for the
beautiful young Dunya who is to be, God willing, his third
wife."

"Dunya?" repeated the visitor in a Russian accent with an
inquiring frown. "Isn't that a Russian name? Is she a Russian
girl then? Did her parents come from Russia?" "Pure Arab
stock," said Yehuda Prosper Bey. "Her family's an Arab
family and a good one—Masrur. The name Dunya is an
Arabic word meaning 'world,' and Mahmoud Effendi says
he would give the whole world for one of her smiles."

From the entrance to the clinic Gabriel looked out and saw
the white glare of the walls shimmering in the naked light of
the sun and the wheels of Mahmoud Effendi's carriage
spraying the cripples on the pavement with a fine gray dust,
like the dust that rose from the paths between the graves on
the Mount of Olives. "The whole world indeed!" said the

visitor with a sarcastic smile. "I'm already familiar with the exaggerations of the Arab mind from reading *The Arabian Nights.*" Yehuda Prosper Bey burst out laughing. "To give this world," he said, pointing to the clouds of gray dust outside, "for a smile of love is no exaggeration, my dear fellow. I wouldn't even call it noble or generous. Only an idiot would take this world in exchange for a smile. Only an idiot would take it for nothing, *baksheesh, pourboire!*"

"*Baksheesh, pourboire*—here in the Levant everything gets mixed up," said the judge, who had come to say good-bye to Yehuda Prosper's son, about to sail for France to study medicine. Dan Gutkin was then the youngest judge on the Supreme Court bench, and his name had already appeared on the King of England's birthday honors list as an Officer of the British Empire. "It's only in the demotic Arabic of the Levant that the word *baksheesh* is used to designate three quite different things—bribes, charity, and tips, but any self-respecting Arab with a little respect for his language, even if he isn't an expert at literary Arabic, will use the word *baksheesh* only for the first of these, for the bribe. If he means charity he'll say '*zakaat,*' and if he means a tip he'll say '*rashum al hidamaat*'—which is the *pourboire*. The *pourboire,* or tip"—here the judge's face assumed the stern, grave, and emphatic expression which in court was reserved exclusively for the reading of his verdict and outside it for those remarks he did not expect to be taken seriously—"the *pourboire,* as I was saying, is one of the two basic criteria for evaluating the civilization of a people or a country. The other is prostitution. Yes—prostitution and tipping."

Gabriel broke the rules of tipping in Paris the first day he set foot on its pavements despite the fact that he had been instructed in all their particulars by Judge Dan Gutkin, who had seen fit to initiate him into the conventions of the *pourboire* and the etiquette of prostitution in the great city when he came to say good-bye to him before he left for France. He broke them in the big public lavatory in the Métro station. You had to tip the attendant whenever you went into one of the cubicles, but to his surprise the attendant standing there to open the door of the cubicle for him and hand him the paper to wipe himself was a woman in a white smock and cap who, in addition to attending to the duties mentioned above and keeping the place clean, also polished the gentlemen's boots for them on a stand set up for this purpose in the corridor next to the big mirrors. When he emerged from the cubicle and saw her face he was flooded with a feeling of warmth and compassion: the lines of her eyes and her smile reminded him of his mother when she was in a good mood and sang the songs of her schooldays to herself. The woman asked him if he would like to have his shoes shined, and he felt a momentary pang at the thought that his mother too might one day have to clean public lavatories and polish strangers' boots for a living. But when he had seated himself on the high comfortable chair and placed his foot on the copper-decorated polishing stool, his apprehensions disappeared. His mother would never go to clean public lavatories, not even if she were suddenly left for some catastrophic reason without a roof over her head or a crust of bread to eat and she had no other way at all of earning her living. She would send her elder sister, Pnina, to do it. She herself wouldn't go out to work at all, not even if she were offered the most respectable and prestigious job in the world—say, for example, to be the headmistress of the Evelina de Rothschild School for Girls. And what if Aunt Pnina were dead? In that case Mrs. Gentilla Luria could be trusted to find herself another Pnina. "I wasn't brought into this world to clean public lavatories!" he heard his mother's voice in his inner ear. "And this woman devotedly—yes, devotedly!— polishing my shoes, she was brought into the world to clean public lavatories?" he heard his own voice answering his mother in front of the lavatory attendant who was good-humoredly getting on with the job she had not been brought into the world to do, her face alight with a bright, kind smile. It was this bright kindness in her response to her customers, as if she were a hostess happy to welcome her guests and offer them home-baked cookies to eat, that chiefly touched Gabriel's heart. She conveyed the impression of a well-brought-up girl from a good family, spoiled and softened by the luxuries of the big city, who had been forced by some financial catastrophe to go out and work at a menial job because she had never been trained for a profession, and who continued in the performance of this menial service to display the same good manners and desire to please she had learned at home.

"I'm a stranger here, from another country," he said. "I've just arrived in Paris."

"I too am a stranger here," she said, lifting her shining eyes to him. She looked at least fifty, but there was still something youthful about her. "And I too arrived here recently from my country."

"And I thought you were a Frenchwoman and this was your native city."

"No, no," she laughed. "I'm not French and I wasn't born in the big city. I'm a countrywoman from Brittany, from the little village of Carnac."

These words, for some reason, had the effect of moving Gabriel's heart even more than before, and when he stood up to go he rummaged in his pocket and gave her a whole handful of coins. "No, no!" she cried, sorting out the tip which was due her. "Put the rest back in your pocket at once," and she began explaining the whole business of the percentages due for service, which he already knew. "But I want to give it all to you," he said, blushing with embarrassment. "Don't be a fool," she said gently. "You're a young man and you need your money, especially in a big strange city. Money can give you the most important thing in the world—freedom!"

"It must be terribly hard," said Gabriel, feeling a great fool, "to have to slave your life away in a public lavatory."

"You're quite wrong, young man," she said. "I've never felt freer before. I've never been as happy in my whole life as I am now."

The brightness in her eyes accompanied him on his way to the hotel like a kind of reconciliation, softening the sting of the contradiction between the freedom which was the most important thing in the world to her and the slavery to the public lavatory, where she was happier than she had ever been before in her life. "I suppose there must be something religious at the bottom of it," he said to himself, recalling stories about nuns who devoted themselves to all kinds of difficult and disgusting tasks out of religious ecstasy. In this too, however, he was due for a surprise. Arriving for a superfluous shoe-shine on All Saints' Day, he remarked that thanks to all those saints even antireligious students could enjoy a day's holiday and freedom from their studies.

"I never had the honor of meeting any of the saints you speak of," she answered surprisingly with her bright, innocent look, "but if they're anything like the saints I do know, I can tell you that it wasn't holidays and freedom they brought to the world, but slavery. The saints I knew made my life a hell on earth, and the person who saved me from it was a woman they regarded as a witch, a pagan sorceress."

The saints she knew were her mother and her husband. Her mother's virtues were famous not only in the village of her birth but in the whole province, in all the villages hugging the coastline of the Wild Coast and Morbihan Bay, and after she had donated a hundred thousand francs for the reconstruction of the ancient village church the priest himself said that she deserved to be canonized as a Catholic saint. Most of the land in the district belonged to her, but she never gave her own daughter a penny to buy herself a sweet in the village shop, which was because she was a saint. Because she was a saint she brought her daughter up on stories of the strange and awful agonies lying in wait for the souls of the damned in the world to come, and because she was a saint she married her off, when her time came, to the sole heir of the owner of the adjacent farm. Her husband was a saint not because of what he did for the sake of his faith, but because of what he didn't do for its sake. He was a great believer in the liberation of Brittany from the French yoke. If only he could have, he would have banished the French together with their language and customs from all of Brittany and ruled it himself with a strong hand and an outstretched arm and tremendous majesty, from the Atlantic Ocean to the city of Nantes, like the Grand Duke of Brittany Nomino, whose fame and glory had spread throughout the world. He would have aroused his fellow Bretons from their apathy, sold his father's lands and the rest of the family property, and bought guns for the war of liberation with the proceeds; he would have organized and equipped with his own money whole fighting battalions of peasants and workers, conquered first the village police station, then the provincial prefecture, and then on and on until he ruled the whole land and was famous throughout the world. But the first thing was to take the village police station. All these dreams of glory, all this heroism, all this fame and splendor he sacrificed—because he, too, was a saint—on the altar of his family. When his sick old mother and father heard that he intended selling all the family estates it hit them very hard, and when they realized that the money from the sale of the land was to be used to buy guns to break into the village police station their horror and outrage knew no bounds. If he had put his great idea into practice it would have been the death of them. But he was not so selfish and ambitious as to sacrifice his family on the altar of his ideals: on the contrary, he offered up his own life, every single moment of it slipping by wasted and profitless never to return, as a sacrifice on the altar of his family— which consisted, after his marriage, mainly of his wife. The

sorrows of his martyred life and blasted hopes he drowned
by day in alcohol and by night in violent arguments with his
wife, in the course of which he slapped her face and beat her
black and blue—especially after the waning of his sexual
powers. To tell the truth, even when he was a young man in
his prime it was not in the marriage bed that her husband's
greatest glory lay, but it was only after his sexual powers had
dwindled away to nothing that she began to get a real taste
of the glories of his strong right arm. Caught between these
two saints, her mother and her husband, her life flickered
and faded until the old maid Leontine saved her from the
pair of them. It was Leontine who helped her to run away
from home and, what was more important, it was Leontine
who freed her from the bonds of fear that had tied her to
her mother and her husband all her life and gave her the
courage to act.

"How did she do it?" asked Gabriel.

"I don't know," said the shoe-shiner. "It's a special kind of
power she has. In our village people think she's a witch, a
kind of sorceress with magic powers."

Ever since the embarrassment of the first time, Gabriel
had been careful to give her exactly the tip due her, but
when he offered it to her now she lifted her shining eyes to
him from the low stool on which she sat and said with a
smile, "Today you can give me as much as you like because
it's All Saints' Day."

"As for Calvin's attitude to the Catholic saints . . ." said one
of the two gentlemen passing Gabriel in the corridor, and
behind the door in the interval between one polite knock
and the next he heard the steps of the pastor who was
regarded by the hotel manageress as such an important
man. If she had been a Catholic and not a Huguenot, she
would probably have called him a "saint" instead of a "great
man." As the footsteps approached the door he thought he

heard someone singing, as if the important pastor were humming the tune of a song to himself—not a psalm or a Christian hymn but a popular Hebrew song that had been a favorite of Gabriel's in the days when he was a student at the Ezra Teachers' Seminary, "In the Wood on the Hill of the Three." He had suffered a similar delusion once before, when he was out walking on the Wild Coast at night and he heard voices coming from the bay. Then he thought he heard the voices singing, "Here in the land of our fathers' longing all our hopes will come true . . ." and it was only when he drew closer to the young people sitting in the boat that he realized they were singing the Breton folk song "It's Written in the Sky." Then a vague terror had gripped his heart but now that it had all happened before and he knew that it was only a delusion he was amused by the comical tricks played on him by his imagination and he could already hear himself telling his mother about the curious thing that had happened to him in the French town of Noyon on the northeastern outskirts of Paris. He had been working as a porter for the big removal firm of Calberson, delivering a parcel to a Huguenot pastor staying in a hostel for Protestant clergymen. Behind the door he heard the Christian minister walking up and down and praying softly to his God. When he bent down to knock on the door the words of the song reached his ears, and imagine his surprise on discovering that it wasn't a prayer at all but the tune of a popular song, and not just any popular song but the favorite of his own youth, "In the Wood on the Hill of the Three." The Christian priest was walking around and around his room and singing to himself, "Oh, young man, do not touch me, My heart feels an awful foreboding, In the Wood on the Hill of the Three, The vision of beauty appeared, Slender as a palm, white as ivory, In the Wood on the Hill of the Three . . ." His mother would look at him sorrowfully, and a little angrily too, and say with a sigh, "Oh, Gabby, Gabby, you and your Oriental fantasies! Tell me, what makes you any better than your father, the old Turkish adulterer? Well, what's the wonder? Flesh of his flesh you are, and bone of his bone."

The door opened and the minister held out his hand to take the parcel, rummaging with his other hand in his pocket for a few coins to tip the porter. When he lifted his head Gabriel saw, beneath the brim of his black hat, the face of little Srulik, of Israel Shoshan, his old friend from the distant days of Rabbi Avremale's Little Yeshiva, and Rav Kook's Yeshiva, and the Ezra Teachers' Seminary.

Little Srulik's face suddenly appearing beneath this black hat with the same expression, strained and hesitant and defeated but at the same time stubbornly rebellious, as it had worn during their last year at the Ezra Teachers' Seminary, when his friend was suffering the worst agonies of his great and foolish love, flooded Gabriel—together with the shock of his stunned disbelief—with a wave of warmth and gaiety, but his burst of happy laughter was checked for a moment by little Srulik's panic. A grayish pallor spread over his pink cheeks protruding on either side of the Chinese-slanting eyes behind his big round spectacles, and he fell backward, bumping into the table and holding on to it with one hand while with the other, which still held the tip he had been about to give the porter, he shaded his eyes as if to protect them from the terrible apparition that had suddenly sprung up before him. When he had recovered he muttered something about modern man carrying his modern cross printed across his back, and Gabriel burst out laughing again and said, "Srulik, Srulik! Leave all that boring non-sense about modern man and modern crosses alone and tell me, for God's sake, what on earth are you doing here?"

"What am I doing here?" repeated Srulik, setting his spectacles straight on his nose and smoothing his cheeks, which began to blossom into their habitual pinkness again. "I'm preparing a lecture on the Last Supper. I have a few ideas of my own on the meaning of the Last Supper which are, I believe, rather original and could contribute something to an understanding of the redemption of the soul by and in the Messiah . . ." In growing excitement and enthusiasm he began to develop the main points of his lecture for Gabriel, who leaned the parcel against the bed, sat down in a chair, crossed his arms, and said to himself, "Maybe I really am dead?" The terror he had just seen on little Srulik's face at the sight of him was the terror of a man suddenly accosted by a ghost. Gabriel had once read something about the ways in which you can test yourself to see if you are still alive, or if your soul hasn't perhaps escaped from your body without being aware of it. The most reliable of these methods, according to that book, was the shadow-test: if you can find your shadow it means there is a body to cast it. When he read these things in order to amuse himself with the curiosities of folklore he never dreamed that the question would one day be a real one for him. "Things have come to a pretty pass," he thought, and burst out laughing in a kind of hilarity that knew no bounds. "Here I am looking for my own shadow! Maybe little Srulik's dead too, like me, only he doesn't know it?" His hilarity grew as he looked around the room and failed to find any definite shadow either for himself or for Srulik. In the grayish light of the eternal mists surrounding the towns of the north and hiding the face of the sun from them, all he could see were soft, delicate shades of color merging into each other with no dividing lines between them.

A Voyage to Ur
of the Chaldees

To Shula

Points of Reference

1.

Overture in the B'nai B'rith Library

THE FIRST CASUALTY in the nocturnal battle for control of the airspace over the Street of the Prophets (which raged between the Chopin waltzes emerging from the home of Dr. Landau, the eye specialist, and the love songs of Farid el-Atrash blaring from the newly installed radio sets in the Arab cafés) was our landlady, Mrs. Gentilla Luria.

On clear summer nights, the piano strains escaping from the innermost recesses of the Landau residence, secluded behind its high garden wall, would float all the way down the Street of the Prophets and into our windows, opened wide to the stars. Sometimes the notes dropping from the keyboard would splash into the Arab tunes streaming up from the Damascus Gate and the Mussrara Quarter into my round east-facing window, and the night air would vibrate with a growing tension. For the Western rhythms did not blend with the Oriental tunes to create a smoothly flowing harmony—as sometimes happens when music absorbs a melody from a foreign culture and succeeds in assimilating and digesting it—but instead produced an explosive compound which needed only a spark to ignite it.

As soon as the first notes fell from the piano like cool, smooth marbles into the tremulous vibrato of the guitar

strings accompanying the Arab crooner (some said that he
wasn't an Arab at all, but an Egyptian Jew, and some said
that he was a Druze), Mrs. Luria would succumb to a violent
headache, requiring the immediate attention of her sister,
Pnina. "Hurry up and soak the handkerchief in cold
water"—this was the handkerchief which would be bound
around her head like a turban to relieve its sufferings—"and
close the windows! Hurry, hurry! Can't you hear—the doctoress's Polish owl is at it again! I'll see him in hell, and his
lady-friend with him! Such a thing could never have happened if my husband were still alive. He would have told the
mayor, Ragueb Bey Nashashibi himself, to stop that creature
from banging on the piano and preventing the whole street
from getting a decent night's sleep. Have you ever heard
such a thing? An entire street should suffer just because the
only lover Dr. Landau's wife can find is a Polish owl who's
good for nothing but thumping on a piano! At least if he
would play a proper tune to warm a person's heart. But no,
he's not capable of that either. And what's the wonder? If he
was a proper pianist he wouldn't need that hysterical cat
who's never managed to find herself a real man—nothing
but broken vessels who imagine their moanings and groanings are works of art."

I never met any of the "broken vessels" who had sheltered
under Mrs. Landau's wing before the "Polish owl," but with
regard to the latter's musical ability Mrs. Luria's description
did justice to only one part of the external truth, and had
less to do with his actual talents than with his relations with
the public—in other words, his stage fright. So great was
this stage fright that it paralyzed his arms and made his
fingers play notes that were forced and frozen, and sometimes even wrong, giving him a bad reputation. Alone in his
room, however, especially at night, he was wonderful. Half
awake, half asleep, I would suddenly hear a clear note falling into the open window frame like a star coming out,

immediately filling the empty blackness with waves of secret longing, vibrating to the bottom of my being and stopping my breath with the materialization of the second note in the light of the second star, and then another and another, until the whole of space filled up again with rhythmic waves of longing for the missing points of light needed to complete the constellation of a sign of the Zodiac: the sign of Gemini. But scarcely had this been done than the piano began to play again, scattering here and there, in no discernible order, droplets of sound which crystallized into points of light on the trembling threads of longing to draw another sign—the sign of Aries, and next to it the signs of Leo and Taurus and Virgo. Only when the music died away did the dread come slowly back to take its place, the dread of the infinite spaces of the cold, dark void separating the stars which were meaninglessly suspended on nothing.

I had never met Dr. Landau's wife, the terrible woman who so infuriated Gabriel's mother, and of all the mysteries of the big house on the corner of Abyssinian Road, she was the only one who exerted no fascination on me; I felt nothing but pity for the old eye doctor who had fallen into her snares.

On my way to the library, when I passed his house, I imagined for some reason that one of the two old women crossing the road was the doctor's wife, and the other his sister-in-law. But six months later, when I was sitting in the reading room, it turned out that the two ladies in question were actually the aunts—his father's sisters—of Israel Shoshan, the little librarian of the B'nai B'rith Library. The elder sister's name was Elka, the younger's Ethel, and both sisters had something about them that was not of this world. When I first saw them in Abyssinian Road they seemed like visitors from another planet, not only because of their clothes but also because of their movements, and especially because of the look in their eyes, which was like the look of a convict emerging into the street after many years in jail and seeing that although it is still the street of bygone days, it now exists in another time, and therefore belongs to another world. In order to overcome the intense desire to return to the world of fantasy, and to find her way in this remote and alien land into which she had been cast, Elka would glance about her with constant alertness, and throw herself briskly and resolutely into daring acts—such as crossing the Street of the Prophets on the corner of Abyssinian Road, opposite the garden wall of Dr. Landau's house—dragging her sister willy-nilly behind her. Even before they started to cross the road, when they were still walking straight ahead, it was obvious that Elka was the bellwether, with Ethel trailing behind, unable to separate herself from her sister despite her resistance and resentment—a resentment that expressed itself chiefly in the way she mockingly imitated her elder sister's words, to the accompaniment of a dismissive gesture of her hand. When Elka stopped and said, "We'll cross the road here," Ethel stopped too and said derisively, "We'll cross here, we'll cross here, yes, of course, right here—just at the most dangerous spot!" And indeed, at that very moment the noise of a car engine was heard straining up the hill from the Damascus Gate, but Elka set out boldly nevertheless, scurrying across the street with rapid little steps, while Ethel took her life into her hands, following behind, muttering to herself.

This audacity immediately found its reward in the person of Dr. Ketter, who was walking straight ahead with his nose in a book. As they were crossing the road I saw three people emerging from my Uncle Zerah's bookshop: Uncle Zerah himself, in the company of a young female student, turning toward Princess Mary Street; while Dr. Ketter proceeded in a straight line along the sidewalk, where he bumped into the two women who had just arrived puffing and panting from the other side of the road. Booklets large and small peeped out of his pockets, and in his hands he held two big books, one on top of the other. The uppermost was open and he was reading it as he walked, but this did not prevent him from doffing his hat with a flourish, without taking his eyes off the book, stopping, or deviating from his course. The little librarian's aunts were not the only ones to receive so gallant a greeting. Dr. Ketter doffed his hat to all the women he encountered on his way—the women, not the men. Absorbed in his book, he took no notice of the men who crossed his path, not even when they greeted him; but whenever the flutter of a passing skirt caught the corner of his downcast eye, his right hand rose automatically to the brim of his hat. Thus it came about that Daoud Ibn Mahmoud, the chauffeur, that most manly of men, was chivalrously greeted by the doctor one day as he returned from the dry cleaner's with two leather skirts belonging to Dr. Landau's daughter over his arm. Dr. Ketter raised his hat with a sweeping gesture and continued on his way without taking his eyes off his book, leaving Daoud Ibn Mahmoud on the horns of an insoluble dilemma. Upon emerging from the car with the skirts over his arm, the chauffeur noticed the courteous doffing of the doctor's hat, and wished to return the greeting by immediately doffing his own peaked cap, but by the time he managed to free his arm of the skirts and raise his hand to the peak of his cap, Dr. Ketter had already turned away with—so it seemed to him—a grim expression of anger and offense on his face, which was still there at their next meeting, when Daoud Ibn Mahmoud attempted to anticipate the doctor's greeting with a loud and long salaam, according to all the rules of ritual and etiquette, and failed to receive so much as a nod in reply.

"Good afternoon, Dr. Ketter, good afternoon, Dr. Ketter," the sisters cried in an animated chorus, and giggled to each other. They were about to continue on their way to Abyssinian Road when Elka suddenly began running after him with pattering little steps, taking no notice of her sister's exhortations: "Elka, come back at once. Come back, I tell you, and stop making a fool of yourself." She caught up with him outside the Café Gat and pulled him once or twice by the sleeve until he lifted his eyes from his book. "Dr. Ketter," she said, "I have a piece of good advice for you. Important, useful advice: instead of holding those heavy books in your hands, why don't you hang a shelf on your chest?" He looked at her in astonishment, raised his hat with a muttered "Thank you, thank you very much," and continued on his way. In his habitual inattention to everything happening around him, he did not appear to have grasped the meaning of this female apparition at all, nor what she had come to tell him, but many years later we realized that the words of the late lamented Elka had, indeed, eventually succeeded in breaching his protective armor and penetrating his mind: the last time we saw him he had a bookshelf strung around his neck on a piece of rope and resting on his stomach, thereby enabling him—exactly as Elka, may she rest in peace, had foreseen—both to carry a large number of books on his perambulations and change them as required, and to doff his hat to every skirt he caught a glimpse of on his way without any danger of his burden slipping and falling to the ground.

I do not know why I imagined that Elka of all people was the old eye doctor's wife. Perhaps it was simply due to a coincidence: before I set out for the library I heard our landlady complaining about Dr. Landau's wife, who harbored a collection of failed musicians in her house with the sole purpose of disturbing Mrs. Gentilla Luria's repose. Immediately afterward, encountering Elka next to Dr. Landau's house, I made a connection between her and the doctor, and attributed everything I had heard from Mrs. Gentilla Luria about the doctor's wife to her. It was easy, too, for me to interpret her behavior in the light of what I had heard, and see the way she imposed her advice on Dr. Ketter, and dragged Ethel behind her, as examples of her domineering nature. But only half an hour later in the reading room, when I discovered that the two women were the little librarian's aunts, I could not imagine how on earth I had made such a mistake. Elka, with her sister, Ethel, bringing up the rear, would come to visit him in the library about once a month, shortly before closing time, and after the last of the borrowers and readers had left, they would remain to spend an hour or two in his company. Why did they come to visit their nephew Srulik at work, rather than at home? Because after his father left the country they had sworn never to cross his threshold again. According to them, the only reason he had gone abroad was to escape his wife. Since their sister-in-law had banished their brother from his home, they had sworn never to visit her or speak to her. Actually, it was not in their nature to hold a grudge, and they were soon quite ready, even eager, to forget their oath—but by then Srulik's mother would not give them a chance to do so.

The pair of them looked like a couple of giant butterflies, whose wings had crumpled and shriveled the moment they were poised for flight, but went on shining brightly through the wrinkles of the crushed stuff they were made of. The stuff of their wings was nearly always American, and not only the stuff but every stitch of clothing they wore: the blouses and skirts and dresses and petticoats and hats and stockings and sometimes even the shoes had all arrived in parcels from America, and no sooner had they arrived than they were donned, just as they were, by Aunt Elka and Aunt Ethel and taken out for a dress-rehearsal parade from Shaarei Hessed Street to the B'nai B'rith Library in Abyssinian Road. All these brightly colored, striped and checked and spotted clothes had previously adorned the bodies of three young American women, and no doubt they had not seemed particularly startling then, since the youthful garments were

quite compatible with the body in its prime. Here they spar-
kled like the mirror image of the aunts' naked souls in all
their youthfulness, ignoring the bodies in between. And
since the aunts did not take the trouble to iron the contents
of the parcels before they put them on—because, one might
say, of a fundamental attitude that cast inessentials aside and
went straight to the heart of the matter, perceiving the
quality of the cloth and penetrating to the core of the color
and grasping the significance of the forms beyond the
chance vicissitudes of time—the garments covering the outside of the old bodies reflected the youthfulness of the souls
dwelling within, despite all the wrinkles and stains and accumulated dust of the years. And this withered burgeoning of
the bloom of youth gave off a distinctive aroma, it too composed of elements diverse and distant from each other. Like
their appearance, the smell of the aunts too gave the impression of a certain perfection, strange and remote as a sudden
glimmer from another world, a perfection absolute and indi-
visible although it was composed of details that were mutually incompatible, if not actually antagonistic. A perfection
that was the sum of its component parts, but at the same
time transcended them, like the melody that transcends the
combination of instruments which bring it into being: the
smell of the aunts filtered through the smell of the old
clothes lying in closed chest drawers and mingled with the
worm-eaten wood and the delicate Roger & Gallet eau de
cologne and the smell of the laundry soap and the cistern
water and the moss and the musty stone and the moldy
bread and the henna paste and the Lysol and the honey. A
few years after my discovery that they were the little librarian's aunts, after I had sat in the reading room of the B'nai
B'rith Library and laughed with them to my heart's content,
little Srulik's nostrils were suddenly assailed, in a distant
land and another time, by their distinctive scent. He was
standing on the platform and addressing the eminent eccle-

siastics who filled the big hall to bursting: ". . . the Holy Trinity, the central dogma of our religion which states that the One God exists in Three Persons and One Substance; the Holy Trinity which is held, as we know, to be a mystery in the strict sense of the word, in that it can neither be known by unaided human reason apart from revelation, nor be cogently demonstrated by reason after it has been revealed . . ." when suddenly the scent of the aunts assailed his nostrils so clearly and vividly that he was amazed that the audience did not sense it, and that it was not as plain as day to the men of God assembled there that this smell was the simplest, most human and logical proof of this mystery of our faith—a proof able to open the eyes of even the dullest man. Although it seemed to him at that moment not only that he had been granted the revelation of the smell, but also that he was about to be granted the revelation of his aunts' physical presence as well, he nevertheless continued with his prepared speech: "On the other hand, it is maintained that though the mystery transcends reason it is not contrary to it since it is not incompatible with the principles of rational thought. The term 'Trinity,' as we know, first appeared in a Greek text by Theophilus of Antioch in about A.D. 180 . . ." This happened to Srulik in the French town of Noyon, the birthplace of John Calvin, in the middle of his sermon on Calvin's interpretation of the Last Supper, the closing address of the Great Council of Presbyterian Churches. The smell of his aunts seemed to him, on second thought, incongruous and irrelevant—not, indeed, with regard to the Holy Trinity, or the Last Supper, but with regard to the clergymen present. The latter exuded a smell of starched and ironed shirts, and their thoughts were already turning to the luncheon awaiting them at the end of the sermon.

On their visits to their nephew at his place of employment, the aunts would organize light refreshments in the reading room, a meal to which Aunt Elka, who had spent many years perfecting her English, would refer by the elegant title of "five-o'clock tea," which made us all laugh. The librarian was quite willing to include a few of the laggard readers, too, in Elka's "five-o'clock." There were only two of them whom he categorically refused to allow to remain after closing time: he would simply show them the door. "Gentlemen," he would say when he saw them still absorbed in their books, indifferent to the ringing of the bell. (He had a bell like a school janitor's, and at closing time he would go to the door of the reading room and ring it as loudly as he could. During summer vacation he would allow me the honor of sounding the closing bell, and this was the first time in my life that I felt, with a thrill of wonder and fear, that I was holding in my hands a power far superior to my own actual strength, a power that had been endowed on me by Divine Grace: I rang, and the pure, clear, crystalline peals filled the gloomy reading room like a bright stream of spring. I rang, and all these grownups, each of whom was far stronger than I, some of whom were even men of consequence in the city, obeyed me immediately and stood up, collected their belongings and left. Yesterday, when I was crossing the Street of the Prophets and saw the traffic cop stopping the cars with a majestic gesture of his hand, I felt that he was just as proud of himself as I had been when, as a child, I rang the closing bell. Here he was, a little policeman who occupied the lowest rung in the hierarchy, whose salary was never enough to last the month, and who would never be able to afford the purchase of the most dilapidated of used cars—let alone its monthly maintenance—standing in the middle of the road and with a sweep of his hand stopping all the cars, including those belonging to people of far superior station. The handsome policeman was stopping the traffic with a proud gesture of his hand on exactly the same corner where, thirty years before, the aunts had crossed the street at the moment when the noise of a lone car engine was heard straining up the hill—a car that belonged, of course, to Dan Gutkin, Esq., Supreme Court judge and Officer of the British Empire.) "Gentlemen," the little librarian would say to the two readers in question, "you heard the bell, didn't you, so why are you still sitting here? Get up and leave at once!" For at the sound of the bell both gentlemen would stick their noses more deeply into their books; it would invariably take them by surprise, a premature and unexpected blow, and they seemed to think that by going on reading and ignoring it completely, they could make it disappear. Thus death must seize those who love life and are in full possession of their faculties, even if they are as old as Methuselah—suddenly, prematurely, and as if inadvertently.

As soon as they had grudgingly departed, the librarian would slam the door angrily and contemptuously behind them. It always seemed to me that the door was about to hit them on the back, and that it was really with a kick in the pants that he would have liked to expel this "pair of starchy old souls," as he called them—although actually they were both young and nice-looking, each in his own way. True, they were starchy not only in their clothes but also in their way of life, which was strictly organized and rigorously calculated down to the last moment and cent, and the librarian once told me that what infuriated him even more than their stinginess with money was their stinginess with reading, never wasting a moment on anything unnecessary to the advancement of their academic careers. Still, they were not unique in this respect: there were others of their ilk in the reading room, who for some reason did not enrage the librarian to such an extent; some of them were even allowed to stay on for Aunt Elka's five-o'clock tea. The truth was that these two succeeded in driving little Srulik wild with fury by their praise of Professor Talmi, proving themselves to be not only his students but also his disciples. The librarian could not imagine a more loathsome creature than the possessor of a "starchy old soul" who was also an admirer of Professor Talmi.

"Here we are!" Aunt Elka would announce as soon as the two students had beaten a retreat, and Ethel would repeat "Here we are!" and the two of them would burst out laughing. During the entire course of the visit they would enthusiastically recount, to the accompaniment of merry peals of laughter, everything that had happened to them on their way. To be exact: Elka would recount, while Ethel emphatically repeated the most important words—to the delight of Srulik, who would narrow his eyes or widen them in astonishment behind his spectacles, suck in his breath, beat his little fists on the table, and join uproariously in their laughter. They realized, of course, that his astonishment at their every word was an exaggeration, an act intended to give them pleasure, but this knowledge detracted nothing, and even added to their enjoyment—for they themselves, like children telling their parents about their adventures on the way home from school, seemed to see everything that happened to them as a game inseparable from the condition of life itself. The librarian would go on listening attentively and admiringly even when his aunts proceeded to the inevitable attack on his mother, an attack that invariably began with birth. "You know, Srulik," Elka would commence, "your mother was already a child of four when I was born."

"Yes, yes, a child of four," repeated Ethel, wagging her finger like a little pupil imitating her teacher.

"Ay, ay, ay," cried Srulik, swaying to and fro in amazement, "she was already a child of four!"

"Certainly," said Elka, "your mother is at least a year older than your father, and your father is three years older than me. In other words, she was four years old when I was born, and six years old when Ethel was born!"

"When I was born, she was already six years old!"

repeated Ethel solemnly, beaming with satisfaction at the art of arithmetic capable of bringing such pleasant discoveries to the world, and Srulik, who knew that his mother was a good few years younger than her sister-in-law Ethel, made no attempt to fight for the absolute truth and defend his mother's relative youthfulness, but joined enthusiastically in his aunts' arithmetical games. He did not argue with them even when they wrongly accused his mother of having chased his father out of the house, even though they knew very well that she had not yet recovered from the shock of his sudden disappearance, and that her only hope was that one day he would return as suddenly as he had left. Srulik would let them unburden themselves freely of all the grievances and complaints that had accumulated since their last visit two or three weeks before (feeling as he did so a vague pang of anxiety at the thought of the future: where would they go and to whom would they unburden themselves when he was gone?) until it was time for the basket entrusted to Ethel to reveal its contents. For the aunts had come to take pleasure in Srulik and to give him pleasure, and not to depress him and burden him with their troubles, and whatever they had said against his mother was intended only to let her, Rachelie, know—via her son—that they were not about to allow anyone to "spit in their soup," even though they had grown up as orphans.

"Haven't you had enough of those petty calculations of who's older than who yet?" Elka rounded on Ethel, who was not, in fact, to blame for initiating this war of the ages, and who had not said anything that was not an echo of her sister's words. "What on earth's the matter with you? Did you come here to bore poor Srulik with idiocies about when you were six years old and stupid stories about the days of the Turks? Well, what are you waiting for? Start taking the things out of the basket. And now"—she turned to Srulik— "guess what we have for you today!" Her eyes were melting

with pride in this son of her brother's, who had attained the
glorious and exalted post of librarian in the B'nai B'rith
Library. The object of her admiration, however, did not in
any way share in the feeling. One day, when I was helping
him to carry the tattered books to the binder's, he told me
that there were three types of people in the world he
detested, and that all three of them were combined in his
own person: he hated myopic people with thick glasses, men
with straight fair hair, and anyone called Srulik. Walking
down the street with the bundles of books in our arms, we
both laughed out loud. But although his words drew my
attention for the first time to his fine, silky hair, they did
nothing to change my feelings toward him in person, or
toward nearsighted people and men with straight fair hair
in general: I have no reason to hate either one or the other.
As far as questions of taste are concerned, I have always had
a soft spot for straight fair hair.

His remarks about his work in the library and the reading
room, on the other hand, had a profound effect on me, but it
took years for me to realize this—although at the time I did
feel a certain surprise at the strange light they seemed to
cast on things. After we had delivered the books to the
binder's, instead of saying that he had to go back to work,
the librarian said: "And now I have to bury myself again."
He referred to the library, and especially the reading room,
as "the graveyard," and to the readers who spent their days
there as "the living dead." In general he divided the readers,
as well as the books, into two categories: the living and the
dead. The living readers were those who read everywhere
but in the reading room, and who read books that added life
to their lives; while the dead were those who spent their lives
in the reading room of the B'nai B'rith Library, and they, of
course, read dead books that added death to their deaths.
These things he revealed to me (a child who happened to
live in the house belonging to the family of his friend Ga-

briel Luria), but not to his Aunt Elka; for just as he made no
attempt to correct her calculation of her own age in relation
to his mother's, neither did he try to disillusion her about his
supposed pride and happiness in his work. If, for him, the
library was nothing but a tomb, Aunt Elka, at least, could
rejoice in her nephew's lot and his position in the world. Had
he left the library and become a prosperous businessman,
she would have seen it not as an improvement but as a
shameful decline in his way of life, for as far as Elka was
concerned there was nothing to touch the prestige of an
intellectual holding down a job of cultural significance, such
as that her dear nephew Srulik had attained. Whenever she
heard of someone who had acquired a knowledge of English
or French—and the knowledge of languages seemed to her
the very pinnacle of book-learning—his prestige rose sky-
high in her eyes, and she would jealously declare: "Yes, yes,
that's all very well, but he's still not a patch on our Srulik."
On the other hand, rumors of someone's sudden enrich-
ment did not move her at all or give rise to the slightest
jealousy in her breast—only to the kind of speculation that
manifested itself in the ironic question, "Thanks to what
good deeds, I wonder?" As one might inquire, upon hearing
of a person's arrest: "What for? What did he do? What crime
has he been accused of?" For in Elka's eyes wealth, like
arrest, was first of all a sign of some "good deed" that had
preceded it, the manifest result of some hidden infection,
revealing itself in the form of an abscess blossoming on the
body.

Unfortunately for Elka, she was only too well acquainted
with two such abscesses, which had blossomed on either side
of her: Mendel Wiesel, her neighbor to the left, and Zalman
Segal, her neighbor to the right.

Mendel Wiesel had grown rich schnorring—that is, collecting money for charity—while Zalman Segal had grown
rich on speculation, and there was no difference between

them but the fact that one was a scoundrel with a hat, beard, and sidelocks and the other a scoundrel who went clean-shaven and hatless. As far as Mendel Wiesel was concerned, the width of his beard and the length of his sidelocks was matched by the depth of his ignorance, which was cele-brated throughout Jerusalem. You could believe anything you heard about him, and to the vile deeds that were already well-known you could add a long list of secret abuses too modest to expose themselves to the light of day. You should never believe, on the other hand, the stories you heard about the vast knowledge, deep wisdom, and great gifts of Zalman Segal. Such stories were invented by politicians and busy-bodies to justify the affection they felt for this land specula-tor and the respect in which they held him. Since there were Jews who wanted a house in Jerusalem, and idealistic pioneers, honest young men from good families, who came to Eretz Israel to cultivate an ungrateful soil under a cruel sun, to sacrifice the best years of their lives and expend their strength and dry up the marrow of their bones, and shrivel up and turn black like dried figs doing hard labor that even convicts could not have endured, and all this in order to "redeem the land," as they said; since there were some Jews who wanted a house in Jerusalem, and others who gave their lives for their country, this crook Zalman Segal had to get rich with the help of a bunch of petty bureaucrats who were no better than he was. And why did they run to him, every time there were lands and houses to be purchased from the Arab effendis? Why him, of all people? To this question they had a ready reply: Zalman Segal was in the unique position of being an expert both on Arab affairs and on the British rulers of the country. There was no one to touch him when it came to mastery of the Arab language, familiarity with the rituals of Oriental bargaining, and understanding of the intricacies of the Moslem mind. And such was his genius—according to these politicians—that in addition to the foregoing, he was also an expert on the English language, and had excellent connections with the British officials, who loved him like the apple of their eye.

And where had he acquired this great knowledge? In the Café Gat, which was both his Al-Azhar and his Oxford universities. Between washing the dishes and peeling the potatoes he sat at the feet of Massuda, the cook's assistant, and between serving the drinks and clearing the tables he studied British political theory from the mouth of the sage Yosef Shvilli. From Massuda he learned to say: *"Ahallan wa-sahallan! Kif hal-ak el-yom?"* and Professor Yosef Shvilli taught him how to copy an address in English.

"To copy an address in English—wonderful, wonderful!" cried Ethel, lifting her finger and widening her eyes in imitation of a teacher marveling at the latest little genius she has discovered among her pupils. "That saint Mendel Wiesel has been trying to write an address in English for forty years and he hasn't succeeded yet!" Ethel would interrupt the flow of Elka's speech with interjections of this kind not only when the time came to underline the theme with a choral response, but also when she felt that her sister was losing her balance and slipping from the simple pleasure of storytelling into an excitement and anger liable to lead, God forbid, to a violent outburst. Signs of rage began to manifest themselves in her flashing eyes, in the red blotches on her throat, and in the way in which she spat out the "z" of "Al-Azhar." More than she feared Elka's rages, however, Ethel feared "that business," and whenever she sensed it coming, she was no longer content with the interjections suitable to her part in the choir, but energetically interrupted her elder sister with the cry: "Hold your tongue—you're starting on that business again!" And if this command did not have the desired effect she would even pounce with hand outstretched to stop her sister's mouth, turning to Srulik with the cry: "Don't pay any attention to her nonsense! Tell her to hold her tongue!" "That business" was the business of *"that man's"* relations with Aunt Elka. *That man* had ways of contacting her that were peculiar to himself. For example, he would knock on the windowpane after midnight in a special way, knocks that were meant only for her and reached her ears alone, or he would send her signs in the milk the milkman poured into the jug every morning; or he would talk to her through the light bulbs, or sometimes even come to sit beside her, bold as brass, in the presence of other people, who ignored him as totally as he ignored them. As soon as Elka began to talk about *him,* Ethel would pounce on her to stop her mouth. Something that horrified her only slightly less than *that man* was the matter of a cure for cancer. Elka had long ago discovered a cure for cancer, which she wished to make public in order to save all the poor souls doomed to suffer and die from it, but she was prevented from doing so by the wall surrounding her. For years she had been racking her brains to find a way of circumventing or breaching this wall, which was, of course, the barrier set up by the speculators, "the Zalmans of every kind," and their allies the politicians. For, the moment she published her cure for cancer, the Zalmans and their accomplices would take control of it. Liberation from the deadly enemy, the terrible cancer, would be transformed into one more tool in the hand of the politicians to dominate the suffering and the downtrodden, while the Zalmans would be given a wonderful opportunity to get rich quickly.

Apart from "that business" and the cancer cure chained to and dragging behind it, Aunt Ethel had no need to shut her sister's mouth, a mere remark of the kind alluding to Mendel Wiesel and his difficulties with "English addresses" sufficing to turn Elka from her wrath and bring her back to the enjoyment of recounting her adventures on the way to the library, and describing her neighbors on her right and left. As long as the visit lasted Ethel would go on digging into the basket and producing a stream of canned delicacies (they too, like the aunts' apparel, having crossed the high seas from the distant shores of America) while Elka fed us with entertaining stories, at the same time keeping an eye on her little sister to make sure that she did not neglect her duties and deprive the company of bodily nourishment by participating too actively in the spiritual side of things. In the middle of her story about the encounter with Dr. Ketter, when we were all enjoying the idea of the bookshelf, and the two sisters were as usual dissolving in gales of laughter which brought tears to their eyes, Elka suddenly cried to Ethel: "Before you open the can of pineapple, run quickly to the lavatory!" And turning to Srulik she added: "She's perfectly capable, you know, of wetting her pants from laughter!" And beneath the lines of laughter one could perceive the anxiety that had entered Elka's blood more than fifty years before, when they had been orphaned and she had begun to worry about her younger sister. But just as the intervening years had not succeeded in dulling the pang suddenly piercing Elka's soul in the midst of her laughter, so too they were incapable of blunting the sting of the insult to the soul of the infant Ethel, an insult that stared, in all its primal innocence, through the wrinkles netting the face fifty years older than it. Ethel lowered her big gentle eyes and her mouth pursed tearfully. She averted her face and, swallowing her tears, gave her sister tit for tat: "You pee in your pants yourself. You'd better go to the lavatory before you wet yourself!" "That's exactly where I'm going," retorted Elka, standing up and looking around her triumphantly, "and in the meantime you open the can of pineapple!"

"I won't open it. Open it yourself. Who do you think you are, anyway? I'm not your servant. Isn't it enough that I carried that heavy basket all the way here?" In fact, Elka would have been perfectly willing to share the load, but for some reason Ethel refused, and when Srulik asked her why, she replied angrily: "You can't trust her with anything. She's quite liable to forget herself on the way and lose everything you give her." Just as it seemed that the exchange between the sisters was about to develop into a full-fledged row, Ethel rose to her feet and, cupping her hand around her mouth, trumpeted: "Para-para-parapam! Parapam-parapam-para-pam!" and, like a soldier marching after her commander, followed Elka to the lavatory.

Exits to the lavatory did not always end in peals of laugh-ter. Sometimes, when one of them discreetly left the room, the other seized the opportunity to complain about her sister to Srulik, who, for all his attempts to defend the absent accused, showed complete understanding for the point of view of the plaintiff too. He told me more than once that he not only understood but also sympathized completely with what was going on in the heart of each of them, since he had experienced the same thing himself. He was as familiar with Elka's sudden pang of anxiety as he was with Ethel's burn-ing insult. He had experienced Ethel's misery whenever his absentminded father had suddenly roused himself from his reflections on sacred architecture to say to him, in front of all his friends, "Yes, and before you go off to Herodian don't forget to go to the lavatory, and take a sweater." And as for Elka's sudden anxiety, ever since his father's disappearance it had gripped him almost daily, and precisely when his chores were over and he was free to relax in the Café Gat or enjoy a game of chess with Police Officer Gordon. All of a sudden, just when he was savoring the move that would end up by checkmating Gordon, his heart would be gripped in a vise of anxiety for his mother lying ill in bed alone at home. In his mind's eye he could already see her slipping and falling as she tried to get out of bed to make herself a cup of tea, lying there helpless on the floor, unable to get up, while her beloved son relaxed on an upholstered seat in the Café Gat, enjoying the attentions of the waiters and passing the time of day in a game of chess with the British officer. And the very same anxiety had caused him, on more than one occasion, to shame her in front of precisely those people from whom she was trying her best to hide her affliction. Indeed, it would never have occurred to anyone who was not fully acquainted with the facts that this slender and well-groomed woman—since her illness she had taken greater pains than ever over her appearance—intermittently lost the use of her legs. As soon as he noticed the frightened fluttering of her eyelids and the frown on her forehead, he would jump to his feet with the words "Come, Mother, let me help you to the kitchen" in front of all her visitors. And once, with the tall shadow of Haim Long-Life already at the door, he had called out: "Don't bother getting up. I'll bring the chamber pot here." It was an insult she had never forgotten, even though Haim Long-Life, who had come to tell them about the new invention that had popped into his brain, had not even heard his cry.

The aunts having returned from the lavatory in a light-hearted mood, we all tackled the pineapple. All these twi-light feasts in the library reading room were topped off by canned pineapple, Aunt Elka's particular favorite, for dessert, while whatever remained in the depths of the basket was presented to Srulik, "to eat and enjoy in good health." All the parcels that arrived once every two or three months from America were equitably shared by the aunts with their nephew, and since they contained not only cans of food and packets of tea and coffee and chocolate, but also used clothes, they would keep the female apparel for themselves and give him the men's suits, which he would stuff, together with the cans, into the bottom drawer of the cupboard behind his chair. Whenever he felt the need of a new garment, the little librarian would burrow into this drawer, pull out some crumpled article, and hurry to his friend Antigonus the tailor, for a "fitting and alteration," an operation which invariably meant the shortening and taking in of every coat, suit, and pair of trousers, at the end of which the librarian always appeared—whenever I saw him in the days of my childhood—to be walking sideways, thrusting one shoulder forward and dragging one leg behind him, as if he had to push his way through a dense crowd invisible to anyone but himself. Meeting him thirty years later, I was astonished at the sight of his elegant suit, made to measure from fine English cloth. In the last years of his life he looked not only neater and more elegant, but also stronger and more energetic than he had in the bloom of his youth and the prime of his manhood, midway through the journey of his life, which seemed to him like a dead end closed to the world and open only to the tomb of the library.

The librarian's lopsided gait was due not just to the "fittings" of Antigonus the tailor, but also to his own impatience, which grew more acute from fitting to fitting, until he announced: "That's enough. The suit's fine. Stop unpicking and begin sewing, for God's sake, because this is the last fitting I'm coming to." Antigonus the tailor, for his part, would have been prepared for another ten sessions, if only the suit would fit. He was ready to do anything for his friend Israel Shoshan (for such was Srulik's full name), even the thing he hated most in the world, which was altering old suits to fit new measurements. Antigonus the tailor would say that this kind of alteration was harder than crossing the Red Sea, while making a new suit was like "singing a new song unto the Lord, a song of the saved." He prayed for the day when both he and the librarian would be saved: free of the fetters of the clothes parcels from America.

In contrast to Antigonus the tailor, Mendel Wiesel, the aunts' left-hand neighbor, was spellbound by these parcels. When the aunts came home from the post office, carrying the latest parcel between them, he would prowl about like a chained dog sniffing a bone. Even though he knew by now that he had no chance of getting hold of the sender's address, and despite all his efforts to ignore what was happening in his neighbors' house, he could not overcome his avidity; and if he did not actually rush out of his door and pounce on the parcel—as he had done at first—he would gaze at it in awe from inside his house, lurking at the windows and peering through the curtains. It was this passion of Mendel Wiesel's for the parcels from America, and especially his tireless attempts to obtain the address of the American uncle, that had brought about the rupture between Aunt Elka and Srulik's mother many years before his father disappeared. Aunt Elka, the only member of the family who kept in touch with her eldest brother, who lived in America, had never asked him for anything, nor had it ever occurred to her to do so. On the contrary: in all her letters she begged him to stop sending these superfluous parcels. She and Ethel had no need of charity, since they had more than enough of their own. They earned a good living from the "pots and plates and ashtrays"—Aunt Elka hammered bas-reliefs on copper and Aunt Ethel helped her—and it was ridiculous for him to starve himself and his wife and children simply in order to "send them canned pineapple," which they could very well do without. In her letters Elka of course exaggerated the extent of her profits, so that he would not "upset himself over there in America." All her letters were intended only to calm his fears and anxieties. Her eldest brother, Maurice, was a great worrier, even worse than she was, and he had a heart of gold. That was all she needed, for him to deprive himself in order to make that shameless schnorrer Mendel Wiesel a little richer. Once the crook in question realized that he would never get the address out of Elka, he began to send his wife to bribe Ethel to sell it to her. But Ethel was on her guard. "I don't know where it is," she would say. "When Elka comes home you can ask her, and she'll sell it to you." For Ethel, this was the fruit of years of training and education. With the sisters left orphaned and alone in the big house, all the neighbors tried to rob them with a show of love and kindness. With senti-mental expressions on their faces, with heartfelt sighs of sympathy, with sweet voices and soft caresses, they began to rob them of everything they could lay their hands on. As soon as Elka's eyes were opened to their hypocritical masks and false voices, she trained her little sister always to say: "I don't know. Wait until Elka comes home." Ethel was well trained from childhood, but not her sister-in-law Rachelie, Srulik's mother. Rachelie, who was the child of wealthy par-ents, did not understand such things. On the eve of the New Year, she was in the habit of sending greeting cards to all her relations, friends, and acquaintances. When she discovered that she had a brother-in-law in America, and that he was the source of all the cans of food with which Elka presented her once every two or three months, she wrote him a greet-ing card too, and asked Elka for his address. At that moment the rupture occurred. "Give me the card," said Elka, "and I'll send it to Maurice. I can't give you the address, because Mendel Wiesel will get it out of you by a trick—he or his wife or his son or one of his henchmen schnorring all over the country for him. One of them will certainly catch you in their traps. You don't know them. You don't know the world. You simply can't imagine what people are capable of doing for money!"

What people were capable of doing for money Rachelie knew only too well, from her experience with her own mother—her mother who had cheated her of her share in her father's legacy. And knowing Elka, she knew that she would never be capable of treating her as her mother had done, because she was totally disinterested in money for its own sake. "I really can't see why it would be such a catastro-phe if the address fell into Mendel Wiesel's hands," said Rachelie in a voice trembling with insult, "but if you want me to keep it a secret, I promise you that I will never disclose

Maurice's address to a living soul." With these words
Rachelie had sworn a solemn oath to Elka, which it seemed
to her was more than enough to inspire her confidence. But
Elka did not give her the address, or even answer her—
except with the kind of smile one gives a little girl promising
faithfully to guard the house against all the robbers lying in
wait for her parents to go out. In general, Elka saw the world
as divided into two: the members of the household and the
others, the world inside the house and the world outside it.
Since the world outside was always lying in wait to destroy
the world inside, and since the members of the household
were unaware of the dangers threatening them, Elka saw
herself as responsible for their safety and well-being, and at
the same time, the moment she came to regard anyone as a
member of the household, she no longer made any difference between herself and him, between what was hers and
what was his. The librarian told me that he had always, even
in his infancy, felt more at home at Elka's than in his own
house. In Elka's house he could do whatever he liked whenever he liked, at any hour of the day or night, and not only
he but also his friends whom she included in the members of
the household by virtue of his love for them. They would
meet at Elka's, and when the arguments went on into the
small hours, anyone who did not feel like dragging himself
home would stay and sleep in his aunt's house. For several
months, while he was preparing for the entrance exams to
the University of Beirut, Yankele Blum stayed with Aunt
Elka, who at the same time took the opportunity of feeding
and clothing him from the American parcels. In those days
Yankele Blum did not have a penny to his name, and if he
put his hand into the pocket of his American trousers and
found a few pence there as well, they were no doubt part of
the income from the pots and plates and ashtrays that Aunt
Elka hammered out in the little niche that everyone called
her studio.

With the same abolition of barriers, Aunt Elka was capa-

ble of turning up for a visit at all kinds of unheard-of hours,
and until the crisis of Uncle Maurice's address Srulik's
mother never said a word but always welcomed her warmly
even though she was disrupting her daily routine. But far
worse than the domestic upsets she caused was the way Elka
"wormed her way into the marrow of your bones," as
Rachelie (who had taken to calling her sisters-in-law "those
old maids") claimed after their falling-out. The little librarian's mother was very sensitive about her privacy. Just as she
could not bear anyone poking about in her soul, so she could
not stand a stranger touching her body, which was liable to
turn any bus trip or cinema line into a nightmare for her as
soon as the sweaty bodies of strangers began pressing up
against her. Any kind of crush would give rise in her,
together with the revulsion and nausea, to a great urge to
run away and hide in her own private corner. But there was
no escaping Elka. "That old maid," Rachelie complained,
"comes storming into the house like a whirlwind and jumps
down your gullet before you know where you are." Thirsty
from her walk in the blazing sun, Elka would make straight
for Rachelie's cup of tea and take a sip without any inhibitions at all, as if it were the most natural thing in the world.
And if her eye happened to fall on a new blouse lying on the
sofa as she drank, she would pounce on it immediately and
rush to the mirror to try it on. In the kitchen she would
freely taste the contents of the pots, and if any crumbs got
stuck in her teeth, she would not hesitate to use Rachelie's
toothbrush. Rachelie, of course, never showed her disapproval; but the moment the "whirlwind" left the house she
would pour the dregs of the tea down the drain and make
herself a fresh cup, thrust the new blouse into the laundry
basket, and throw the toothbrush into the garbage pail. She
counted her toothbrush among her most intimate possessions, and except for her husband she never let anyone touch
it, not even her children. To the latter she would say, even

before the breakup: "Don't listen to Aunt Elka and don't behave like she does. She breathes a spirit of anarchy, and life is not anarchy."

After every visit of Aunt Elka's, Rachelie would fall prostrate on the sofa. It would take her at least half an hour to gather the strength to reestablish order in her home and compose her thoughts after the confusion sown by the old maid's anarchic spirit. Unlike Rachelie, who was thrown off balance by the slightest breath of wind, Elka was capable of concentrating on her work even in the midst of the commotion created in her home by Srulik and his friends during the period of their studies at the Teachers' Seminary. While they turned the world upside down, argued at the tops of their voices, sang and shouted and wrestled and acted charades, she would sit in her little niche and hammer out her pots and plates and ashtrays. I myself saw her at work several times when the librarian sent me to fetch the books she had forgotten to return, which were usually found underneath her bed. She was in the habit of reading in bed, and when she turned over to go to sleep she would push the book, which had dropped to the floor, under the bed with one hand while pulling up the covers with the other.

I would volunteer to go around to Elka's to fetch her library books simply in order to see her at work. She would hammer bas-reliefs on copper utensils of all shapes and sizes, plates, mugs, bowls, pots, coffeepots, casseroles, ashtrays, trays, and even on the handles of soup ladles, all of which lay scattered around her studio in gleaming piles, their color changing with the variations in the light streaming through the rose-shaped grille of the round window which peeped like an eye from the corner of the ceiling. From the depths of the dim corners the heart of the copper sent out dull tawny gleams, and as the eye approached the center of the light pouring from the ceiling it set off a dance of flashing arrows of pink and gold and red and yellow and orange, and all these flashes of copper and bronze would reverberate with waves of metallic sound in melodious response to the passage of a cart outside, the footsteps of a person entering, and the delicate, rhythmic taps of Elka's hand. In her right hand she would hold a little hammer with which she banged on the heads of the chisels and burins taking their turn in her left, and making their respective marks on copper: tiny holes and grooves and lines and points. And on the smooth, blank hollow of the bowl, the image of the picture she had seen in her imagination would gradually take shape. In the Bezalel Art School, where she had acquired her craft, she had been taught a few conventional scenes which were reproduced by all the graduates of the school: the shepherd playing his pipe with three sheep bringing up the rear, the caravan of camels following a man riding a little donkey, Rachel's tomb in the shadow of a leafy tree, and David's Tower seen from various angles—all of them framed by a pattern of little Magen Davids and ram's horns. It was, perhaps, the same urge as the one her sister-in-law called a "spirit of anarchy" that had caused Aunt Elka to question the teachings of the art school when she was still a student there. By the time I knew her she had long abandoned the conventional style, returning to it only when obliged to do so, as she said, "to earn her bread," in compliance with specific orders from souvenir merchants. Her copper reliefs made me think of the scenes I saw in my imagination when reading the Book of Esther: sumptuous feasts worthy of a king who reigned from India to Ethiopia, over a hundred twenty-seven provinces. On a great copper tray, set upon little wooden legs and serving as a table, she hammered the image of a woman dancing to the music of lutes and harps and drums before the king reclining beneath the trees of his garden. Like visible electric wires vibrating with an invisible current, her fingers holding the hammer and chisel would conduct the picture she saw in her mind's eye to the copper surface, and what had once existed only in Aunt Elka's imagination was imprinted on the copper in the form of a relief possessing its own independent reality.

Once I saw her hammering a picture onto a burnished copper ashtray without any preliminary sketches, right after a row with Ethel, who had pounced upon her to shut her mouth. Elka had been laughing and talking animatedly when she suddenly began on the subject of *that man,* who was making signals to her through the rosette of the window grille. Ethel, perceiving by the look in her sister's eye that she was about to topple off the common path, bounded forward with her hand outstretched, just as she would have leapt to shut the door of a railway car upon sensing that her elder sister (the sole surviving member of her family, all the others having gone off and left her, whether for the world to come or for other countries in this one) was about to jump off the train in order to wander alone in distant fields beyond a yawning, unbridged chasm. "All right, all right, I'm stopping," replied Aunt Elka to the hand about to land on her mouth. "I won't say any more. I'm going to work." She turned her back to Ethel, sat down on her stool, and reached for the pile of utensils on her right. Her fingers pulled out a heavy copper ashtray of a ruddy orange hue, and began tapping energetically, to a quick, deliberate rhythm. The chisel seemed to be engraving a series of little lines slanting from the center of the ashtray to the rim, like sunrays. Some days later, when I saw the completed relief, I was stunned. On a little hill, its body and crowned head facing forward, stood a peacock, spreading its tail in a magnificent fan over the entire surface of the ashtray.

2.

Dreams of Ur of the Chaldees

AS I HAVE ALREADY MENTIONED, I had never met Dr. Landau's wife, that terrible woman who so infuriated Gabriel Luria's mother. On my way to the library, however, I often encountered the doctor's daughter, emerging from the garden gate alone or in the company of the Polish owl, alias the pianist Paul Dornoy, or leaning on her father's arm.

To this day I don't really know what is meant by the verse "The Holy One, blessed be He, made the sun come out of its sheath," but on my way to the B'nai B'rith Library, when the green iron gate suddenly opened and the doctor's daughter stepped out of it, I sensed the meaning of the sun coming out of its sheath: at the sight of her face and the sound of her voice the world suddenly filled with light and became wider and higher and freer and better. Her big brown eyes and her enchanting smile, above all, seemed to say to every child who crossed her path that whatever he wanted and whatever he did was just fine. Sometimes the old judge's big car drew up at the gate just as she was coming out of it, and Daoud Ibn Mahmoud, the chauffeur, would jump out and open the door for her respectfully. Sometimes the judge's chauffeur would give Paul Dornoy or one of her other friends a lift. Long after the little librarian disappeared from the B'nai

B'rith Library, when Gabriel Luria returned from Paris, Dr. Landau's daughter would stop by the yard of our house almost every day to take Gabriel somewhere in the judge's car. Once I said to Gabriel that it seemed as if Daoud Ibn Mahmoud was not the old judge's chauffeur, but the chauffeur of Dr. Landau's daughter, who was gracious enough to put the car and its driver from time to time at the judge's disposal.

"And why not?" said Gabriel, "She's his daughter, isn't she? Judge Dan Gutkin's daughter, the famous Orita."

Instantly, the whole picture changed. If she was the old judge's daughter, she couldn't be Dr. Landau's daughter. "So what's she doing in Dr. Landau's house all the time?" I asked Gabriel. "Exactly the question," said Gabriel, smiling beneath his square mustache, "posed by Srulik, the friend of my youth, in the letter informing me of Orita's marriage. Two or three years after I went to Paris, Orita Gutkin married her father's best friend, the famous eye doctor. What does Orita Gutkin do in Dr. Landau's house? What women do in their houses, I imagine. Mrs. Orita Landau. Yes. Orita. What a name! You may think that the old judge decided to give his daughter a modern Hebrew name, but he was actually giving way to an old-fashioned superstition. When she was born her father was busy reading the Kabbalistic Book of Zohar, and he no doubt wished to endow her with the radiance of Zohar and the light of Orith in order to overcome the darkness of Lilith. All this probably sounds like a lot of nonsense, and it means nothing to me, but there are people who attach enormous importance to names in general, and to their own names in particular. Orita was always very fond of her name. When I got Srulik's letter with the news of her marriage to a man twenty-six years older than she, I wasn't in the least surprised. Even before I left for Paris, in fact when we were still studying together at the Teachers' Seminary, I sensed that there was something going on between them, and at my farewell party she herself confirmed it."

It was then, on the night of Gabriel's farewell party before he set sail for Paris to pursue his medical studies, that the spark was ignited and the great days of hope began for his friend Israel Shoshan. When Orita Gutkin went out to the verandah accompanied by Dr. Landau, she was talking, naturally, of painters and painting, for in those days anything unrelated to the art of painting brought a yawn to her lips. A strange new word, "cubism," which kept on coming up in her conversation, gave her particular pleasure and made her eyes flash: any painter who was not a cubist was not a painter at all, and any art not based on cubism did not deserve to be called art. Dr. Landau listened to her with an anxious frown. His distress appeared to increase with every gleam of admiration flashing from her eyes. "But what is this cubism, the devil take it?" he suddenly thundered in his celebrated roar. "I've never heard such an idiotic word in my life!"

" 'Cubism' comes from the word 'cuba,' " said Orita, who had intended at first to pronounce the word in English (for she had been born in England while her father was studying at the universities of London and Oxford, and had learned her first lessons in the English language), but suddenly remembering that there was a word in Hebrew derived from the Greek root common to both, had mispronounced it "cuba." "Cuba," muttered Dr. Landau to himself, "Cuba, Puerto Rico, Jamaica—are you referring to the art of the West Indies?"

Like the great eye doctor, the little librarian too had never heard the word "cubism" before and had no idea what it meant, but even before Dr. Landau took off for the West Indies, Srulik recalled a Talmudic commentary from his days as a student at Rabbi Kook's Yeshiva: "The following are debarred from bearing witness: the cube (i.e., dice) player and the usurer." Without intending to interrupt their conversation he suddenly exclaimed: "The cube! Of course, the art based on the concept of the cube, on the geometric division of space. And just as the sages said, 'Make a fence around the Law,' so the modern painters say, 'Make a cube around art'!" Before the words were out of his mouth he was overcome with embarrassment at the nonsense he had spoken, but his embarrassment quickly turned to elation when Orita gave him the full benefit of her luminous regard and instead of answering him with the contempt he deserved, or dismissing him with a scornful grimace, clapped her hands and cried: "Wonderful, wonderful—that's it exactly! I see that you are the only person in this country who understands modern art. Even the painters here are still living at the end of the last century. Listen: we must meet and discuss cubism. You know what? Come and see me on Tuesday morning, not too early—let's say half past nine, and we'll go for a walk to Mount Scopus. You can tell me what you think of Apollinaire's latest book on cubist painters."

No more, no less. Not in a dream but in reality Orita Gutkin was making a date with him, and all because of a couple of idiotic remarks that had unwittingly escaped his lips. Where intelligence failed, imbecility did the trick. In his excitement he found nothing to say but a muttered remark about some important business awaiting him at eleven o'clock at night, and immediately he bounded down the verandah steps and began running down the Street of the Prophets and into Abyssinian Road with its double curve, like two waves chasing one another and catching up and suddenly turning to stone as they flowed. Only when he reached the B'nai B'rith Library did he realize that he had left the keys at home, and without stopping to take a breath he broke into a light trot all the way home and back again, this time with the keys in his pocket. But this was not the end of his exertions on that great night. An exhaustive search through all the catalogues of books and periodicals produced no reference to Apollinaire's last book (or for that matter his first), nor the faintest allusion to the author himself or cubism and its painters, as if none of them had ever existed except in Orita's imagination, which had sent forth a spark to the world—a spark which had missed its mark and hit him instead of Dr. Landau. And no sooner had that spark died than another one was lit, which sent him, still running, to the home of Gabriel Luria. His sole hope of finding Apollinaire's latest book on cubism, or some article mentioning it, now lay with the French consul's wife, who received all the latest periodicals from France, and his only way of reaching her was through Gabriel and the good offices of his father, Yehuda Prosper Bey. It was now two o'clock on Monday morning, which left only thirty-one hours to nine o'clock on Tuesday morning, and in the space of these thirty-one hours he had to reach the consul's wife and track down this Apollinaire so that he would have something to say about him when he met Orita.

In his haste to reach Gabriel right away in order to wake him up and explain to him the urgency of his appointment with the French consul's wife, which had to be made for the earliest possible hour that very morning, Srulik did not notice what was happening in the shadows of the wall of Dr. Landau's house. But when he had already passed the gate and returned, still running, to the Street of the Prophets, his ears caught whispered snatches of conversation in the limpid stillness of Jerusalem before dawn: a deep, muffled male voice and the light laugh of a woman in response, musical and resonant as the laughter of Orita. "I must be really tired," said Srulik to himself, "I'm beginning to hallucinate. I'm hearing voices." And a verse from another time rose into his memory, for some reason connected to the Song of Songs: "And he was delirious all that night, all that night he was delirious."

Yes, Orita. Orita had been asleep for hours, ever since

coming home with her father from the party given by Yehuda Prosper Bey for his son Gabriel, who was about to sail for foreign shores. In her dreams she saw cubist paintings. And if she could not sleep she sat up in bed, leaning against her folded pillow, and read charming interpretations of cubist paintings in the book by Apollinaire. And if, by chance, in the course of pondering the cubist paintings, the countenance of her beloved rose before her eyes and she got up in the middle of the night to seek him in the streets and marketplaces of the town, it was not at Dr. Landau's gate that she would knock, not that cranky old man who insulted cubism and called it idiotic, not that eye doctor who was old enough to be her father.

It was no doubt fatigue that made his ears ring with imaginary voices, but actually he did not feel tired at all. On the contrary: his limbs were all aflutter with a tingling kind of lightness, although logically he should have been dead-tired, for usually he was tired even before night fell, even before his legs had carried him to Gabriel's house—even, in fact, before getting out of bed that morning. On that distant morning, lost somewhere in the depths of the time before the flood, when he woke up tired to a tired world, he had no idea that before the dawn of the next day he would be running about the streets as energetic and alert as a hunting dog that had just been set loose. That morning, it was above all the thought of the ironing that tired him; not the ironing itself, but the thought that woke with him the moment he opened his eyes and said to himself: now I have to iron my shirt, or at least the collar. "Oh, the dead end of my life," he cried, and instead of letting his head drop back onto the pillow he leapt up and with one breath attacked both key points at once: the kerosene-ring and the Primus stove. On the kerosene-ring he put the kettle to boil and on the Primus he put the iron to heat.

"The dead end of my life"—he had awakened to these

words every morning, ever since the day he found himself in
a literal dead end on his way to the orphanage. The Moriah
Orphanage was situated in the Bucharan Quarter, and the
first time he had to go there to meet the director, he had
hurried through an alley in Beth Israel which he thought
would lead him straight to the orphanage, and logically,
indeed it should have done so—but it ended in a blank wall,
apparently the back wall of some building. When he stood
facing the stone wall blocking the narrow lane, the smell of
rotting fruit from a nearby barrow assailing his nostrils, he
said to himself, "The dead end of my life." And suddenly he
understood the meaning of the weight oppressing his chest
every morning when he woke: ever since he had completed
his studies, from the very first step he had taken on the
highroad of his life, leading to the infinite spaces of the
future, at the very point of departure, he had run into a
blank wall. Not one by one, but all together, the difficulties
had blocked his way like an avalanche of rocks. And all his
efforts, all his humiliations, not only had failed to allow him
to forge ahead and breach the stone wall, but had barely
sufficed to keep him treading in the same place. "So many
humiliations, so much effort, just to survive, just to hang on
to this miserable existence in this moldy swamp"—and the
smell of mold rose into his nostrils from the corners of the
damp bedroom wall: the "rheumatic wall," his mother called
it, the wall that burst out in spots of mildew like a leopard,
after all the efforts, all the operations and excavations and
layers of cement and plaster.

If not for his mother, he wouldn't have bothered. He
himself did not care either about the damp wall or about all
the other exhausting problems. He had made do all these
years with three hours' work in the afternoons in the library,
and he would have been content to go on making do with
whatever came to hand, so long as he could devote his true
efforts to "the most important things, the essential things,

the things for which he, Israel Shoshan, had been destined
from his mother's womb..." But first of all, he would have
taken off. He had made up his mind that as soon as he
finished his studies he would leave home and roam all over
the country; he would travel it far and wide, he would visit
every spot, particularly the archaeological digs that had
recently begun, and he would be "free as an eagle on high"
to occupy himself with "the quintessential, the basic, fundamental thing which he was destined to do." The thought of
the travels awaiting him when he graduated made him
shiver with delight, gave him the same kind of thrill he had
felt when he took his first ride in an automobile. He was
already a first-year student at the seminary and he had
never been in a motorcar before—and only once, when he
had fallen ill as a child and been taken to the hospital, had
he been in a horse-drawn carriage. The shiver of delight at
the journey itself, the sensation of motion in space and
freedom, the mystery of the landscapes appearing before
you and disappearing behind you, and the longing to travel
on, beyond the shifting horizons—all these were enhanced
by a kind of philosophy connected to the "essential, fundamental thing," a kind of metaphysic of God's command to
Abraham: "Get thee out!" Man, the human personality, and
indeed, the "liberty of the soul"—these were the dizzy
heights to which he aspired in his meditations on the journey awaiting him, for what was life itself, in essence, if not a
journey? The soul accomplished its journey on this earth in
the body allotted it, and the journey always began in severance and separation.

Severance was the starting point, the birth of human
individuality and independence. This severing began on the
loftiest and most abstract plane and continued on the lowest
and most basic. In the beginning, the soul was severed from
its root, from the universal soul, and sent to the body allotted it, to its vehicle. Even at this initial stage all kinds of

errors and confusions were already evident in the bill of consignment, such as a tiny, dwarfish soul sent to drive a giant truck, and on the other hand a great soul obliged to squeeze itself into a shaky little car. But setting these initial confusions aside for the moment, we can clearly see how the driver's heavenly departure is immediately reflected on earth in the parting of his vehicle from its workshop—the baby parted from its mother's navel, and later the man departing his father's house at the command: "Get thee out of thy country, and from thy kindred, and from thy father's house." He, Israel Shoshan, was ready. All he was waiting for was the starting-signal: "Get thee out!"

The "basic, fundamental" thing was, in fact, closely connected to "Get thee out," and he already had the essential outlines of the entire project drawn up. Not that he had whispered a word of it to a living soul, of course. It was a kind of research project, a life's work which would examine the verse "Get thee out" in all its aspects, beginning with the geographic aspect, in a study of all the places connected with Father Abraham, from Ur of the Chaldees to Hebron, and ending with the metaphysical aspect of the voyage of the soul toward its fulfillment. And the thrill he felt in anticipation was, he knew, but a pale reflection of the delights of the journey awaiting him.

But once the signal was given the road was blocked and he found himself facing a blank wall. It began with a telephone call. One day toward the end of his last year at the seminary, when the secretary came into the classroom and announced that Israel Shoshan was wanted on the telephone, his heart sank with fear: something terrible had happened at home. Nobody called him, little Srulik, to the telephone, or sent him express letters or telegrams or urgent messengers except to inform him of a calamity, an accident, a tragedy in the family—and to appeal to him for help. At best, a registered letter might contain a final warning before legal steps were taken for the recovery of an unpaid tax or bill. In order to phone him at school, his mother would have had to get dressed and go to the pharmacist, whose help she would probably have needed to look up the number in the telephone directory and dial it for her—not because she didn't know how to read or dial numbers, but because of her agitation and panic. She used this black anonymous object only at extreme moments, when she had to summon the doctor or the ambulance or the police to separate quarreling neighbors, and by the time she reached it she was already breathless and flustered by the event itself, the hurry, and the prospect of the conversation upon the outcome of which the failure or success of her mission depended. Her heavy breathing echoed in the instrument, buzzing around her frail, gentle, melodious voice. "Hello, Israel, this is Mother. How are you, my dear?"—an irrelevant question which was intended to reassure him. For good measure she added: "Don't panic. I only wanted to ask you to come right home after school, without going to work first. It's something connected with your father. No, he's not ill. He's gone away." Srulik, of course, did not wait for the last class, but ran straight home. His father would disappear from home from time to time, not because of domestic discord, but simply out of absentmindedness, like a child so absorbed in his game that he forgets to go home to eat. At work, too, he behaved like a child, throwing himself energetically into work that interested him and putting off whatever bored him, with the result that he was perpetually in financial difficulties although he was considered one of the best carpenters in town and an outstanding pupil of the Old Man—the famous Markel Cohen, Gabriel Luria's maternal grandfather, whose favorite apprentice he had once been. This time, however, it was no ordinary disappearance. The telephone call itself was enough to confirm his worst fears: that his father had taken off and left home together with his Temple. As a child

Srulik had been hurt to the quick, as if at the twist of a knife in his heart, when he heard the neighbors referring to his father behind his back as "the Temple-builder" because of the wooden model he had spent years constructing accord-ing to the descriptions in the Bible and Maimonides, and the habit he had of singing to himself as he worked: "The Temple will be rebuilt, the City of Zion renewed . . ." The Temple-builder had taken his Temple and left the country with it. He claimed that he was going to Vienna to study cabinetmaking, but after his departure Srulik had heard from a number of newcomers to the country that his father was not in Vienna but in the villages of Poland, and that he was not studying cabinetmaking but showing his model of the Temple to Jews who, there too, called him the Temple-builder.

With his father gone, Grandma Shifra's role became more important than ever. True, there had never been a time when they did not require her assistance, since the Temple-builder had never earned enough to provide for his family. But after his father's disappearance, their dependence on his maternal grandmother's charity increased, since what Srulik himself earned at the library was barely enough to cover his school fees and pocket money. And week after week the same scene repeated itself: after putting it off from day to day, his mother would finally pull herself together and go round to her mother's on Thursday morning to receive the weekly handout in time for the Sabbath. In Grandma Shifra's house she would sit on the big sofa in the big room, place at her feet the straw basket to be filled with the food her mother's money would buy, fold her hands in her lap, bow her shoulders, and blink her eyes with the same expres-sion of painful anticipation that she wore when mounting the dentist's chair. In contrast to the dentist, who would sometimes dig and drill and sometimes not, her mother never skipped her weekly ration of digging and drilling,

which never deviated from the established ritual order—
beginning with expressions of commiseration in the way her
daughter looked, fading away in the prime of her life, and
ending with an enumeration of the catastrophes that had
befallen her as the punishment only to be expected for her
disobedience to her mother and insistence on marrying that
artisan, that worthless rascal, that irresponsible good-for-
nothing, that fool who was known to the whole world by the
ridiculous name of Temple-builder. At this stage of her
discourse she would go up to the drawer where she kept her
papers and take out the brown receipt book where Srulik's
mother would sign that on such and such a date she had
received such and such a sum, on account of the money
coming to her from her father's will. His mother's hand
would shake as she signed, and after his father's disappearance her knees would at this stage fail her to such an
extent from weakness and backache that she would have to
go straight home with her empty basket in her hand to lie
down, leaving the Sabbath shopping for Srulik to do when
he came home from school. It was quite clear to him that he
himself, even if he was literally dying of hunger, would never
go to beg for Grandma Shifra's charity. If he ever went to
her, it would be to claim what the wicked old woman had
robbed her sick daughter of, to extract his mother's lawful
inheritance from her by force, with compound interest, with
a high hand, and in the eyes of all the world.

The urgent need to recover his mother's stolen property
from his grandmother would awake in him every morning as
he hurried to boil the kettle on the kerosene-ring. This
boiling of the water for his early-morning coffee penetrated
to the marrow of his being and went on palpitating in his
blood all his life, right up to his last years on earth, when
there was not a kerosene-ring or a Primus to be seen. It took
at least twenty minutes from the moment he lit the kerosene-
ring until the amount of water needed for two cups of coffee

began to boil. So he would hurl himself at the kerosene-ring the moment he opened his eyes on a new day, and then do everything else—wash, dress, prepare his books and his sandwich for the ten-o'clock break—after which he would return to the kerosene-ring to listen for the eagerly awaited sound of the water boiling in the kettle. This rush to light the wick on waking remained imprinted on his limbs, losing none of its force in the years to come, even after the kerosene-ring had been replaced by an electric kettle or a gas-cooker which boiled water in a few minutes. And if in his student years, anxious not to be late for his first class, he would return too soon to the kerosene-ring, only to discover that the kettle was still far from boiling, in the years to come he would often wait too long and find the kettle empty, with all the water evaporated. In the last years of his life, when his own body was no longer capable of leaping for the stove, the moment he opened his eyes in the morning he would call impatiently to his wife: "Paula, put the water on to boil!"—even when the aroma of the coffee had already begun to spread through the house.

He could, of course, have boiled the water more quickly on the Primus, but the noise would have awakened his mother. Since his father's disappearance the pains in her back had increased to such an extent that they kept her awake at night, and she fell asleep only at dawn. There was also a quiet Primus in the kitchen, but it had been broken when Srulik was a child and had never been used since. It needed a new head, but there was never enough money to buy one. If he ever had any money, he would buy not only a new head for the old Primus, but a quiet Primus as well, brand-new from its head to its three feet, which would burn with a beautiful, silent, bright blue flame. This morning, having come home too late to iron his shirt the night before, he had no choice but to light the noisy old Primus in order to heat up the iron, and his mother did indeed wake up with the noise of the pumping. But this time she woke in a good mood, without any pains, and said, "You know what, Srulik, I've just had a wonderful dream. I dreamed that your father came home!" The roar of the Primus which had woken his mother and with her all her longings for his father, began to flicker and expire before the iron had time to get hot, and when it was dead Srulik remembered that there was not enough kerosene in the container, and that he had even said to himself a few days before that it was time to buy a gallon or two, but he didn't have the time or the money. "Never mind," mumbled his mother as she slid back into sleep with the dying of the flame, "it won't be so terrible if you go to the seminary with a creased shirt for once. You'll easily pass your exams anyway. The Temple-builder never went out in a well-pressed shirt in his life. The best-pressed shirt in the world, a shirt I had spent a whole hour ironing, would suddenly look creased when he put it on. I really don't know why everything looked creased on him: trousers, sleeves, collars . . ."

She was right, of course: he passed his final exams with honors despite his creased shirt-collar, and she too recovered sufficiently to resume the weekly torture of her visits to her mother, and there was only one week left—the last week of slavery—separating him from the great voyage to Ur of the Chaldees, when Rosa suddenly appeared in the seminary courtyard. From the classroom window he saw her coming through the gate, pale and breathless, and his heart immediately skipped a beat in the knowledge that something terrible had happened to his mother—although there might have been many other explanations for Rosa's appearance at the seminary. She was sometimes summoned to assist the cook, for example. And if it was not on her own business that she had entered the gate this time, but on a mission for someone else, surely it was more likely that she had come to call Gabriel Luria, since she not only worked in his house twice a week, but was also the sister of Señor Moïse, his father's kawass? Having crossed the threshold of the gate, she hesitated for a moment, apparently at a loss, and Srulik felt that he should hurry out to her, but before he could do so she appealed to that imbecile, Professor Zvi Sadeh, the geography teacher, who emerged into the courtyard with his briefcase and his cane and his self-importance. For all her agitation, she bowed her head and waited respectfully for his reply: the poor woman revered anyone who knew how to read and write, and how much more so a gentleman like Zvi Sadeh, who was not only a teacher, but a teacher of teachers. Srulik, who was well acquainted with both of them and knew that she had more innate intelligence and common sense in her little finger than he had in the whole of his big head— not to speak of other human qualities—was filled with anger at the sight of her abnegation before this fool with a diploma, even with a kind of general, absolute despair, as if he had seen the face of humanity itself reflected with horrifying clarity in the scene. "All these great men, these saviors and doctors and leaders, are as capable of bringing salvation to the masses who worship them as Dr. Sadeh is of bringing back Rosa's father, who was murdered by Arabs twenty years ago." What did Arab murderers have to do with it? In the sudden shock of his despair the connection seemed direct and obvious. "All is lost," Srulik said to himself. "There's no hope. The crooked cannot be straightened and the missing cannot be counted."

Dr. Sadeh said something to Rosa and pointed his cane toward the secretary's office; she nodded her kerchiefed head and disappeared into the building. When five whole minutes had gone by and the classroom door had not been opened, Srulik breathed a sigh of relief: his fears were groundless. If the anxiety that had gripped him at the sight of Rosa coming through the gate had no basis in reality, it must have stemmed from his chronic nervousness, the inner tension which made him quail before every leaf blown in the wind. "It's a miracle that Rosa didn't come into the classroom," he said to himself, an effervescent gaiety beginning to replace his fading anxiety as a luminous picture from bygone days floated to the surface of his mind. Once, many years before, his father had prevented a shop from being burgled and helped catch the thieves. The incident was reported in the papers, and when he was called by the police as a witness, the whole neighborhood came to court to see him—everyone except for Grandma Shifra. A little girl in a blue dress ran down the long courthouse corridor, and everyone smiled at her and called her Orita. Even the policemen drew back and made way for her gladly because she was the judge's daughter. While giving his evidence and describing how in pursuing the thieves he had fallen into a pit full of junk, his father said, "It was a miracle I didn't break both my legs." The judge, who had listened up to then with a blank, expressionless face, suddenly smiled and remarked, "That's the way things are nowadays. The miracle today is the catastrophe that could have happened and didn't take place." At the thought "It's a miracle that Rosa didn't come into the classroom," Srulik was flooded with light and joy and a tremor of the strange happiness he had tasted then, which was not spoiled despite the absence of the little girl in the blue dress. When he saw her running down the corridor, he had hoped that she would come into the courtroom and see him and his father in all his glory, but the little Orita had disappeared behind some other door.

It was Grandma Shifra who had bitterly disappointed him then. After all his father's boldness and heroism, after he had been written about in the newspapers and commended in court, after all the neighbors and all the shopkeepers, from Beth Israel to the Bucharan Quarter, had come to shake his hand and congratulate him—Srulik was sure that his grandmother's eyes would finally be opened and that she would see what kind of a man his father was. He was sure that in her heart she regretted all the insulting things she had said to his face and behind his back, that inside herself she was both sorry and glad: sorry for the sins she had sinned against him in thought and deed, and glad that his glory had now shone forth over the entire neighborhood. She was thinking only of the best way to recompense him, of the lovely surprise she had in store for him. Since he suffered from a chronic lack of good tools of his own, and was always having to run to the workshops of others, she was probably renting a big, airy workshop for him in the middle of the new commercial center and filling it with the most up-to-date machinery money could buy. Only after everything was ready, then and only then, would she invite them all to come with her, and she still wouldn't give the surprise away. Outside the workshop door she would present him with the keys and say: "Here, it's yours. Open the door—what are you waiting for?" But that very same day, when they came back from the court, he overheard her saying to his mother: "Naturally! Catching thieves—what else is he good for? I've always said he was a ruffian. From the moment I set eyes on him I knew that the man standing before me was a man of strife and contention to the whole earth." Just like that. She always had the apt phrase, the relevant biblical quotation ready. When she heard that the Temple-builder had gone away and left her daughter destitute and penniless, she was overjoyed that all her dire prophecies had come true, in her own lifetime, and more speedily than she had dared hope. This wicked old woman was immune to all the ills and misfortunes in the world. Every day people younger and better than she were run over in the streets, sweet young girls died a thousand deaths in hospitals, while this old witch went from strength to strength. Then, when he heard her say that his father was good for nothing but playing cops and robbers, he had yelled: "I wish you were dead!" and his

mother had shut him up. He had cursed his grandmother
with all his might and all his heart and soul, and he had
believed that his curse would come true. He was even afraid
that if she died within the next few days he would be
arrested and put on trial for murder. Ten years had passed
since then and she was still blooming, while her daughter
wilted. Who knows, she was quite likely to outlive him, her
own grandson, too—and what's more, to have the pleasure
of knowing that it was she he was thinking of at the moment
of his death.

Afraid that his teacher and classmates would think him
mad, Srulik suppressed a loud burst of laughter. That
would really be the last straw, the best trick yet played by that
bastard fate—to teach him, little Srulik, a lesson and finish
him off at the very moment when he was thinking of his
hatred for his Grandma Shifra and his anger against his
teacher, Zvi Sadeh. What last image would he take with him
of life on this earth? Not a beautiful, beloved image, not
something lofty and precious and good, but something contemptible and hateful and stupid and petty that in the last
analysis was not important to him or the least bit interesting.
If he was destined to die now, at this moment, he would wish
to think of something pleasant, to see a series of images that
would be good to take with him as souvenirs, and for whose
sake his life would have been worth living. It was quite
illogical, of course, and once the game was over it made no
difference one way or the other, but nevertheless it was very
important to him, if he was going to die now, to contemplate
something pleasant, some memory capable of warming his
heart—but to his annoyance, his anger against his grandmother was replaced by the bad taste left by his conversation
with Professor Talmi. A few days before, when plans for "the
great voyage to Ur of the Chaldees" were ready (in his
notebook he called it the "great voyage" but in his heart he
preferred the word "trip" for its associations of pleasure and

freedom), he wanted to discuss the whole idea with Professor Talmi. In fact, Talmi was the only person in the world to whom he was not just willing but actually eager to reveal his project. For it was in the wake of one of Talmi's articles that the idea had first come to Srulik, and the only things that had made this last year at the seminary worthwhile were Talmi's lectures on "the spiritual crisis of our times."

But the eagerly anticipated meeting, which took place at the Café Gat, had not been a success. The more he talked, the more Srulik felt that his words awoke no echo, and that he was banging his head against a stone wall: Professor Talmi saw no need for all this traveling in order to understand the idea behind the story of Father Abraham—especially since there was not the faintest chance of discovering any new texts either in Ur of the Chaldees or in Haran. On the other hand, he began to tell Srulik about a number of texts he himself had discovered the year before in the British Museum, texts that were capable of revolutionizing all our ideas; and he confided to him that he was busy writing a book on the subject, which was going to "explode like a bomb on the heads of all the scholars in the world." At this stage Talmi sank into a kind of melancholy that made him look like a wrinkled and bespectacled baby about to burst into tears, and began talking about his troubles: to be precise, the troubles caused him by his wife, who would not allow him to finish the last chapter and was holding up the explosion of his bombshell. Now that the bad taste left by the meeting had returned to his mouth, Srulik made up his mind to request a second interview in order to "make everything clear." The failure of the previous meeting was certainly due to Professor Talmi's bad mood because of his troubles with his wife. But Srulik, too, was to blame for not having explained his ideas properly. Next time he would succeed in getting through to him.

When the classroom door opened and the secretary asked

for Israel Shoshan, he knew that Rosa was standing behind her, and before the latter had a chance to open her mouth he was already running in the direction of home, with Rosa puffing and panting behind him. "Your mother," she said to him as they ran, "your mother fell on the floor and she can't get up." She was red in the face with exertion and he was afraid that something would happen to her too. "Listen, Rosa." He stopped and said, "I'll go on ahead. You don't have to run like that. It's not good for your health. You can walk slowly and come later." Rosa nodded but kept running after him and trying to catch up with him anyway. He decided to slow down, and the moment he did so she tripped over a coil of electric cable lying on the sidewalk in front of Judge Gutkin's house; if he hadn't been there beside her to support her with both hands, she would have fallen flat on her face. One of the workers dragging the cable into the gate yelled at her: "What's the matter with you? Haven't you got eyes in your head?" If he had had the time Srulik would have taught the rude fellow a lesson: What did he mean by obstructing the public highway and then on top of it shouting at Rosa? The closer he came to home the more his dread increased, and as he crossed the threshold he had to stop himself from asking Rosa if his mother was still alive.

His mother was sitting up in bed, pale and smiling wanly, and he wanted to jump for joy. While Rosa was running to fetch him, his mother had managed to get up by herself and sit on her bed, and before sitting down she had even gone to the kitchen and made herself a cup of tea. When he saw her alive and sitting up and smiling—a weak smile, true, but one that reflected full consciousness and a lucid mind—he ran up to her and kissed her again and again in a transport of joy—the joy of deliverance from the nightmare that had gripped him the moment he saw Rosa in the seminary court-yard, and whose full terror he realized only now that he was saved from it. Already a few months earlier he had heard the doctor say that his mother should not be left alone. There should always be someone with her, not because she was gravely ill, but because from time to time—and there was no way of foreseeing when—she was liable to lose control over her legs and would require assistance to get into bed "until it passed." The doctor had spoken of the need to prevent a "hard fall," and Srulik understood that he was referring to the danger of her falling backward when she was alone, and breaking her neck. Now that the nightmare was over and it appeared that she not only had not broken her neck but had not even been badly bruised, everything else seemed simple, easy, a matter of organization. From now on he would have to organize things so there would always be someone with her, get some sort of duty roster going—but first of all, he had to fetch the doctor to examine her. As if reading his mind Rosa said, "I'll stay here with your mother while you go to fetch the doctor." In his relief he wanted to kiss Rosa too, but he suddenly felt embarrassed and set off at a run.

As Srulik had expected, the doctor found no damage from the fall except for shock and weakness, and he had nothing new to say on the subject of the need to keep a vigilant eye on his mother or the chances of a recovery. Before leaving he whispered in Srulik's ear—and this was not new either—only that he would like him to drop in for a chat one day next week, and Srulik understood that the chat would be about the desirability of doing further tests on his mother and perhaps even hospitalizing her. But on his way to the doctor's something happened: the way was the same way he had been taking to school for the past three years, since the doctor's house lay just behind the seminary, in the street parallel to it, and in order to reach it he had to hurry up the steep incline of the Street of the Prophets and pass the judge's house. The coil of electric cable upon which Rosa had previously stumbled had already been dragged inside, and on the other side of the fence he saw the worker putting up colored lights. "Let her come out," he said to himself, more out of habit than anything else—as he did twice a day when he passed the gate—but this time, as if in answer to his routine prayer, she did come sailing out, and met him face to face. She was angry and agitated, as if she had just emerged from losing a quarrel, and when she encountered him she composed herself and said: "Oh, is it you, Srulik? Why do you look so happy?" "It's a miracle," he said, feeling that his heart was about to burst out of his mouth. "My mother fell and wasn't killed. She wasn't hurt at all." At the same time he remembered that when he had first set eyes on her ten years before—a little girl in a blue dress running down the corridor—he had heard her father say to his: "The miracle today is the catastrophe that could have happened and didn't take place." She frowned as if she were trying to comprehend some obscure riddle, and suddenly burst out laughing. "You really are awfully amusing," she said, and it was only then that he realized that his words had sounded to her like some sort of joke whose point she hadn't immediately caught: some joker in the street had announced to her that he was deliriously happy because his mother had not been killed or his grandmother had not fallen out of bed.

"You don't know how miserable I am." Now she was serious again. "I've had a terrible fight with my father. He's decided that he needs the car the whole month long, after promising me I could have it for at least three days for a long trip."

"I'm getting ready for a trip too. A long trip. Very long. Much longer than three days." When he had revealed his project to Professor Talmi on that unfortunate occasion he had not imagined telling anyone else about it, much less Orita. "Let's go together, then. I'm game!" And indeed, she looked ready to set out immediately. "When do we leave?"

"I haven't decided yet," he said, marveling that his heart had not yet flown out of his mouth like a fluttering bird from its cage. The abstract idea was taking on flesh before his very eyes. "There are still a couple of things I have to organize. And first I have to talk to the doctor."

"And about how long will your preparations take?" She was impatient and practical.

"I imagine four or five weeks," he said, a little alarmed at committing himself to so near a date. After all, the doctor might diagnose something seriously wrong with his mother, and nothing had yet been done about arranging the duty roster of people to stay with her.

"Five weeks?" cried Orita, all the wind suddenly taken out of her sails. Why, in less than five weeks her father's car would be at her disposal! She waved him a hasty good-bye and ran across the road toward the Café Gat or Gabriel Luria's house, and Srulik went on running to the doctor's, murmuring to himself, "This is a great day, the day beyond the great river, the day beyond the day, the day beyond."

Even after the doctor had left and his mother had eaten the food Rosa prepared for her, and in fact all that day, whenever he had a moment to spare, he found himself murmuring, "The day beyond." He felt as if he were full to the brim with something great and precious, which he was loath to waste on trivial cares and concerns. It was only in the evening, when his mother had fallen asleep, that he went out into the yard and, like a man taking his treasures out one by one and arranging them carefully before him (not only in order to enjoy them to the fullest but also to reckon up their value), he passed the images of the day before his eyes, beginning with Rosa's appearance and ending with Orita's. But while Rosa's image remained clearly before him, including details he had not even noticed at the time, such as the brassy henna color of the hair peeping out of her kerchief, Orita's refused to stand still at his command: the picture frame was filled with the shock of her presence, which had struck him like a whirlwind at the gate and stopped his

breath with the wild beating of his heart. Within this fragrant whirlpool he caught fleeting glimpses of the gleam of
her big brown eyes, of the smile on her lips, slightly parted
even when her mouth was closed because of the fullness of
her drooping lower lip, the shining lock of hair perpetually
falling over her left eye and tossed back again, the glow of
the flesh pulled tightly over her high cheekbones. And when
he tried to force these rays of light to stay inside the picture
frame, the Orita of the greatest moment in his life, the
moment when she had asked him to take her with him
wherever he went, vanished, to be replaced by other images
of Orita, from other, previous occasions—the usual Orita of
his thoughts, the Orita he wished to see when he offered up
the routine daily prayer: "Let her come out."

A cold, crisp winter's day and she comes out in leather
boots, a tartan skirt, and a blue scarf fluttering in the wind
and getting mixed up with the black flames of her hair, and
draped over her shoulders the sheepskin coat she received as
a gift from Sheik Zay'iin on the occasion of the reconciliation feast her father arranged between two tribes next to
Beersheba. The coat was not given to her because of her
father: she won it herself in the riding and marksmanship
contests. She smiles at him and the sky opens and sings
between her lips; she waves at him and the mountains of
Moab rise and fall to the rhythm of the dance. The pouring
abundance of all the worlds, taut and trembling, is balanced
on a razor's edge. One false move from him, the blink of an
eye out of step with the delicate rhythm, and he is thrown
from the twinkling stars of the benevolent smile into the
jagged abyss of the smile of contempt. A double-edged
sword of a smile, sending you to heaven or to hell.

He had noticed the changes in this smile even before
Gabriel had introduced them, in those bygone days when he
thought he would never be able to speak to her unless some
miracle breached the invisible wall surrounding her as

impregnably as the stone wall around her father's house. There seemed to be a hidden thread connecting her eyes to her lips, and the least emotion taking place inside her would strike this thread and make it vibrate: a tiny tremor here, and a merciful smile would flood her face—a tiny tremor there, and her lips would purse and her eyes narrow in the scorn and disgust particularly reserved for importunate suitors. Nothing in the world, it seemed, was more loathsome and detestable to her than the attentions of a man she did not like. One such smile of contempt, for instance, was enough to seal the fate of Yankele Blum, who since then had not even dared to greet her in the street. But there were others, of course, less sensitive to the drooping of her lips and twitching of her eyelids, like Dr. Yaakov Talmi—he was not yet a professor then—who failed to grasp the sentence passed on him by her undisguised disdain. Srulik could not decide if Talmi was really too blind to see what Orita's smiles meant, or if he simply ignored what his eyes told him. In either case, it was certain that he interpreted the signs in the way most pleasing to him, and went on courting her with all the obstinacy and thick-skinned impertinence at his command—until she insulted him in public, and in the presence of the people who were most important to him: the officials of the British Mandate. She did it as if she were crushing a bothersome fly after failing to chase it away by waving her hand, not as an act of premeditated malice or arrogance. In general, her behavior and facial expressions were distinguished by an utter lack of premeditation, an absence of anything false, affected, or forced. She had inherited some of her most prominent features from her father: the high cheekbones, the chin and mouth. But in contrast to his cold, blank expression, her most fleeting sensation was reflected on her face; and it was always astonishing to see the two of them together because of the differences despite the resemblance, or the resemblance despite the differences. The features were the same, but each of them, as it were, made different use of the vessel they had been given: while the father used his as a lid to hide the contents of the pot, the daughter made hers a mirror to reflect what was happening inside, and the wonder was that not only the same feature but also the identical movement, the same twisting of the lip for example, would close his face and open hers.

Her sister, Yael, who was two years older, resembled their father too, but nevertheless she was far less like Orita than could have been imagined. Yael wasn't ugly, and some people were even attracted by "something strange and special" they saw in her, but ultimately this paternal inheritance had conferred a heaviness and sternness on her face, especially about the mouth and chin. These features might have been a burden to Orita too, but for the miraculous sculpting of Nature, who had apparently decided to show all mortal artists what she could do with the most intractable lines if she felt like it, and how could she not feel like carving the face of Orita? The heavy lower lip and cleft chin which imparted firmness to her father's face and gravity to her sister's gave hers a kind of mischievous eagerness, a cheeky, provocative sensuality.

Srulik's prolonged observation of her father had revealed yet another marvel in this mysterious game of resemblances, something so absurd that it could only deepen his harrowing sense that everything depended on the slightest of contradictions. He came to know the judge's face when he went to court sessions in hopes of meeting her as she got in or out of her father's car, or even simply of being near someone who shared in her life, or of hearing her surname spoken. He would sit in the audience and contemplate those stern, impenetrable features which had left their imprint on Orita, and the better he came to know them the more he realized that the judge's face reflected a greater delicacy than his daughter's; that the crude, rough-hewn features offered a nobler image than their tender, beautiful reproduction. For then it seemed to him that the inscrutability of the judge's face was hiding and guarding something extraordinary in its subtlety, something quintessentially spiritual, while the transparency of his daughter's breathed the breath of the flesh. At the same time he realized that it was precisely this exhalation of the earthy and elemental which attracted him, this quiver of sensuality reflected in her whole being—in her body, her movements, her speech, and her laughter. She had a dancer's body, fuller in the hips than the chest, and her legs were long and strong. She had even studied dancing for a while with Elsa Revlon, the modern dancer who had come from Germany, which only emphasized the innate perfection of every movement and posture of her body.

Orita did not know, of course, what an earthquake was provoked in little Srulik's heart by every swing of her hips, every tremor of the leg resting on the counter rail while she chatted with the proprietor of the Café Gat or anyone else who happened to drop in, every lift of her breast when she breathed, every inclination of her neck revealing the tip of an earlobe, every peal of laughter coming out of her mouth, every flutter of an eyelash reflected in the windowpane, every flash of a smile for good or ill. And since she did not know, she could never have imagined the terrific efforts it cost him to keep her from knowing, from sensing or feeling or guessing one fraction of what was going on in his heart. And all from fear. Not fear of humiliation, for he was beyond caring about that. He was ready for anything, not only ready but eager to do anything for her and at her command, to make himself a laughingstock and be disgraced forever, if only she would allow him to be in her company. His terrible fear was of a sentence of banishment from her presence, a dark dread that the moment she became aware of his sentiments she would send him packing just like Yankele Blum and Yaakov Talmi and the rest of the poor wretches who had courted her against her will. Srulik knew this by instinct, and he had been confirmed in his intuition by a remark of hers about all kinds of little cockroaches who wanted to be rapists—a remark she had made after sending Dr. Talmi to the devil. Furthermore, when he stepped into her shoes and saw things from her point of view, he realized that she had no choice but to squash the said cockroach and wash it down the drain so that it would not continue revolting her. Until Dr. Talmi had begun pursuing her, he was nothing but one of the people who came to see her father, someone who made no difference one way or the other, just another scholar, quite young and gifted, who might even say something interesting and intelligent once in a while at the dinner table, but from the moment he began to court her he turned into a cockroach—and quite naturally so. Suddenly he had forced her to turn her attention from the things he said to the person who said them, and the person himself could not seem to be anything in her eyes but a little cockroach, a pale worm. The two tufts of hair waving on either side of his bald head like a pair of feelers, the frail, boneless body, the soft hands without power or competence, fluttering feebly at his sides like the wings of a helpless insect. And all of sudden— dear God almighty!—this insect sidles up to her with his feelers groping in the air and his feeble wings fluttering, and begins to carry on in a way he no doubt considers irresistible, squeaking and buzzing sweet nothings in her ear, and proposing in all seriousness—ah, the horror of it!— no less than to go to bed with her, and as he wrote in that frightful letter, "to love her forever and ever." She tries to shake him off, but the disgusting creature refuses to go away, and back he comes, creeping and crawling, reaching out with his sticky pincers, and if she doesn't crush him immediately, this hell will open up and swallow her "forever and ever."

And what did the cockroach in question do after he had

been crushed? First of all he got married in a hurry, and then he told his wife and all the world—even the people who had witnessed all his humiliations—that Orita was "not normal, a girl full of sexual complexes." He spread his hints liberally in all directions, and his listeners were free to come to their own conclusions as they saw fit: if they decided she was a lesbian, she was a lesbian; if they decided she was frigid, she was frigid.

"And so, my dear Srulik," Srulik would say to his reflection in the mirror before going out to one of the places where, according to all his calculations, he had the best chance of finding Orita, "where do your strength and manhood lie? In the fact that you are not a cockroach." Concluding that Orita should now be at Gabriel Luria's house, he hurries there as fast as his legs can carry him, on the pretext that Gabriel's library books have been overdue for a month. The Street of the Prophets splits open lengthwise and Srulik sinks into the chasm made by the earthquake which devastates his heart at the sight of Orita sprawled on the leather couch on Gabriel Luria's verandah. "Oh, hello, Orita, you're here, are you?" he says calmly—with neither demonstrative indifference nor exaggerated emotion, but cordially and friendly—and immediately awards himself a medal for unprecedented self-control and heroism of the highest degree, the Victoria Cross for succeeding in greeting her without a tremor in his voice on the one hand or a note of cold hostility on the other. For succeeding, that is, with one elegant, efficient blow, in crushing the deadliest of his enemies: the cockroach.

"You know," he says, sitting at her feet on the sofa before his knees give way beneath him, "I had an important idea today, a great idea!" "What?" cries Orita, her eyes lighting up. And the earth quakes again, this time even more violently than before. The Dead Sea sees it and flees, the Jordan

is driven back, the mountains of Jerusalem skip like rams—
and Srulik shoots like a comet into the sky between the sun
and the moon in Orita's eyes. Lofty and exalted, the mighty
Srulik glides, and the earth trembles before him. Omnipo-
tent, Srulik awaits the bidding of the sun and the moon.

"To form a select, elite group of people and teach them
the great secret," says the Master.

"I'll join," says Orita. "What secret?"

"The great secret of how not to be a cockroach."

Orita bursts into peals of clear, ringing laughter and all
the stars turn into resonant drops in the melodious sea of
the sky.

"You and your queer ideas," she says to him, and then she
turns to Gabriel and adds: "I think that Srulik is so amusing
because nothing is really important to him." Srulik smiles
and she says to him: "Yes, the reason you can be so amiable
and easygoing is that nothing in the world really touches
your heart." Touched to the quick of his heart, his soul,
Srulik immediately awards himself another medal—the
medal for heroism in the secret service.

"And where is this great secret hidden?" inquires Gabriel,
and with his question the antique clock inside the house
emits four sonorous peals. "I'll be late for work—I have to
run," says Srulik. "We'll talk about it next time." Children
with books to change must be waiting in front of the locked
library door by now, and he came here only for a minute to
breathe, to fill his lungs with alpine air before diving back
into his sea of troubles, one deeper than the next.

"The great secret is hidden in the mirror," said Srulik
to himself when he saw his reflection in the big mirror in the
Café Gat. After closing the library at eight o'clock, he
dropped into the café on his way home. According to their
hastily improvised schedule Rosa would stay with his mother
until nine in the evening, so he had almost an entire hour to
himself, to rest and study the map of his situation so that he

could chart his route out of these narrow straits and into the open horizons of Ur of the Chaldees.

"Seeing is believing," he said to himself, as his father used to say when he wanted to show a customer what a table or cabinet would look like, and with exactly the same gesture he pulled a pencil and notebook from his inside pocket and began sketching, not furniture or the articles of worship in the Temple, but a diagram of his present situation and the necessary sequence of action. If he had had a few colored pencils with him the map would have looked better, but even in black and white it came out quite well. Once it was completed it appeared that the situation was not so desperate nor the outlook so dark as he had imagined, and the longer he studied it the lighter his heart became and the greater the stirrings of joy at the imminent realization of his hopes. One more examination from the right angle and the glad tidings would leap out from between the lines: the great journey, so eagerly awaited, was not only not precluded by his miserable troubles, but actually made imperative by them; and as he had already said to Orita the day before, all the necessary arrangements would take no more than two months to complete. Obviously, he would first have to go to the doctor, to obtain as clear and definite information as possible about his mother's illness and her chances for a speedy recovery. All the rest was only a question of the organization of the "shifts"—which is how he referred to the need for someone always to be with her—to be shared among himself, his sister, and Grandma Shifra. For a moment he thought of including Elka and Ethel in these shifts. And when he set out on his great journey, their neighbor Rosa would replace him, and he would pay her in full for every hour that she spent with his mother. He would pay her for three months in advance. In the last analysis it was only a problem of money, and he could earn the necessary amount by working overtime. If he worked from morning to night and night to

morning for two months at anything he could get, there was
no doubt that he could pay Rosa for three months in
advance, as well as cover the initial expenses of his journey.

And what if at the end of two months, after working night
and day at anything that came his way, however odious, and
earning enough money, and paying Rosa in full, and after
organizing all the shifts in the most satisfactory way among
his sister and Grandma Shifra and Rosa (and who knows, in
the meantime his mother might even recover, or at least
improve, as she had done before, in which case she would no
longer require all these elaborate arrangements!), and after
everything was ready for the voyage back to the origins of
the first Hebrew—what if, after all this, Orita suddenly
changed her mind? What if she suddenly decided not to go
with little Srulik to Ur of the Chaldees, but to stay here in
Jerusalem with her English acquaintances, or take a trip to
Paris with one of her artist friends?

First of all: it wasn't Srulik who had proposed the idea to
her, but she who had proposed it to him; not she who had
consented to accompany him, but he who had consented to
take her with him on his journey. It had happened only
yesterday: there he was, walking distractedly past her house,
when the gate suddenly opened and Orita stood there as
large as life, crying enthusiastically, impatiently: "Let's go
together, then. I'm game! When do we leave?" The café
walls expanded from the Euphrates to the Tigris and the
ceiling rose to the stars in a joyful flood of memory: . . . *I
remember thee, the kindness of thy youth, the love of thine espousals,
when thou wentest after me in the wilderness, in a land that was not
sown, beyond the river toward the sunrising. Thus, alone together
in the heart of the desert, to drown in the fathomless light of those
eyes and to die and to live.* And once more, like yesterday, when
he tried to recall that great moment, Orita's image refused
to take shape in his memory, and all kinds of details which
had surrounded her at that time and place appeared

instead, claiming his attention and attaching themselves to what had slipped his mind. When Orita spoke of joining him he saw through the opening in the fence a worker sitting in the garden, fixing colored light bulbs to an electric cable. It was the same worker who had shouted at Rosa fifteen minutes earlier, when they were hurrying home from the seminary. The worker had dragged the cable into the judge's garden, where he was now busy hanging the lights from the trees in preparation for the big party. Yes, of course, it was obviously for the party Gabriel had told him about. The news that the Supreme Court judge Dan Gutkin had been named O.B.E. had already been published in the newspapers—"Officer of the British Empire," highest of the titles awarded by His Majesty on his official birthday to a chosen few of those who served him throughout that part of his Empire east of the Suez and west of the Persian Gulf. For the occasion His Honor the Judge, O.B.E., was giving a garden party which promised to be the grandest affair Jerusalem high society had ever seen, and which would be attended by the full flower of the said high society, beginning with the High Commissioner himself, and ending with all the mayors and notables of the various communities and the foreign consuls residing in the capital city. In order to prevent the intrusion of the gate-crashers who always appear at these affairs, and to protect the heads of government and army officers who would gather there, a guard of British policemen would be stationed around the house to bar entry to any but the invited guests. As soon as news of the garden party reached the ears of the Yishuv, a panic-stricken stampede for invitations broke out, and anyone who discovered that his honor had sunk so low, that his name had been dragged through the dust by not being included on the official guest list, set out with urgent haste to correct the omission and lay his hands on an invitation. On this subject Gabriel told Srulik a story concerning Professor Yaakov

Talmi. A week before, when he came home from the seminary, Gabriel had found the young scholar in question sitting on the verandah, engaged in animated conversation with his father and Señor Moïse. The unexpected guest had displayed an astonishing knowledge of the old Bey's family tree, going back in a direct line to the Holy Ari, as well as the extent of his glories and greatness in the days of the Turks, who had awarded him the title of Bey, which in terms of the British Empire of our own day was more or less equivalent to that of Sir. Which meant that the old man was the equal in rank of no less a personage than the High Commissioner himself! And in addition to all this, Talmi showed the keenest enthusiasm, accompanied by much waving of his hands and creasing of his brows, for the old man's brilliant innovations on the subject of Moses. But to Gabriel's great surprise, his father did not respond to his guest's enthusiasm with any enthusiasm of his own. Yehuda Prosper Bey, who in his old age could think of nothing but our master Moses; who was happy to sit for hours on end with anyone at all—be he deaf, dumb, or child—who was prepared to listen to his commentaries and interpretations on the history of his hero; who could not control his passion, even to the extent of exposing himself repeatedly to the wrath of his wife, who immediately retaliated by snatching the hat off his head and stamping on it, because there was nothing in the world that infuriated her more than our master Moses—this same Yehuda Prosper Bey suddenly withdrew behind a wall of affable politeness precisely when confronted by this important guest, *the* expert on the subject closest to his heart, who had fallen into his lap like a veritable gift from the gods. The old man seemed not only unenthusiastic, but even eager to put off the entire conversation to another day. It was only after the guest had gone, promising to come back the very next day, that Gabriel discovered how quick the senses of this former man of the world, close to the seat of power and active in society in his day, were to awaken from their long and profound slumbers and deploy themselves in the full force of their erstwhile subtlety and sharpness. "I smell favors and honors cooking here," he pronounced in his hoarse, ancient voice. "But what can I possibly give him today, and what is it that he wants to get out of me? I would have said that he was about to ask me to exert my influence with Gutkin to send him an invitation, but he surely doesn't need me for that. He knows the judge well enough to ask him himself. And if something has happened between them, I would have to speak to Gutkin first in any case, to find out if he was worthy of my recommendation. And even if they have fallen out, he would be invited not as a friend of the family but as one of the professors on the list of important scholars, unless Gutkin has given explicit instructions to the court secretary to cross his name off the list. And if Gutkin went to all that trouble, then Talmi must have done something to deserve being crossed off the list and he wouldn't get my recommendation anyway." Gutkin had indeed taken the trouble to have Talmi's name crossed off the list of invitees, and the old man's entire train of thought was perfectly accurate except for one detail of which he was ignorant, and which would not have made him change his mind in any case—on the contrary, it would probably have increased his determination not to give Professor Talmi any kind of recommendation whatsoever. For the professor's name would not have been crossed off the list, nor would the mere mention of it have infuriated the judge, if Talmi had not pressed his attentions on Orita.

Since the whole business was distasteful and repugnant to her, Orita saw no reason at the time to tell her father about Talmi's attentions or the manner in which she was obliged to rid herself of them. This had happened at the home of the old English painter Holmes on the way to Bethlehem. Holmes, who had built his house next to the Greek monas-

tery of Mar Elias, and who had spent fifty years painting
landscapes of the country, especially those he saw from his
garden—the Judean desert and Herodian and Bethlehem
on one side, the Mount of Olives and Mount Scopus and
Jerusalem on the other—would from time to time invite
young painters from Bezalel and others, art and nature
lovers, to show them his work. Orita, as we know, was an
enthusiastic advocate of modern art, which painted the soul
of things without trying to make photographic copies of
their outer forms, and since she also believed that anyone
who was not a modernist was not an artist, one might have
supposed that the work of the old painter Holmes would
have seemed trivial and devoid of merit in her eyes. Nevertheless, her heart leapt within her at the sight of these
delicate sketches. She wished to make a thorough examination of the landscapes hanging between the arched windows
overlooking the very same landscapes, in order to understand what it was about them that made her soul vibrate,
despite her artistic ideology. Yes, the old man had great
technical ability and undoubted powers of execution, but
that didn't make it art. So what was it about these precise
sketches that radiated a kind of aura, breathed a kind of
atmosphere that made you feel that you were looking at
the Judean desert through the eyes of Holmes, as if in
every sketch the painter was making you a gift of his eye,
which was an innocent eye, and saw in the Judean desert a
dream and a holiness. She was on the point of clarifying the
meaning of this contradiction, all she needed was another
moment or two, when suddenly, instead of Holmes's
sketches, Professor Talmi's face appeared before her eyes.
Without a word she escaped immediately to the opposite
wall, but he was after her in a flash, pressing her into the
corner and with a self-satisfied smirk pronouncing words of
wisdom on everything she saw around her. She pursed her
lips and made no response, she turned her head away from

him to the sketch of the Valley of Hinnom, but Talmi kept on pouring an eloquent stream of words into her ear. He spoke of the art of painting and she stuck her nose into the Valley of Hinnom and tried to ignore the guttural voice burbling on at her right. The names of Lord Cardon and Lady Ashley surfaced on the stream, which came as no surprise to Orita, since such great names were bound to appear sooner or later in Professor Talmi's discourse—the names of the noblest, most exalted members of the English aristocracy who all, according to him, had vied for his favors when he was working on his doctoral thesis at Cambridge University. The deeper she gazed into the Valley of Hinnom, the louder he spoke, bombarding her with the sensational news that Lady Ashley never bought a painting without consulting him first, and describing how she would detain him for hours on end in order to hear all about the latest developments in modern art from his lips. Since she was unable to jump right into the Valley of Hinnom through the glass covering it, Orita turned around and found herself face to face with Professor Talmi on one side and the British consul on the other—he and his wife and another tall, stooped Englishman whom she did not know but who was apparently even more important than the consul himself, judging by the appraising manner in which Talmi looked him up and down, attempting, no doubt, to ascertain whether the news of the high esteem in which he was held by the Lady with royal connections had reached his ears. Talmi's fluttering hand came to rest, as if by chance, upon Orita's elbow, and she could bear it no longer: with one rude blow she shook off the limp, offending hand, and to its owner she said, "You know, I have never had the honor of meeting Lady Ashley myself, but according to what I have heard I always supposed her to be a capricious, hysterical old bitch. At this moment, however, it seems to me that she must be a saint. If she really put up with you for hours on end, as you say she did, if she didn't send you straight to hell after five minutes, she must be a saint, and not only a saint but a martyr too. But I am not a saint or a martyr or a masochist"—Orita's voice rose to a scream—"so go away! Get out of my sight!" But the scream was superfluous. The little professor had disappeared, vanished into thin air, and she never saw him again. She breathed a sigh of relief at the thought that she would never have to hear the pet name Rita rolling about unbidden and unwanted in that mouth again. At the height of his courtship she had lived in fear of hearing his three taps on her door, loud and discreet at once, and before she could reply, his head would pop into the room with the smiling, belated question: "May I come in, Rita?" "To you I'm Orit Gutkin," she would say, but he would take no notice and call her Rita, as only her family and closest friends did. His intrusion into the intimacy of her nickname angered her even more than his intrusion into her room, for against it she was completely powerless. Her attitude toward her name was the opposite of Srulik's to his. Ever since he could remember, Srulik had felt that his name was something alien to him which had been imposed on him against his will. He was called after his paternal grandfather, Israel Haim, who in his time had been called after his maternal grandfather. Something that reflected the spirit of other men in other times and other places, something not only foreign but antagonistic to his own essential self, clung to this name and trailed after it like a plague. Whereas Orita sensed something of herself, her essence, in her name, and the name Rita carried an echo of those inner circles beyond the veil, which no stranger might approach unpunished. If she could do nothing to prevent Talmi from using her pet name to her face before she banished him from her presence, she was even more powerless to prevent him from taking her name in vain behind her back after his banishment, but she really did not care. Long after she got rid of him, and even after he married, rumors of his spite would reach her ears from time to time without provoking any reaction in or from her, as if these slanders had nothing to do with her. She was happy to be relieved of Talmi's presence, and as long as her eyes did not have to suffer the sight of him, or her ears the sound of his voice, or her nose the smell of his breath, she did not care what he did or said. In his own world he was at liberty to do and say as he saw fit, so long as he did not try to impinge his world on hers. And as time passed without any such attempt on his part, he ceased to exist as far as she was concerned.

One day, when she came home for lunch and went into the dining room, she felt her knees giving way beneath her. Professor Talmi, with his pale, bespectacled smile and his soft fluttering hands, was seated at the table next to her mother like a nightmare come true. Once she had dreamed that a huge, repulsive cockroach had dropped onto the table in front of her and begun advancing toward her. She hit it with the book in her hand, sure that the force of the blow had killed it on the spot, and indeed, when she lifted the book she saw its flattened corpse—but it suddenly began filling out, standing up, and advancing toward her again, alive as ever. "You know," she said afterward to Gabriel Luria, "when I went into the dining room and saw Talmi sitting there I was more horrified than in the dream. I felt as if the cockroach of my nightmare was turning into a waking reality." She froze in the doorway, throttled the scream trying to break out of her throat, and then fled to her room and shut the door behind her. Her father, who had no idea of what had passed between them, was shocked at his daughter's behavior toward his guest. He paled, apologized on her behalf for her inability to join them for lunch, and then went into her room to scold her. "But the man simply disgusts me. It's as if you were asking me to sit down and eat with a monster or an insect," she said to him, and when she saw that this argument did not satisfy her father, who considered that, under the circumstances, the least she could have done was to apologize to his invited guest for not joining them, she told him the whole story. Even then the judge would not have broken off relations with Talmi—although he would not, of course, have brought the two of them together at his table again—and he would have seen no harm in inviting him to his party, until Orita added: "And after that he began spreading lies about me all over town."

"Are you sure?" asked her father.

"Yes," said Orita. "You understand, Daddy, if I turn down such an attractive man there must be something wrong with me. Talmi began throwing out all kinds of hints that I was a lesbian, frigid, God knows what—in short, that I wasn't normal." As soon as he heard this the judge gave instructions to his secretary to cross Talmi's name off the list of people to be invited to the garden party.

The worker putting up lights for the party, which was to take place in a month's time, popped up in Srulik's memory despite his efforts to conjure up Orita, the Orita of yesterday, of the great day, the day beyond the great river, the day beyond the day, the day beyond all days. Orita, who at the greatest moment of his life had asked him to take her with him immediately, wherever he went, continued to elude his mind's eye like a name that slips away from you just when you need it most, and instead there appeared the clear picture of the worker sitting with his back to the gate, and something in his bowed shoulders and his squatting posture seemed familiar. "Maybe I know him from somewhere," said Srulik to himself, and suddenly he heard the voice of Orit at the great moment, he did not see her face but only heard her voice saying, "I've had a terrible fight with my father. . . . The car won't be available for a whole month. . . ." And then he saw the connection in a flash, the connection he had not noticed the day before at the moment of the meeting, which now enabled him to see the whole thing from Orit's point of view. The car would not be available for a month because in addition to its usual work in the judge's service, it would be needed for the preparations for the garden party. The chauffeur had to deliver all the invitations by hand, and he also had to go to the police and the other government offices to take care of the official side of the reception. And because of all these arrangements, Orit had to give up the trip she had been promised: not actually give it up, but postpone it. But to postpone for four or five weeks something on which she had set her heart and which had already been promised her was quite out of the question. Orita could not countenance such things. Her mother liked to tell the story of "My bed, my Nancy": When Rita was still a baby, a tiny one-year-old who could barely walk and tottered about like a pigeon, she already knew exactly what she wanted, and it was impossible to distract her from whatever it was she had laid her eyes on. When the object she desired was not given to her to play with, she would bend down and beat the floor furiously with her little hand. With her plump little hand and her tiny fingers she would bang on the floor and utter angry sounds. God alone knew where she had learned such tricks and from whom she had inherited her impatient willfulness. Her father was a model of cold, calm deliberation, whereas her mother, who had submitted her whole life long to her father's will, and then her husband's, could certainly never have transmitted such a character to her daughter. When Rita was a small child she had an English nanny named Nancy, and Nancy slept with her in the same room. When the time came to transfer Rita from her little bed to a bigger one, and from the nursery to a bedroom with her sister, Yael, and from the care of the nanny to that of the governess, nothing about the new arrangements pleased her. When they picked her up and carried her to her new room, she stood on the bed, hanging on to the railings, and screaming, "I want my bed, I want my Nancy." For forty-eight hours she would not utter a word except for the cry "My bed, my Nancy!" That was Rita as a baby, and that was how she had remained when she grew up. If she took a fancy to something, whether it was an idea or a concrete object, a specific painting or a carved bench, she took a fancy to it with all her heart and soul and might and main, and she wanted it right now. Rita wanted her trip at the time it had been promised her, and as soon as she realized that she would not get it out of her father, she ran outside, beside herself with disappointment and resolved to go away at the first opportunity that came her way and with the first person she met. And before she even left the house, at the garden gate, she bumped into little Srulik, radiant with happiness and joy— or so it seemed to her—and the minute she heard him say that he was planning a long and interesting trip, she jumped on the opportunity that had fallen into her lap at just the right time and cried: "Let's go together, then! I'm game!"

"And what if the first person she bumped into wasn't me but, for instance, Yankele Blum or Yaakov Talmi, and he had proposed a trip to her?" Srulik asked himself, full of satisfaction with himself and what had happened to him and the answer to his question and the hour-long interval he had to himself to sit here in the Café Gat, and with the Café Gat itself and the whole world. And the answer was self-evident, because as far as Orita was concerned Talmi was beyond the pale, not a human being at all, but a loathsome kind of vermin, and how on earth could anyone compare Srulik to Talmi anyway? True, he was short like Talmi, and even if he was a centimeter or two taller, it was hardly noticeable. It was not in this that the difference between them lay, but in the nature of the man and the essence contained within those small dimensions. In contrast to Talmi's pale, soft, sloppy fleshiness, Srulik's body was firm and muscular and shapely, and his hands were "good hands," as his father said. When the Temple-builder said "good hands" he meant hands that felt the material, that were sensitive to its form and handled it in accordance with its nature and needs and function. Only "good hands" were capable and dexterous, and this had nothing to do with their size or the muscular strength of the arms, so that you would always find big, strong hands that were incapable of "holding a hammer or knocking a nail into the wall," in the words of the Temple-builder. And in fact, Srulik's muscles were strong (although he was no hero, and he would never be able to hold his own against someone like Gabriel Luria, for example; but he was still stronger than most of the boys in his class, all of whom were taller than he by two or three centimeters at least—and anyway, however strong you were you would always find someone stronger), but his hand was small. And in this small hand you would find more manual dexterity than in many big hands, never mind Talmi with his two left hands. In the matter of Talmi's hands he had once heard Gabriel make a remark that opened his eyes, although it had annoyed him at the time. It was in the middle of Talmi's lecture on "Personality and Circumstances in Modern Historiography." Srulik was completely carried away by the brilliant lecture—it was perhaps the lecture that had most influenced and impressed him of all those he had heard in his life—and when Gabby tugged at his sleeve and began to whisper in his ear Srulik was as angry as if he had been roused from a good dream into a poor and miserable reality. Gabby was apparently not impressed by what he heard, and even if he was, he could not take his eyes off the devastation inflicted by the lecturer on anything that fell into his hands. The pages crumpled and got mixed up with each other, the stick he lifted to point at the map hanging on the wall caught on the hooks and broke in his efforts to extricate it, and even the zipper of his portfolio, although made of metal, was no match for the lecturer's hand, which succeeded in bending it so that it could be moved neither backward nor forward. "Look," said Gabby to Srulik, "see how blind Talmi's hands are and how deaf his body is." Talmi's hands—those pale, weak hands which could be considered delicate only because of the common and widespread confusion identifying weakness with delicacy and delicacy with feebleness—were crude and destructive in their contact with the tangible world surrounding him because they were blind to it, and in their blindness they did not fit in with it but bumped into it: they groped and stumbled, they clutched and grabbed always from the wrong angle. And like the hands, the rest of the body was insensitive to its situation, to the atmosphere of the place and time in which it found itself. Since he grasped only the content of spoken words and did not hear the background music throbbing beneath them and above and beyond them, and sounding in the abysses gaping in the silences between them, Talmi was always out of time with the essential rhythm of Orita's being, and did not get the hint until she told him in no uncertain terms exactly what she thought of him, on the occasion of Lady Ashley's canonization for martyrdom.

But Srulik's hands were not blind, and his body not only attended to the waves emanating from Orita's being, but trembled and danced to their rhythm. And if she was always glad to see him and smiled in pleasurable anticipation even before he opened his mouth, it was only because when he was in her presence everything he said and did floated on the currents of her waves and took on the colors of her aura; the memory of the lights going on in her eyes and the ringing peals of her laughter when she heard him speak of the circle for the study of the Great Secret made his heart soar and throb with the delightful feeling that he was cut out for her from every point of view, tailor-made to meet her needs, perfect, and lacking in nothing, and if in the secret of his heart there was something left to be desired, it was a very trivial and trifling thing: two or three centimeters to add to his height, and perhaps the removal of these eternal spectacles on his nose. But even just as he was, with the superfluous spectacles and without the added centimeters, he was all right, and quite satisfied with himself. And even if he was a little on the short side, what of it? Napoleon too, as everyone knew, was no Goliath. The popular wisdom of the Middle East had already taken note of the fact that physical height reduced mental capacities; as the ancient Arab proverb had it, *"Tawil wa-habil"*: tall and stupid. Nor was that all: everybody knew that the short were endowed with sexual organs of the most respectable proportions, and who had not read in the biography of Toulouse-Lautrec (ever since hearing of Orita's passion for modern art Srulik had snatched up everything he could lay his hands on related to the subject) that this giant among artists, whom fate had cruelly given the legs of a dwarf, was known to all the admiring prostitutes as "the prick on chicken-legs." And he wore glasses too. As far as glasses were concerned, they gave Srulik an air of importance. As their neighbor Rosa had once remarked, you could see he was "a thinking man" from the flashing of his glasses. Having arrived at this lofty degree of self-satisfaction, he pushed his chair back so that he could look at his reflection in the big mirror which took up one whole wall of the café, saying to himself as he did so: "And now, my dear Srulik, let's see what this bespectacled Napoleon looks like! Let's see what's happened to this Napoleonic squinter to make him so happy that he could die, no less." Happily dying of happiness, for that is how he imagines the height of happiness to himself: to clasp Orita in his arms in a close embrace with their bodies tightly entwined, and to drown in her eyes and thus to die, to sink into the light of those big, beautiful brown eyes, into the deep lake of those doe's eyes, and die.

This contemplation of his inside from the outside—with the help of a mirror if available, or by the force of his imagination if not—he called "the great secret of how not to be a cockroach; the great secret hidden in the mirror." And even if he did not aspire to the contemplation of the Great Secret itself, he would always find all kinds of little secrets at every step of the way, secrets so unexpected that the very surprise they caused him was enough to remove the danger of becoming a cockroach. Last week, for example, he was suddenly confronted with the unexpected secret of the tiny dot and the great pain when he went up to the mirror to stuff the hole in an aching tooth with brandy-soaked cotton. That huge, excruciating pain took up no space at all in the material world. One little spot on his tooth, a hole the size of a pinhead at the end of a nerve against an ocean of pain. So the scholastic dialecticians were right after all when they calculated that all the angels of heaven could dance on the head of a pin! As against one point of light in the pupil of Orita's eye a whole world of happiness opened up in his heart, and at one smile of grace on her lips all the stars of the galaxy lit up inside him with the Glad Tidings, and the whole universe with its chasms of pain and peaks of joy was contained within this little creature, Srulik Shoshan, this bespectacled squinter who suddenly took himself for Napoleon simply because Orita, instead of brushing him off or scowling, had smiled and exchanged a few words with him.

What had actually happened here? If we dropped into the Café Gat and sat down for a while and smoked a cigarette and looked into the mirror taking up the whole wall opposite us and saw this little fellow reflected there as large as life, and coolly and lucidly considered his fate over the past few days, we would find that the observing Personal Providence up there, who was no less sharp-witted and cunning than the object of His observations down here, that this

exalted Srulik up there had made up his mind that it was
time to teach the lowly little Srulik down here a lesson,
because his heart was puffed up with pride and he was
getting too big for his boots: he wanted to discover what
none of the scholars of his generation, or the generations
preceding them, had discovered before him—the secret of
Father Abraham; to travel far, far away, to fly away with Orita
because it was Orita for whom his soul pined. This little
nonentity, who had no title or high degree, no deeds of valor
or works of note, who possessed neither wealth nor prestige,
the son of the Temple-builder, a penniless, eccentric carpenter, had set his heart on Orita Gutkin, the high-society
beauty, the capricious, sharp-tongued girl who had dis-
dained bigger and better men than he. He wanted her to
love him, no less, love him and him only, love him and die
with him, clasped in his arms. Before she had even had a
chance to live with him, he was already killing her off, along
with himself. How selfish could you get?! You want to die—
die, nobody's stopping you, but what are you killing her for?
She wants to live, and to live with the person she wants to live
with, not the one you want her to want. No, no, Srulik, my
friend: the time has come to teach you a lesson. Now that you
have completed your studies you imagine that you are free as
a bird to fly away in pursuit of your dreams, take off and
leave home with Orita. But your father has beaten you to it,
my lad, he has flown the coop and forced you to stay at
home, bound by the chains of a wretched livelihood and the
need to take care of your sick mother. As for Orita, see how I
mock you and drop her into your hands just when they are
tied and cannot take hold of her, just when you are running
to fetch the doctor for your mother—purely and simply to
show you how right your illiterate neighbor Rosa was in what
she said about God. In Ladino there's a proverb—she said to
him one day—that God gives nuts to those who haven't got
the teeth to crack them. Yes, yes, Srulik, my lad: you will

learn by your own bitter experience the meaning of the verse "Thine eyes shall look and fail with longing," or if you prefer the Greek drama you studied last year at the seminary, you can call it by the more pretentious name "The Tortures of Tantalus." And if you are sick and tired of all these remnants of the Bible and the Greek drama, of all these worlds' dead and gone generations before you were born, and you would rather relate to yourself in terms of your own time, you can call it in ordinary language—the language of Orita—"the irony of fate."

Little Srulik in the mirror suddenly stood up without a word, and we stood up with him, firmly resolved not to let fate make a mockery of us any longer. "I'll show him," Srulik decided on the spot, "I'll show Rosa's God if I haven't got the teeth to crack the nut he gave me." It was only a question of the right way of setting about things, and thanks to the right way of setting about things he would embark on his great journey with Orita not in four or five weeks but the very next week, and the whole plan of action he had just mapped out with all its arrows pointing this way and that was null and void—and he took out his notebook and ripped out the page with the plan and tore it to shreds, which he crammed into the ashtray. Finished with the shifts between himself and his sister, Rina, and Rosa and Grandma Shifra, and all the other clumsy and complicated arrangements! He would simply hire a cab and move his mother, with everything she required, to Grandma Shifra's or to his sister's, and be done with it. And he would be free to crack all the nuts in the world. He wasn't going to put it off a minute longer. This very evening the entire operation would be over and early next morning he would go to Orita and say, "Come on, we're off."

"Wonderful! I'm ready. Where are we going?"

"We're going to Ur of the Chaldees."

"Where's Ur of the Chaldees?"

"In Iraq."

"Iraq? Why Iraq, of all places? Well, let it be Iraq. Baghdad's in Iraq, isn't it? Baghdad—the city of Haroun al-Rashid, of *The Thousand and One Nights!* Wonderful, wonderful! When I was a little girl I read *The Arabian Nights* in an edition for children"—she called it by the name of the English translation, because she had read the book in English—"and later I read the unexpurgated edition of Burton's translation with all the obscenities and erotica. Wonderful! Sit down here until I finish packing my case— the little one will be enough, won't it? It won't take more than a minute."

He went into the yard and his heart leapt with joy: his father had come home. Through the lighted window he saw his mother's eyes luminous and radiant as at the happiest hours of her life, and between her and Rosa, who had her back to the window, his father's hat was hanging on the back of the chair, and the two women were talking to him. His father pushed the chair backward, as he always did when sitting at the table, and only the left sleeve of his jacket was visible through the window. An ancient joy, dead these many years, revived and flooded him in all its details, steeped in a violet-blue radiance. He was a child of six dressed in a new suit still smelling of the clothes shop. It was made of an orange checked material, and had a pair of little trousers and a splendid jacket with a buckled belt, but best of all were the pockets. The little jacket had four pockets, two above and two below, in honor of his first day at school. On the way home he took a piece of candy out of the bottom right-hand pocket and popped it into his mouth, then smoothed the clear cellophane wrapper and spread it in front of his eyes and saw the courtyard steeped in a violet-blue light like a light coming from another world, from Paradise. An exultant glee seized him at the sight of his father's hat hanging on the back of the chair on the side facing the window. It was

the middle of the day and his father was here, and not at
work. He ran inside crying, "Daddy, Daddy," and fell right
into the arms of his father, who lifted him into the air with
one quick, terrifying, delightful swoop. He glided high
above the world on his father's strong hands and saw the dust
on top of the cupboard. His mother's eyes followed him from
below, full of light touched by a line of anxiety lest some
harm befall him up there. He floated in a heaven of delight,
which opened up into a still-higher heaven, like a happiness
that opens the way into a still-greater happiness, like the
sorrow that opens the way to a sorrow more profound. That
moment of joy high above the cupboard and the sideboard
opened his eyes to the meaning of the seven heavens, heaven
within heaven and heaven beyond heaven, about which he
learned many years later. There was a secret surprise sparkling in his parents' eyes. To celebrate his first day at school
his father had made him a wooden rocking-horse the likes
of which you would not find in all the toy shops of Jaffa,
King George, and Princess Mary streets put together, for
beauty and splendor and height. It was almost as tall as a real
pony, and they began taking turns to rock on it, first Srulik
and then his mother and then his father and then Rina, who
came home from school an hour later than he did because
she was already in the third grade. The sight of the hat
hanging on the back of the chair, on the side facing the
window, which had flooded him with a surge of sudden joy,
revived the violet-blue light in which the candy wrapper of
his first day of school had steeped the whole yard so vividly
that his hand tried to smooth out the creases in the cellophane paper, which were making the door look blurred,
and a tremor of obscure anxiety ran through him as he
sensed the movement of his arm trying to flex the little
fingers of the hand which was no longer there to smooth out
the wrinkles in the cellophane paper which was no longer
there the better to see the marvelous sight in violet-blue

which was no longer there, but which nevertheless went on existing more clearly and vividly than those things that were physically present. The desire to move a limb that no longer existed within the framework of a time that had passed reminded him of things he had come across in his reading as examples of superstitions related to a primitive way of thinking, which accepted as gospel the tales of the world to come and heaven and hell and all the rest of the nonsense engendered by such fictions. Somewhere or other he had read that hellfire was the fire of lust. If a man was sentenced to roast in hell because of this sin, his Personal Providence sent him to the appropriate department and there he showed him all his desires, laid out in every shape and form and posture and position, winking and beckoning, awaiting his pleasure and inviting him to satisfy every nuance of his every desire—except that he lacked the tools to satisfy his lusts. He had no mouth to kiss and bite, no hand to fondle and feel, no member to penetrate and sow his seed, and no means whatsoever to extinguish the growing flames of the fire. But if his Personal Providence weighed up the good deeds of his ward in the balance and found that they out-weighed the bad, then he sent him to a heaven not far from hell. Heaven, as we know, is separated from hell by no more than a hairbreadth, and the scene was exactly the same, but for the fact that here our hero, in other words little Srulik, was permanently and inextricably attached, coiled and clutched and sunk and dug and planted into the root of the soul of Orita, which was glowing with a radiant light, more alive and tangible and concrete than all the bodies and objects in the material world. And the flavor of the happi-ness which he tasted with the sensation of his childhood memory coming back to him at the sight of his father's hat hanging on the back of the chair was nothing but a pale reflection of that image of Paradise.

Srulik crossed the threshold of the thin partition with a light bound and stopped at the sight of the uninvited guest who had taken his father's place and with whom his mother was engaged in such animated and bright-faced conversation. His mother had always been glad to receive guests, and since his father's disappearance she was moved by the sight of anyone who had been a friend of his or connected with him in any way coming into the yard. A light would go on in her eyes at living contact with the living person who had been somehow associated with the life of his father, who at this moment was nothing more to her than a memory of the past and a hope for the future. Happiness of this kind is often—although not always—encountered among people who have lost someone they love when they are visited by one of his friends: they love the person who was beloved of their beloved and their hearts are gladdened by his presence. From this point of view, his absent father was dead, but for the knowledge that he was alive in some other place and the hope that he would come back someday; and for anyone who believed in the immortality of the soul the difference was even smaller: both of them, the dead and the departed, remain with us as a memory and a hope alone, and there is no difference between them but for the knowledge— founded on faith alone—that the one continues to live his life somewhere else on this earth, where we are bound to meet him again one day, while the other continues to live another life in another world, where we are bound to meet him again someday. For his mother, a visit from a friend of his father's was like a premonition of the future realization of the hope she cherished in her heart, a kind of foretaste of the return of her departed husband, and accordingly a meeting of this kind would move her so much that it upset her balance and deprived her of her wits, as in the present case when she went so far in welcoming the visitor that—as Srulik was later to discover—she committed a fatal mistake which upset the cornerstone of all his plans.

The visitor was none other than Haim Long-Life, who owed his nickname to the fact that "Haim" in Hebrew means "life" and the fact that he was a very tall man. His surname was Raban, and he was the elder brother of Berl Raban, the director of Dr. Landau's eye clinic. Unlike Berl, the great admirer of Joshua, son of Nun, who took no interest in anything but what was written in the Book of Joshua about the conquest of the Land and its division among the tribes of Israel, in contrast to this brother preoccupied with idle fantasies about ancient legends and imaginary heroes, Haim Long-Life thought of nothing but the quickest and easiest way of making a lot of money so that he could spend the rest of his long life in ease and comfort, and to this end all he had to do was find the proper invention, discover the "right patent." He spent his entire life trying to discover the "right patent." It was one of these right patents of Haim Long-Life's that had ruined Srulik's father's life—which is what his mother had claimed many years before, when his father had first begun to think about building his model of the Temple. While admitting that his father had inherited his general daydreaming inclination from his teacher, Markel Cohen, that old carpenter from the Old City of Jerusalem, she insisted that the actual idea of building the wooden model of the Temple and the impulse to do it had come from Haim Long-Life. One day, when Haim Long-Life was sitting in his father's workshop in his bow tie—he always went about in a bow tie, which gave him the air of a permanent guest at some official function, of a man who had just emerged from the wedding reception of the daughter of the Paraguayan consul, or who was just about to go to the birthday party of the wife of the president of the Bethlehem Rotary Club— when he was sitting thus and watching his father carve the ornamental pediment of a wardrobe, he had suddenly exclaimed: "Yes, that's it—I've found the right patent!" The right patent, like all other inventions of genius, was simplicity itself, and was sure to bring vast profits to them and their children and their children's children after them. Srulik's father would carve the model of the Temple in wood, and he, Haim Long-Life, would take a large, grand shop in Jaffa Street to serve as a kind of museum for the Temple, and anyone who wanted to see its marvels would have to pay an entrance fee. And even if the entrance fee were no more than, say, half a grush a head, and if the daily trade were no more than fifty customers, they would already be assured of a livelihood without any trouble or effort or slavery or fawning or misery. And many years later, when all the people of Zion had passed before the Temple, Haim Long-Life and the Temple-builder would be able to go on a world tour; and by the time they came home from this grand tour, there would be a new generation in Zion who did not know Haim Long-Life's Temple, and the whole thing would begin all over again.

In short, he had scarcely finished expounding his idea before Srulik's father was convinced, and not only convinced but on fire with the enthusiasm that earned him the name Temple-builder, and consumed his life and destroyed his family. And it was no wonder that Haim Long-Life had succeeded in seducing his father. This Haim Long-Life was capable, by virtue of his imagination and tongue and bow tie, of making the driest of timber merchants and the sharpest of spice traders enthusiastic about his patents. As far as he was concerned, his troubles started not before he had persuaded them but afterward. As soon as he had talked the owner of the capital into his schemes, and obtained an advance against the future profits of their business partnership, he would go to Beirut to rest from the exertions of his persuasions and enjoy a foretaste, if only for two or three days, of the good life awaiting him after the patent was transformed from theory into practice. Once the two or three days had passed, and the advance payment, together with a couple of little loans picked up here and there, was gone, he took no further interest in the said patent, and began to occupy his mind instead with new patents for different business projects. Any humdrum work, all the trivial cares and concerns connected with translating the patent from imagination to reality, bored him to tears. There was no truth in the claims of his creditors that he was nothing but a crook, out to defraud them of their money by dazzling them with all kinds of tall tales about the huge profits in store. On the contrary: whenever the idea for a new patent popped into his brain, he resolved, quite sincerely, that this time he would throw himself body and soul into translating it into a practical proposition—only to be defeated time and time again by the dullness and boredom of sheer reality.

And what was Srulik's mother's complaint? She claimed that all Haim Long-Life's creditors, all those avaricious merchants who wanted only to exploit his inventions for their own profit, had lost nothing but their money, while her husband, who had been infected by the idea itself, had ruined his life and been deprived of his family. She would say this to Haim Long-Life's face, without bitterness or belligerence but as an undeniable statement of fact, inevitable as a natural phenomenon. As if she were saying that her husband had come home from work soaked to the marrow because he had gone out in the pouring rain without taking his coat. Just as it was in the nature of rain to consist of drops of water which fell from the sky and made things wet, so it was in the nature of her husband to work without a coat, and when he was working he was oblivious to any changes in the weather. Everyone would laugh when she said these things— her husband and Haim Long-Life and even she herself. "Yes, and is there water in the shop?" asked Haim Long-Life before standing up to leave and taking his hat from the back of the chair. "Of course there is," said Srulik's mother. "There's a tap and a basin in the shop." "That's the main thing," said Haim Long-Life. "Fresh, running water." As he left he muttered happily to himself: "Fresh, running water."

At the sound of the question "Yes, and is there water in the shop?"—even before his mother told him the reason for Haim Long-Life's unexpected visit—Srulik flared into a rage, first of all against himself, and then to the same degree against his mother and the lanky inventor, when an escape-hatch suddenly came into view among the fumes of his anger. Haim Long-Life had come to ask his mother for the keys to his father's workshop "for a while" and she, of course, had agreed without asking any questions: not what he needed the shop for, nor what "a while" meant—days, or weeks, or maybe months. And what, after all, did Srulik want of his mother? Could he really have expected her to turn down the friend of his father's youth, who had gone on to become the friend of the whole family? And what differ-ence did it make to her anyway? If he asked, it meant he needed the shop for one of his patents, and for her part she was glad that she could be of help. And what difference did it make how long he wanted it for? There was no danger that Haim Long-Life would persist for any length of time with any of his patents.

"There isn't a penny in the house and you rush to hand father's workshop over to Haim Long-Life, just like that!" Srulik yelled at his mother, unable to control the rage against himself which was swelling inside him. How on earth could he have forgotten the workshop? Of all the ways and means he had considered for breaking through the wall barring his way, he had never even thought of his father's workshop standing idle and abandoned, when the rent he could get for it was more than everything he could earn in six months at the library and all the extra work put together—assuming that he could get extra work at the orphanage or anywhere else! How had it happened that even he, the witty, brilliant Srulik, whose great ideas amazed even Orita, how had it happened that he too was groping in the dark until the inventor arrived and opened his eyes to

the simplest, easiest, best, and most efficient solution of all!
The very next day he would go straight to the shop and take
back the keys. But in any case Haim Long-Life deserved a
prize for his brilliant invention! He would pay him a certain
percentage of the rent—the fee paid to the broker, for example. Three percent, perhaps.

The next day, before setting out, Srulik arranged for Rosa
to stay with his mother for eight hours. The four hours he
was at the library, and another four to retrieve the keys and
go to the broker. If everything went smoothly, he might even
have time to go round to Orita and tell her that he was
setting out on the great journey not in five or six weeks, but
in five or six days!

When he arrived at the workshop he found it locked and
barred, and his heart sank at the sight of the meager cypress
tree standing outside as it had in the days of his childhood.
Even then, in the distant days of his childhood, he had been
sorry for this miserable cypress sentenced to grow and spend
all its life in this corner of all places, without any possibility
of its moving even a few steps to the left or right, which
would have changed its fate completely. It grew right next to
the public lavatory that served the whole of the commercial
center, and all the apprentices who were too lazy to use the
toilet itself would huddle in the corner and pee on the tree.
And as if that were not enough, sooty streams of oil from the
garage higher up the street would come trickling down to
mingle with the urine and collect in pools at its feet. And still
it stood here, planted in a basin of urine and gasoline and
motor oil and scrap iron, trying to hold its head high like all
the cypresses that were well-off in the world simply because
someone had planted them somewhere else. "Something
must be done to help it," thought Srulik, and he imagined
himself uprooting the tree and planting it on the borders of
the Russian Compound. "But I could never save all the
cypresses choking to death through no fault of their own.
And what about all the wild crocuses sprouting in the mid-

dle of the road, where donkeys come to trample them before they have a chance to bloom! As far as the crocus which can never escape the donkey's hoof is concerned, it's no consolation at all that a whole population of crocuses goes on living and blooming in the fields around.

"If I had found the shop open and Haim Long-Life sitting inside it, everything wouldn't seem so abandoned and forlorn," said Srulik to himself, sensing how the business of renting the workshop with all its tools was dragging out while he was so pressed for time. When he was a child he had loved going to visit his father in the workshop. From the fallen chips of wood he would make himself toys: buses, cars, and airplanes; and then he would take them home and paint them with watercolors. Once he had sat with his father in the darkness of the workshop and watched the flame of a candle. He had forgotten why he had been taken to the shop at night, and why there was no light and his father had been obliged to light a candle. But he clearly remembered the candle burning on the bench. In the light of the candle the trumpets and the swords and spears surrounding the rough stone walls gleamed. Another six times around and the wall would crumble. The wall and all the legions surrounding it fell the moment his father lit the Lux lamp with its sizzling white light. As soon as the light flooded the shop the spectacle was dwarfed and the great marvel was reduced to ordinary little objects: the huge stone wall surrounding Jericho became a plank lying on the bench, and all the glittering trumpets and swords and spears of the hosts of Joshua, son of Nun, were only the teeth of the saw leaning against it. And the wonderful light of the flame which had brought the scene into being was itself reduced to a faint flicker smelling of melted wax.

"Joshua, son of Nun," Srulik said to himself, and immediately set off for Dr. Landau's eye clinic. Berl would be able to tell him where to find his brother, Haim Long-Life.

Most of the patients besieging the doors of the clinic

office were, as usual, Arabs, peasants squatting patiently on the floor along the long walls of the corridor, whose benches never had enough room for everybody, with a few Jews with swollen, running, suppurating eyes scattered among them, who made feeble efforts to prevent Srulik from going into Berl's office, crying: "There's a line, there's a line, go and get a number from the doorman." "The whole world is obstructing me," said Srulik to himself, and with growing fury, without taking the trouble to explain that he had not come for medical treatment, he ran down the corridor, stumbling into peasant women baring their breasts to suckle bleary-eyed babies, and entered Berl's office.

Berl Raban was sitting at his desk with a peculiar smile on his pale face. Opposite him stood Reb Yitzhok, his face showing red through the tangle of his beard and sidelocks, and he too appeared to be smiling between his beard and mustache. At first sight they seemed to be enjoying some joke that had just passed between them, and it was only afterward that Srulik learned that he had walked in at a moment when the two of them were ready to tear each other to pieces—as one might lift up his eyes in the street and see a pair of turtledoves stretching their necks on a windowsill and imagine them to be making love, whereas actually they are preparing for a cruel battle in which one of them will peck the other to death. He had walked in right in the middle of the war, the language war. Reb Yitzhok, who had come for the treatment of a cataract, insisted on speaking Yiddish, while Berl insisted on understanding only Hebrew.

"Now you know exactly who a Jew is," said Berl to Srulik, as if he had come simply in order to hear this answer: "A Jew is someone who is forbidden to speak Hebrew."

Berl's voice was always hoarse and low, and when he was excited it did not rise but grew even more muffled than before. When arguments broke out between him and Dr. Landau, he would grow hoarser with every roar that burst from the doctor's throat, until in the end his voice sounded like a kind of bubbling, sizzling mutter, a kind of background music to the roars. The doctor, who was already a little hard of hearing and had difficulty in understanding even clearly pronounced remarks, did not hear Berl's arguments at all in the advanced stages of the argument, and if he wanted nevertheless to know what his opponent was saying, he was obliged to stop thundering and put his ear right next to Berl's mouth, which would infuriate him even more than the arguments themselves. "You're whispering on purpose, hissing like a snake, to make me put my ear next to your mouth," the doctor would complain in the heat of the argument, as if he thought it was some kind of rhetorical trick to distract his attention, although he knew that it was no such thing. Perhaps it was an innate characteristic, or perhaps Berl's voice had been smothered by the permanent shouting match which had been going on around him for as long as he could remember, and which caused him such physical revulsion that he would sometimes get a sore throat and go hoarse because of someone else's shouts. In any case, the husky whisper of Berl's voice told Srulik that he was in the middle of a fight with Reb Yitzhok, and accordingly he made haste to call out, "I'm looking for Haim Long-Life, where can I find him?" before Berl could continue the argument. Berl stared at him for a moment in astonishment, as if trying in vain to find the connection between Haim Long-Life and the language war raging in the office. And when he discovered that there was indeed no connection at all, and that Srulik had come only to find out the whereabouts of his brother, he grew even more indignant and gasped in a broken, smothered voice: "Am I my brother's keeper?"

Srulik's heart sank within him: time was running out and now the direct route to Haim Long-Life had been blocked. Although it was not Haim Long-Life himself Srulik sought, of course, but the keys to his father's workshop, which his

mother had so idiotically given him. If only he could get
hold of them he would run straight to the broker and ask for
an advance on the rent, and if he discovered that it was going
to be a drawn-out, complicated business, he wouldn't even
wait for all the papers to be signed. The advance payment
would be enough to make all the arrangements: he would
pay Rosa for everything she had done up to now and for
another month in advance just to be on the safe side, move
his mother to his sister's and hurry to Orita to tell her that he
was ready to set out.

"Actually it's not your brother I want, but the keys to my
father's shop, which are in his possession," said Srulik, more
to himself than to Berl, and so saying he turned to leave.
Berl started, said in a whisper something Srulik did not
hear, and when Srulik pricked up his ears, repeated: "Wait
for me at the Café Cancan. I'll be there in half an hour." "All
right," said Srulik, sensing that Berl wanted to tell him
something about Haim Long-Life in the café that he could
not say there in the clinic office. As he left he saw Berl
getting ready to charge into battle again against his enemy,
Reb Yitzhok. It was only after he had shut the door behind
him and begun to make his way toward the café that he
saw—in the very same scene which remained imprinted on
his mind's eye—how much Berl Raban resembled Reb
Yitzhok. The bony, stooping Berl, whose gleaming bald
head paralleled the flashing of his eyes, whose hollow cheeks
gave the long, deep line of his lips the air of a perpetual
smile even when he was seething with rage, whose chin
strove upward to unite with the tip of his nose above the
cavern of his toothless mouth, might have looked exactly
like Reb Yitzhok if he had grown a wild beard and sidelocks
and worn a black hat on top of a white skullcap and draped
his body in a caftan. And vice versa: if Reb Yitzhok had cut
his beard and sidelocks and thrown off his skullcap and hat
and caftan and displayed to the world the sight of his bony,

stubborn body through a thin shirt with rolled-up sleeves, he would have looked exactly like Berl.

No sooner had he left the office than a bitter, helpless rage against both Berl Raban and himself began seething and swelling inside him. Instead of dismissing him with a biblical verse, Berl should have told him at once where he could find Haim Long-Life. After all, every minute was precious to him from every point of view, even the financial one, since every minute that he was running around town Rosa was sitting with his mother, and he would have to pay her for it in the end. Every delay in finding Haim Long-Life postponed Rosa's payment. And this Berl, instead of being grateful for the favor they had done his brother and apologizing for the unnecessary trouble it had caused and trying with all his might to remedy the fault and find his brother "from underneath the ground," as Daoud Ibn Mahmoud, the chauffeur, would say when the judge or Orita asked him for something ("I will find it for you and bring it to you from underneath the ground, *ya Sidi,*"), instead of saying "I'll find my brother, Haim Long-Life, and bring him to you from underneath the ground," Berl had to show off and drag in quotations from the Bible, and then make himself important and mysterious and drive Srulik wild with postponements and delays. Meetings in the Café Cancan—that was all he needed!

This is what he might have said to him if Berl had known what he was talking about. But it was plain as day that Berl didn't have the faintest idea of what had taken place. He didn't know that his brother had taken the keys to the shop, and he didn't know that he, Srulik, needed the keys, and perhaps he didn't even know where his brother was. In that case, why had he made an appointment with him in the Café Cancan? He certainly knew nothing about the keys, but he apparently did know where to find his brother, and this he was not prepared to disclose in the presence of Reb Yitzhok, because there was something fishy going on. It was this last point that gave rise to Srulik's bitter anger against himself for never being quick and alert enough with regard to the situation in which he found himself—a failing that always led to a waste of time, unnecessary trouble, and avoidable problems. Instead of bursting into the office like that and announcing what he wanted at the top of his voice, he should have taken Berl aside and asked him if he could spare him a moment. And since he had not done that, he should at least, after Berl said, "Wait for me at the Café Cancan, I'll be there in half an hour," have explained to him that he simply didn't have the time, and instead suggested retiring for a moment to Dr. Landau's office, or the head nurse's room, or any other corner, so that he could get the necessary information at once, which was, after all, nothing but an address. Haim Long-Life's address, that was all he wanted. With this thought, Srulik turned on his heel and began hurrying back to the eye clinic, but as he did so he sensed the utter idiocy of rushing urgently back to Berl's office now: the return and the second charge through the crowds of patients waiting their turn in the corridor and the dragging of Berl from his office into one of the other rooms would take no less time than walking to the Café Cancan and waiting there, and at the same time he would make an unnecessary fuss which would annoy Berl—and what was worse, would arouse the fury of Dr. Landau against the pair of them, himself and Berl Raban. And so Srulik turned on his heel again and made for the café, bathed in a sweat of helpless anger against himself.

On the way to the Cancan, which was on the corner of Jaffa Street and Melissanda Street, Srulik passed the Café Gat and peeped inside by force of habit. Orita wasn't there, nor was Gabriel Luria. Gabriel was no doubt busy with the preparations for his trip to Paris. He was going to study at the medical school of the Sorbonne, and he must be reading some anatomical text now, or improving his knowledge of

French. What Orita was doing now it was impossible to
know. In the corner of the café sat Boulos Effendi smoking a
hookah with his usual tranquillity—the Arab tranquillity
which stemmed from a life of being and not of doing, like
that of a protected and well-fed house cat dozing calmly in
its corner. Gordon, the commander of the Mahaneh Yehuda
police station, was standing at the counter and showing the
proprietor, Yosef Shvilli, some photographs that he had
taken, and he, too, exuded tranquillity. The life of this
Englishman, as opposed to that of the Arab, was a life of
action and adventure—during the past twenty years he had
served in the remotest corners of the Empire, from the Suez
Canal to Hong Kong—but it was a calm activity, free of the
urgent and frenzied distortions of an unquiet soul. At the
sight of Srulik standing in the doorway he smiled invitingly
and called, "Hello, Israel, come in. I'll buy you a whiskey and
soda and while you drink it you can have a look at a few of
the pictures I took in Wadi Kelt and Jericho."

"Thank you very much, I'd love to stay and have a drink
with you but I'm in a hurry," said Srulik, and he felt a
delicate pleasure invading him at the sound of "Jericho,"
diluting the bitterness and dissolving the burning anger. He
leaned forward, saw the three people sitting next to the
mirror that took up the whole of the inner wall, and added:
"Actually, I think I will have a look at those photos. I have a
quarter of an hour till my appointment in the Café Cancan."

"Why didn't you make your appointment here?" asked
Gordon, just as Srulik was thinking that he really should
have suggested to Berl that they meet at the Café Gat. "In
the Cancan," continued Gordon, "they don't know how to
serve drinks. They haven't even got a barman, and the ones
who call themselves barmen in the other cafés aren't much
good either. The only barman in town who deserves the
name is Joseph." Yosef Shvilli stroked his mustache complacently, with a proper sense of his own worth. He had devoted

the best years of his life to learning the bartender's art, which he had been taught by the greatest master of cocktail-mixing from the Persian Gulf to the Bay of Hong Kong: Little John, the chief bartender of the flagship of the Indian Ocean fleet. For fifteen years Yosef Shvilli had sailed the Indian Ocean and sat at the feet of the famous Little John, until he had landed in Jerusalem and opened his café, and who was capable of competing with him in this town? All the greatest of the land, the government secretary and the judges and the army officers and the consuls, it was not for nothing that they were his clients. Nobody who knew the first thing about drinking would set foot in any other establishment. "Yes, yes, you're quite right, this is a good place," said Srulik, for whom it was a good place not because of Yosef's bartending skills, but in spite of the drinks and the nauseating smell of alcohol permanently floating over the counter.

When Gordon handed him a photograph of the Jericho mound, Srulik smiled at the thought that if anyone were to ask him now to describe one of the happiest moments of his life, he would have to answer, in all honesty, "Right now I can't think of a single moment in my life happier than when I first entered the Café Gat." It was then that he had first spoken to Orita, and that she had invited him to go for a drive with her to Jericho in her father's car, which happened to be free that day. The trip did not come off because Daoud Ibn Mahmoud arrived half an hour later without the car, which had broken down on the way to the café and had to be taken to the garage. The cancellation of the trip itself did not particularly sadden Srulik, since he was not free to go along in any case—although there is no doubt that if the car had not broken down he would have left everything and driven off in it with Orita and her sister, Yael—but on the other hand, like a dream too good to be true, his dearest wish was suddenly realized by none other than Yosef Shvilli, who led him to the table where the judge's daughters were sitting. Ever since his childhood there were many things in the world Srulik knew would always be beyond his reach, impossible, unattainable dreams, and the things he knew he would never be given he tried to make for himself—toys, for example. Already then he knew that the toys in the shop window in Jaffa Street (the shop next to the Café Cancan, where he had to be in a quarter of an hour's time) would never be his, for his father had no money to buy them. "Oh, Daddy, look what a lovely airplane," he would cry at the first sight of the wonderful silver airplane in the window, perfect down to the last detail, beginning with the tires on the wheels and ending with the helmet on the head of the pilot smiling under his mustache in the cockpit. And his father would smile sadly and say, "Yes, it's a fine airplane, good, clean workmanship," for he too longed to buy the airplane for his son but he did not have the money for it, and Srulik said no more about it. He knew that his pleas would only make his father miserable without bringing the airplane any closer. And so he pulled him away from the window, crying, "Come on, Daddy, let's go to the workshop," and there, among the chips and sawdust on the floor he would seek the bits of wood that would be right for the body of the plane, its wings and tail, and even the head of the pilot, which he would make himself, with his own hands. His sister, Rina, two years older than he, was completely different in this respect, in fact the absolute opposite. When she wanted something she would fight for it with all her strength and without any consideration at all for the feelings of her parents or the lack of money in the house. That's what she was like as a schoolgirl when she wanted a wristwatch, and that's what she was like when she grew up and got married and made up her mind to have an "elegant wedding." She always fought tooth and nail for her wishes, banging her head against the walls barring her way to their fulfillment, but all these stubborn battles did not get her far. Even then, in the fight for the wristwatch, Srulik had realized the futility of all these battles. Once Rina had set her heart on a watch, during the year when other girls in her class began coming to school with watches on their wrists, and had caused a chain of explosions which almost brought the house down. She demanded her due with tears and screams and slamming doors which reverberated throughout the courtyard and reached the ears of the neighbors on the other side of the street. She threw her school sandwiches in her mother's face, and when Srulik tried to interfere, she hurled her satchel at his head. "We haven't got any money because you don't want to work!" she screamed at her father. "Instead of working you spend all day playing with that Temple of yours like a baby playing with building blocks!" He tried to calm his daughter's fury and explain to her that he worked on the Temple model only in the evenings, after working hours, and that he did not have enough work not because he was lazy but because of the disastrous state of the economy. Every day skilled workers came knocking at his door ready to work for next to nothing; self-employed carpenters were shutting up their shops and walking the streets with a saw on their backs crying, "Carpenter, carpenter," ready to do little repair jobs for pennies because people had no money to order furniture—not to mention the competition of the Arab workers and the Bethlehem carpenters. And in spite of all this he, thank God, was not yet wandering the streets with a saw on his back, and his family was not hungry for bread; they had not only all the bread they could eat, thank God, but even butter to spread on it. But the more her father tried to explain that a watch was not a necessity but a luxury, and that these things had no end, and that however hard she tried to emulate the rich girls in her class she would always find girls richer than she, just as they themselves would always be looked down on by girls richer than they, the more enraged Rina would grow until her big pale-blue eyes, just like Grandma Shifra's, would shoot arrows of blind hatred at her father, just like her grandmother's did when she was having a quarrel with her son-in-law. And thus Srulik's father would sometimes find himself the target of the fury of a pair of beautiful blue eyes which kept on changing their framework: looking out at him first from the withered face of his mother-in-law, and then from the blooming face of his daughter, and whichever the case might be, in the end he would grab his hat and rush out of the house to take refuge in his workshop. "You don't understand anything, anything, anything!" Rina would shriek at her father with all the power of her lungs; the power of Rina's lungs, like the fury of her big blue eyes, was a hereditary gift from the grandmother she hated. (Fortunately for her, Grandma Shifra's heredity combined in her with the musical ear and the love of singing she inherited from her father, who was mad about music and loved to sing while he worked. Since Grandma Shifra was tone-deaf, the power of her lungs served only to shout down her opponent in a fight, whereas Rina sang as much as she shouted.) "It's got nothing to do with being rich!" And Rina, too, was right, for she would have been no less intent on the wristwatch if it had cost a penny. She did not want to display riches, she wanted to be like all the other girls. The tyranny of fashion is no less harsh than the tyranny of money, especially among children who subject themselves gladly to its dictates.

Haim Long-Life appeared in the thick of the battle, at the moment when Rina seized the bowl of fruit on the table and hurled it to the floor in response to her father's argument that she had nothing to complain about, that instead of lamenting the unobtainable watch she should count her blessings and be glad that she was still at school while the neighbor's daughters were obliged to clean floors and wash dishes in cafés to help their father support the family. "And what about all the little girls in India!" shrieked Rina to the accompaniment of the shattering china. "Why don't you mention all the children dying of hunger in India? Only yesterday you told me that in India alone three million little children die of hunger every year!" This approach of her father's would drive her out of her mind with rage: she felt in her bones that this argument was completely irrelevant to the circumstances of her own life, that it was neither pertinent nor just, but she simply did not know how to refute it— especially since as far as her father was concerned it was not only an argument but part of his very being. With every crisis that befell him, her father, after the initial shock was over, would pull himself together and find consolation in the fact that nothing worse had happened to him. People were starving to death in the streets of Bombay and Shanghai in broad daylight; earthquakes destroyed entire cities and buried their inhabitants alive; fine young boys were killed in wars, and what was sometimes even worse, were left crippled, broken vessels for the rest of their lives; people were run over in traffic accidents—and what, in the end, had happened to him? The landlord had sued him for not paying more than six months' rent for the shop, and the court had issued an eviction order against him. So what? It wasn't so terrible! If he couldn't get hold of the money he would work at home until things improved and then he would find a better workshop, in the center of town. If it made him happy that no earthquake had flattened Jerusalem and buried him alive, and that he had a piece of bread to eat and a ragged coat to wear while on the other side of the world people were dying of hunger, then good for him. She, Rina, was not living in the slums of Bombay, and there were no earthquakes in Jerusalem, and when all the girls in her class came to school wearing wristwatches, she wanted one too, and that was that. She simply was not prepared to be the object of their ridicule, or their pity either.

When she grabbed the fruit bowl and threw it on the floor, her father concluded that it was time for him to flee to his shop, her mother began to see her way clear to procuring the wristwatch so vital to Rina and domestic peace, and Haim Long-Life, who had just come in with his soft step and his bow tie, stood rooted to the spot, charmed and fascinated. Srulik, who had seen him through the window even before he entered the room, wanted to deter Rina and stop her in time, before they were exposed to the visitor "in all their shame," but he was too late. And even if he had been in time, he would never have succeeded in stopping Rina. When she lost her temper, she was beyond caring about anyone, including her father and mother, let alone some stranger and what he might see, hear, or think.

As soon as he saw him through the window, Srulik noticed that Haim Long-Life was slightly ill at ease. He thought Haim must be uneasy because of the shouting and quarreling coming from the house, but the truth was that the inventor was embarrassed because he had come to ask for a loan at the end of the month, when the Temple-builder probably didn't have a penny in his pocket. Nevertheless, he had no alternative but to try his luck, and if worse came to worst and he failed to procure a loan of even twenty grush, at least he would be invited to lunch.

The sight of Rina rampaging cast a spell on him which completely banished his embarrassment. Haim Long-Life could not take his eyes off the raging girl, her stamping feet, her flushed face, her eyes flashing sparks of fury, her firm little breasts rising and falling with her heaving breath, and Srulik suddenly saw, to his astonishment, that this old man—he thought of him as an old man then because he was a friend of his father's—was inflamed with desire for Rina. Apart from his feeling at the time that it was improper for an old man to get carried away by carnal lust, especially for a girl young enough to be his daughter (a violation of the laws of nature, which joined young to young and old to old), Srulik sensed that he was witnessing something strange and astonishing which cast an unexpected light on human behavior in general, and on these people—Haim Long-Life and Rina, with whom he had spent all his life—in particular. They seemed to him like puppets controlled by forces stronger than they. Naturally he had often heard, and even sometimes used himself, expressions such as "appetites stronger than he was" or "a slave to his passions"; but what had been up to then a manner of speaking or an abstract idea was suddenly transformed before his eyes into a concrete reality, as if he were seeing bacteria under a microscope for the first time after knowing of their existence for years by hearsay alone. Once his father had bought him a cheap Japanese toy, a wind-up horse made of tin and operated by a spring. When you turned the key, the unfortunate horse would go round in circles in the direction opposite to the inclination of his neck, as if trying to free himself of the mechanism that forced him to turn round and round when all he wanted was to run straight to the stable. This horse did not last long, since the spring was far stronger than the tin body containing it, and after a few circuits the body broke in half. With his long, curved neck and his drooping face, Haim Long-Life resembled this Japanese horse, and it seemed to Srulik that he too was about to break in half, just as Rina would explode if she did not get what she wanted. Srulik saw this clearly because he himself did not share either Haim Long-Life's lust for his sister or the latter's lust for a wristwatch. At that moment not only was he angry with Rina, he hated her. And he was fed up with his father and mother too, who—instead of teaching her a lesson, slapping her face until she learned what it meant to be so spoiled and selfish, extorting wristwatches from a poor father who didn't even have the money to pay the rent for his workshop— behaved, each in his own way, as if they were guilty and acknowledged their guilt and wanted to do all they could to atone for it. She had everything coming to her, this Rina! She even left her dirty laundry for their mother, as if it were self-evident that a mother's role included washing her daughter's panties, and when she was sometimes obliged to wash her things herself she did it with a sulky, martyred expression like the victim of some terrible injustice. If only, at least, she had persevered with her passions and enthusiasm toward some great goal, he could have forgiven her, even admired her—as in the matter of her playing and singing. She had inherited their father's fine ear for music and his melodious voice, and she liked singing, but in this too she had not gone far. Girls whose natural gifts were far inferior to hers had become famous singers thanks to their perseverance and dedication. But Rina had never been able to persevere in the attainment of any goal unless she could see it right in front of her eyes. She sang simply when she felt like singing. When she was in a good mood—and she was generally in a good mood in company—she would sing for anyone who happened to be present. But as for investing any effort in developing her voice or mastering the notes in order to reach a professional standard one day, this seemed to her completely senseless and pointless, no less abstract than the concepts "expectation," "hope," or "future." She was innocent of all ambition, and it was this, to tell the truth, that was the source of her peculiar charm. And since in addition to her lack of ambition she had never learned how to deploy any degree of cunning in order to get what she wanted, to plan and scheme—in short, to "behave rationally," as people say—each of her desires cast her into violent battles, frontal attacks, and (when her parents were not there to satisfy her whims) to beating her head against stone walls.

In the end Rina got her wristwatch. After her father had escaped to his shop, her mother delved into the depths of the bureau, in the shabby old leather purse which held her most precious possessions—mainly faded photographs and tattered letters from the happiest years of her life—and

came up with the watch she had once received as a present
from the old witch herself, Grandma Shifra: an excellent
watch, a gold Omega, but not the kind of watch upon which
little Rina had set her heart. It was a heavy, square watch
whereas the fashion among the girls at school was for a little
round watch with a black leather strap. "It's a granny's watch,
not a girl's watch!" cried Rina in despair. "That's all I need, to
go to school with a granny's watch. Why not a granny's shoes
too, with long white laces tied around the ankle!" And again
her mother felt in the wrong, and she decided to sell her gold
watch and buy a modern one instead.

The sale of the gold watch was the only business transac-
tion their mother had ever executed in her life, and it cost
her more in nervous energy and willpower than she would
have believed possible. She detested anything that
reminded her in any way of her mother, who was an expert
haggler. Grandma Shifra's bargaining powers were unique
and exceptional, especially when it came to little shopkeepers, peddlers, and artisans. She regarded every penny
she managed to save on a kilo of sugar, a porter's tip, or the
washerwoman's fee as a victory, and any day on which she
was deprived of a victory of this kind was a sad and bitter
one for her. She would sometimes haggle over the prices of
things she had not the least intention of buying, and would
come home as a consequence laden with all kinds of superfluous knickknacks which gave her nothing but the pleasure
of knowing that she had beaten the hawker down. Ever since
she was a child, Srulik's mother had dreaded the moment
when her own mother charged into the fray, her lips curling
in scornful disgust as the shopkeeper unrolled the bolt of
cloth, her judiciously feeling fingers recoiling from the
material in horror, as if they had just come into contact with
some loathsome vermin. Already then she had tried to
escape from the house when her mother held a rummage
sale of all the junk and rags she wanted to get rid of, and
began telling lies about every bit of rubbish on display with-

out batting an eye, and for no reason at all but the enjoyment of practicing the art of deception. Nor did she shrink from administering a stinging, soul-searing slap in the face when her daughter stood in the way of her business transactions, as happened in the incident of the boy and the book. When this young boy came to the basement of their house to buy a table and chair for his room, he grew enthusiastic at the sight of a tattered old book lying in the corner and was just about to pay more for it than he had for the chair, when the little girl burst out: "Don't buy it, she's lying! She won't let you open it because of all the pages missing in the middle, not because she's afraid you'll damage it. She didn't inherit it from her grandfather—she's lying, she's lying! I found it myself when I was playing in the Russian Compound." Even then, as a child, when she was sent to buy something at the shop, she could never remember the price: she would come home dreading the moment when Grandma Shifra would ask her: "How much did it cost?" and she would not know the right answer. One of the greatest joys of their mother's life was her liberation from the tyranny of how much things cost, her ability to live in blissful ignorance of the price of a loaf of bread or a packet of butter. At the end of the month the grocer sent the bill, and that was that.

In her best dress and broad-brimmed hat Srulik's mother went from one watchmaker to the next, smiling shyly, her heart beating and her knees giving way beneath her. The more she tried to avoid arguments, the more eager she was to sell the gold watch as quickly as possible, the more the watchmakers shunned it. The first one she went to—who knew her and the watch as well since he himself had mended it—was the best of them. He admitted its value and beauty, but he simply did not have the money to spare at the moment to buy it from her. He was quite willing, however, to display it in his window until it found a buyer, in return for a small commission. "How long will it take to find a buyer?" she inquired. "No way of knowing," replied the watchmaker, "someone could come this very day, and it might take three months." At which Rina fell into a rage again—three months seemed to her like an eternity, it may just as well have been three years or three centuries as far as she was concerned— and her mother resumed her rounds with a feeling of gloomy trepidation. Despite her friendly smile the second watch- maker looked at her suspiciously and dismissed her with the sentence "I don't buy secondhand goods," and she left his shop, her cheeks burning with shame, as if she had been caught out trying to pass on stolen goods. "And in truth," she said to herself, "how does he know that the watch wasn't stolen, and how could I possibly prove it? Perhaps I should have explained to him exactly how it came into my hands and why I'm trying to sell it?" She turned this question over and over in her mind, wondering how she should approach the next watchmaker, and what she should say to prevent him from suspecting her—but all these efforts were superfluous because the third watchmaker was not in the least suspicious. He was perfectly friendly and even eager, but the minute he saw the watch he turned up his nose and said: "Not modern." He screwed the magnifying glass into his eye, and as he opened the case and examined the inner mechanism he explained that in the world of trade an inferior modern watch was preferable to a superior watch that was out of fashion. From the gist of his words she learned that he would be doing her a great favor to rid her of this watch on which the whole fashionable world had turned its back. At that moment a ragged child peered enviously into the shop, and she felt a great urge to give him the gold watch for a present. If she had not needed the money, she would have given him the watch. Nothing would have afforded her greater plea- sure at that moment than to give the watch to the child who so obviously coveted it, especially since apart from the happi- ness it would bring to the child, it would rid her of the watch, which she had come to regard as a loathsome and intolerable burden, something she had to cast off as quickly as possible and at any price. In the end, after a week of running round town, she was delighted when a venerable old watchmaker agreed to exchange the gold watch for a modern "young girl's" wristwatch, even though she was perfectly well aware that her own watch was worth at least three times as much as Rina's.

This picture of his beloved mother going out in her best dress with an ingratiating smile on her face to sell her gold watch, and tottering home a few hours later on her aching legs, pale, insulted, and humiliated in her own eyes, was always associated in Srulik's memory with the matter of Rina's relationship to Haim Long-Life, and not only because the two things had happened during the same period of time. Just as his mother was helpless in the hands of the watchmakers, so Haim Long-Life was helpless in the hands of little Rinaleh. But Rina—despite her temper tantrums and the frank egoism with which she pursued her desires— never revealed anything like the hardness frequently displayed by Orita toward those who were dependent on her good graces, especially toward Yaakov Talmi, who was not only contemptible, but also loathsome and repulsive in her eyes from the moment that she sensed his weakness for her. Haim Long-Life was not contemptible in Rina's eyes, only funny. But the more aware she became of his weakness for her and his dependence on her, the sorrier she felt for him and the dearer he became to her, like a faithful, ridiculous, pathetic old dog.

Since he didn't have a penny to his name, Haim Long-Life, with all the goodwill in the world, could be of no material assistance to Rina in the matter of the wristwatch. On the other hand, he did have a great idea. "I've got it—a fantastic patent!" he cried, and began stalking around the room, assiduously chewing an apple which he had picked up from the floor amid the debris of the broken fruit bowl.

He picked up all the fruit and arranged it in a row in front of him, and as he developed his idea in his head he ate the whole apple without realizing what he was doing. He had arrived hungry, hoping at the very least to be invited to lunch; but lunch had been forgotten in the scene created by Rina, in the wake of which the Temple-builder had escaped to his workshop and Rina had made off to her best friend's house, while her mother had dropped exhausted onto the sofa. Haim Long-Life sat down next to her on the sofa and began to expound the details of the idea for watches which had popped into his brain, to the accompaniment of the crunching of the apple and the clicking of his false teeth. All the great sorrow felt by Rinaleh on account of the watch, together with the pandemonium she had created because of it, he explained, only went to show that in our day and age the watch—particularly for the female sex—was as much a piece of jewelry as an instrument for measuring time, in which case, why not go whole hog? If it was an ornament then it contained limitless possibilities, from every point of view: colors, shapes, and styles. Thus, for example, you could make watches with frames or faces in red, green, yellow, brown, or any other color, and women could match their watches to their dresses and change them when they changed their costumes; a watch for the morning and a watch for the evening and a watch for in between. And we could make them in all kinds of different shapes as well: square, round, oval, triangular, hexagonal, and every possible geometrical form—and why only wristwatches? Why not, for example, arm watches and ankle watches and breast watches? We would make, in different shapes and sizes, bracelet-watches and ring-watches and pendant-watches and choker-watches and earring-watches and anklet-watches and tiara-watches and even garter-watches. "Forgive me," said Srulik's mother after recovering her strength somewhat, lowering her eyes as she spoke in an attempt to ignore the loud and reckless activity of her interlocutor's masticating jaws. "I quite forgot to offer you something to eat. Perhaps I can boil you an egg?"

"No, no," protested Haim Long-Life. "Thank you. I'm not hungry. And anyway I've already told you long ago that I hate boiled eggs. I'm not all that keen on eggs at the best of times, but if you haven't got anything better, I wouldn't mind an omelette with onions and tomatoes. One egg will be enough for me today." And all this time Srulik sat and wondered at this Haim Long-Life, who spent his life floating on the wings of his imagination and building castles in the air, and who at the same time regarded himself as the most realistic and practical person in the world; a man who didn't have the money to buy himself lunch and ravenously devoured the apples he hated, and who was nevertheless convinced of his ability to earn at one stroke more than all the merchants of Jerusalem put together. "I'll never sink into that kind of Jerusalem daydreaming," Srulik would repeat to himself whenever he reflected on his own course in life, and he would make up his mind that he would never follow in the footsteps of his father or his father's lanky friend or, needless to say, his mother, who didn't have a practical bone in her body. Each of them symbolized this "Jerusalem daydreaming" in his eyes—not because he had anything against them but, on the contrary, out of love and sympathy for them, out of the grief it caused him to see these dear souls stumbling with every step they took in the practical world because each one of them was sunk in his own fantasy, and Haim Long-Life most of all. In the course of time the watch patent became a family joke, in which Haim Long-Life himself participated, although his jokes at his own expense did not detract one iota from his enduring faith in the value of his patent and the fact that one day it would make him a fortune "at one stroke." Srulik's mother would say that it was lucky for her husband that he wasn't a millionaire watch manufacturer, for otherwise he would undoubtedly have fallen for the watch patent and lost all his millions on it. At the moment, having no money to lose, he lost working hours only on the Temple patent—and Rina would laugh and promise the inventor that she would marry him if he would give her a pair of watch-earrings for a present. Haim Long-Life would laugh with her and say, "If only you knew, my dear, how close it was, you wouldn't make any promises." And in the meantime even the wristwatch she had received as a present from her mother, the watch she had longed for and for whose sake she had turned the house upside down and caused all those explosions and scandals, had ceased to interest her, and sometimes she would even forget it and go to school without it.

Haim Long-Life's watch patent was remembered by the old convert, Dr. Israel Shoshan, three or four days before he gave up the ghost, when he was telling me, while hawking and spitting and coughing up the remnants of his sole remaining lung, about Henrietta van Eckern of Amersfoort and Gabriel Luria, who had appeared to him in Noyon in a French porter's uniform, and other anecdotes of his travels abroad. The last time he had been abroad was two years before, when he went to Amsterdam for lung surgery. The surgeons there—among the best in the world, to whom he had been sent by the heads of the Calvinist Church—had removed his infected lung (although he knew very well that he was suffering from lung cancer, Dr. Shoshan never allowed the word "cancer" to pass his lips, as though it were as taboo as the Ineffable Name of God). One day, as he was strolling about the streets of Amsterdam after he had recovered from the surgery and was feeling fit again, it occurred to him to go and visit Henrietta, whom he had not seen for years. He began walking to the railway station in order to inquire about trains to Amersfoort, and as he was reflecting that he had better phone Henrietta first, before descending on her like a bolt from the blue, he remembered that he had to buy a present for his wife, Paula. "First of all I'll buy something for Paula," he said to himself, and went into a jewelry shop, a large, fancy shop in the center of town. One of the assistants, a young girl, turned to him with a smile and he froze where he stood. On the pearl necklace around her neck hung a square watch, orange as the color of her dress. The old priest looked around himself and saw that the other shop assistants too were wearing colored watches set into pieces of jewelry.

For decades Haim Long-Life had not entered his thoughts, neither his waking thoughts nor his dreams at night, and now all of a sudden, in broad daylight and in full possession of his faculties, Dr. Israel Shoshan found himself in the middle of one of the forgotten Haim Long-Life's daydreams. A fantasy dreamed up by Haim Long-Life on an empty stomach in the home of his friend the poor carpenter in an alley branching off from the Street of the Prophets in Jerusalem had come true forty-five years later in Amsterdam and Paris and London, and tears of pity for the inventor who had died poor and despised came into the eyes of the tough old convert, who had not shed a tear for himself even when he realized that the cancer had spread to his only remaining lung. The young shop assistant who showed him watch after watch set into different pieces of jewelry thought that he was wiping his eyes because of the smoke from her cigarette, and she apologized and quickly put it out in a clock-ashtray. When he wanted to tell her about his father's old friend the inventor, he suddenly realized that the tears he was shedding were not only in memory of Haim Long-Life, but also in memory of the boy he had once been, nearly fifty years before; the boy to whom I now return, as he peered into the doorway of the Café Gat on his way to the Café Cancan, and was hailed by Gordon, the commander of

the Mahaneh Yehuda police, who invited him to come in
and have a look at the photos he had taken of the Jericho
mound.

Srulik did not have time to waste in cafés on that particular day of his life. While their neighbor Rosa sat with his
mother—in return for the payment she would receive in due
course, for it was unthinkable that he of all people should
exploit the kindness of this poverty-stricken woman who
lived from hand to mouth cleaning other people's floors and
washing their dishes and doing their laundry—he was running around town looking for Haim Long-Life in order to
recover the keys to his father's workshop, which he intended
to rent out. Since Haim Long-Life was not in his father's
shop, Srulik had gone to ask Berl where he was, and Berl
had promised to meet him at the Cancan in half an hour and
inform him of his brother's whereabouts.

Yael Gutkin was sitting in the corner of the café and
copying something out of the newspaper. "She must be copying a poem by Eshbaal Ashtoreth in her clear, backward-
sloping hand," said Srulik to himself at the moment Yael
raised her head and smiled at him with her kind eyes, which
made him feel guilty even as it warmed his heart. He felt
guilty because he knew that he did not deserve her good
opinion of him. As opposed to Orita's brown eyes, which
would wreak havoc in his heart even when they were not
looking at him, Yael's blue ones—which were similar to her
sister's despite the difference in color—would flood him
with a serenity which stemmed neither from their blueness
nor from the radiation of any inner serenity on her part,
since Yael herself, especially at this time of her life, was tense
and nervous. For all her resemblance to her sister, and above
and beyond it, the look in Yael's eyes, like her manner of
speaking, her walk, and her movements in general, flowed
on a different wave and sang to a different melody. The look
in Yael's eyes always spoke to Srulik about the duty of a man

to bring out the good in himself and the world around him, and in so doing it would shut the lid on the boiling pot and send him floating off on waves of serenity, between his feelings of guilt on the one hand and the pressure of the seething pot on the other. "You're a good, intelligent boy, Srulik," her look would tell him, "a dear soul"—this was how Yael referred to everyone she liked: "Rosa is a dear soul; Srulik is a dear soul," and so on—"and there is so much to be done for this nation and this country and for all the wretched and oppressed of the earth: if only you and I and each one of us did the little we could, the world would be a better place to live in, less evil and odious." And Yael's look would say all this to him, and more, without any connection to the actual subject of conversation between them, which might be about anything or nothing: How's your mother, and What did the doctor say, and What do you intend doing now that you've graduated, and What do you think of Holmes's latest exhibition. Yael did not like making speeches, or listening to them either, about justice and righteousness, the redemption of the land and the Jewish people, the conquest of labor and the fraternity of nations, the revolution of the toiling masses, or the need to practice what you preached. She herself, however, lived under the constant pressure of the duty to behave properly, to lend a hand, to work for someone or something, a duty that preoccupied her to such an extent that she completely neglected her appearance and her clothes. She would put on whatever came to hand when she got out of bed in the morning, and in her absentmindedness she would sometimes go out in a skirt whose hem had come undone, a blouse without buttons, or a sweater worn inside out. Because of Yael's good taste and discriminating eye, Orita would drag her along whenever she went shopping. Yael always found time to help her sister choose the right blouse to match her skirt and the right bag to match her shoes, but she never had the time to do these things for herself. It was her duty to help her younger sister, and all kinds of other people as well—but she did not consider that she had any duty to beautify herself or make herself look elegant. On the contrary, she regarded anything to do with her personal appearance as an irrelevant nuisance, and until Orita forced her to buy a new dress or pair of shoes she never even realized that she needed them. "My God! What on earth have you done to your hair?" shrieked Orita when she suddenly saw her sister, in a shabby leather coat, on the corner of Princess Mary Street on her way home from the hairdresser, her hair shorn and cropped. "You're making yourself ugly on purpose! Don't try to sell me all that stuff about not having the patience to look after long hair or get into a decent dress. You simply want to deny your femininity."

"Really, Rita, it's about time you stopped with all those boring psychological clichés. If I tell you that I feel more comfortable like this then I feel more comfortable like this and that's all there is to it." More than the shabby leather coat and the cropped hair—which actually suited Yael and drew attention to her long neck—Orita was saddened by the sight of the wrinkles which had appeared on her sister's face, on her forehead and in the corners of her eyes, after she had accompanied a group of workers who had gone to work on the Jericho Road. Nine months in the sun of the Judean desert had ruined her complexion: her proud little snub nose had turned into a permanently peeling pink blob, and the agonized narrowing of her blue eyes against the cruel light had engraved crow's-feet in their corners and frown marks in the middle of her forehead. "You went to cook for the labor brigade only because you hate cooking and you don't even know how," Orita would say when she wanted to tease her. In all Orita's other jokes and witticisms about the Jericho Road—many of them far sharper than the remark about her cooking—Yael would join with good grace, but for some reason this particular sally hurt her. Yael, who enjoyed good food and had a discerning palate, detested anything to do with the art of cooking itself, which was the most important subject in her mother's life. "The moment I dread most of all," she said once to Srulik, "is when she starts telling everybody about her philological studies in Cambridge." The turn of this linguistic tale would invariably come round with the serving of the dessert. After her guests had expressed their admiration for the excellence of the dishes set before them by their hostess—who always insisted on doing all the actual cooking herself, leaving the cook only the routine kitchen jobs—Mrs. Gutkin would modestly incline her head and, smiling the sad, resigned smile of a condemned man listening to his sentence being read out in court, would say: "Yes, yes. On this nonsense, on cooking and frying and baking, I've wasted my life! When I studied philology at Cambridge University all my professors were sure that I had a brilliant academic career ahead of me. I was always so embarrassed; whenever the head of the Philology Department praised me to my face I would blush to the roots of my hair. I never really believed that I deserved to have such a fuss made about me. But I did feel that despite my limitations I had a vocation for philological research, and that I was capable of making some modest contribution to the field. I would never have imagined, when I was a young student at Cambridge, that instead of occupying myself with philology I would spend my entire life among the pots and the pans in the kitchen."

It sometimes happened that philology had to wait its turn because of the ignorance of new guests, who had been invited for the first time to dine at the judge's table and were not yet acquainted with the rites and customs of the house. When, for whatever reason, the culinary compliments were dilatory—usually because the diners were busy talking to the judge—his wife would frown and inquire of the person

next to her, in the tone of concern one usually reserves for
the ill, if there was anything wrong with the soup. She was
afraid that the soup was too spicy. And what about the gefilte
fish? Did he find it a little too heavy, perhaps? Fish cooked in
this way could sometimes be indigestible and keep a person
awake all night! Perhaps it might be best to take the gefilte
fish back to the kitchen (the gefilte fish, so firm and light, so
piquantly and delicately flavored, which melted so deli-
ciously in the mouth and slid so smoothly down the throat,
the celebrated gefilte fish, the very crown and culmination of
her culinary art) and ask the cook to make something simple
to prepare and easy to digest instead—an omelette perhaps?
As soon as the echoes of his wife's concern reached the
judge's ears he would interrupt his conversation and give the
signal for the chorus of praise to commence: "Ida!" he would
cry, for that was her name, "Ida! I haven't tasted fish like this
for years! Even my mother, God rest her soul, who made the
best gefilte fish in the Jewish Quarter of the Old City, didn't
always succeed in making fish like this! What do you say, Mr.
Holmes," he shouted into the ear of the old English painter,
hard of hearing these many years, sitting on his right, "how
do you like the fish?" And after this subtle hint all the judge's
guests, even the most inexperienced or absentminded
among them, came forward to present their tributes,
whether in so many words, or whether by smacking their
lips, nodding their heads, or grunting in appreciation—
which immediately led to: "When I was studying philology
in Cambridge . . ."

If the judge was so hasty in arousing the anticipated
praise of his guests, it was not only in order to satisfy his
wife, but also—and mainly—for fear that Orita would pre-
cede him. On Yaeli's score he had no fears. He knew that the
more irritating she found her mother's philology and the
guests at his table, the more she would withdraw into her
shell and more silent she would become. Not so Orita. So far
from annoying Orita, the philological issue amused her, and

this being the case, it was quite out of the question to leave the initiation of their guests into the kind of table manners expected of them to her tender mercies. For in her amusement she was quite likely to shame her mother in public, and it was this that upset the judge, who did not usually mind the scandals provoked by his daughter's gaiety, and even relished them. Orita had even learned to cook for fun: laughing and joking, and after driving her mother mad and bringing her to the brink of despair and wreaking havoc in the "old philologist's holy of holies"—which is how she referred to the kitchen so hated by her sister, who would sometimes go without a cup of tea rather than set foot in it— Orita learned to cook all kinds of savory dishes and bake cakes and whip up soufflés. "Now, if I had gone out with the labor brigade, I would have made a cream cake for Louidor the Silent's dessert," said Orita in response to her sister's declaration that she had gone not out of idealism (for she detested the idea no less than the word that expressed it), but simply to see that Louidor the Silent had a hot meal after a hard day's work.

Yaeli had actually wanted to say "to make a hot meal for Louidor the Silent and all the other boys who can't take care of themselves," but Orita burst into her loud, musical laughter straight after "Louidor the Silent," and ever since then the expression "a hot meal for Louidor the Silent" had gone to join the store of family jokes invented by Orita. Whenever she wanted to refer to her sister's idealism she would say, "Of course, for the sake of providing a hot meal for Louidor the Silent . . ." and in the course of time "Louidor the Silent" became a synonym for "ideals" and "idealism" in general, used even by Yael herself in speaking of people "who sacrifice everything for the sake of Louidor the Silent" and of herself when she announced: "I'll never be willing to sacrifice the freedom of my opinions and feelings and thoughts on the altar of Louidor the Silent."

The joke behind the joke was that not only had Yaeli never

been Louidor the Silent's girlfriend, but that she hardly knew him, and to the extent that she had met him and exchanged a few words with him in the Café Cancan or on the labor detail, she had never found him particularly interesting, for either good or ill. He was a habitué of the Cancan, and since he was weak and retiring it had not occurred to the leaders of the labor detail—who were habitués of the same café—to attach him to the group going out to the Judean desert, but in this matter he suddenly found his tongue: he informed them that he wanted to go with them, and after immense efforts of persuasion, and stubborn and eloquent pleas, they agreed in the end to let him come. On one of his Jerusalem leaves—they would come to town once a month—he told Yael that the hardest thing to bear was the lack of a proper meal in the cold evenings. When the sun came down, after a day of back-breaking work in the cruel desert sun, a sudden cold descended and chilled to the bone their exhausted, sweating bodies, avid for a hot meal—but unfortunately none of the others in his crew knew any more about cooking than Louidor himself, and so they were forced to make do with cold, dry rations. When the rumor spread among the crew that "a cook was coming soon," Louidor did not know that the cook was Yael and that the few words he had exchanged with her were responsible for her decision to come and cook for them.

Later on he vanished from the Café Cancan and Yaeli never saw him again. Just as Louidor could never have imagined that his name had become a humorous term for a noble idea in the judge's home, so Yaeli had no idea that he was avoiding the Café Cancan because of her, and that she never saw him anywhere else because he not only made every effort to keep out of her way, but also was intent on wiping out the memory of the favor she had done him, which had turned into a nightmare. She did not have the faintest idea of what she had done to him that night, with a casual act of kindness to which she had not given a second thought.

It happened a few days after they had finished laying the road and returned to Jerusalem. As she was walking back to her room that night—she had left home even before going out to the Jericho road—she saw a huddled figure half lying, half sitting on a bench in the Russian Compound. It was Louidor the Silent. "What's wrong, Louidor? Why don't you go home to bed?" He mumbled something and looked at her strangely from the black circles surrounding his sunken eyes. "Aren't you feeling well? Are you ill?" She realized that he was shivering all over. He must have been on his way home and must have collapsed on the bench. "Come with me," she said to him. "I live here, in the lane on the other side of the gate. He went with her to her room, where she ordered him to get undressed and get into bed, and in the meantime she made some hot tea. "I'll sleep here, on the couch," she said, and began to take off her clothes. Suddenly he clasped her to him in a strong embrace and covered her with feverish kisses. "What's the matter with you? Have you gone mad?" Yaeli cried, and violently pushed him away. "Go right back to bed and stop this nonsense." He went back to bed on trembling legs and turned his face to the wall and she tucked him in and said, "And now good night and pleasant dreams." And indeed, as soon as Yaeli lay down on the couch she fell fast asleep, but Louidor the Silent did not close his eyes all night long; he tossed and turned, got up and paced about the room, drew the curtain and looked outside, and with the first light of dawn, unable to endure her deep sleep and rhythmic breathing any longer, he got up and fled through the streets, petrified in the dreams of dawn on the threshold of waking. At the same time Fat Pesach, one of the two owners of the Café Cancan, came out to prepare breakfast for the early-morning workers. Walking with his measured tread down the lane past the Russian Compound, he saw the

door of Yaeli's room opening quietly and Louidor the Silent
emerging from it "as flustered as the saintly Joseph fleeing
from Potiphar's wife"—as he told the story later, rolling his
bulging eyes with a conspiratorial air, to all the habitués of
the Café Cancan.

"Oh, it's you, Shoshan!" called Fat Pesach as Srulik entered
the café and went to sit down next to Yael. "It's been a long
time since we saw you here." Smiling broadly and exposing
the wide gaps between his short teeth, his eyes beaming
above his full cheeks and his belly wobbling over his twinkling feet, he hurried to serve this prodigal son come back to
the fold from the Café Gat. Srulik would often wonder at the
agility of this corpulent body, which knew how to dance not
only the horah and the krakowiak but also the tango and the
waltz better than his thinner customers, and whose fat fingers performed delicate tasks—removing a speck from an
eye or screwing a screw into the depths of a kerosene-ring—
far more deftly than the long, lean fingers of his partner
Yom-tov the Sad. In contrast to Yom-tov, whose sadness
seemed to deepen with every new customer who entered the
café, Fat Pesach would hurry forward with a welcoming
smile, willingly take the orders, and serve the food and
drink with a seasoning of gossip to taste and a pinch of
flattery to whet the appetite.

"Let's see, Shoshan, how long has it been since you were
last here?" Unable to answer with any degree of precision
himself, Srulik could rely only on the elephantine memory
of Fat Pesach: "Just a moment—it was Hanukkah! Six
months ago at least." And as he spoke Srulik remembered
that it was indeed Hanukkah. It was Hanukkah when he
had sat for the first time at Orita's table in the Café Gat, and
she had asked him to come along on the trip to Jericho. "So
you're spending your time with the high society in the Café
Gat? With the British gentlemen and Arab effendis? A little
bird told me that you did very well in your examinations,

and that you're organizing an archaeological expedition to Ur of the Chaldees. Yes—who was it now? Just a minute—don't tell me!—it was Gabriel Luria!" A sharp pain cut off Srulik's breath at the sound of Gabriel's name, spoiling his pleasure at Pesach's remarks about his success in his examinations and organization of an archaeological expedition. One of the café owner's tried and tested ways of gratifying his interlocutor was to exaggerate the good things he found to say about him by one or two degrees while preserving the essential truth of the facts. Thus his intention of visiting Ur of the Chaldees was transformed into the "organization of an archaeological expedition," and despite the deliberate exaggeration Srulik would have gone on basking in the warmth of the fat man's welcome but for the introduction of Gabriel Luria's name, which proved beyond the shadow of a doubt that his worst fears had come true: Orita had run straight to Gabriel and asked him to join them on their journey. Fat Pesach, of course, had no idea of what he was doing to Srulik, and only wanted to make him happy. Even when he gossiped he did it only to please his listeners, never out of any ill will toward those he was gossiping about. He was fond of Louidor, for example, and would lend him money on the sly, trembling lest his partner find out, while as for Yael, he regarded her as the very flower of his establishment. Nevertheless, he could not keep his great and wonderful secret to himself, and as soon as one of the regulars walked in, the fat man would quiver all over in anticipation of the enormous pleasure he was about to give him with the dainty morsel of Potiphar's wife, which he was going to serve up for dessert—free, gratis, and for nothing.

Together with the pain of the knowledge that if Orita came with him alone, it would be only because Gabriel did not wish or was not able to accept her invitation to join them, Srulik's heart swelled with compassion for Louidor the Silent. For Srulik knew that the poor wretch deserved neither the halo bestowed upon him by Pesach nor the envy of all the lions of the Café Cancan, who saw this weirdo who had mysteriously disappeared from sight as Yaeli's secret lover. Louidor and Srulik did not know each other; that is to say, they had never been introduced and had met only by chance, usually in the Cancan, as strangers who did not even greet each other. Srulik did not know if Louidor would recognize him at all, and it had never occurred to him to seek his confidence, but nevertheless he had heard the whole story with his own ears straight from the confessional, where the confessor had heard it from the mouth of Louidor the Silent himself.

The confessor in question was Rosa, and the confessional a wooden partition she had put up in the corner of the yard, behind which she kept the laundry she did at home. Rosa usually worked as a laundress in the homes of her employers, but the young bachelors who lived in rooms without laundry facilities would bring their washing to her at home, and she would do it for them at a reduced rate. Louidor the Silent was one of them, but unlike the others, who came in the evenings, Louidor for some reason would turn up with his little bundle early in the morning. When Srulik himself got up early to study for an exam or to bring his mother a cup of tea in bed (a cup of tea at dawn was the best remedy for the pain of her aching heart), he would sometimes see Louidor through the bars of the kitchen window depositing his little bundle behind the screen and then sitting down on it to wait until Rosa noticed him and came to exchange a few words with him. He would tell her about himself in the third person, opening with: "Listen to what happened to a friend of mine." And when he failed to begin, Rosa would take the initiative and ask: "How's your friend?" When Srulik got up early one morning to iron his shirt before his last exam, he heard everything that had happened to this "friend," and what astonished him most of all was the old woman's reaction.

"You know that my friend is in love with a girl called Ofra." Thus Louidor began his story that morning because he was too discreet to mention Yaeli by name. This friend could no longer contain the great love he felt in his heart, and he made up his mind a thousand times to disclose it to her, to Ofra, but at the last minute, when he was already standing on her doorstep, he would always retreat because he didn't have the courage to go through with it. In the end he decided to write her a letter telling her all he felt and push it under her door. He went up the path leading through the Russian Compound to her room, and when he was only a few steps away from it he heard a woman's footsteps coming up behind him. "It's her," his heart told him even before he turned his head, and when he did so he saw her figure hurrying up the path behind him. "It's the finger of God," he said to himself. "Now or never!" And so great was his emotion that he began to tremble all over, shivering as violently as when he had come down with malaria on the Plain of Jericho. He took a step toward her and felt that his trembling knees were about to give way beneath him. Fortunately for him there was a bench under the tree next to the path, and he dropped onto it. At that moment she caught up with him and looked at him suspiciously. When she recognized him her eyes lit up and she said gently, "What's the matter, why don't you go home to bed?" And he almost died of happiness. "It's the finger of God!" he said to himself, and he wanted to tell her everything; but he could not speak and all that came out of his mouth was the sound of his chattering teeth. "Aren't you feeling well? Are you ill? Come with me, I live here, in the lane on the other side of the gate," and as in a dream too good to be true, in Paradise, he followed her, repeating to himself, "The finger of God, the finger of God!" Hand in hand they entered her room, and she pointed to the bed and told him to undress and get into it, while she made him something hot to drink. And while he

sipped the hot tea, she drew the curtain on the other side of
the table and began to take off her clothes behind it. As she
was doing so she sent him a warm smile, which did more to
cure his shivering and shaking than all the hot drinks in the
world, and sent him lunging toward her. At that moment her
look changed: instead of love and warmth there was a terrible contempt in her eyes, a kind of disdain and disgust, as if
it were not he, the desired and beloved, who was embracing
her, but some kind of revolting frog. This look seemed to
split his soul in two, as if she had severed his member from
his body and flung it out the window like a loathsome insect.

"And now good night and pleasant dreams," she said to
him, and he collapsed in a terrible fear. Suddenly he realized that it was not the finger of God but the hand of Satan
which had been sent to torture him. He fell onto the bed,
choking back with his fists the groans that escaped from his
mouth. A moment later he heard her lying down on the
couch and covering herself with a blanket, and before he
could swallow his groans and turn to face her, she was
already fast asleep. And then he stood up, resolved to rape
her in her sleep: there she was, stretched out before him with
nothing but a nightgown on her body, and he could do what
he liked to her, whatever he had imagined in the best of his
daydreams—but as soon as he approached her the look of
contempt and disgust he had seen in her eyes came between
them and made him go limp. The whole world became too
hard and bleak to bear, and he went up to the window and
drew the curtain, but no abyss gaped there to receive him,
only the gravel of the path below the first-floor window.

Throughout the story of the "friend who was in love with a
girl called Ofra," Louidor the Silent went on sitting behind
the partition on his little bundle of washing, while Rosa
listened standing.

"You tell your friend," said Rosa in her rusty voice, "that
instead of jumping out of the window he should go straight
to Luna."

"What are you saying, Rosa," exclaimed the horrified Louidor, "why on earth should he go to a prostitute? Excuse me, Rosa, but you don't know what you're talking about. You don't understand at all . . ."

"I know exactly what I'm talking about. You tell him exactly what I'm telling you now. Tell him that Luna will revive him on the spot. And once he's erect he won't want to jump out of the window anymore. And let him forget about Ofra. You tell him from me: Rosa says you must forget about Ofra. Rosa says that Ofra's not for you, and you're not for her. Ofra is a bitch, and she did a wicked thing to you."

At the sound of the warm welcome accorded by Fat Pesach to Mr. Shoshan on his return to the fold from the Café Gat, Yaeli lifted her head from the newspaper out of which she was copying a poem by the young poet Eshbaal Ashtoreth in her clear, backward-sloping hand, and smiled at Srulik with her kind eyes. "We haven't seen you here for ages," she said to him in her voice so similar to Orita's. "Come and sit next to me."

Srulik went up to her table and the minute he sat down on the creaking chair—all the chairs in the Cancan creaked and groaned and squeaked—a terrifying thought flashed through his mind: What if the same thing that had happened to Louidor with Yaeli should happen to him with Orita, and Louidor's single nightmare turned into a three-month-long hell for him? No, no: nothing like that could ever happen to him, it was quite impossible, for Srulik was Srulik and not Louidor the Silent, and Orita was Orita and not Yaeli. And why, in fact, hadn't Yaeli gone to bed with Louidor? He felt a tremendous urge to turn to her and say: Please tell me, my dear Yaeli, why didn't you go to bed with poor Louidor? You'll no doubt reply that you didn't go to bed with him because you don't love him and don't desire him and Louidor the Silent doesn't give rise in you to even a passing sinful thought. And to this I reply that precisely because of this, the question arises with regard to you—

you and not some other woman. You, after all, are a good woman, an idealist (I say this in all seriousness, I use the word you hate so much just because you really are what it says, while all kinds of bastards put it up for sale on the black markets all over the world). I swear to you, Yaeli, that you are the dearest soul I know. And it is as such that I address my question to you. When you came across someone you knew on your way home at night, a solitary soul who seemed to you in need of help, you didn't hesitate for a moment, and without even thinking about it, on the kind of impulse that is second nature to you, you took him to your room and put him in your bed in order to help him and make him better. But once he was in your bed it suddenly dawned upon you, to your astonishment, that he was sick not of a germ, but of his love for you, and that what would make him better was not a cup of tea, but going to bed with you. In which case, why didn't you go to bed with him? Why did you refuse to give him the only medicine he needed, which could have cured him and made him better? Yes, yes, I know it would have been repellent to you, but that's not a good enough reason to withhold help from someone who needs it: every nurse in a hospital does things that disgust her twenty times a day simply because the patient in her care needs them to be done for him. And while she does it the nurse does not make disgusted faces or wrinkle her nose because of the smell. She looks kindly on her patient and smiles at him! And you yourself have already done things you hate for him and his friends: Orita claims, and you don't deny it, that there's nothing in the world you detest more than cooking, and nevertheless, "for the sake of a hot meal for Louidor the Silent," you spent nine months, from morning to night, doing the thing you hated most in the world! And not in the shade of your mother's cool, airy kitchen either, but in the burning sun of the Jordan Valley; and not with the most modern and efficient cooking utensils, but with the primitive tools of the desert Arabs. Yes, yes: I know that you did it not for just anyone, but for a comrade who had committed himself body and soul to our national and social and historical ideals, for the sake of the redemption of the land and the people, for the sake of justice and righteousness. And I say these things without any cynicism, I say them in all seriousness and with profound admiration—I would even say "holy reverence" if I knew what holy reverence was. And in view of all this, the question becomes even graver: this same comrade comes to you and says, "It's not a warm meal that I need, but your warm body, and when you lie next to me and offer me a cup of tea instead of your loins, you put me through the agonies of hell, and with your kind heart and good deeds and laudable intentions you become as diabolical as Satan himself"—and what do you say to him then? You could say, of course, that the kind of help he requires he can get from any whore in the street—which is exactly what Rosa told him—and that you are not a whore. True enough, but in that case any common prostitute would have brought more benefit to the man himself and the cause he serves than all the idealistic women like you in the world! "No, no," you will say, "you've got it all wrong. You yourself heard him telling Rosa that when my sleeping body was at his mercy and he wanted to rape me, he lost his erection when he had the opportunity to do so simply because of the memory of the look of disdain and disgust in my eyes. And as for Rosa's advice about going to a prostitute, all she wanted was to cure him of the fear that he had become completely impotent because of me—a fear any prostitute could cure him of in a moment with her professional expertise. In other words: Louidor the Silent would never have been satisfied with an anonymous body, like the embalmers in ancient Egypt who would rape the dead bodies of the ladies they had to embalm, and succeeded in doing to them after their deaths what they had wished in vain to do to them while they were alive. He wanted at least a live body which would respond to him, he wanted at least the kind of sexual collaboration that expresses itself in passive acquiescence, in the lack of physical resistance. If he was neither loved nor desired, Louidor wanted at least to be sure that he did not disgust me."

"Fat Pesach is very put out that you finally showed up just when I'm sitting here," said Yaeli when the latter hurried off to the kitchen to make a cup of cocoa for the long-lost customer. Srulik was very fond of cocoa, and besides, when he was hungry and didn't have enough money to order something to eat and something to drink, he had come to appreciate the peculiar quality of the drink in question, which somehow managed to satisfy his hunger while at the same time quenching his thirst. "Otherwise he could have told you the story about Potiphar's wife." They both laughed, and Srulik for some reason said to himself, "It's now or never," and asked her the question that had been bothering him: "Tell me, Yaeli, why didn't you go to bed with Louidor the Silent?"

Yaeli frowned as at a sudden, painful memory, and her shining eyes stared into the distance in silent reverie. Then she said: "There was a moment when I said to myself that I should go to bed with him, that it would be the best deed of my life, but I simply wasn't capable of it, and as you see everything worked out all right, thank God. I'm simply incapable of going to bed with a man I don't love. I can't even stand the touch of a man I don't feel anything for, which is why I don't like going to dances. I know it sounds a bit like a romantic cliché, and perhaps it's petit-bourgeois of me, but I can't help it. And anyway—why should I have to apologize? He got over it quickly enough."

"And what about the touch of my hand? Can you stand that?" asked Srulik just as Fat Pesach brought his cup of steaming, fragrant cocoa.

"What a bastard you are," cried Yaeli. "Haven't you got

anything better to do than try to force confessions out of me? You know very well that I wanted you from the minute I set eyes on you," and she leaned over and planted a kiss on his cheek in front of Fat Pesach, who dissolved in a beaming short-toothed smile and showed no inclination to return to the counter until Yaeli said, "That's all for today. There's nothing more to see."

"Perhaps I should go to Ur of the Chaldees with Yaeli instead of Orita?" said Srulik to himself, and immediately he banished the vague temptation to tell her the whole truth about Louidor the Silent's condition. In spite of her single moment of insight into what was happening inside him— when she had tried without success to force herself to respond to him—she really and truly thought that "everything had worked out all right, and Louidor had gotten over it quickly enough." It was better that she didn't know what she had done to him. If he told her what he knew, Srulik would only cause her grief and pain without doing any good at all to Louidor. And really—how could she be blamed if this silent oddball was pining away for love of her, sinking further every day into insane fantasies? He had always been a weird, enigmatic creature. The last time Haim Long-Life came to visit them, when he asked Srulik's mother for the keys to his father's shop, he told them that he had seen Louidor the Silent wandering around the market in Ramleh dressed like an Arab fellah. All his peculiarities were part of his very nature. He had come into the world together with a predisposition to madness, and if Yaeli had done anything at all to him, it was only to reinforce and accelerate his innate tendencies; and if by chance he had met not her but some other girl, it would have been not Yaeli but this other girl who would have triggered the identical reaction. Nor was it at all clear that there was any connection between Louidor's love for Yaeli and the night he had spent in her room, and the fact that he was roaming around the markets of Ramleh dressed like an Arab. All kinds of young men, healthy in body and mind, who had never in their lives had anything to do with Yaeli lived among the Arabs in various places all over the country. There was Pesach Bar-Adon, for example. Pesach Bar-Adon, whose manhood nobody would deny, who was pursued by women, had spent the last year and a half wandering with the Bedouin tribes in the mountains of Gilad and Hauran, and by now he looked like a real Bedouin shepherd, right down to the braids in his hair. Gabby Luria said that he had even begun publishing stories about Bedouin life under the Bedouin pen name Aziz Effendi. And even the story that Louidor was running around dressed like a fellah was far from certain. The only proof was the testimony of Haim Long-Life, and Haim Long-Life, who always walked around wrapped in his dreams of inventions, could be mistaken. He may have met an Arab fellah who resembled Louidor the Silent in Ramleh, or he may have seen this resemblance only in his mind's eye, in which case the whole story was simply a figment of the inventor's imagination.

The inventor's brother appeared in the doorway just as Yaeli was addressing Fat Pesach with the words "That's all for today. There's nothing more to see," and Srulik was looking at her profile, at her long neck, her sunburnt little snub nose, her clear, kind eyes, and saying to himself: "There's no need to travel to Ur of the Chaldees with Yaeli; I can sit right here with Yaeli. With Yaeli I can bring Ur of the Chaldees here, to the creaking chairs of the Cancan." This unexpected discovery astonished him to such an extent that Berl's appearance at the door seemed to him superfluous. At the sight of the lean, stooping man hurrying inside between the tables and chairs, Srulik wondered how until one moment ago he had been awaiting him with such anxious impatience. His bemusement grew and suddenly turned into a feeling of insult as he realized that Berl was no less taken aback by his presence there. Angry and agitated, Berl made a beeline for Yaeli and gave him, Srulik, a look of astonishment as if he were wondering what on earth he was doing there. As for Srulik, he would have liked to give this Berl a piece of his mind and tell him, without beating around the bush: "Listen here, Berl. It wasn't me who wanted to meet you here, but you who made the appointment with me. Only half an hour ago, in the clinic, you said to me: 'Wait for me in the Café Cancan.' As a matter of fact, I haven't got the time for meetings in cafés. I'm in a hurry, and the only thing I'm interested in is where I can find your brother, Haim Long-Life—that's all! And this one little thing you could perfectly well have told me right there in the clinic, without any need to make appointments in the Café Cancan!" But before Srulik could even open his mouth Berl said to Yaeli:

"You have no idea what trouble your sister is causing me. She came sweeping into the clinic this morning like a whirlwind and dragged Dr. Landau off on some trip or other. And off he went, leaving me to deal with all the mess on my own and without even telling me how long this trip of theirs was supposed to last. And today of all days—the Ramallah district day, when I've got every fellah from Nebi Samwil to Anata on my hands!"

The constant, smoldering fear that Gabriel Luria would go off on a trip with Orita before him exploded in a burst of laughter. Srulik laughed and wiped away his tears, laughed and said, "So Orita is going on a trip with Dr. Landau, with Dr. Landau of all people, who isn't ashamed of admitting in public that he likes van Gogh and hates modern painting, old Dr. Landau, who's still living at the end of the last century, Dr. Landau, who insults cubism and calls it 'idiotic'!"

His laughter rang in his ears, sounding amazingly like the peals of Aunt Elka's laughter, and beyond it he heard Yaeli say, "Wait, wait. It's not the end yet. Rita will still drag Dr.

Landau up the aisle and into the marriage bed!" The more
Srulik laughed, the more clearly he saw the lines of Aunt
Elka's face in his imagination, until he actually expected to
hear her voice saying to him, as she used to say to Aunt
Ethel: "And now run quickly to the toilet before you wet your
pants."

"Yes," said Berl to Srulik, "I remember now: you're looking for Haim. I couldn't tell you in the clinic. Haim is simply
hiding from his creditors and the court process servers. He's
sleeping in your father's shop, but you won't find him there
before eight or nine at night. He only goes there after all the
shops in the commercial center are closed. He doesn't want
anyone there to know where he sleeps. He's afraid of
informers."

And it was only then, when Berl pronounced the words
"his creditors and the court process servers," that Srulik
remembered something that had completely slipped his
mind—that the court had issued an eviction order against
his father, and this in the wake of a previous order confiscat-
ing all his "assets." And this was what was written in the
court order: "In view of your failure to comply with the final
warning prior to seizure that was sent to you, and your
failure to pay the sums owing for your debts, I am hereby
obliged to put into effect the injunction against you and
confiscate all your property, both movable and immovable."
Dr. Landau had vanished in the wake of Orita, and his
dreams of the rent to pay for the voyage to Ur of the Chaldees had vanished in the wake of Dr. Landau. Srulik wiped
away the tears of laughter that welled up again at the
thought of his mother, that timid and innocent lamb, who
had succeeded in spite of everything in pulling the wool
over the eyes of the landlord. She had told him that his
father had gone away to "find the money" to pay his debts,
and thereby succeeded in postponing the eviction and the
confiscation orders until his return "in a few weeks' time."

The climax of the whole affair, which had become a standing joke in the family, was Rosa's reply to the process server. When the latter entered the courtyard with his shabby official briefcase containing the two court orders and asked Rosa, "Where does Mr. Abraham Shoshan live?" she had given him the blank look reserved exclusively for representatives of authority, and dryly replied: "There's no one here by that name. You've got the wrong address. I live on this side of the courtyard, and over there, on the opposite side, lives Mr. Temple-Builder."

3.

The Last Dream

FREE AND PURIFIED of any image of Orita, a married woman by now and mother of a three-year-old daughter, the little librarian felt the urge to get up and go to Ur of the Chaldees reawaken in him one fine day at the time when I already knew him, and his aunts used to come to the reading room every few weeks to hold their tea parties. It was a great day for Aunt Elka. She burst into the library with her eyes sparkling beneath the broad purple brim of her straw hat and cried: "Srulik! Today I sold the peacock ashtray for seven pounds!"

"Yes indeed, seven pounds!" repeated Aunt Ethel, puffing and panting in her wake, and in her excitement she plunked both her baskets down on the pile of books stacked on the librarian's desk. "Yehuda Prosper Bey paid her seven pounds for the ashtray."

"Wonderful, wonderful!" cried Srulik, clapping his hands. "In that case, you earn more in one day than I do in a whole month."

"Not in one day but in three hours. I made that ashtray in three hours. When I began hammering I had no idea what would come out," Elka said, laughing. "It's a pity that buyers like Yehuda Prosper Bey don't come along every day."

"Yes, a buyer like Yehuda Prosper Bey doesn't come along every day." Aunt Ethel made haste to confirm her words. "Yehuda Prosper Bey is a buyer in a class of his own." He had come into Elka's studio accompanied by Señor Moïse, looked around and fingered objects here and there until his eyes fell on the peacock ashtray lying underneath the bench, and stopped right there. That was enough for Señor Moïse: after moving his long legs with alacrity, bumping into pots and bowls on his way, he raised the ashtray from the dust, wiped it with his sleeve and held it up to the light so that his master could see it properly. "I'll pay you seven pounds for it," the old Bey said to Elka in his deep, hoarse voice. She could hardly believe her ears. She had intended asking a pound and half and was prepared to go down to a pound. "It's too much," she said. "Don't be a fool," said the old man. "For you it's a lot of money, but the ashtray is worth far more than seven pounds."

Even after the seven notes were folded in her hand Elka could not believe her good fortune, and as soon as the old Bey and his faithful retainer, with the peacock ashtray tucked under his arm, had turned Zalman Segal's corner and disappeared from sight, she quickly locked the front door and escaped through the kitchen with Ethel in case the old man had second thoughts and came to ask for his money back. Throughout the "five-o'clock" the aunts were busy calculating how much money they could make if they had a buyer like Yehuda Prosper Bey for every one of Elka's articles, taking into account the fact that when she felt like it Elka could turn out three a day. Toward the end of the tea party, when the time had come for Ethel to open the cans of pineapple, Elka sank into an enigmatic silence, and a strange, remote gleam came into her eyes: an image of thirty years before, an image associated with another sale, had suddenly surfaced in her memory. She told us that she remembered herself in the Old City, in the middle of a big

crowd of Jews and Arabs surrounding a Turkish crier. The
Turkish crier was an officer of the court, displaying a few
miserable wares on the steps of David's Citadel in a public
auction of the effects of an Arab murderer condemned to
death by hanging at the Jaffa Gate. In the heap of wretched
rags lay a gleaming dagger. Everyone stared at it but no one
touched it or bid for it. The crowd suddenly parted to make
way for a man in the prime of his years, with an erect
bearing and a bold look in his eye. This proud, handsome
man was Yehuda Prosper Bey, who began walking slowly
between the two walls of eyes silently fixed on him toward
the auctioneer standing on the steps and holding out the
dagger. He bought the dagger and turned away without
paying any attention to the crowd, which shrank even farther back with a murmur of awe.

On that great day, even before the arrival of his aunts and
before hearing the story about Yehuda Prosper Bey, the little
librarian had been seized by a ferment of feverish gaiety,
which continued to seethe and bubble inside him as he
listened with his usual fascination to their stories, nodding
his head, raising his eyebrows and exclaiming "Ay-yay-yay!"
at the news of Elka's amazing commercial success. This
ferment had commenced when he was busy entering in the
card index of the catalogue, the titles of new books that had
arrived that morning from England, and his eye had fallen
on one of the titles: *Dead Towns and Living Men.* "Dead towns
and living men!" he repeated to himself, and his heart leapt
at the image that appeared before his eyes—the image of
himself walking among the ruins of Ur of the Chaldees.
The image came even before he began to write down the
particulars of the book and noted the name of the author:
Sir Charles Leonard Woolley, the celebrated archaeologist
who had conducted a dig at Ur of the Chaldees many years
before. It was a long time since Srulik had opened a book
with such eager anticipation, an eagerness which did not

wane even after he began reading the titles of the chapters and discovered that the book dealt not with the dig at Ur of the Chaldees but with the beginnings of the author's archaeological career in other places—in Egypt and Carchemish. Apart from the obscure biblical verse "Is not Calno as Carchemish?" the name Carchemish awoke no echo whatsoever in Srulik's memory. But the exotic name in itself, preserving in its strangeness the flavor of its remote, ancient world while its appearance here, in Latin letters, endowed it with a defined and concrete existence in the contemporary world, even if only as a ruin, aroused Srulik's longings to such an extent that he stopped filling in the catalogue card and opened the book at the chapter on Carchemish and read: "In 1912 T. E. Lawrence and I drove from Aleppo northwards in the old-fashioned covered touring-wagons which had not yet been displaced by the motor—and the railway-line, too, had still to be built—and after two days' journey were welcomed at Jerablus, then a squalid little village built alongside the ruins of Carchemish. We were welcomed, because although I was new to the country Lawrence had worked there throughout the previous season with Hogarth and Campbell Thompson and was therefore an old friend." At this point Aunt Elka arrived with the news of the fantastic price she had obtained for the peacock ashtray, and Ethel put her two baskets down on the pile of books. As he listened with his usual wide-eyed amazement Srulik reached under the basket for the book, in order to go on reading, and something happened which in the ferment of his expectation he took as an omen, the finger of God pointing the way: instead of *Dead Towns and Living Men* he pulled out another book, also by Sir Charles Leonard Woolley, which was called *Abraham—Recent Discoveries and Hebrew Origins.* While Elka was reminiscing about events of thirty years before, he opened the book and began to read: "Chance has ordained that of all the periods of Sumerian history this of Abraham is most fully represented by monuments of every sort, by the ruins of houses and of temples and by written texts . . . Only to those who have seen the Mesopotamian desert will this evocation of the ancient world seem well-nigh incredible, so complete is the contrast between past and present. The transformation of a great city into a tangle of shapeless mounds shrouded in drift-sand or littered with broken pottery and brick is not easy to understand, but it is yet more difficult to realize that this blank waste ever blossomed and bore fruit . . ." One of God's fingers had already pointed out the book to him, and here was a second divine finger appearing in a metallic flash of copper lightning: as Aunt Elka spoke of the quality of the copper of which she had made the ashtray, and the ease with which she had hammered out the delicate design of the peacock's feathers, the page he was secretly reading inadvertently closed, and when he opened the book in another place he looked down and saw his finger pointing to the word "copper" like a printed echo of his aunt's words, like a seal confirming the beginning of his road to Ur of the Chaldees. "The owner of the house, No. 3 Straight Street, which I have described as typical of its class, was a copper merchant," Srulik went on reading in the book lying on his knees under the table. "In late years he had entered into partnership with one Eanasir, whose house backed on his own (since that faced on Old Street, and to get from the one to the other meant a long detour, they had opened a communicating door in the party wall and could consult one another without loss of time), and the two were engaged in the import of raw copper for the local market. In ancient times copper had been got from Oman in the Persian Gulf, a naturally mixed ore that gave a hard alloy excellent for casting, but that source had long been cut off, and now it was from sources further afield and especially from the Anatolian mountains in the north that the ingots came. The firm had their resident agents abroad who brought the metal from the mines, sent it down country on pack-asses and loaded it into boats on the Euphrates."

At the end of the visit, when the aunts got up to leave, as Ethel presented Srulik with a can of pineapple she had brought for him, and Elka, as usual, searched through the books on his desk for the right one to suit her present mood, he said to himself, "And now Elka will take Woolley's book on Abraham," and he was not in the least surprised at the immediate fulfillment of his prophecy. It was a direct and natural continuation of the twice-proved feeling that the voyage to Ur of the Chaldees was just around the corner, a third sign to reinforce the two previous omens. Although Srulik wanted to go on reading it, he allowed his aunt to take it home with her, since in any case, before reading this summing-up that compared the results of twelve years of digging to what was written about Father Abraham in the Bible, he intended studying the details of all the archae-ological finds themselves, which appeared in volumes four and five of *The Excavations at Ur of the Chaldees,* published jointly by the British Museum and the University of Penn-sylvania. Even the fate of the excavations themselves, which had been undertaken years after the discovery of the site of Abraham's birthplace, seemed to him a sign of the fate of his own journey, which was about to take place despite the fact that it had appeared to be doomed. For the site of Ur of the Chaldees had been discovered by Mr. J. E. Taylor, the British consul in Basra, in the year 1854, whereas the excavations had not begun until sixty years later, and all because of Mr. Taylor's poor sense of timing. He had discovered Ur in the south of the land of Shinar just when the archaeologist Layard had discovered the magnificent palaces of the kings of Assyria in the north, digging up from the depths of the earth and bringing to light those colossal man-headed bulls and those rows of bas-reliefs displayed in the British Museum today. The brick houses and broken cuneiform tablets of the city of Abraham's birth seemed an insignificant find by comparison, a poor recompense for the cost of excavations and the efforts of scholars, and accordingly the world ignored Taylor's discovery and came back to it sixty years later. Ur was already a very ancient city when Abraham was born there to his father, Terah, but it was not yet Ur of the Chaldees, for the Chaldeans conquered it many years after his death, and in Abraham's time it was still Ur of the Sumerians. And this too, the fact that there were no Chaldeans as yet in Ur of the Chaldees at the time of Abraham, whereas now, in his own time, they were already extinct, seemed to Srulik for some reason an auspicious omen that his journey to Ur of the Chaldees would take place after all hopes of going there with Orita had faded from his heart.

The librarian sent me to his Aunt Elka to recover Woolley's book about Abraham a few weeks after the manifestation of all these signs and omens, which in the fever of his expectation Srulik had tended to see in everything that happened to him, on the very day that his path suddenly opened up before him, and from the most unexpected of all possible directions—that of his sister, Rina, who suddenly announced that she was ready to take her mother in for a number of months. When he heard Rina saying to his mother, in so many words, "I want you to come and stay with me for a few months at least," and felt that all the mountains of obstacles on his path were now falling down as flat as the walls of Jericho at the trumpeting of the rams' horns, he remembered one of Rosa's sayings, to wit, that even a broom could shoot if God wished it so, and he blushed at the thought that the broom in question was his beloved sister, Rina, who was not to blame for anything, who bore her own burden of troubles, far heavier and more painful than his renunciation of his heart's desire. Years ago, when he completed his studies and gave up his trip to Ur of the Chaldees because he could not desert his sick mother, who needed his care and financial support, the idea of moving her over to his sister's place had seemed impossible. At that time Rina was living with her husband and three children in one room full of screams and tears and diapers hanging up to dry around the kerosene stove, and as if that were not enough, a few days before Srulik's graduation Rina's husband had been badly hurt in an accident at his workplace. An iron bar had fallen on his back and injured his spine, and in addition to all the usual worries and cares about the family's health and daily bread, she now had to contend with the gnawing anxiety that her husband, Oded, might remain an invalid for the rest of his days. After a few months Oded had recovered almost completely, but he was unable to return to his previous work. He was an expert roof tiler, and since he was no longer capable of climbing to the tops of buildings and leaping about all day on planks suspended in space, he became a driver in the Public Works Department. Until he met Oded, Srulik had never given a second thought to tiled roofs, but ever since meeting him he never passed a house topped with a tiled roof without considering its form and fit. Oded would fit a roof to a house like a hatter making a hat to order, tailored to fit not only the size of the customer's head, but also to suit his character; and just as not only the size and shape of the hat but also the manner and angle at which it was worn testified to the character of the wearer and complemented his personality, so too the roof should fit its house in its dimensions, height, slope, angles, gutters, and even the color of its tiles—if only it had been possible to find the proper variety of shades on the market. If there was one thing Oded regretted during all the years he spent at his trade, it was this lamentable lack of choice: there were only red tiles to be had on the market, while he was of the opinion that the houses built of the pinkish stone called in Arabic *misi ahmar* should rightly be topped with gray tiles and not red ones. Some years before his accident Oded had taken an enforced leave from roof laying for the simple reason that during an entire year not one single house had been built in Jerusalem with a tiled roof. The fashion of flat roofs had swept the town, and during the height of its triumph not a single architect had dared to come out against it, and even if a rebel like the architect Gutkin, the judge's brother, had dared to suggest a tiled roof, his client refused, for fear of being considered backward in his taste and ideas and lacking in the spirit of progress. Oded could have continued working in construction during this period too, putting up scaffolding and laying stones, had it not been for the suffering caused him by the fashionable flat roofs; these flat-roofed houses looked to him not like a bare-headed man but like a man without a cranium: an unfinished creature, an ugly, open-ended abortion. If, at least, the building had finished properly, like a block, in a straight line, he would somehow have resigned himself to these monstrosities with the tops of their heads sliced off. But the flat cement roofs were always full of all kinds of protuberances, pipes and rods and water tanks sticking up in all their ugliness—like the stuffing sticking out of a doll with its skull torn off, showing the world that its head was stuffed with straw.

Oded would say that the flat roofs at least had one thing in their favor, for it was thanks to them that he had met and married Rina. The fashion for flat roofs having conquered Jerusalem, he was left without work, and when he went to look for a job in the workshops of the commercial center, he met Haim Long-Life, who turned him into a ballroom dancing master, and it was in his capacity as a ballroom dancing master that he met Rina, who came to him for lessons. Oded had always been a first-rate dancer, cutting a fine figure at parties and dances, but the possibility of converting this pleasure into a livelihood would never have occurred to him had he not come across the lanky inventor, who planned and organized the whole enterprise for him. Haim Long-Life arranged everything, beginning with the artistic sign, the work of a Bezalel art student, which bore the legend "Ballroom Dancing Institute, Under the Direction of the Dancer Oded"; including finding the room opposite the English Hospital and equipping it with a gramophone and records; and ending with providing the pupils and appointing himself business and administrative director of the Institute. And once the Ballroom Dancing Institute became a reality, it was such an instant and brilliant success that it surpassed the wildest dreams of its originator and business and administrative director, Mr. Haim Long-Life—let alone the hopes of its artistic director, Oded the Dancer, who, although an artist to his fingertips, lacked the creative imagination of his partner, who considered himself a hardheaded businessman.

From the first week of the Institute's opening it was clear that one teacher and a single room would not be enough for all the students who signed on, and Haim Long-Life rented an entire three-room apartment on the corner of Rav Kook and Jaffa streets, while Oded found himself an assistant in the person of his best friend, Ezra Choo-Choo, the glazier and frame-maker. Ezra was called Choo-Choo because whenever a dance tune reached his ears, never mind from how far away, he would be swept away by its rhythm and cluck his tongue in time to it, "Choo-choo-choo." In his abandonment to the rhythms of music and dance Ezra Choo-Choo differed from the controlled and reserved Oded, and the difference between them opened the eyes of Haim Long-Life to a new way of looking at things—things of which he had been unaware until his association with the Ballroom Dancing Institute. Haim Long-Life, who was prone to philosophic reflections even in the midst of his business activities—and, in contrast to most men of action of a certain type, who begin to speculate on the deeper meaning of things only when their transactions fail—even when he was riding high on a wave of mounting success, confided to Rina that his observations of the two dancers had led him to a number of important conclusions touching on religion and philosophy, classicism and romanticism, and mythology and art. Until the arrival of Ezra Choo-Choo, Haim Long-Life had not realized, despite the long hours he spent watching him, how controlled and restrained Oded's movements were. Oded would approach his partner with a measured tread, his chin tucked in and his back straight, and he would maintain this erect posture throughout the entire dance. The faster the rhythm grew, the more strictly he controlled the steps keeping time to it. And when it reached its climax, instead of being swept away by it, Oded would pause, vibrating with inner tension, capable in his perfect poise of instantly changing direction and executing dazzling steps which drew gasps of admiration from his audience. His tour de force was the waltz, and especially the "Russian waltz": as he whirled around the room with his partner—like the earth revolving on its own axis as it circles the sun—the tempo of the music would quicken and Oded would spin faster and faster until he stopped dead as the music reached its climax, caught his still-turning partner in his arms, poised for the next wave to begin, and went on dancing in the opposite direction, from right to left, in perfect control both of the rhythm coursing through his limbs and the force of inertia impelling his body to continue in the previous direction, from left to right. It reminded Haim Long-Life of the Viennese horse-trainer in the French circus that had come to Jerusalem that year: the trainer would send the horses galloping around the ring and suddenly, with an air-rending, breath-stopping crack of his whip, he would bring them to a standstill, trembling with tension, necks outstretched and manes flying. But Oded when he danced was both the rhythmically galloping horse and the trainer at once, and his movements combined the prancing effervescence of the horse with the proud, aristocratic airs of the trainer, airs which received their fullest expression in the Spanish dances: tango, *paso doble,* and flamenco. Tapping his heels to the beat of the castanets on the cracked old record (several times in his diary, Haim Long-Life had already made a note of the need to buy a new supply of records until the business expanded to such an extent that they could afford a "live orchestra"), his head inclining slightly forward, his chin tucked in, his look grave, back erect, thighs and hips contracted and chest expanded, Oded would approach his partner, stopping and stamping, proud and fierce as a lover or a bullfighter courting death in the arena.

Ezra Choo-Choo's dances too were performed to the very same rhythms of tango, jazz, Charleston, waltz, *paso doble,* and rumba—but the dancer was different. No one seeing Ezra Choo-Choo walking down the street or cutting a piece of glass in his shop would have imagined that this plump, bespectacled young man could dance. With the first notes sounded by the wheezing record Ezra would begin to tap his feet, and when he went up to ask his partner to dance, he himself was already dancing. At the height of the dance, possessed by the rhythm coursing through his body, he would abandon himself entirely: his feet danced, his hands flapped, his body writhed, and—what surprised Haim Long-Life most of all—even his neck waggled and his eyes rolled behind the fog of sweat dripping from his spectacles. Once he had familiarized himself with the room, he no longer needed his spectacles, and in the tempest of the dance his naked eyes had a hypnotized look as they rolled about in his swaying head, spellbound by the music and blind to the outside world from which, nevertheless, flowed the waves that aroused the rhythm of his interior dance. At first Haim Long-Life called this the "Ezra Choo-Choo style" as opposed to the "Oded style" of dancing: but after going

into the question more profoundly he concluded that it
would be more appropriate to name them the "School of
Ezra" and the "School of Oded" on the subject of dance.

In everything concerning the study of ballroom dancing
there was no more diligent student than Haim Long-Life.
As long as the Institute lasted, he would devote every
moment he had to spare from his administrative duties to
observing the lessons. Ensconced in the shabby, faded armchair in the corner of the room, he would sit with one long
leg crossed over the other, puffing on his fat cigar—during
periods of prosperity he smoked nothing but Dutch cigars
made of Cuban tobacco, and in the many lean years too he
tried not to deprive himself of this pleasant habit with its
soul-satisfying aroma—and watched the dancers with a sad
and beaten look. He had a sad look even when he was happy,
and sitting there with his long, sagging face he looked like
an old goat in a bow tie. In addition to his theoretical study
and research and philosophical conclusions, he attempted
from time to time to master the practical side of the subject
as well, and there was nothing in the whole world that made
Rina laugh more than the sight of Oded trying to teach
Haim Long-Life to dance. Whenever Haim Long-Life lifted
one of his long legs Rina would fall into fits of side-splitting
laughter, and once she even wet herself at the sight of the
inventor kicking to the left, kicking to the right, and caper-
ing lopsidedly as he tried to learn the rumba. Oded thought
that there was something wrong with Haim Long-Life's ear
for music. "Look," he would say to him, "all you need to
dance is an ear. It's simply a question of rhythm: you beat
time to the music with your feet. All you have to do is keep in
step, and that's all. The rest is cosmetics. Your troubles begin
with your poor ear for music."

"I have an excellent ear for music," said Haim Long-Life
in helpless anger. "There's nothing wrong with my ear—on
the contrary, my ear is perfect. My trouble begins when I try
to dance or sing. I've simply got a rotten instrument."

"What instrument?" asked Oded, seeing a piano in his mind's eye, since his partner had been harping lately on the need for a piano and even hinting that very soon, if business continued to prosper, they would be able to afford one for the Institute.

"My performing instrument," said Haim Long-Life, "this body of mine, that instead of helping me to dance hinders me at every step."

"A performing instrument, the body," repeated Oded uneasily, as if he had suddenly heard of an unexpected danger lurking in a place hitherto considered safe; as if a peephole had been opened into the future and he had peeped through it and seen the terrible danger threatening him, the danger of losing his control over his body in the accident that almost cut off the connection between the soul and its performing instrument. "And I thought you were talking about the piano."

"Oh yes, of course—it's a good thing you reminded me: we have to get hold of a piano. A dance hall without a piano is unthinkable."

But the "dance hall" remained without a piano to the end. On the other hand Oded received as a gift from Haim Long-Life something for which he had longed for years without being able to afford it—a gold Ronson cigarette lighter. Ezra Choo-Choo had had one for ages, even though he had always earned less than Oded—but then Ezra wasn't Oded. Just as Ezra was different from Oded when it came to dancing, so he differed from him in his attitude toward the objects of his desires: from the minute that the desire for a gold Ronson lighter awoke in him, Ezra Choo-Choo did not rest until he acquired the object in question, which cost him, including the interest on the credit, over two months' wages. And since it was the same with a camera or a new pair of trousers, and his wages were never enough to satisfy all his wants, Ezra Choo-Choo's expensive ties and jewelry and accessories meant that he dried himself with a ragged towel, patched his last sheet ten times over, and sometimes went for days on end without his dinner. When he came to stay in Oded's room after his landlady refused to wait any longer for the rent he owed her, the first thing he did was to sit down on the couch, take an English cigarette out of a silver cigarette case, light it with a gold Ronson lighter, and smoke it on an empty stomach. At the height of the roofing season, when Oded was working overtime and earning twice and three times as much as Ezra, he would never have dreamed of allowing himself to buy a gold cigarette lighter because he had promised his father before he died that he would save money in the busy season and put half his wages aside for a rainy day—and the remaining half was not enough to live on and buy a gold lighter as well. And for all his joy at Haim Long-Life's unexpected gift, it also had the effect of deepening the guilt gnawing at his heart ever since his transformation from a roof tiler into a ballroom dancing teacher. "It's wrong to take money for dancing," he said to Rina. "You silly boy," she replied in astonishment, "why on earth should you think so?"

"Dancing isn't a business," he said. "Dancing doesn't belong to the world of money. Dancing is something you do for enjoyment, something people do together when they're happy. When you're having fun together and it makes you happy you shouldn't take money for it."

"But you enjoy tiling roofs too, and you take money for that."

"That's something else entirely," he replied. "That's a trade, a way of earning a living." He wanted to give her an example of what he meant, but since the only one that came to mind was that it was as wrong for him to take money for dancing as it would be to ask for money for going to bed with a woman, he held his tongue and began humming his late father's favorite tune, "Be Happy and Rejoice in Your Festivals," and as he hummed he thought of King David leaping and dancing with all his might before the Ark of the Lord, and he came to the conclusion that it would be the worst kind of mean-spirited baseness to demand money for the marvelous grace that this festive joy bestowed on the soul as it made the body dance. He looked at the gold cigarette lighter, gripped it in his hand, lit Rina a cigarette, and told her a story about his childhood. Like Oded, his father before him had been a roof tiler, and in the dead seasons he had been reduced to looking for all kinds of odd jobs. Between one job and the next the family went hungry. Once, after a long stretch of unemployment, he had found work in the slaughterhouse. He worked late and came home after midnight with meat in his bag. Oded remembered how his father woke him up in the middle of the night crying, "Wake up, Oded! There's a good hot meal." "Get up, children, here's something to eat!" cried his mother, bringing every child in his bed a plate of meatballs and potatoes in gravy.

This dish of meatballs and potatoes in gravy which he had eaten in bed in the middle of the night was the best meal of Oded's life. Even the sumptuous and sophisticated meals he had consumed in the palatial Shephard's Hotel in Beirut— where he had spent his honeymoon with Rina, chaperoned by the faithful Haim Long-Life—had not tasted so delicious to him. His heart contracted when he remembered the children sitting up in their beds and eating their midnight feast, and his father sitting at the table and puffing cigarette smoke toward the oil lamp shedding its soft, orange glow on his mother asking happily: "Who wants another meatball?" All the luxury of Shephard's Hotel, the magnificence of its rooms and halls, the polish of its waiters, the uniforms of its bellboys, and the caps of its chambermaids, which so delighted Haim Long-Life, oppressed Oded with a sense of sin that increased with every bill paid by his partner with a nonchalant air and a tip that made the waiter bow and scrape obsequiously. Without knowing the details—since

Haim Long-Life, unwilling to trouble the bridegroom with
sordid money matters on his honeymoon, was careful to
keep them from him—Oded could not help keeping anxious count of the swelling bill, or thinking that with all this
money disappearing into the till of the hotel and the pockets
of the waiters he could have furnished an apartment and
paid a few years' rent in advance—as well as putting aside a
tidy sum "for a rainy day." When he asked Rina if she would
agree to be his wife, the idea of a honeymoon had not even
entered his head, and he would never in his wildest dreams
have imagined himself whirling around the dance floor of
Shephard's Hotel to the applause of tired old gentlemen and
ladies with raddled, painted faces (for some reason the hotel
was full of elderly guests)—if only for the simple reason that
he had never heard of such a thing as a honeymoon in his
life until Haim Long-Life announced its existence. He had
intended renting an apartment and furnishing it, and was
firmly resolved, too, to keep the promise he had made his
father to put something aside every week, so that his own
family would never be reduced to the miserable circumstances he had known as a child when his father was unem-
ployed.

But Haim Long-Life, who at the news of the wedding
wiped a happy tear from his admiring eye, thought otherwise. "I'll see to it that you have a honeymoon fit for a king,"
he said, "something you've never dreamed of." He never
took his eyes off the young couple, and everyone at Shephard's Hotel, from the reception clerk down to the regular
patron Mrs. Benson, who had met him during his previous
stays at the hotel, thought that this elderly gentleman was
the bride's rich uncle, a misapprehension he made no
attempt to correct. The first day they arrived at the hotel he
explained to Oded that he must buy a gift for Rina. "I've
already bought her an evening gown," said Oded. "A dress
isn't a gift," said Haim Long-Life. "Dresses are included in

the basic things a husband owes his wife by law—food, apparel, and conjugal relations. Come with me to the jewelry shop in the lobby and we'll buy her something nice, a bracelet—or even better, an elegant, beautiful wristwatch." For himself Haim Long-Life bought a cane—not to make an impression or for the air of mystery and dignity it gave him, but for the "painful twinges in the side" which had been afflicting him with increasing frequency ever since his attempts to master the passionate Latin dances which captivated him more than any waltz or fox-trot. When he descended the red-carpeted staircase flourishing his cane, the conductor mistook him for the Austrian ambassador coming down for a cocktail before dinner, and quickly struck up the latter's favorite tune: "Ah, Gypsy, You Have Stolen My Heart." It was Mrs. Benson who corrected the conductor's mistake and informed him that the gentleman in question was not the Austrian ambassador but Mr. Raban, the Jerusalem industrialist, who in addition to being a financier was also a patron of the arts with a special interest in a famous dancing company. In general, Mrs. Benson was always popping up wherever Haim Long-Life happened to be. She would place her chair next to his, with the result that it was in her company that he spent all the hours during which the young couple were secluded in their room. She was sitting next to him on the night of the ballroom dancing competition in the Hall of Mirrors. As far as Oded and Rina were concerned it was not a serious competition, or even a competition at all, since there was no one for them to compete against, despite the dozen or so young couples who arrived at the hotel especially for the event and mingled with the wealthy old guests swaying on the floor and flapping their arms like scarecrows in the wind. Free of any tension, and completely ignoring the couples milling around them in a steam of perfumed perspiration, Rina and Oded chatted and laughed aloud as they danced. From the beginning of

the second or third round it was already obvious to everyone
that Rina and Oded would win first prize in all the events,
and nevertheless Mrs. Benson was surprised to see how
tense and nervous the old uncle was in comparison to the
young dancers in their carefree grace. Haim Long-Life
looked as anxious as a father for a son about to undergo the
examination that would determine his entire future. Above
his stiff collar and bow tie his tense face twitched spas-
modically, and his big dreamy eyes alternately frowned in
pain and smiled. At the end he was gasping for breath,
doubled over with the pain in his side, and when the cheers
of applause burst out as the young couple approached the
judges' platform, a groan escaped his lips and tears flooded
his eyes.

It was this excitement, apparently, that was behind the
unexpected sharpness of his retort to words spoken by
Oded in all innocence and sincerity. When they went out
onto the terrace after the competition and sat down on
chairs facing the sea, Oded started speaking about the sense
of sin which gave him no rest, not even at the moment of
their victory in the competition, and it was then that Haim
Long-Life suddenly lost his temper and exclaimed: "Sinner!
Of course you're a sinner! You're worse than a sinner—
you're a criminal!"

Rina gasped as if she had received a sudden slap in the
face. Pale and trembling she screamed at him: "You wicked
old man—what do you want of Oded, why are you abusing
him all of a sudden?"

"Don't get excited, Rinaleh," said Oded, "he's right."

"Of course I'm right," said Haim Long-Life, "but not
from your point of view. You don't even realize what a criminal you are to spoil the finest days of your life, to destroy
such rare and privileged moments of grace with your anxiety for the future: don't worry—the troubles will catch up
with you whether you worry about them or not."

And sure enough they did, far more quickly than Oded had feared. Three or four days before the end of the honeymoon, Haim Long-Life woke them up with the urgent announcement that they had to leave the hotel at once, "before eleven, because Mrs. Benson gets up at eleven o'clock." Although he did not explain what Mrs. Benson's hour of rising had to do with their leaving the hotel, it was evident from the tone of his voice that their lives would not be worth living from the moment she opened her eyes, and so they got up immediately and decamped. Even before they reached Jerusalem, Haim Long-Life informed them that the Ballroom Dancing Institute would have to close down until such time as he, the administrative director, "straightened things out." He gave Oded a sum of money, his "share of the working capital," which was supposed to enable the young couple to rent an apartment and furnish it, and to tide them over until he "straightened things out." The thorniest of the problems to be straightened out proved to be the piano investors, of whose existence Oded knew nothing until long after his return from his honeymoon, and in return for whose investments Haim Long-Life had promised to acquire a grand piano and furnish the Institute with a live orchestra shortly before setting out to accompany the young couple on their honeymoon. In the meantime, until these problems were straightened out, Haim Long-Life was obliged to go underground—an underground then situated in the cellar of the home of Yehuda Prosper Bey. The turn of the underground in the Temple-builder's shop came only seven years later, when Rina gave birth to her third son and Srulik graduated from the Teachers' Seminary. This was the most difficult time of Rina's life: she and Oded and their three small children were living in one room full of screams and tears and diapers hanging up to dry around a kerosene stove, and as if that weren't enough, Oded had been incapacitated by an accident at work only a few days before

Srulik met Orita in the Street of the Prophets and she announced her intention of accompanying him on his journey to Ur of the Chaldees.

In those days, when Srulik, full of plans for going away, felt a stab of guilt whenever he thought of Oded lying helpless in bed and smiling, thanks to the tranquilizers and painkillers, at Rina washing diapers and smiling back at him as she stifled her tears, he could never have imagined in his wildest dreams that a few years later it would be Rina and Oded of all people who would liberate him from the bondage of caring for his mother and open the road to Ur of the Chaldees before him. After Rina had taken her mother to her home—Oded came to fetch her in the Public Works Department van—the little librarian sent me on an urgent errand to Aunt Elka's to get Sir Charles Leonard Woolley's book *Abraham*, which was still, naturally, under her bed, where it had been lying ever since she had come to the library to celebrate the sale of the peacock ashtray to Yehuda Prosper Bey and taken it away from Srulik.

"Tell her I need the book at once," said Srulik, and in reply to her anticipated argument that she had not yet had time to finish it, he added: "She's had more than enough time to read it three times over and learn the names of all the kings of Ur of the Chaldees by heart and engrave a copper picture of the temple of Nin-Gal, the moon goddess, into the bargain." On the way to the librarian's aunts' house, the beautiful name sang inside me, "Nin-Gal, Nin-Gal, Nin-Gal," but when I arrived it transpired, giving rise in me to an obscure and growing sense of dread, that all his instructions, including the moon goddess with the beautiful name, were completely superfluous. Elka had forgotten that she had ever taken a book by the name of *Abraham* home from the library, and when I reminded her that it had been on the day she had sold the peacock ashtray to Yehuda Prosper Bey for seven pounds, she began to search for it in all kinds of

drawers, pulling things out and throwing them on the floor,
instead of going straight to the obvious place underneath
her bed. As her movements grew more agitated, nervous,
and reckless, and the pile of crumpled clothes on the floor
grew higher, I went up to the bed myself, bent down, and
lifted the bedspread. A bristling cat greeted me with a hiss,
and I recoiled in fright. I bumped into the bench at the
entrance to the alcove and a shadow slipped between the
dusty copper vessels piled higgledy-piggledy in the studio, a
shadow which materialized in the corner in the form of
another cat, staring at me with terrified eyes and ready to
retreat or attack if necessary. The house was full of cats, but
the obscure sense of dread had begun before I saw them, in
fact even before I entered. In contrast to the entrances to the
neighboring houses, through which people went in and out,
the door of the librarian's aunts' house, with its faded, peeling blue paint and the closed window beside it, was
shrouded in the aura of a domain beyond the pale, whose
strangeness was underlined by the stares of the children
following me as I approached and entered. Once inside, I
was depressed above all by the sight of the studio—the little
alcove in which Elka had once beaten her copper vessels.
Time was when I had eagerly volunteered to fetch Elka's
library books simply in order to see her at work: on my way I
would look forward to the moment when I would enter and
see the gleaming piles of beaten copper vessels, their color
changing with the variations in the light streaming through
the rose-shaped grille of the round window peeping like an
eye from the corner of the ceiling. From the depths of the
dim corners the heart of the copper would send out dull
tawny gleams, and as the eye approached the center of the
light pouring from the ceiling it set off a dance of flashing
arrows of pink and gold and red and yellow and orange, and
all these flashes of copper and bronze would reverberate
with waves of metallic sound in melodious response to the

passage of a cart outside, the footsteps of a person entering, and the sensitive, rhythmic little taps of Elka's hand hammering pictures in bas-relief on the surface of the copper. But now the round window peeping like an eye from the corner of the ceiling was shrouded with cobwebs from within and covered on the outside with a thick layer of dust, which had coagulated around the circumference and allowed only a dim, grayish shaft of light to penetrate through the center of the glass. And just as formerly the clarity of the light was echoed by the clear ringing of the metal and the reflections of the colors danced to the reverberating sounds, so now the dullness of the light was echoed by the dulling of the sounds, and the lack of dancing reflections mirrored the muffling of the echoes. Underneath the dusty rags filling the alcove, all the coppery gleams and metallic sounds lay dying, and on top of them the cat arched and bristled. Like the ancient archaeological stratum of a rich and splendid metropolis overlaid by the mean ruins of a poor, dirty village, the beaten copper lay buried below the rags, and the cat arching above them, like the Bedouin leading his camel over the ruins of Ur of the Chaldees, had no idea of the precious treasures hidden beneath his feet.

Like the circle of light growing smaller and smaller in the window of the alcove, because of the steady encroachment of the layers of dust from the circumference to the center, the circle of life in the house was steadily narrowing and withdrawing from the circumference of the walls to the table at the center. All around stood barriers of chairs and armchairs and crooked, slapdash shelves collapsing beneath the weight of clothes piled onto them, and the table in the middle of the room could be approached only by a narrow passageway leading directly from the front door. It seemed that every garment that had ever been pulled out of the corner of its drawer had stayed where it fell, and no object removed from its place had ever been returned to it: and consequently Elka was now busy all day long looking for lost things and bumping into long-forgotten objects suddenly popping up from the past like uninvited memories. "When people grow old," said Elka in response to my astonished expression, "they are always looking for something—their spectacles or their purse or the book they put down only a moment ago on the table," and from the look in her eyes it was evident that the muddle barring her path in the house was paralleled by the straying of her soul in the chaos of all the memories that had been pulled out of the corners of her mind and left to lie where they fell, only to accost her and trip her up with the images of long-forgotten events suddenly looming up like misplaced objects on her path.

"But you always used to put your books under your bed," I said. "Yes, yes," she replied impatiently, "but now Tzippi the Ginger is living there. You know, Tzippi the Ginger is cleverer than anyone: she knows exactly where I want to go, and before I have time to turn around, she's already there. When I have to sew something, for instance, Tzip skips over to sit on the sewing machine before I've taken a single step in that direction. And she sits there and watches over me until I'm finished and keeps the others from pestering me. She has to keep a special eye on Black Bella. That little devil wants me to play with her all day long, especially when I'm busy. The minute I sit down to sew she's up to her tricks, pulling the thread, rolling around in the material and making a proper nuisance of herself. If it wasn't for Tzip putting her in her place and driving her away, I wouldn't even be able to get lunch ready."

"Tzippi the Ginger! Bella the Black!" cried Ethel, making a mocking face, and turning to me she said: "Don't take any notice of her nonsense. As if it wasn't enough all these years with the cancer cure and that man of hers—now she has to drive me out of my mind with her Tzippi the Ginger, who's so clever that she knows more about cancer than all the professors in the world!" Elka nodded her head and winked at me as if to say that this was indeed the case in spite of her sister's objections, and added: "It all has to do with the sense of smell. The sense of smell will save us all."

"The sense of smell, the sense of smell!" repeated Ethel, and she lunged forward to stop her sister's mouth. "Instead of shutting me up, run and make the child a cup of cocoa," said Elka, and she herself went up to the sideboard to look for something good for me to eat. Once distracted from the subject of the lost book for which I had come, their spirits rose, and both of them, despite the quarrels and arguments between them, were as full of noisy gaiety and joyful hospitality as ever. In all the thirty years which have passed since then I do not remember coming across many homes in which an uninvited guest was made to feel so welcome. When Ethel went to prepare the drink for me she discovered that they had run out of cocoa, and she immediately called from the kitchen: "Elka, run to the store to buy some cocoa," and Elka, to my astonishment, obeyed her without putting up any opposition. She hurried to the store with her tottering little steps, not because her abandonment of her art had led to a falling off in her authority over her sister, but on the contrary, because of Ethel's ever-increasing dependency on her. Since the arrival on the scene of Tzippi the Ginger, who was going to save us all by her sense of smell, and the mischievous little Black Bella and all their colorful friends, Ethel had gradually stopped going out alone in general, and stopped doing the shopping in particular. For all her eagerness to accompany Elka wherever she went, and all her bitterness and offended feelings when she was left behind, she was unwilling to go out by herself—and thus it was Elka who went to buy the cocoa, while Ethel prepared it and brought it to the table.

As if to prove to me that she deserved all Elka's praise, Tzippi the Ginger emerged from beneath the bed and with two bounds reached the table and sat down on an engraved copper tray (the only piece of copper to be seen in the house; all the others were buried under the rags in the alcove) apparently intended for the cookies that Elka had purchased together with the cocoa. Tzippi sat there in the middle of the tray, curled her tail around her, and in her wisdom, which could see into Elka's heart and tell the end from the beginning, she raised her eyes to the packet from which the cookies were about to fall right into her mouth. "Be off with you, you cheeky little thing!" scolded Ethel, and immediately she turned on Elka: "It's all your fault. You spoil her so much that she thinks she can do whatever she likes. Look—she's already soiled the beautiful tray!" "The beautiful tray," muttered Elka, brushing her sister's words contemptuously aside, and at the same time stealing an inquiring glance at the tray.

"It really is beautiful," I said to Elka, and I wanted to add that it was a pity that all her beautiful things were buried under dirty old rags that the cats slept on, and a pity that she had stopped making them, but I held my tongue because I sensed that any mention of the subject would enrage Elka. In any case she was already angry because of what her sister had said.

"The tray is beautiful," she said to me, "but Tzippi is far more beautiful, and what is even more important, Tzippi is a living soul. The beautiful tray feels nothing, but my beautiful Tzippi feels pain when those wicked children, the bastards of that schnorrer Mendel Wiesel, throw stones at her and torment her. And if I don't take care of her, who will?"

As I listened to Elka while watching the graceful bounds of Tzippi the Ginger, who had apparently decided to remove herself from the tray until tempers cooled, I saw under the hem of the bedspread, at the edge of the rags of the cat's bed, a squarish protuberance, which I immediately realized must be the book *Abraham*. I bent down and pulled the rags—which appeared to be the remains of a blouse covered with beds of roses—and the English archaeologist's book was revealed as one dreadful wound: its covers and pages all torn and mutilated, scratched and bitten like a body mauled by feline teeth and claws.

"Look how pale the child's gone!" cried Elka with a note of concern in her voice. "Don't be upset—it's nothing terrible. Tzip had a little fun, so what? It's not a living creature after all—it feels no pain. What is it when all's said and done? A book, lifeless paper! You can tell our Srulik that I'll buy the library a new copy. You can always get a new copy of a book." It occurred to her to give me a note for Srulik promising to buy a new copy of the book soon, and to throw the old one away, but I snatched it from her hands. I knew that Srulik needed the book immediately in order to plan his trip to Ur of the Chaldees, and I saw that despite its wounds it was still possible to read it. Apart from a bunch of pages that had been torn out of the beginning of the book—including the title page, the table of contents, and part of the introduction, which was later found buried farther down among the rags under the bed—all the pages, even the most crumpled and torn, were still in their places. At the sight of the mutilated book my heart seethed with rage against Elka, and when she announced that she would come part of the way back to the library with me—she always accompanied her guests when they left—I felt like telling her that there was no need for her to do so; but I didn't dare. Ethel, who wanted to accompany me too, was firmly commanded to "stay at home and tidy the house." Elka sensed my anger and all the way we walked together she tried to appease me by saying that it was wrong to mourn for inanimate objects, for "inanimate objects were not living creatures," but her words only made me angrier. It was only after she stopped at the turn in the road and waved good-bye that my anger melted, giving way to a flood of pity for her—she looked so poor and pathetic with her thin feet in their shabby slippers and her appeasing smile and her bony hand sticking out of her threadbare sleeve: that artist's hand which knew the secret of transmitting the marvelous world existing in her imagination from her mind's eye onto the copper and making it into a graven image possessing a reality of its own, independent of this frail, lonely, little old woman, ridiculed by her neighbors who had both feet planted firmly on the ground. One of their children pointed at her now and said to his friend: "Look, there's the cats' mother," and both of them burst out laughing. "Shhhh," hissed his mother in an audible whisper, "it's not nice to point at people and make fun of them out loud."

I placed the mutilated book wrapped up in newspaper on the desk of the little librarian, who was on his knees rummaging in the bottom drawer of the cupboard where he kept his aunts' American presents. He glanced at it and said: "The only problem left is the problem of the suitcase."

"Here's the book," I said. "It got a little torn there and I repaired it." I had not brought the book straight to the library, but had taken it home first and done the best I could to stick the torn pages together and mend the cover, and so its appearance had improved considerably. I had intended hiding from him everything I had seen and heard in the house—especially the fact that Elka was now known in the neighborhood as "the cats' mother," but since I did not know how to account for the state of the book I decided to admit a little of the truth, and tell him that Elka had taken in one marmalade cat, called Tzippi the Ginger, and that this cat had played with the book one day when both Srulik's aunts had gone out. To my relief, he paid no attention to my expurgated account and did not even bother to remove the book from its newspaper wrapping. "Yes, yes, I see. Now all I have to do is get hold of a decent suitcase, and I'll be ready to set out. I'll read the book on the train." He sat on the floor in the middle of the pile of clothes, and as he rummaged in it he told me with growing enthusiasm, his eyes flashing sparks of happiness behind the thick lenses of his spectacles, about his journey to Ur of the Chaldees. Everything was ready; all he needed now was a decent suitcase: one small, strong suitcase would be enough for all his needs. The first thing he did after moving his mother to his sister's house was make a list of everything he would require, and the more he thought about it the longer the list grew. If he had taken everything he thought he might need, his journey from Jerusalem to Ur of the Chaldees would have come to resemble Sir Moses Montefiore's journey from London to Jerusalem. Sir Moses Montefiore in his time had arrived in Jerusalem with an entire caravan of carriages and carts, and if he had lived to the present day—and in the case of a man like Montefiore this was not so hypothetical a proposition as it sounded, for someone who managed to survive in this world of ours for over a hundred years might well have succeeded in drawing his life out for a few more decades— he would probably have filled several train cars with his possessions and entourage. At first Srulik thought of taking books about all the excavations in Mesopotamia, and these alone would have easily taken up an entire car on the train. The thought of himself traveling to Ur of the Chaldees in a railway car resembling the reading room of the B'nai B'rith Library depressed him to such an extent that he felt like setting the library on fire. Suddenly, in the darkest depths of depression, he had an illumination: he would go just as he was, with the shirt on his back—with no luggage at all! As the Arabs said, *khafif*—he would travel light! And if he were rich, he would not have taken even one little suitcase, haversack, or briefcase. A checkbook in his pocket, and that would have been it. For money you could get anything anywhere; there was no need to encumber yourself with baggage and boxes and bundles. Since, however, he was not rich and could not afford to throw away his shirt when it was dirty and buy himself a new one instead, he needed one small suitcase to hold his toilet articles, underwear and a change of clothes, the Bible, and Sir Charles Leonard Woolley's *Abraham*, which summed up all the findings at Ur of the Chaldees and their implications regarding the biblical sources about the father of the Hebrew nation. Actually, he too could have set out without a suitcase—not like the rich man who can buy himself a new pair of trousers for every one that gets dirty, but like the Bedouin who can travel for hundreds of miles without any luggage at all—but for his sensitivity to the cleanliness of his person and apparel, which required him to take at least toilet articles and two changes of clothes. Two suitcases which would have suited his needs had once reposed in the attic of their house, but they had disappeared on the day his father left home. In one of them the Temple-builder had undoubtedly packed his model of the Temple. Yes, and what was he, Srulik, doing here on the floor in the middle of this heap of used American clothes? He was looking for one more or less respectable suit to wear when he was in Baghdad. In Ur of the Chaldees he would wear his ordinary working clothes, but from time to time he would have to leave the excavation site for study and research in the museums. He himself would not mind in the least appearing in the museums too in his working clothes, but the people in charge there were presumably either British officials, notorious for their formality and strict observance of the rules governing the proper attire for every place and pursuit, or Iraqi clerks who valued a man according to his tie and the crease in his trousers and who would have no hesitation about throwing out any impudent upstart who dared attempt entry without a tie around his neck. There would be place in the suitcase for a tie and one respectable suit.

Since there were no suitcases left at home, Srulik set out to purchase one at Simon Garji's; but on the way there he changed his mind and, instead of entering the luggage manufacturer's alley, turned around and went to the home of his old friend Gabriel Luria. He had enough money to buy a suitcase, of course, but every penny spent here instead of there seemed to him a deplorable waste. The price of a suitcase in Jerusalem could support him for a month in Ur of the Chaldees. There was a chance, of course, that once he was on the spot he would be able to get a job working on the dig, and thereby count himself among those happy few lucky enough to be able to do what they wish in this world and earn their bread from it as well—but he could not rely on this, especially since he did not even know for certain if there was actually a dig going on in Ur of the Chaldees at the moment. On the other hand he was absolutely certain that there were plenty of suitcases lying around the vast basement of Gabriel Luria's house. A few years before, on the eve of Gabriel's journey to Paris to study medicine, Srulik had gone down to the basement with him, and he clearly remembered seeing five or six suitcases left behind after Gabriel had taken the three he needed for his trip. "Let's hope the old man's at home," Srulik said to himself as he went in at the gate and began climbing the verandah stairs. He had a feeling that the old Bey, Gabriel's father, would be more willing to lend him a suitcase than would his mother, and this feeling persisted despite the fact that there were no grounds whatsoever for it in his past experience, and that whenever he had asked her for anything up to now she had agreed without any hesitation and had even been happy to help. He knew exactly which suitcase he would choose—he had had his eye on it even then, when he was planning his trip with Orita. It was a small light-brown camelskin case, with sky-blue trimming around the edges— the perfect choice for the voyage to Ur of the Chaldees, right down to the colors of the desert in which the first Hebrews had led their nomadic lives.

In answer to his prayers the old Bey's bald head appeared at the top of the stairs, followed by his fierce black mustache, and then all the rest of him sank in his red armchair as he passed his amber worry beads through his fingers and chatted serenely with Señor Moïse, Rosa's brother, who was sitting opposite him and applying brass polish to the peacock ashtray, streaming with light in the setting sun. "At this very moment we were speaking about your aunt, Miss Elka," said the old man in his hoarse, ancient voice. "You know, Mr. Israel, your aunt must have been favored by divine grace to make such beautiful things, things which satisfy a man's soul and allow him to peek, as it were, past the veil of the seven heavens. When my friend the former governor of Jerusalem, Sir Ronald Storrs, saw the peacock ashtray, he admired it so much that he wanted to buy it from me for twenty-five pounds, but I didn't buy the ashtray to make a profit on it. And it occurred to me—and this is what I was speaking of to Señor Moïse when you climbed up the steps—to commission a big work from Miss Elka and to pay her a generous fee for it, enough to keep her in style for eighteen months. This is what I want Miss Elka to make for me: a big copper tray for a tabletop with enough room for twelve people to recline around it at their ease, and on the tray a big and most wonderful picture: the picture of Moses and Aaron standing before Pharaoh at the moment when Moses commands Aaron, 'Take thy rod and cast it before Pharaoh, and it shall become a serpent,' and Aaron casts his rod down before Pharaoh, and before his servants, and it becomes a serpent."

"Yes, yes," said Srulik, wondering how to turn the conversation to the subject of the suitcase. "And how is Gabriel? How is he doing in his studies in Paris?" The old man sank into a heavy silence, and beads of sweat broke out on his forehead, sparkling and glinting in the flashes of light coming from the ashtray in Señor Moïse's hands. "I have no satisfaction in my beloved son," said the old man. "He has abandoned his studies, and I have already written to him to say that if he does not return to work and study at once, I will disinherit him."

"I'm going off soon to study myself," said Srulik, "in a few days' time." The road to the suitcase now lay open before him, but Srulik was nevertheless obliged to come back for it the next day, because the old Bey did not know where to find the key to the basement. Gabriel's mother had gone out to see Dr. Landau at the eye clinic, and the old man did not know where his Ashkenazi wife kept the keys hidden. "Tomorrow morning," said the old man, "the basement will be open. I'm leaving for Jaffa, and Señor Moïse will have to get a few things out of the basement for me. If you come at nine o'clock in the morning, or nine-thirty, the suitcase will be ready and waiting for you here on the table."

When Srulik climbed the steps to the verandah of Gabriel's house at seven minutes to nine the next morning, something round and black like a cat suddenly flew down and pounced on him. Srulik paled, fell backward, and held on to the railing. Yehuda Prosper Bey's bowler hat landed at his feet, instantly followed by Señor Moïse, who made haste to pick it up and dust it with the little brush he removed from his inside pocket, and straighten out the dents with his bony fingers. Srulik had arrived in the middle of a quarrel between Gabriel's mother and father. Mrs. Gentilla Luria, that delicate-looking woman with the dreamy eyes, was standing in the doorway and hurling various items of his traveling costume at her aged husband sitting in the armchair on the verandah, ready to set off for Jaffa, to the accompaniment of a volley of Yiddish curses flavored with a little Ladino abuse. Señor Moïse stood between them, trying to calm the woman's frenzy with soothing gestures and soft words—"Begging your pardon but it isn't right, it isn't becoming, either to your dignity or to that of your husband"—and at the same time on the alert to absorb any further missiles that came his way in case the attack was renewed.

Srulik stole away before the antagonists had time to notice him, and turned in the direction of the library. He decided to finish whatever remained to be done there first, and to go back for the suitcase later, after the old man had left for Jaffa and his wife had calmed down. The book *Abraham* was still lying wrapped up in newspaper on his desk, and when he removed the wrappings and the book was exposed like an open wound, a woman burst in crying, "Come quickly! We have to call an ambulance!" He did not know who she was, although her face was vaguely familiar. She looked at him and said, "I'm Mina Wiesel, your Aunt Elka's neighbor. Your aunt has had a paralytic stroke. She's lying on the floor unable to speak or move. I wanted to call an ambulance, but Ethel wouldn't let me. She won't let me fetch a doctor. She's kneeling down next to Elka, talking to her and trying to open her mouth. She keeps on trying to open Elka's mouth. She chased us out of the house, me and Bilha Segal and all the neighbors, and locked the door. You must come at once. You're the only person she'll open the door to, or allow to call a doctor. Come quickly. Elka's life is in danger. Every minute counts." Srulik dropped the book and ran, leaving the door open behind him.

4.

The End of Awakenings in the Street of the Prophets

MY JOY ON WAKING that summer in the Street of the Prophets, in the house of Gabriel's father, the old Turkish Bey, facing the window of his dreamy-eyed mother, was lost to me many years ago, lingering on only in the longings of memory and the fatuous hope that it may return one day.

That summer I saw Gabriel for the first time in my life.

Long after the little librarian had disappeared from the B'nai B'rith Library without leaving a trace, Gabriel Jonathan Luria came home from Paris the moment I was drawing water from the well. This was a great and strange day in my life, the day on which my eyes beheld, on the other side of the street, the King of Kings, Haile Selassie, Elect of God, Conquering Lion of the Tribe of Judah, the Emperor of Ethiopia. Ever since that day, the wave of vague longings connected with that joy on waking has brought surging into the forefront of my mind the vivid expectation of the clear outline and strong voice of Gabriel Luria, sitting on the verandah in the red plush chair next to the three-legged iron table and preparing himself for his morning shave. Until Gabriel returned from Paris, the waves of expectation rising and swelling on that joy of waking to a new morning were diffuse and open to any surprise hiding behind the fence, in the secret stones of the house, or around the bend in the road, just like the flood of longing that inundated me with the opening of every new book I brought home from the library; and like the latter, the former too had a smell. But unlike the smell of the paper, with its expectations of the adventures hidden in the library books, the yearnings of the morning breathed the fresh, delicate smell of dew drying on stones and thistles and olive trees, joined, once Gabriel came home and cast his shadow on the crest of the wave of longings flowing from the joy of awakening in that summer in the Street of the Prophets, by the scent of his shaving soap and the aroma of his cigarette smoke.

Gabriel himself no longer felt any joy on waking, and for years it had been difficult even to look at him when he opened his eyes in the morning because of the anger glaring from his sleep-creased face, a kind of hostility toward the world into which he was constrained to wake. The moment he opened his eyes he would jump out of bed with a decisive and vigorous bound, which may have appeared full of joy to anyone not seeing the expression on his face as he leapt from sleep to wakefulness—the expression of a man jumping into an abyss from which there was no return. As soon as his feet touched the bottom of the abyss—which happened to coincide with the floor beside his bed—this bold leap would crumble, and from then until he had his breakfast coffee it would increasingly disintegrate as he staggered about the room, stumbling on an ill-placed stool and supporting himself against the wardrobe door and the solid walls. It was as if he had lost control over his body in general and each of his limbs in particular, a control he would not regain until he had drunk his first cup of coffee of the day—for Gabriel needed two cups of coffee in order to consolidate his position in the kingdom of the day. Until his first cup of coffee—

so his mother said in her moments of grace—he was in the world of outer darkness and primeval chaos and there was no point in trying to talk to him; but when she was angry she would say that until his first cup of coffee he revealed all the wickedness he had inherited from his father, for he was bone of the bone and flesh of the flesh of that lecherous old Turk. He himself warned me to keep out of his way when he got up in the morning. "Until the first cup of coffee," he explained, "there is no king in Israel, and every man does as he sees fit." His legs, still numb with sleep, slipped away from him and flopped about, one in this direction and one in that, while his rebellious member reared its head and poked impertinently out of his pajama fly without so much as a by your leave. And as he put it back in its place with one disobedient hand, leaning on the wall with the other, King Gabriel himself, floating in the void somewhere on the threshold of waking, tried to command the orifices and doorways of the world to open so that he could pass through them. But his eyes were still cobwebbed with sleep and in pursuit of fleeing dreams, his ears stopped with the echoes of ghostly voices, his nostrils breathing the base matter of the flesh, and his mouth full of dust and ashes.

He was simply incapable of saying a single word until he had a cup of coffee, and when he was obliged to do so, even by the arrival of a person he loved, it was not a word that came out of his hoarse throat but an angry growl. His rage was not only that of a king before gaining control over his rebellious subjects, but also—and chiefly—that of a king about to don the crown that had fallen to his lot, and take up the burden of that ancient heritage which so oppressed him whenever he woke up in the morning and felt the full weight of its hated chains in all their heaviness. For it was then, and then only, on the threshold of waking, that he discovered in himself all the qualities he so detested in his mother, such as these very difficulties in waking, which he inherited directly from her, and from which he had suffered so much in his childhood days (those distant, blessed days, bathed in the joy of waking) when he needed her to get him ready for school. As much as he loved the light in her eyes when she was happy, so he had never been able to endure the way she looked on waking, when she staggered about disheveled and unkempt, with a sour expression on her face and a staring, glassy look in her eyes. Throughout his childhood he had tried to avoid her when she got up in the morning, so as not to see her stumbling with blind, glazed eyes to the basin, hiccuping and scratching under her armpits. The nature of these hiccups and armpit-scratching became apparent to him when he unwillingly found himself beginning to imitate his mother's awakenings in his own person. The hiccups were directed toward the air of waking, whereas the armpit-scratching had to do with the air of sleep, and both were the result of that sensitivity to the environment felt precisely by a strong and healthy body. When Gabriel hiccuped on the way to his first cup of coffee, it was a sign of an imminent change in the weather: sometimes the hiccup preceded the change by a number of hours, and sometimes it announced not a change in the temperature but a change in the direction of the winds.

There are always winds blowing in Jerusalem, but we usually feel only the broad currents, woven like thick ropes from thousands of interlocking fibers, while Gabriel sensed even the isolated jets suddenly coming from far away and in their flight from one place to another hitting him by chance on the neck or the back, so that this strong and healthy man suddenly found himself with a bad back, or a pain in the neck or the loins. His susceptibility was largely dependent on his mood. When he was in a good mood no wind could prevail over him, but when he was feeling fragile his body— the weakest link in the combination of earthly vessels and divine abundance—was at the mercy of every passing

breeze, and the morning hiccups acted as a kind of regula-
tor, adjusting his body to the air of the waking world in
which he would have to function that day. For a whole week
after his return home the hot eastern winds had given him
deep and continuous hiccups before his first cup of coffee,
while blowing into his face a childhood scene that had risen
to the surface of his memory in France, at the sound of the
word *"pourboire"* on the lips of the mistress of the farm: from
the entrance to Dr. Landau's eye clinic the ten-year-old Gabriel looked out and saw against the white glare of the walls
shimmering in the naked light of the sun the wheels of
Mahmoud Effendi's carriage spraying the crippled beggars
on the sidewalk with a fine gray dust, like the dust rising
from the paths between the gravestones on the Mount of
Olives. As he drank the coffee he would remember what
Leontine had said to him when he came to live in her room:
"A sensitive gentleman like you will no doubt be susceptible
to the winds at night," and later on, while heating up his
shaving water on the kerosene stove, he would unconsciously
begin to sing the children's song she loved so much: "On my
way I met the corn-reaper's daughter, On my way I met the
hay-reaper's daughter."

As opposed to the hiccups, which addressed themselves
to the beginning of the waking day, the armpit-scratching—
as mentioned above—was related to the ending of the night's
sleep, and just as he took the trouble to hide his member,
which reared its head of its own accord, so he tried to
postpone the scratching of his armpits to the privacy of the
bathroom, where he went to wash between one cup of coffee
and the next. In itself it was nothing: most of us probably
give ourselves a scratch or two under our armpits before
proceeding to wash away the sweat of the night with its odor;
and if, in fact, Gabriel differed from the rest of us, it was
only in the enormous burden of meaning that he attached to
this routine and insignificant physical act. First and foremost

was the memory of the astonished revulsion and shame with which, as a child, he had watched his mother staggering blindly on waking, hiccuping and scratching herself under the armpits, to the washbasin, and above all the astounding sight which met his eyes one day through the half-open bathroom door. Next to the basin stood his mother sniffing the tips of her fingers, which had just been rummaging in her armpits, and as she sniffed, her half-closed eyes gazed into a world so remote that they were utterly blind to everything around her. He did not even have to decide, it was so self-evident to him, that he would never present so shameful a spectacle to the world; but when he reached the age of forty, and especially after returning to his parents' home, the fact that he himself had now become the chief actor in this degrading bathroom scene no longer even caused him any surprise. For he had long ago come to realize that a number of his mother's characteristics, especially the ones he hated most—such as her deplorable habits on waking, her fits of rage, the glazing of her eyes when she was lost to the world around her, and even her slowness in eating—were appearing with increasing frequency in his own behavior, without his being able to do anything about it and without their manifestation in his own person detracting in the least from the revulsion they aroused in him: all he could do was hide them as much as possible. Once he had shut the bathroom door behind him and sniffed the smell of his armpits adhering to his fingertips, he would smile to himself at the thought that for all the loftiness of his mind and profundity of his awareness, he was no different from a dog smelling the folds of its own flesh or Mrs. Luria when she woke up in the morning. Apart from learned hypotheses or random guesses, there was no knowing exactly what the smell of its own body meant to the dog, and because of the revulsion and shame involved, it would never have occurred to Gabriel to ask his mother the meaning of her armpit-scratching, but as far as he was concerned, something extraordinary happened to him. The smell of the sweat in his armpits plunged him back into the atmosphere of the sleep from which he had just been fished by his first cup of coffee. After a sound night's sleep he sensed no smell at all, as if the identity between his being and smell were complete, and if he did sometimes catch a whiff, it was extremely subtle and pleasant—whereas if he had a troubled, sleepless night he would feel it in the sourness of his sweat. And there were also mornings when the smell, like the bluish-white vapors rising from the valleys of Judah and Benjamin at the approaches to the Jebusite city, would envelop him again in the world of the dream he had forgotten the instant he opened his eyes, and return him to precisely the point at which he had awakened. If a mist of disturbing images surrounded him to plunge him back into the bitter lake of a dream from which he had escaped only by the skin of his teeth, he would say to himself, "The sweat of the soul, the sweat of the soul," but in any case, even after a night of happy dreams, he would make haste to soap his armpits immediately after washing his face, passing the soap over his chest at the same time. His morning toilet always included his entire upper torso, even during the period when he was staying in Leontine's room, which lacked any kind of faucet, and where every toilet obliged him to draw water from the pump at the other end of the farm and carry it back in a jug to the tub in the room. Leontine, who had no need of washing herself, except on feast days and festivals, couldn't get over Gabriel's dawn exertions at the ancient pump. The struggles of his awakenings were already familiar to her from the days of his greatness, when he was her mistress's exalted guest and slept in the master's antique bed, and since she knew from experience that there was nothing he liked better in the mornings than a cup of coffee in bed, while he lazily stretched his limbs, she was convinced that his scrupulousness over his morning ablutions and his diligence at the pump stemmed from some religious duty imposed on him from above, and she accordingly asked him one day, about a week before he left the farm to return home, if he belonged to some monastic order which demanded the purification of the armpits every day. At first he did not understand her question, since she asked it in Breton dialect, but when she repeated it in French they both burst out laughing, he in his loud, strong voice and she with the full, free, uninhibited peals of laughter that made her seem so much younger than her years. Leontine would sometimes suddenly address him in the ancient language of Brittany, which was no longer comprehensible even to the young people of the region who had been educated in French schools, and he never really understood her motive for doing so. Sometimes she would switch over to Breton when she felt especially close to him, as if she were talking to Marcel, her son, who had been killed twenty years before in the battle for the Marne, sometimes in the absentmindedness of her old age or with an air of childish mischievousness, and sometimes with a deliberate intention, accompanied by a twinkling of her smiling eyes, whose meaning was beyond his comprehension. This time she asked her question in the Breton tongue as if she were talking to herself, and trying to clarify and explain to herself something that concerned her personally. When she repeated in French, "Tell me, do you belong to some monastic order which obliges you to wash your armpits so thoroughly every morning?" and the two of them burst out laughing, her eyes were alight with strange gleams, and for many days afterward he would suddenly burst out laughing when he remembered the occasion. Her question astounded him. Later, he told the old judge's daughter that this remark of Leontine's, this trivial question followed by the peculiar joke about the Knights of the Order of the Armpit, astounded him no less—and perhaps, from a certain point of view, more—than the sight of little Srulik's face under the hat of a Huguenot pastor in the Calvinist hostel of Noyon.

"What did you reply to her?" asked Mrs. Orita Landau.

"I didn't reply at all," said Gabriel. "I told you, I was stunned. But afterward I replied to her a number of times in my dreams at night."

"And what did you reply in your dreams?" asked Orita.

"I don't remember," said Gabriel. "The minute I open my eyes, I forget the answer I made in my dream. Sometimes the smell of my armpits when I wake up returns me to my dream, but when I wash it's all wiped out."

"And what would you say to her now, waking and not dreaming?"

Instead of replying Gabriel looked at her with that look of his which was at once very close and very remote, and began humming the tune of the prayer "Who Distinguisheth Between the Sacred and the Profane," which he didn't actually like, and then passed from it to "And Purify Our Hearts," which he liked better. "You never tell me anything about yourself," she said with growing resentment, and with both her hands she resolutely seized his hand holding the cigarette and cried: "But this time you won't get out of it. This time you'll tell me." However, when he went on to tell her the strange story of the meeting in the ecclesiastical hostel she forgot her resolve in a growing fascination with the story of the distant pastor—not necessarily because of the relationship that had once existed between them, but because it was Gabriel telling the story.

When he was in a good mood, and in the company of kindred souls who wanted to listen, Gabriel would tell stories, and when Gabriel told stories no one could tear himself away, except for his mother, who would suddenly interrupt him in the middle—just as she had interrupted his late father, the old Bey, in the middle of his remarks about our master Moses—for any nonsense that happened to be on her mind, such as the Primus stove which had begun to smoke and needed a new head, or the Arab peddlers who had begun to raise their prices recently, and in general were getting too big for their Arab boots. Between the balustrade of the verandah on one side, and the three-legged iron table on the other, in the same shabby, dark red plush armchair where his father had sat before his death, crying, "Our master Moses, our master Moses," and where the old judge sat when he came to call on the old man's widow, I first saw Gabriel on his return from abroad sitting and telling a story, the story about the pastor in Noyon, to the old judge's daughter. Before he began his story, he would draw deeply on his cigarette and exhale the smoke partly through his nostrils and partly, as he spoke, through his mouth, at the same time wetting his throat with a sip of coffee from the cup on the table by his side. He would stroke his thick eyebrows and square mustache with his fingers, his smooth-shaven face would break into a smile as he remembered the incident he was about to relate. His calm, deliberate voice would bestow on his tale an epic breadth and strength, into which it was pleasant to sink confidently, however shocking the subject matter, and as the listener was swept away on the rhythmic waves of the narrative he would find himself transformed into the spectator of a play with one actor taking all the parts—for as Gabriel entered into the spirit of his tale the epic would gradually turn into a drama. If his lively imagination—what his mother referred to as his "Oriental fantasies"—was an inheritance, as she averred, from his father, the lecherous old Turk, there could be no doubt that he had inherited his gifts of mimicry from his mother. In describing the pastor who opened the door to him in Noyon, he rose from his chair to look for his hat, which he set on his head dead-center and low on the brow, in the manner of the said ecclesiastic, and began walking with the latter's hurried little steps, turning first this way, then that, at the same time imitating his voice. At this stage, when little Srulik's voice came out of Gabriel's mouth humming the tune of "The Wood on the Hill of the Three" under the Protestant clergyman's hat, Dr. Landau's wife was already in stitches, wiping the tears of laughter from her eyes. At the climax of the story, with Gabriel acting both as the porter bringing the clergyman a parcel and as the clergyman opening the door to take the parcel from the porter, the pair of them meeting face to face, his mother's voice was suddenly heard from inside the house. "Stop that shouting! My head's splitting, and he stands there shouting at the top of his voice like his savage Turk of a father. It wasn't enough with the doctoress's Polish owl pecking my brain to pieces all night with his accursed piano. Now this one has to come from Paris to shatter my head with his roars in the morning too, and all for the sake of making an impression on that stuck-up doctoress! And what's the wonder? A man who does nothing to earn his bread all day, and not just any man but a healthy, strapping fellow like his father the lecherous Turk, has enough strength and energy and time to entertain all the doctoresses in the world. The only one he's never got any time for is his mother, not even to sit down for a minute and tell her something about what's going on in the world."

Her outbursts of rage against him were astonishingly like her furious attacks on his father in his time, and when she was at the height of her rage it sometimes seemed that the knowledge that her husband was already dead and gone did nothing at all to detract from the intensity of her emotions, which were indifferent to logic and oblivious to any subtle distinctions between the dead father and his living son. The truth is that she was glad he had not completed his studies in Paris and had come home to her, but when she was in the grip of one of her rages this fact—like all his deeds and attributes—was transformed from an advantage to a fault, and in the heat of her anger she spared him nothing, but hurled the worst insults and gravest accusations she could think of at him, in accordance with the volume and particular nuance of her rage, and without the least regard for the truth. "It's me she's getting at, of course, not you," said the doctor's wife with a smile, and after a pause she added with a mischievous wink: "She's right, you know—you're not doing what you should be doing. And now I'll be off before the Consul's wife sweeps me away with her fiery breath." Before she left she planted a quick kiss on his mouth and called from the verandah steps, "Oh, that dreadful mustache, when are you going to shave it off? I'll never get used to it. You can go and work in the Café Gat now. I passed by there and saw that there's nobody there you know to disturb you. The only person to disturb you will be me—in, let's say, one and a half or two hours' time I'll come and carry you off to lunch at our place." When she had complained earlier on that he never told her anything about himself, she meant, among other things, the nature of his occupation, for even Orita, who was one of the very few people who had realized that Gabriel was "working" on something, did not know exactly what this "work" was: since at the period of Gabriel's return she was in the grip of enthusiasm for the art of the Far East, she took it for granted that his "work" was somehow related to Far Eastern art, although the exact nature of the relationship was not yet clear to her. Gabriel did nothing to disabuse her of this notion, just as he made no attempt to prove to his mother—or the rest of the world, who all thought as she did that he was just another Jerusalem dreamer and idler—that he was always doing his "work," and that there was nothing that depressed him more than the sight of those wastrels who did not know what to do with the most precious gift in their possession, the span allotted to them in this life on earth.

When Orita began cross-examining him about what he was doing, he would cover his eyes with his hand and then

run his fingers through his hair, as if trying to shake off
great fatigue or depressing thoughts, and then, with the
same hand, make a dismissive gesture, as if to indicate the
unsatisfactory or insignificant nature of his affairs, at
the same time turning the conversation into channels connected with her and not him. With others close to him he
would deal in more or less the same way, while with casual
acquaintances his manner made it quite clear that in spite of
his natural friendliness and frankness his daily affairs were
no more their business than were the intimate reflections of
his heart. And if anyone was impertinent enough to persist
in prying into his secrets, Gabriel would put him in his place
with a brutality that forever removed any urge to conduct
further explorations into the intimate mysteries of the soul
of the affable and charming Gabriel Luria. On the other
hand, he was capable in a casual conversation with a total
stranger of disclosing things about himself which Orita, for
example, in spite of her assiduous efforts, had never succeeded in getting out of him. Sometimes, when a benevolent
breeze brushed him with its wings as it blew through Jerusalem, he would tell her, too, things she had long wanted to
know, but he would formulate them in such a way, in a
cadence and a music so remote from her ken, that their
meaning was quite beyond her comprehension—leading her
to repeat, more than once and in a tone of growing resentment, the question he had just answered in full.

"So what is this work waiting for you in the Café Gat?" his
mother, who had been eavesdropping from her window,
demanded, emerging from the house the moment the old
judge's daughter tripped down the verandah steps and
turned in the direction of her husband's eye clinic. "It's
something to do with the bookkeeping of the commercial
college and the French factory," said her son, to allay her
suspicions and satisfy her curiosity. Once and once only had
he attempted to give his mother a proper answer to her
questions about the nature of his occupation; this was on the

very day of his return home, about ten days or a fortnight before Orita found out by chance that he was back and came rushing, beside herself with excitement, to see him. Even before he opened his mouth to answer her, as soon as she saw the weary frown on the face of her son, the familiar gesture of the hand covering his closed eyes, Mrs. Gentilla Luria knew that her worst fears were about to come true. And when the words "Bible" and "Torah" reached her ears, together with a few remarks about our need to understand today precisely the things most remote from us—in other words the whole bloody and disgusting business of the laws of the priests and the sacrifices, which demanded a new, fresh insight, more directly related to the sources than all the ancient commentaries—when these words penetrated the dread gripping her heart, it was already clear to her beyond the shadow of a doubt that all the daydreaming idleness of her senile old father had been transmitted directly to her only son. She could thank her lucky stars that Gabriel was punctilious about his external appearance at least, that he shaved carefully every day and made sure his collars were properly pressed and his trousers sharply creased. And it did not take long before she realized that she had another miracle to be thankful for too: unlike her senile father, who displayed his Jerusalem daydreaming in broad daylight, for all the world to see, her son kept his ravings to himself. These two things did much to disperse the clouds of her great dread, although they did not wipe it entirely from her heart. On a number of occasions she was on the point of disclosing her fears to the old judge, and stopped herself in time only when she realized that he himself, His Worship Supreme Court Judge Dan Gutkin, O.B.E., was tainted by the same Jerusalem daydreaming, which had begun to manifest itself with increasing conspicuousness from one visit to the next, especially since the death of Yehuda Prosper Bey.

After her husband's death she even discovered, to her

astonishment, signs of the same Jerusalem daydreaming in
Dr. Landau, the eye doctor: the clinic, as usual, was full of
patients, who for lack of room on the benches were sitting
and awaiting their turn on the floor and the stairs; the
nurses and doctors were rushed off their feet, and Dr. Landau himself—pale and red-eyed after performing two
urgent operations the night before on Arab children from
Hebron—barely had time to attend to the most serious cases
demanding his care, when all of a sudden, in the middle of
the commotion, and precisely at the moment when Mrs.
Gentilla Luria came in to receive her weekly treatment, he
plunged into an argument with the administrative director,
that stoop-shouldered Berl Raban, about some verse or
other in the Bible. The one claimed it said this, and the other
insisted it said that, as if it were really so important what it
said—and Dr. Landau was not satisfied until he left her
there, right in the middle of her treatment, and ran into the
office after Berl with the eye-dropper in his hand to open
the Bible and see for himself. It was a miracle for her that the
verse happened to be written the way Dr. Landau wanted it
to be written, otherwise in his rage he would probably have
mixed the bottles up and dropped some poison into her eyes
that would have blinded her entirely and darkened her
world until the end of her days. "And really," she said to
Gabriel when he came onto the verandah after his morning
wash and she poured him his second cup of coffee, "I'm not
at all sure that he didn't get the bottles mixed up in his
excitement over that verse, even though he beat that hunch-
back Berl in the argument. From the minute he put the
drops in I felt that something was wrong, and it's already
been twenty-four hours and I still have a peculiar feeling in
my eyes. I can see I'll have to go to the clinic again this week.
Well, I ask you: Is such a thing possible? An intelligent,
advanced man like him to show such Jerusalem daydreaming, to get as excited as your senile grandfather over some-

thing said thousands of years ago by the Prophet Jeremiah, who was no more, when all is said and done, than a peasant from the hills around Anata or Nebi Samwil. There was an old Arab fellah from Anata in the clinic, standing there and shaking his fists and cursing all the effendis in his village, and I thought to myself that that was what the Prophet Jeremiah must have looked like when he came to Jerusalem to give the king and all the effendis running the Temple a piece of his mind. Anata is the biblical Anatoth after all, and its inhabitants are probably descended from the people of Anatoth. Who knows if that old fellah isn't a descendant of the Prophet Jeremiah's? I don't remember anymore if that old scandal-maker Jeremiah had wives and children. I really should open the Bible and have a look. But I can promise you that even if it doesn't say anything about wives or children, that whole village was crawling with his bastards. I know them, those old scandal-mongers, all those searchers after sins and preachers of sermons who've appointed themselves to be God's policemen on earth. I told him, Dr. Landau, that my eyes were more important to me than all the prophets put together. Dr. Landau, I said to him, when you're attending to my eyes I'll thank you to think about the proper drops and not about some old biblical verse! And what's the matter with you, may I ask? Don't wrinkle up your nose at me, if you please! And I don't want to hear any more complaints from you about my coffee not being strong enough for you."

When Gabriel told Dr. Landau's wife that his second cup of breakfast coffee determined his mood for the rest of the day, she thought he was making fun of her. Actually, the orientation of his thoughts began even before this, when he concluded the morning ablutions which differentiated between the sleeping and waking worlds, and enabled him to concentrate all his resources clearly on the chosen chapter of the day, in which, by the time he picked up his second cup of coffee, he was already completely absorbed. Sometimes he would lean his little Bible against the sugar bowl and read as he drank, and sometimes he would place some other book there, even one of the medical books from the days of his studies in Paris. On particularly good mornings he did not need a book at all, but would look at the birds flying among the trees next to the fence or the cat preening itself on the cistern lid or the lion cub bearing the imperial scepter in its jaws on the façade of the Ethiopian Consulate above the inscription which said in Ethiopian: "Menelik the Second, Emperor of Ethiopia, Descendant of the Lion of Judah." If a sudden spark welded his musings into an idea, he would hastily jot down a word or two on his cigarette packet, words to which he would return when he came back from his midnight walk, lucid and alert in the silence of the sleeping world around him, and took up one of those big notebooks that looked like account books in order to clothe the fruits of his morning meditations in the language of contemporary words, and thereby add a sentence or two to what was already written in the open notebook before him. It was this thin line, leading from the concentration of his morning meditations to the few sentences added to the commentaries in the notebooks after midnight, that gave light and joy, flavor and focus to his whole day and to all that happened to him during its course.

If, as already mentioned, no one disturbed him during the drinking of his second cup of morning coffee, if none of the thousand and one nuisances that descend upon us every morning to distract us from our true course in life intruded on him as he sipped, and he was permitted to drink his coffee to the dregs and top it off with a cigarette, he would unconsciously begin to hum a contented tune to himself as he removed the empty cup from the three-legged iron table and prepared it for his morning shave, for as the reader will remember, Gabriel, like his late father, the old Bey, before him, shaved sitting down, and on nice days he preferred shaving outside, on the verandah.

If Gabriel's daily ablutions between one cup of coffee and the next were a frontier, a barrier erected to prevent the last waves of sleep from impinging on the awakening continent, his shave was already situated firmly within the daytime domain, and in the joy of my own awakenings during that summer in the Street of the Prophets, I waited every morning for his clear outline and strong voice as he sat down in the red plush armchair and arranged his shaving gear on the table in front of him. I knew then that he was already approachable, and I jumped out of bed and ran onto the verandah not only to learn strange songs in all kinds of languages and hear stories of his childhood and other days from him, but also simply to watch him shave. Since he sat with his back to the balustrade, the top of the street, in the place where it joined Abyssinian Road, was reflected in the upper corner of his shaving mirror, enabling him to see what was going on in the triangle of the world behind his back as he shaved and to make his comments. The slightest movement, the most imperceptible stir, would create havoc in the landscape reflected behind his back, although it made no difference at all to his own lathered face in the mirror. One minute Gabriel's head would be floating by itself in a clear, empty sky, and the next people would be going in and out of the doors of the Café Gat. One after the other, the judge's car stopped on the corner and the chauffeur Daoud Ibn Mahmoud jumped out to have something to drink in his spare time, before his boss required his services again at the end of the court session; a flock of Ethiopian monks sailed past like black candles against the gray stone walls; and Dr. Landau peeped from his window before setting out for the eye clinic.

"Good God, how he's aged, how he's aged!" said Gabriel to the doctor's reflection in the mirror, "and he still has the strength to shout all day in the clinic after a night of two urgent operations. When I was a child I already knew in my bones that this roaring bear was a good man, a kind man who loved children, and nevertheless there was nothing in the whole world that frightened me more than a visit to Dr. Landau."

As Gabriel was puffing out his second lathered cheek for the razor, Dr. Landau, who was on his way to the clinic, met Daoud Ibn Mahmoud on his way into the Café Gat. The slender, elegant chauffeur, who resembled Gabriel in his mustache and way of dressing, looked like a swift-footed deer approaching an old polar bear. The former asked a smiling question, and the eye specialist, whose hearing was not all it should be, bent his head and put his ear almost to Daoud's lips, placing his hand on his shoulder, close to the neck, as if the chauffeur's head were the receiver of a kind of living telephone, which he was intent on aiming directly at his bad ear. The chauffeur's expression changed immediately from that of a self-confident man who knew his own worth, to that of a timid child being tested by the school principal. The old doctor treated everyone, not just the chauffeur, like an overgrown child capable of every kind of folly imaginable. The inclination of his ear, together with the narrowing of his eyes and pursing of his mouth into an expression that could easily be taken for disapproval and disgust with the nonsense he was about to hear—and was, indeed, usually so taken by those who did not know the doctor well and who accordingly began to stutter and stammer in embarrassment—stemmed not from deafness (although by then, at over seventy years of age, Dr. Landau was already rather hard of hearing) but from long years of medical experience in Jerusalem among many diverse communities, beginning with Jews from Kurdistan and ending with Hourani Arabs. They all unburdened themselves before him in their different tongues and dialects and accents, while he had not only to understand the words coming out of their mouths, but also to grasp the hidden, tortuous, and surprising connections between their stories and their eye diseases. During the half-century in which he had treated eye diseases in the Holy City, he had grown accustomed to listening to the discourse of the "seven nations," as he called them, in order to acquaint himself with what was going on in their minds, and there was always some startling new surprise in store for him, even after fifty years of work. To one of these surprises, which led to a towering rage on the part of the doctor and mighty roars that shook the clinic walls, I myself was a witness as a child, when I had an eye infection. Berl Raban, who had learned to assist the doctor in routine treatments, was putting drops into my eye and muttering something while the doctor himself was examining the eyes of a Bedouin girl from the Beersheba area who was sitting on the chair next to me. The girl's father and mother were sitting on the floor, not because there were never enough chairs for all the members of the patients' families, but because they were more comfortable sitting on the floor than on a chair. "The coffee must be pampered," the girl was saying. "Coffee needs pampering. You should never just boil it like the infidels do. You have to pamper it with a gentle little fire, bring it slowly to a bubble and then a boil, you have to listen to its murmurs. You have to love it."

"Your words are true and sweeter than honey," replied the doctor, his face creased with concern. Not only had the girl's eyes not improved since her last visit to the clinic, but the trachoma was worse and the deterioration alarming. "It's not only coffee that needs pampering," he said.

"Quite right," answered the girl. "After they broke my tooth, the Jewish doctor gave me a gold one instead. My father bought me a mirror for a present, and I would look at my beautiful new tooth all day long. I wanted to see if it was happy in my mouth, if it felt comfortable in its new home. I wanted to know how it would eat and drink. How it looked when it laughed, and how it looked when it cried."

The doctor suddenly bent down and began to sniff her eyes. His big face paled and his blue eyes reddened and his wild gray hair flew in all directions like smoke rising from the terrible rage burning inside him. He recoiled, sat down on his high chair, put both hands on his slightly parted knees, and turned to face her parents. For a moment there was an ominous silence. Even Berl, who should have been immune by now to his master's rages, stopped what he was doing and raised the dropper in his hand for fear that it would tremble in the impending storm and put the wrong number of drops in my eye, and his muttering ceased. The Bedouin and his wife cowered on the floor and stared at him guiltily, ready for the punishment about to descend on their heads. "Curs, sons of curs!" The expected roar burst from his lips, and the clinic with all its staff and patients trembled in awe—for who was so brave he would not tremble at the doctor's roar? The Arab cart drivers outside in the street rolled their eyes piously heavenward at the sound of the famous doctor's heathen roar, twirled their mustaches and murmured: "There is no God but Allah and Mohammed is His Prophet." The girl's mother bowed down until her head touched the ground. "You smeared her eyes with garlic skins again, you mongrel sons of Satan! Haven't I warned you over and over again that one day your daughter will go quite blind with your cursed witch-doctor's mumbo-jumbo! No, no! I won't go on treating her! If you come to me, then you do what I tell you to do—and if not, then get the hell out of here, and stop hurting my eyes with your whore-pimps' faces! Wait a minute, you old witch, and I'll show you what it means to smear trachoma with garlic and onions! It was you who did it, wasn't it?" The old Bedouin woman, crouching on all fours on the floor before the wrathful god of Jewish medicine, groaned in anticipation of the pain of the blow which did not fall: the doctor was content with a few rough shakes of the shoulder under the headdress falling over the nape of her neck. Before she stood up she managed to plant a hasty kiss on the hem of his coat, since the doctor, still shaking with rage, refused to allow her to kiss his hand. "I've got nothing against their beliefs and medicines," he once said to Judge Dan Gutkin. "What angers me is that they don't even know their own medical traditions, and what infuriates me most of all is that they're not faithful to themselves. With their tortuous Oriental cunning they want to enjoy both worlds at once and deceive them both—their world and ours." And they went on trying to enjoy and deceive both worlds at once, with the unholy combination of the tattered remnants of their own traditions grafted onto the doctor's treatment in the clinic, even after they had tasted his wrath, because they knew that the same hand that had shaken them so roughly in order to make them mend their ways was a benevolent hand, and that it would go on taking care of them in spite of everything. In these hard cases, the doctor would order the patient's hospitalization— as he did in the case of the Bedouin girl—in order to prevent the family from recklessly ruining the results of his prolonged and tireless care and to give himself a little rest. And the girl too needed rest. She deserved a little pampering.

"You have to pamper the coffee and see if the gold tooth is happy in its new home," he muttered to himself, marveling anew at the young girl's words; and to Berl Raban he said: "Ah, Berleh, Berleh! I, who like nothing better than silence, have to shout the whole day long. Tell me, Berl, why is it that I always have to do the exact opposite of what I want to do?" Many years before, Gabriel had heard him ask the very same question, when he came to say good-bye to him on the eve of his departure for Paris. Dr. Landau and Judge Dan Gutkin were among the guests invited to a little farewell party given

by Yehuda Prosper Bey for the son of his old age. Orita, the
judge's daughter, came later, together with Srulik Shoshan,
Yankele Blum, and the rest of Gabriel's friends. After
instructing the young man in the niceties of tipping and the
ins and outs of prostitution in the metropolis, the judge
entered into a conversation with the old Bey about the ety-
mology of the word "baksheesh," while Dr. Landau began
telling Gabriel about his own student days. "The whole road
of my life—you hear!" (here his voice rose to a near roar)
"the whole road of my life has led me in the exact opposite
direction to the inclinations of my heart." Although he had
spent most of his youth in Germany and had been brought
up and educated in the German language, the Russian
accent of the land of his birth was apparent both in his
Hebrew, which he had begun learning while still in Germany, and in the Arabic which he had learned in the course
of his work in Jerusalem. As a matter of fact, the love of his
life was painting, and if he had had any talent he might have
become a painter, but he had never succeeded in drawing so
much as a simple chair. Since it was not given to him to make
things that were good and beautiful to the eye, he hoped
that it would be granted him, at least, to study the mysteries
of the eye itself. But instead of sitting in the peace and quiet
of a laboratory and conducting research, he had been sentenced to struggle against the filth and corruption of an
outlying province of the decrepit Turkish Empire. Empires
come and empires go, but the chaos surrounding him went
on forever. When he completed his studies, it had not even
occurred to him to open an eye clinic. He did not see himself standing and examining the eyes of Berliners in order
to provide them with the right glasses, and he certainly
never saw himself, not even in his worst nightmares, curing
the eye infections of a lot of Houranis and Bedouins, of
whom he had never even heard. First of all he planned a
long holiday in Paris and Rome, and then he intended to

return to Berlin and begin research on something that particularly interested him in the field of color perception. The eye perceives whatever it perceives, and the owner of the eye sees colors and shapes and interprets them: this is a red roof, this is a green tree, and so on. He intended to pursue this research in collaboration with his friend Heinrich: he would concentrate on the perception of color, Heinrich on the perception of form, and they would publish their results together. For the moment, Heinrich, his best friend, was to accompany him to Rome and Paris on a long vacation. Heinrich Strauss, like Albert Landau, was also an art lover, but while he himself was supremely interested in art, Heinrich was by nature more inclined to questions of politics and society. Heinrich wanted to reform the state and society, which were the source of most of the ills plaguing mankind, while he himself took no interest at all in these problems. As far as Albert Landau was concerned, all that mattered was people. There were beautiful people and ugly people, good people and bad people, strong people and weak people—and to him it made no difference at all if the person standing before him was a German or a Hottentot, rich or poor; nor did he see any need for states or rulers, or how they could have it in their power to change human nature. Even if Marx and Engels took over the government from the German kaiser, would they be able to turn ugly people into beautiful ones, or mean people into kind ones? He himself had been born big and strong, and he had always been stronger than most of the children in his class at school and the students studying medicine with him at the university, but he had never sought to dominate those weaker than himself, nor had he had the least desire to beat them up or order them about, and he saw no need for any form of government whatsoever. In this last point Heinrich, who belonged to advanced circles and was particularly active in the anarchist group, agreed with him. Heinrich was only

sorry that his best friend, Albert, did not join the group with
him and work for the common good, because of his exaggerated love of art. And indeed, in those days Albert had
not given a moment's thought to the common good or the
overturning of governments, for all his thoughts were
devoted to the impending trip to Paris and the paintings he
would see in the museums and galleries there, especially
those of the wonderful new young painters, the paintings
that were so full of light and bright, vivid colors pouring like
sparkling wine into a thirsty mouth, the pictures that
transmitted the direct impression of what the eye perceived. In secret, without telling even Heinrich, who in any
case lectured him from time to time (jokingly, of course, but
nevertheless with a trace of concern) about the signs of a
petit-bourgeois mentality still evident in his behavior, he was
busy scraping his pennies together in the hope that when
the great day came he would have enough to buy a couple of
paintings in Paris.

And when the great day came Albert Landau found himself not in a gallery in the Latin Quarter but in Constantinople, buying not an impressionist painting, but a ticket on a
ship bound for Palestine, to take Russian pilgrims to the holy
places trodden by the feet of Jesus Christ.

As he climbed the rungs of the ship's ladder he felt as if he
were in a dream, not his own dream, but the dream of a
stranger. The dream was strange and alien, but far stranger
yet was the fact that he had cast himself into it of his own
free will, not in a state of delirium but in full waking consciousness. All he could say in his own defense was that at the
time he had not contemplated remaining in it for long.
While he was still in the Turkish boat taking him from the
quay to the Russian ship, he had worked out that since the
said ship would take ten days at least to reach Palestine—if it
did not go down in the first storm they encountered and cast
him into the Aegean Sea—and another ten back, he

would have no more than a couple of weeks to spend in Palestine, since he was determined to get back in time to begin his research into the perception of color. Albert had thought then of less than a month; and in the twenty years and more which had passed since then he was still living in somebody else's dream. And all because of a piece of nonsense: a slip of the tongue, a joke made to a girl. If she had been his own girlfriend, he could at least have blamed it on a woman and given the whole affair a romantic turn. But the girl wasn't his girlfriend. She was one of Heinrich's comrades, and she had come on the eve of their departure for Paris to get instructions from him about the role she was to play during his absence. Heinrich expounded on the relations between the anarchists and the socialists and other progressive groups, cursing and abusing the Catholics from time to time as he did so. This Heinrich, who came from a strictly Catholic Bavarian family, was fond of peppering his speech with barbs directed against the Catholic Church. The girl, who did not know Heinrich well, became confused and cried: "But what on earth have the Catholics got to do with it? We're talking about choosing our representatives for the meeting with the socialists!" And then she added: "You really are a queer fish, Heinrich. People are talking about railway workers' wages, and you get in a dig at the Holy Trinity; the subject under discussion is the problem of the relations between students and workers, and you denounce the hypocrisy of the Catholic priests. Leave them alone for a minute and let's get down to business!"

"But how can one leave the Catholics alone," retorted Heinrich, "after they took some Jesus, some little Jewboy from Palestine, and made him into God? The God of the entire universe! Let them send him back where he came from and leave us alone."

That evening they all laughed, but the next morning Albert Landau said to himself, with a feeling of surprise:

"But I'm a Jew like Jesus too, except that he came from
Palestine." He made up his mind on the spot to spend his
vacation not in Paris but in Palestine; a student of Middle
Eastern studies supplied him with the necessary information about the voyage, telling him that in recent years there
was a big movement of Russian Orthodox pilgrims. Russian
peasants from the most remote provinces were streaming to
the Black Sea and sailing from there to the Holy Land. The
name of the ship was *Lazarus,* and from the moment he set
foot on board and found himself surrounded by hundreds
of old peasants, some of whom had been saving their pennies and hoarding their bread for years in order to reach the
Holy Land before they died, he sensed how suitable the
name was for these ghosts of ancient beliefs which had
suddenly taken on flesh and blood before his very eyes, in
this enlightened day and age on the threshold of the twentieth century. This feeling did not leave him, but grew stronger, reaching its climax when he arrived with them at the
goal of their voyage—the river Jordan, where John was baptized and where he baptized Jesus—and saw the hundreds
of pilgrims putting on their winding-sheets and entering
the holy water. Most of them had traveled from Jaffa to
Jerusalem and from Jerusalem to the Jordan on foot, in the
terrible heat, wearing under their sheepskin coats all the
layers of clothes that they wore against the northern cold at
home, without it entering their heads to remove a single
layer. They took them off only in order to put on their
winding-sheets and enter the Jordan River, and by the time
they reached its banks they were already white with the dust
of the valley, which penetrated every pore and covered
everything with a powder the same yellowish-white color as
the old men's beards. The poorest of the pilgrims had made
their journey on the sacks of bread they carried on their
backs—not loaves of bread, but slices, crusts, crumbs, which
they had denied themselves for months and received as alms

in the villages they passed during their long journey over dry land before they reached the sea. It was only in the towns that they received a little money. In the villages the peasants could give them nothing but the crumbs of bread they took out of their own mouths, and these the pilgrims carried in the sacks on their backs. If they were able to add a little oil and a few black olives and cook it up together, they thought it a feast fit for a king.

And when Albert Landau began, by the force of circumstance, to tend to the ills of these pilgrims—for there was no doctor among them, and he could not ignore their ailments and deprive them of what little assistance he was able to offer—he was still convinced that he was enjoying a vacation on the completion of his studies, and nothing had changed except for the place of the vacation and the manner in which he was spending it. An Arab sailor carried him on his back from the ship to the shores of Jaffa, and it was only in Jaffa that he discovered that he was not the only Jew who had just arrived in Palestine, and that not only Russian pilgrims were streaming there, but also Russian Jews: not old men coming to immerse themselves in the Jordan in their winding-sheets, but young men coming to build colonies or settle in the towns and look for work. The latter ran about looking for work everywhere, whereas he was on the run from the work which pursued him everywhere he went. More than twenty years had passed since then, and he was still waiting for the holiday he had dreamed of when he completed his studies. The moment he started treating the pilgrims he was lost. When he reached Jerusalem it was already too late: he could no longer deny his Jewish brothers and Arab cousins the help he had given the Russians. Once he began work he sunk into a bottomless pit, and from then on till the present day he had no option but to continue scraping away at the strange and diverse infections converging on him from the remotest corners of the Levant. He really had no choice in the matter, but when he felt like annoying Berl he would put all the blame on him. If Berl had not latched on to him, he would have gone back to Europe in time to enjoy himself in Paris, but Berl had succeeded in latching on to him the moment he set foot in Jerusalem in the company of the pilgrims. When Berl saw the pilgrims in their rags and tatters sitting in the Russian Compound and eating their moldy crusts of bread dipped in water, he said to the young Dr. Landau: "All that's missing here is Joshua. I've always said that what we need here is Joshua." The doctor stared at the skinny young boy perched on a huge pillar hewn into the rock and abandoned where it lay, cracked and horizontal, since the days of King Herod, and was none the wiser. With the kind of bony, nervous, long-fingered hand that for some reason always goes together with stooped shoulders, Berl pointed at the pilgrims and began reciting, as if he were reading from an open book visible to his eyes alone: "All we need here is Joshua for these people to stand up and say to him, 'From a very far country thy servants are come because of the name of the Lord thy God: for we have heard the fame of him, and all that he did in Egypt, and all that he did to the two kings of the Amorites, that were beyond Jordan, to Sihon king of Heshbon, and to Og king of Bashan, which was at Ashtaroth. Wherefore our elders and all the inhabitants of our country spake to us, saying, 'Take victuals with you for the journey, and go to meet them, and say unto them, We are your servants: therefore now make ye a league with us. This is our bread we took hot for our provision out of our houses on the day we came forth to go unto you; but now, behold, it is dry, and it is moldy: and these bottles of wine, which we filled, were new; and behold, they be rent; and these our garments and our shoes are become old by reason of the very long journey.' I see that the time has come for you to learn something about the Bible, and I, as you see, am in need of a job, so from today I'll be your Bible teacher. We'll begin with the book of Joshua."

And so it was. And since the Bible lessons were not suffi-
cient for Berl to earn a living, Dr. Landau found him a job as
a clerk in the eye clinic. When he felt like teasing Berl by
putting all the blame on him, Berl would flare up and shout:
"Yes, yes, I know. You opened this clinic simply in order to
give me a job. Simply so that I wouldn't have to run around
looking for pupils. Just so that I can dress like a respectable
human being, you work like a dog cleaning out all the filth
left by all the corrupt empires in all the eyes of the Levant.
But for me, you would have gone back to Paris twenty years
ago and wandered round all the galleries and bought all the
Manets and Monets, the Pissarros and Renoirs and Degas
and van Goghs and Toulouse-Lautrecs together. Imagine
what a millionaire you would have been today if you had
bought their paintings then, when they were still starving,
for next to nothing. The only reason you aren't a millionaire
today is that twenty years ago you had to provide a job for
Berl Raban!" Berl no longer had to worry about earning a
living, but he was still looking for pupils to teach them the
Book of Joshua. If all Yehuda Prosper Bey needed was our
master Moses, then all Berl Raban needed was Joshua the
son of Nun. That was all he needed—for Joshua the son of
Nun to come and command the sun to stand still!

The sun suddenly burst into the mirror, hitting sparks of
dazzling white light off the lather piled in snowy heaps on
Gabriel's puffed-out cheek, and he hastily pulled the table
toward him, into the shade, for fear of another flash of light.
The world reflected in the angle of the mirror flew away and
disappeared, and the corner of the Italian Hospital
appeared instead of the picture of Dr. Landau bending his
ear toward the chauffeur outside the Café Gat. From the
mute mirror picture, like an image from a silent movie,
Gabriel understood that Daoud Ibn Mahmoud was offering
to drive the old doctor to the clinic, but the shifting of the
table in the wake of the flash of light had interrupted the
scene before the ending, which he had particularly wanted

to see. He guessed, of course, that the doctor would prefer
to continue his way on foot, and if he had turned his head
for a moment he would have seen not his reflection but the
man himself, as large as life, walking down the street with
his camellike steps, like those of Señor Moïse, but by then
the peculiar fascination exerted by everything reflected in
the mirror had already disappeared: that fascination which
stems not only from the unexpected angles of vision which
suddenly show us a new face in a long-familiar one, but also
from the reflection itself when it conforms exactly to its
source and in the mute mirror frame suddenly presents us
with that marvelous, incomparable magic, the magic we
shall never be able to contain, which is the magic of the thing
in itself.

Like the sun bursting into the mirror, the laughter of
Orita Landau suddenly burst into the street from the
entrance to the Café Gat. It could hardly have been her
father's chauffeur, Daoud Ibn Mahmoud—among whose
many virtues a sense of humor was not conspicuous and, to
the extent that it existed at all, was not of the type that
appealed to Orita—who had given rise to her peals of
laughter, which sounded more like a continuation of something that had happened inside the café, but he, in any case,
joined in wholeheartedly, partly out of the infectious merriment of the sound, and partly out of the affection he bore
her. Until the burst of laughter he was ignorant of her
presence in the café, and when he stopped the car he had
intended going inside and relaxing over a cup of coffee and
a cigarette until the court session was over, but nevertheless
he felt no anger or resentment when, instead of enjoying the
expected rest and drink, he opened the door of the car
again and sat down at the wheel. On the contrary: just as he
had truly and sincerely offered his services to her husband a
moment before, he was truly glad now of the coincidence
(ordained, like all coincidences, by God) which had brought

him here when she needed him and given him the chance to make her happy and take her wherever she wanted to go. Only the anxiety that he might be late, and the judge would have to wait for him at the gate—instead of finding the car standing there ready and waiting, at his service and command—found an echo in his voice and slightly marred his happiness as he asked, in English: "Where to, Madame?" recalling as he did so the out-of-the-way spots to which he had often in the past been required to drive her, over bumpy roads which were never intended for motorcars at all, let alone important motorcars like his. All of a sudden one of those accursed devils would get into her and incite her to drive to some godforsaken village full of benighted, poverty-stricken peasants, where no civilized city-dweller had ever set foot before, never mind members of the upper crust, who had never even heard its name; and once they got there, she would start running about among the rocks and thorns like an untamed colt. If only she would have been content to gaze with incomprehensible admiration at all kinds of base, common things: the millstones, the wooden ploughs, the blind mule turning the threshing sledge, he could have ignored it. But the shame rose hotly to his face whenever this upper-class lady—the daughter of the Supreme Court judge before whom even the British police officers stood up to salute—started conversing and fraternizing with the low-down trash whom he himself had just refused even the privilege of dusting the car. Once, many years before, she had humiliated him so terribly that he had been obliged to complain to the judge. If anyone else had treated him in a similar fashion, he would never have forgiven him. He would have waited all his life to avenge his sullied honor—for she had insulted his honor!—but this fleet-footed deer had done what she did without any premeditation or malice aforethought, out of simple thoughtlessness and because of the wicked little devil that entered her heart through one ear

without going out the other. It came about in the following
way, and Allah the Merciful, the Compassionate, would
surely forgive her for it, as he would forgive all the other sins
she committed in error.

All the important chauffeurs with important jobs—the
drivers of the consuls and bishops and directors of government departments and mayors and the rest of the high-ups
and bigwigs—received uniforms which were fit and proper
for their station in life, whereas he, after having passed all
the tests and beaten all the other candidates and obtaining
the post of chauffeur to the Supreme Court judge, drove his
master for an entire year in ordinary clothes, without His
Worship the Judge indicating by so much as the faintest of
hints when he would finally receive the uniform he so richly
deserved, and this made him very sad. So great was his
sorrow that he lost his appetite and his face fell, until in the
end the judge sat up and took notice and asked him what the
matter was. He told him. His Worship the Judge smiled and
said: "*Ya* Daoud Ibn Mahmoud, do not mope and be sad, for
I have already found you worthy of your post, and you have
already succeeded in all the tests, and you shall receive the
uniform fit and proper to your post in time for the great
reception to be given by the High Commissioner at Government House in honor of the king's birthday."

And indeed, a fortnight before the great reception the
uniform was ready, tailor-made to fit his body, with gold
buttons and gold pips on the epaulettes, beautiful to
behold—but best of all was the cap. Among the caps of the
drivers of all the consuls in Jerusalem you would not find its
like. In every respect and from every point of view it was the
cap not of a chauffeur but of an officer, and not simply an
officer but an officer in the Royal Air Force. It was gray-blue
and it had a stiff peak and high sides, and the only difference between it and an RAF cap was the badge, which was
the badge of the Court. But anyone who did not inspect its

shape and inscription closely would notice the difference, especially since it was always gleaming and polished to a turn with the brass polish that he always kept handy on the shelf in front of him, next to the speedometer, with his driver's license and other documents. Like the badge, his buttons and shoulder pips were always shining too, and he had already been addressed, on more than one occasion, by lady pilgrims from France looking for the way to the Holy Sepulcher, as *"mon capitaine."*

And when the great day came he was no less smartly turned out—you might even say more—than several high-ranking British officers, in whose buckles his sharp eyes were quick to discover spots. These spots were, obviously, the fault not of the officers themselves but of their batmen, who had cheated on the job. If he had been in the place of these officers, he would have punished the batmen, he would have taught them a lesson that they would have remembered for the rest of their lives and shown them what it meant to neglect their work—and not just any work, but the work of preparing for the great reception itself! Look at him, for example. For the past two weeks he had devoted every moment of spare time to intensive practicing. The sergeant major of the law courts had explained to him exactly what he had to do, according to a plan drawn up and decorated with arrows in red and green and blue and yellow, and he had learned all the rules by heart, because he belonged to the superior category of cars which entered the courtyard of Government House, and his own car occupied parking space number 23 on the left. After parking, the driver jumped out, ran lightly round the hood of the car, opened the door and helped his masters out, saluted, closed the door, ran back around the hood, and stood at attention on the left-hand side of the car until his masters entered the building. If he saw the High Commissioner himself passing in his car, he had to draw himself up immediately and salute. For two weeks he had seen himself saluting in the mirror ten or fifteen times a day: drawing himself up, throwing his shoulders back, and saluting at exactly the right angle between the peak of his cap and his forearm—a splendid, vigorous sight. His mother had told him that he was handsome, and in the big wardrobe mirror he saw with his own eyes a Daoud to thrill the heart beneath the peak of his cap set at precisely the right bold manly angle—neither jaunty and frivolous nor flat and dull. Whenever his mother saw him decked out in all his greatness and glory, her eyes would melt with pride and with sorrow that his father had not lived to see him thus, for his father had been murdered by the base and contemptible Ibn Masrur who envied him, and if such curs were allowed to do whatever they felt like, they would destroy the whole world, may their names and memories be blotted out.

When he walked into the café and went up to the bar, he would tip his cap back with one deft motion of his right thumb, and all the Englishmen would call out, "Hello, David, how are you today?" In the mirror in front of him he would see the girls eyeing him as he leaned his elbow on the bar and shifted his weight from one leg to the other with a firm, supple movement of his thigh. Sometimes he would tap his foot like the important officers impatient to receive the service that was their due. He never looked at the cooks and kitchen maids and the other lowly, worthless creatures of their ilk. When they began to flirt with him, joking and giggling, he would turn his back and look in the other direction. He would take a tin of Players out of his pocket and open it elegantly. When he took out a cigarette he would frown thoughtfully. Thus the sergeant major, too, extracted a cigarette, but the sergeant major did not have a lighter, whereas he always had his Ronson in his pocket, and his lighter always lit the first time. Once he had made a bet with Gordon, the commander of the police station, that his lighter would catch twenty times in a row. He had bet him ten grush and won. Twenty times his lighter had ignited at the first go, and the whole café was in an uproar. Gordon was so impressed that he had treated him to two drinks in addition to the money he won on the bet. That's the way it was with him—everything first-class. Just as he took care of the car and kept it in top shape all the time, so he always kept his lighter full of benzene, with an extra flint handy, and the spring perfectly adjusted to the size of the flint. Gordon had a camera, and next month he too would buy himself a first-class Kodak camera with a leather case and all the accessories, even though it cost a lot of money. His camera would be the latest model, better than Gordon's. Gordon, for all his greatness, his camera, and the important police station he commanded, had not been invited to the High Commissioner's reception. What did he amount to in comparison to a Supreme Court judge! With one stroke of his pen a Supreme Court judge could send Gordon and another hundred officers like him to jail like dogs. Gordon had not been invited to the reception, but on the way to Government House, on the street corner next to the Allenby Barracks, where a large crowd had gathered, he was standing and putting on a big act. Waving his camera about over the people's heads, jumping here and there, contorting himself and stretching his neck to the left, then to the right, closing one eye as if with the other he could see Istanbul and Alexandria at once, crouching and winding himself around his camera, straightening up and stretching his neck to the clouds like a cock before crowing—"every cock crows on its own dunghill," as we say—as if it were really such a huge big deal. He could take all his photos and shove them you-know-where. And whenever they met in the café Gordon would call, "Hello, David, how are you today? Come and see the pictures I took last week!" Pulls out a photo and shows it. What is it? Nothing. Not a human face to be seen. A crooked olive tree, a camel drinking water, a ruin from the times of Ibrahim Pasha, a sordid, stinking alley in Kharaat i-Tan-nek—the kind of craziness the devil put into the judge's daughter's head when he went in through one ear and didn't come out the other. And where were the people? Where were the human beings? Aha, says Gordon, so you want to see studies of people—just a minute! And he rummages through the pile and pulls out a picture of an old Bedouin sitting on the edge of a well, then a peasant woman selling onions and garlic, then a Yemenite scrubbing the floor. They could really drive you mad with the kind of pictures they took. Just wait until he bought himself a Kodak, the latest model—and then see what they would say, then they would see photographs! Photographs of handsome men, girls who drew you to them like sweet honey. Things that had some dignity and splendor about them.

Gordon scurried about with his camera on the way to the reception, and he glided past him in his gleaming car with parking ticket number 23 stuck prominently on the front window, and sailed straight into the garden gate with the whole world watching. Ah, what a sight, what a sight! The eye would never weary of looking at the crowds pouring through the gates like rice from a sack, could never take in all the guards of honor lining both sides of the road. It was worth living the whole year simply to see one day like this! The guards of honor alone—how splendid, how splendid! The battalion of bodyguards, the Scots Guard in their kilts and sporrans, the Emir Abdallah's guard mounted on camels, the Royal Horse Guard on their horses, the Royal Signalers Guard and the Police Guard, and all the flags waving in the wind, and the marches and military tunes that filled your heart with courage and glory, and the majestic way Daoud drove between the two rows, sitting erect with his hands holding the wheel properly, without any tricks, with dignity and respect. And the way he drove in and glided

smoothly straight into parking place number 23 on the left,
and everything went as smoothly as the soul sailing in a good
dream. He jumped out and opened the door for his mistress, the judge's wife, may she rest in peace. A good, quiet
woman who had died suddenly six months later. Yes, yes, ten
years had already passed since then. After her came His
Worship the Judge and then the judge's younger daughter in
a long white dress. You could truly say, without any exaggeration, that Orita was the loveliest of all the women and
girls getting out of all the cars put together. The way the
Greek consul's chauffeur opposite stared at her! A frank,
insolent look without any shame at all. They should be put
out, those eyes that stared so boldly! She was in the middle
of bending down to get out, one leg already on the ground,
when suddenly that accursed devil came flying! The son of
Satan, damnation take him, entered her heart and she said,
"You know what, Daoud, I'll stay here in the car for a while."
What had that cursed devil shown her? He had shown her
Yehuda Prosper Bey's car coming in at the gate and turning
around to park in number 48 opposite, on the right hand
side next to the fence. She wanted to stay in the car and see if
Gabriel Ibn Yehuda Bey had come too. If he had, she would
arrange things so that she entered the building together
with him. And so she stayed behind in the backseat of the
car and he shut the door and ran back to the left side of the
car until His Worship the Judge and his wife went inside.
Once they were safely inside, he was at liberty to get back
into the car and sit at the wheel until the end of the reception, but he preferred to stand and wait so that he could
salute the High Commissioner when he rode past in his car.
He stood there adjusting the angle of his cap and preparing
his hand to rise at the right angle, and if only he had listened
to his heart which told him to go on standing in his place . . .
But driver number 21, who was standing next to him—a
plague on that accursed Beirut driver and all his ancestors;

everyone knew that he and his boss, the Brazilian consul, were nothing but a pair of queers—said to him, the devil take him and his good advice: "You can get into the car and sit down, *ya* Daoud, why should you tire your legs out for nothing? You'll have time to smoke a cigarette and a half before the High Commissioner's car arrives." Cursed be the moment that he listened to his advice and sat down in the car, where he removed his cap and put it down on the seat beside him while he took out his handkerchief to wipe the sweat off his brow, for the exertions of the day had been great and the heat heavy. And once he had wiped the sweat from his brow and lit a cigarette, his thoughts began drifting upward with the coils of smoke, higher and higher until they reached the clouds. And here was his father, riding on a cloud with Mount Hebron at his feet. His father said to him: It is good that you have come, my son, for I have missed you. You look well, and you have already warmed my heart with your fine deeds which are an honor to mankind.

Suddenly the command "Present arms!" brought Daoud back with a jolt from the clouds to the car seat. As he jumped out to salute the High Commissioner, he realized that he had left his cap on the seat beside him, and it was forbidden to salute or appear on parade without it. He got back into the car to put on his cap, stretched out his hand to the seat beside him—and the cap wasn't there! Vanished into thin air as if the devil had snatched it away. And while he was turning distractedly here and there, the High Commissioner's car sped past, and in the confusion he heard something like the barking of a dog and the voice of Gabriel Ibn Yehuda Bey, and there was great sorrow in his heart.

The cap was gone. It was only after the reception was over, when they all came back to the car, that the judge's younger daughter said to him: "What, you're looking for your cap? Here it is, on the shelf under the back window." But how did it get to the back window when it was lying here, next to the driver's seat? How had the cap flown to the back window shelf at precisely the moment he needed it most? "Quite simply," said Orita, "I put it there. I tried it on to see how it suited me, and afterward without thinking I put it down under the back window." Some accursed devil, may his name and memory be blotted out and his father's fathers be damned, had entered her heart at precisely that moment in order to torment him and drag his honor through the mud! If anyone else had dared to take his cap from him at that great moment and play with it without his permission and cause him the terrible humiliation of sitting and hiding in the car when the High Commissioner passed by, he would have dealt him a blow that would have laid him flat forever. But this fleet-footed deer had done nothing deliberately, nothing with malice aforethought. She was kindhearted and very sweet, and it was all the fault of the accursed devil who got into her and made her do his bidding. Ten years had passed since then, and she was already the wife of the famous eye doctor and the mother of his son, and there were already wrinkles round her eyes, and she was still set on jaunts and escapades that came straight from Satan. By the time she decided where she wanted to go, it would be time for Daoud to go and pick up her father at the courthouse. "You know," he said to her, "I heard that Gabriel Ibn Yehuda has come back from Paris; he was seen sitting on the verandah of his father's house on the day that Haile Selassie the King of Abyssinia arrived in Jerusalem."

"Why didn't you say so before?" Anyone would think from the tone of her voice that Daoud Ibn Mahmoud was to blame for the fact that a week after Gabriel's return she had not yet heard a thing about it. "We'll go there straightaway. No, no! Stop! I'll run over on foot." The car was on its way down Rav Kook Street toward Jaffa Street, and in order to reach Gabriel's house it would have to continue along Jaffa Street, up Melissanda Street and from there back to the

Street of the Prophets. Orita could get there more quickly on foot if she cut across the alley toward Hasollel Street, turned left and crossed two ancient courtyards leading to the back-yard of our house.

After the flash of light from the mirror came the direct thunderclap of the kiss on the ear. Since Gabriel's face was lathered in readiness for the second round—with him every shave consisted of two rounds, the first from the sideburns down in the direction of the growth, and the second from the Adam's apple upward in the opposite direction—the only place she could find to plant her kiss was on the ear facing her. "This is a fine thing! I have to hear from Daoud that you're back from Paris. A whole week's passed and it never even occurred to you to let me know you were back, and who knows how long it would have taken until you took the trouble to come round to see me? A funny way to behave, I must say! To come home after nine years in secret, like a thief in the night! And will you please finish the shaving ceremony already? Look how long it takes him to shave, the quickest boy in the Middle East! You're doing it on purpose to annoy me. If you shave yourself so thoroughly, why leave the mustache? Do me a personal favor and shave off that mustache for my sake. You know I don't like mus-taches."

He did not do her the favor of shaving off his mustache, but he did take her complaints about the shaving ceremony to heart, and after bringing the second round to a close with astonishing speed ran inside to wash his face and freshen his skin with after-shave. "I'd forgotten the sharpness of your transitions," she said, following all his movements with undisguised pleasure, "I'd forgotten that you were as amus-ing as Mufti." Mufti was her pointer, and the sharp transi-tion really did recall the pointer lying and basking motionlessly in the sun and suddenly, without any inter-mediate stages, leaping up and bounding over the fence.

Gabriel was capable of leaping up from his afternoon nap in order to jot down two or three words on a cigarette box, and once the tail of the idea had been thus caught and chained in words, to go back to bed and fall asleep with the same suddenness with which he had awakened, all in complete contradiction to his terrible difficulties in waking up in the morning. His expression on waking from his nap, too, was completely different from his gloomy, sullen morning looks, and one may have supposed that the difference stemmed from the lightness of this afternoon doze—except that he would wake gladly even after rhythmic snores during the course of the nap had announced to the world that he was sleeping the sleep of the just.

And another way that the afternoon differed from the morning was that in the afternoon he slept crosswise and not lengthwise; and that summer, when the days were fine and not too hot, with a gentle breeze playing through the trees at the bottom of the garden, he would sleep outside on the leather couch, in the shade of the second floor where we lived, which served as a ceiling running the entire length of the verandah. He would set the cushion in the middle of the couch, next to the wall, and sprawl out with his head resting on the doubled-up cushion and his legs crossed on an iron chair placed next to the couch for precisely this purpose. Next to him on the couch he would place a burnished copper ashtray, and thus he would lie gazing at the smoke rising rung after rung like a spiraling stairway whose head was lost in the depths of the infinite clear sky. Once, when the smoke was spiraling upward in this manner, he told me that until that day Daoud Ibn Mahmoud did not know what had really happened to his cap at the crucial moment. When the High Commissioner passed, Orita was horrified to see a tiny puppy almost run over by the wheels of the motorbikes escorting the car. She snatched it up, hid it in the cap, and after the traffic had stopped, handed it over to the sentry. It was the sentry who returned the cap to the back window of the car. Gabriel's thoughts would skip from rung to rung, higher and higher, and the moment they were about to detach themselves from the top of the ladder and fly, the hand holding the cigarette would drop and drag them down in the earthly obligation to put out the burning cigarette. Once the cigarette had been stubbed out in the ashtray and there was no danger of the world surrounding him catching fire in his absence, he was able to take off once more and glide serenely through the higher worlds beyond the dissolving ladder, until he disappeared behind the screen of a rhythmic snore. And he was capable of tearing this screen of snores too, with one abrupt and energetic lurch toward the cigarette box, in order to scribble a few hieroglyphics on its lid: when he was in a hurry to get something down he wrote so fast that the letters were indistinguishable from each other. If he did not throw the box away once it was empty, and these key words with it, he would set it in front of himself after midnight when he sat down to write three or four sentences in the big notebook, which looked like a bookkeeper's ledger, in a clear, straight, precise, rhythmic hand. In the composition of these three or four sentences, which dealt, as we have already mentioned, with his commentary on the Book of Leviticus, and distilled the essence of his thoughts during the day—and to tell the truth he thought of this commentary all the time, sitting at home or walking in the street, getting up or lying down—he would spend two or three of the wee hours after midnight. And in the same clear, clean, upright hand, round and sharp at once, he would also write the dull, trivial things imposed on him by the demands of daily life, such as a letter to the Municipal Water Board about the water seeping into the cellar of the house from a cracked pipe, or a reply to the Land Registry Office in the matter of the title deeds to the house, left unconcluded after his father's death, and the execution of his will.

"You know," Orita Landau would say, "your handwriting never fails to amuse me." The expression "amusing" was one of which Orita was particularly fond, especially in regard to Gabriel. Thus she would declare, "You know, your abrupt mood swings are awfully amusing," or inquire, "Where did you get that amusing shirt from? I suppose Leontine must have dragged it out of the bottom drawer of her antique commode and given it to you as a farewell present." When she saw him writing the shopping list of the groceries he had to buy for his mother at Reb Yitzhok's store, she burst out laughing and cried: "You have no idea how amusing you are! A hulking great man with the shoulders of a boxer sitting and making a list like a good little girl doing an exercise in calligraphy! Not writing but drawing all the letters exactly as her teacher told her to: a semicircle here, a straight line there. But really, why do you write so slowly?"

"It's a metaphysical question," he answered with a smile. "I write slowly because I think quickly. It's a problem of the transition from potentiality to actuality."

"You and your amusing ideas! You never answer me seriously."

"I'm absolutely serious. If I write as quickly as I think, no one will understand my handwriting or its contents. Besides, I don't want to cause suffering. The letters suffer when you treat them roughly and mutilate them. And the paper too, on which you torture them, and the pen, and the eye which regards them. You have to sense things." With the words "sense things" there appeared before his eyes the picture of his mother choosing a loaf of bread with the aid of all her senses, finely honed and developed for this purpose: her eyes which knew how to pick out the exact shade of shiny brown of the perfectly baked loaf, her sharp nose to sniff the good, warm smell, her long fingers to test the tension between the hardness of the crust and the softness of the flesh of the bread, and her little ear alert to the minute crackling noises made by the right loaf when she pressed its crust. At the same time he remembered the suffering she had caused him as a child, his helpless misery when she had forced him to return to the grocer with the hastily purchased loaf of bread and exchange it for one that would stand the test of her sharp senses. "Good God," he said to himself with a smile, "it's frightening, the way I'm beginning to resemble my mother." And as if to reassure himself that things had not yet reached so dire a pass, or to show Orita that he really was as amusing as Mufti, the minute his toilet was completed and he was ready to set out with her he embarked on a series of athletic tricks: first he seized hold of the iron chair, and raising it into the air with a flourish he ran around the verandah bearing it aloft like a torch in the hand of a marathon runner. "Be careful," she cried, "you'll give yourself a hernia." "There's no danger of that," he cried in reply, continuing his curious run, "I haven't told you yet that I concluded my scientific career in France with a first-class porter's diploma from the famous transport firm of Calberson and Company, Limited." After this—a true acrobatic feat—he balanced the chair on the tip of his finger, and then on the point of his upraised chin, stretching his arms out on either side to help his body maintain the equilibrium of the chair balanced on one of its legs on his smoothly shaven and refreshingly perfumed chin. At the conclusion of all these exploits, he put his arm round Orita's waist and the two of them tripped down the stairs to go for a stroll through the streets of Jerusalem. But when he emerged from the garden gate he suddenly cried, "Just a minute! I've forgotten my hat and cane!" and bounded back up the verandah steps to put on his white Panama hat and look for his silver-knobbed cane.

Thus attired and ready to set forth, in a navy-blue blazer which clung to his hips and added breadth to his already broad shoulders because of the shoulder pads fashionable in those days, he took her arm in his right hand, flourished his cane with his left, and the two of them set out for the Café Gat, walking up the Street of the Prophets to the strains of the tune from the days of the Jewish Battalion: "Oh Shoshana, oh Shoshana, how beautiful life is"—except that he changed the "Shoshana" in the song to the Orita walking in step at his side.

In days to come they all vanished—the silver-knobbed cane and the black-banded white Panama hat and the gold-buttoned navy-blue blazer and the white tennis trousers and even the square black mustache balancing the squareness of his chin, but every time one of the songs he used to sing echoes in my heart (and some of the most beautiful of them I heard from him only after he had shaved off his mustache and abandoned his cane), his image rises up before me as I first beheld it on the day of his homecoming, and as it remained until the events that split the world and time in two: bathed in a radiant summer glow.

While Gabriel was still racing round the verandah like a marathon runner holding a chair in his hand, I had already glimpsed a dull reddish-gold gleam and sensed a sharp, smoldering, metallic smell, but I did not pay any attention to them until after his departure with his hat and his cane and the doctor's wife hanging on his arm for a stroll through the streets of Jerusalem. The gleam and the smell both came from the copper ashtray standing on the table. Water from the shaving basin had splashed into the butt-filled ashtray and had given rise to the sharp smell of copper mixed with ash, which I found rather unpleasant although not repellent. Aside from the smell, I was sorry to see this beautiful ashtray serving the degrading function of a receptacle for cigarette ash: the entire inner surface of the ashtray was covered by a bas-relief of a peacock spreading its tail like a fan, and every cigarette placed on its rim would drop its ash onto the curves of the peacock's neck or the tufts of its crown or the tracery of its feathers until the peacock would disappear completely beneath the ashen avalanche, with only the tip of a feather peeping out here and there, like the limbs of a living soul buried alive. In the same way, I was sorry to see the beautiful picture on the cushion cover distorted as if in some inner agony whenever I discovered the cushion after Gabriel's siesta, all crumpled and wrinkled, crushed and squeezed between the wall and the leather couch. The picture showed a captain gazing through binoculars, in the direction of a sailor's outstretched hand, toward a point on the horizon where a ship appeared to be sinking in the light of a glorious sunset, which was painting the linings of the clouds gray and pink and red and gold. And I always felt the same urge to straighten the creased picture and smooth away the wrinkles on the cushion, just as I wanted to empty out the ashtray and wash the ash from the grooves of the peacock's tail.

About the Author

DAVID SHAHAR, a fifth-generation Jerusalemite, is today considered one of Israel's leading contemporary novelists. He received the Prime Minister's Award for Literature in 1969 and 1978; the Agnon Prize, Israel's most prestigious literary award, in 1973; the Prix Médicis Étranger in 1981; the Bialik Prize of the City of Tel-Aviv in 1984; and the Newman Prize of Bar-Ilan University in 1987. Mr. Shahar's other books in English translation include *News from Jerusalem*, a collection of stories, and *His Majesty's Agent. Summer in the Street of the Prophets* and *A Voyage to Ur of the Chaldees* are the first two volumes in a six-volume series, collectively titled *The Palace of Shattered Vessels*, about life in Jerusalem in the 1930s.

About the Translator

DALYA BILU's previous translations include works by David Shahar, Aharon Appelfeld, Yoram Kaniuk, and Yaakov Shabtai. A recipient of the Israeli Minister of Education and Culture's Award for Translation, she lives in Jerusalem.